DUNGEON PLANET

DUNGEON PLANET

Jake Edwin

All rights reserved. No part of this publication may be reproduced, stored in a retrieval system, or transmitted in any form or by any means electronic, mechanical, photocopying, recording, or otherwise without prior written permission from Podium Publishing.

This is a work of fiction. Names, characters, places, and incidents are either products of the author's imagination or used fictitiously. Any resemblance to actual events, locales, or persons, living, dead, or undead, is entirely coincidental.

Copyright © 2024 by Jake Edwin

Cover design by Elias T. Stern

ISBN: 978-1-0394-6597-8

Published in 2024 by Podium Publishing
www.podiumaudio.com

DUNGEON PLANET

PART 1

BOARDING

CHAPTER 1

How in the dark hells does a novice human mage get a job on a starship?

Miles's system indoctrinator had asked him that question the previous night, in response to forwarding the elderly Hurc bureaucrat his candidacy letter.

He'd honestly shared Gart's skepticism. Miles was a novice mage, with only two spells in his index and no combat experience casting them.

Humans were recent émigrés from a world that didn't even have magic before Earth's bower break. He had no work history in the Spiral. He had no qualifications that the real universe recognized. Even his recommendation letter from Gart was lukewarm at best: *He's desperate and his homeworld's a shit heap. Give him a chance.*

Looking at the vessel floating beyond the window of the skydock now, Miles finally had his answer.

It's not much of a starship.

He reached forward and tapped the berth's info panel. Information about the ship flowed out over the black screen, pages of green alien text and diagrams that twisted themselves into English after a few seconds of direct attention.

The *Starlit Kipper* was a tech cruiser built in the Alfaen style. A weave-corroded green metal chassis of dented curves and fins, two cloudy glass-domed observation decks meant to represent eyes, and a euphospher drive that could barely hit thirty astral knots. It was shaped more like a stingray than a kipper, in Miles's view, but artistic fidelity was the least of its problems.

It was a doomed junker. The *Kipper*'s civilian weapons had been removed at some point, and it was apparently four crew members down from the normal complement of eight, with a captain gullible or desperate enough to hire Miles as ship's healer.

When Miles took a closer look at the ship through the viewport, he could see a hole in the hull, badly plugged with some kind of foam. He could barely believe it was spaceworthy. If it was registered for anything other than low-risk scavenger runs, it probably wouldn't be.

Miles tapped on the screen, bringing up a bio for the *Kipper*'s captain.

Name, Rhu-Orlen. Species, Orbellius. A skipper in good standing. Rhu-Orlen had captained various ships over the last twenty years, working as a tech engineer before that.

Tech and magic were competing specializations in the Spiral. Some worlds had physics that had allowed magic before their bower break. Others, like Earth, had systems ruled by technology.

After a world dropped through its false vacuum into the vaster, weirder universe of the Spiral, all of its local laws would inevitably butt up against the prevailing physics of the weave, with fundamental laws jostling and percolating into a new holistic system.

Most of the physics Miles had learned in high school still applied out here in the weave—momentum, states of matter, conservation of energy—but the stuff he'd learned in his first year of college, not so much.

After a bower break, a planet's inhabitants would find themselves in a bubble of their native space where everything worked as they expected, but beyond that, only the natural laws that didn't conflict with the wider weave would prevail. Somehow, through luck, some omniversal law, or by the actions of an unknown intelligence, anyone who dropped through to the Spiral would be able to survive in the common space of the weave, but only some of their technology, or magic, or spirituality, or whatever other unique craft they had on their pre-bower world would work beyond their pocket.

When Earth fell through, the collapse brought the sun, the Solar system, and a few dozen AUs of vanilla spacetime with it, and that was the limit for a lot of Earth's advanced science. Relativity was purely a spacetime phenomenon. Gravity and magnetism still existed out in the weave, but had different underpinnings. Quantum physics stopped at the border of Solar space, and a lot of people were glad to be rid of it. Miles had shocked a few Spiral sapients by recounting the horrors of those particular fundamental laws.

With the bower break had come new technology. Euphospher drives that could propel vessels hundreds of times faster than anything possible in Earth spacetime. Resonance comms allowed instant communication across any distance. The index was maybe the most important for Miles, a device that tapped into the magical truth of what you were, in a way pre-bower Earth had no easy way of describing, and gave you the chance to change it.

An index bypassed the years of training, meditation, ritual scarification, and whatever else the practitioners of the Spiral's many magical traditions normally had to do to attain mastery, at the cost of having to pay for the modifications using delta, a secondary currency of the Spiral, traded among the magic-leaning denizens.

As Miles turned away from the panel and started walking toward the port, he brought up his index and tapped the access button.

There was a buzz of energy through his body, a tingle, and the sense of something in his gut starting to rotate as the index connected with the core of his being.

Name: Miles Asher	**Traditions:** Harmonizer
Fundamental Properties:	
Strength: 0	
Durability: 1	
Speed: 0	
Reactions: 0	
Will: 0	
Authority: 1	
Spells	
Close Wound (Tentative) *A weft of harmonizing energy brings together the free edges of a tear, sealing the join in materials which are co-bondable, such as cellular membranes, metal compounds, woven fabrics, and homogenous molecular surfaces.*	
Temporary Enhancement (Tentative) *A temporary matrix of harmonizing energy alters one of a being's fundamental properties by an amount in accordance with the weaver's Authority.*	
Core Effects	
Eyes of the Émigré *Embeds a matrix of harmonizing energy within the being's mind which will reveal to them the meaning of any plain text or spoken language.*	

It was pretty dire, Miles thought. Almost no magical enhancements to his body, beyond what was needed for his magical tradition. Two spells, and only one persistent magical effect.

A novice mage couldn't be expected to have much in their index, especially an émigré with a limited settlement allowance, but it still seemed particularly lacking to him. He felt like there should have at least been a way to practice his spells up beyond Tentative.

He'd tried to bring Close Wound up to the next stage, Grasping, by cutting and healing his clothes, but either that wasn't enough to raise his ability with it, or he just wasn't doing it enough. Four or five casts were all he could manage before he needed a good meal and a few hours of rest. The overworked technician who'd introduced him to the device had made it sound like overdoing it could be dangerous, but Miles hadn't fully understood how. It'd been couched in language that was unfamiliar and that he found hard to remember.

As it was, he felt like his bare index was as much a liability as an asset. Hopefully, the captain wouldn't ask to see it.

"Show me your index."

Captain Rhu-Orlen was a coral-colored fleshy sphere about the size of a beach ball. They had ten or so hair-like tendrils emerging from goose-pimpled skin and no other features. When they spoke, their tendrils buzzed to create vibrations, and presumably, they sensed their environment through the same threads. The air near them had a hothouse plant smell that Miles remembered from a visit to one of Earth's forest reservations as a child. It wasn't unpleasant.

Orlen was a member of a species called the Orbellius, and with no visible eyes, mouth, or features of any kind, Miles was having trouble sensing their tone. Were they joking? Were they angry at Miles's lack of experience? Maybe they were as disappointed by their first glance at Miles as he had been by his first sight of the *Starlit Kipper*.

They hovered in the *Kipper*'s docking bay in front of him, kept aloft by a quietly whining tech hoverbelt strapped around their equator.

After a few seconds without Miles responding, the captain held out a single tendril toward him.

Miles reluctantly passed the captain his index.

The tendril wrapped around the tablet and lifted it up to face the sphere. It was surprisingly strong, for a limb no thicker than a spaghetti noodle.

Orlen tapped the screen with another tendril, regarded the display for a second, then passed it back.

Miles took it back with relief, locking it before sliding it into a pocket of his cargo pants.

"Your spells are undeveloped."

Tentative.

"I'm new to this," Miles admitted. "My world only had its bower break a year ago."

He hoped he wasn't sinking his chances by being too honest.

"Can you close a wound?"

"Yes. I have a spell for that. I've practiced it, some."

On cloth, but it should work the same way.

The captain used a tendril to touch a device on their belt. Miles hadn't noticed it before, but thought it was probably a communicator. A bead of yellow light appeared on the device, and the captain spoke to someone on the other end.

"Brisk, come to the docking bay,"

"Yeah."

The captain released the comm unit after the reply and didn't speak again.

The two of them remained in place, Miles standing still, feeling increasingly awkward, and the captain hovering in silence. Apparently Rhu-Orlen didn't feel awkward silences the same way Miles did.

"So, do you have any other mages on board?" Miles asked, as much to make conversation as because he was curious.

"No."

Miles nodded. He was both relieved and disappointed.

He knew working alongside a real mage would have made him feel even more inadequate, but it might have been better in the long run to have someone more experienced he could ask questions.

His only real non-human contact on the station was Gart Illaw, his system indoctrinator, and Gart didn't know much about magic. In a universe where technology made lots of things easy, magic use was perpetually out of fashion. If someone wanted to protect themself, they could either connect an index to the core of their being and go through the accelerated process of learning to cast an offensive spell, or they could just buy a weapon. A lot of people apparently just bought the gun.

Magic had two advantages over tech. First, it was universal. A healing spell didn't care whether its target was Orbellius or human; it worked on deeper principles. Magic's other advantage was that it was integral to the individual. Someone could be stripped and dropped on a deserted moon and still have access to all their abilities. Both appealed to Miles, who didn't have many possessions and wasn't sure where he'd be in even a month's time, though that wasn't a selling point for many other people.

Even among the human émigrés on the station, all of whom must have grown up with romanticized ideas of magic, Miles was one of only three who'd bought into a mage line.

Miles had selected the Harmonizer class to start, both because it was the cheapest and because it was the only magical tradition newly bowered worlds were cleared for, but browsing even that limited catalog had shown him a huge range of potential spells, as well as permanent enhancements he could make to his body. The Harmonizer class seemed skewed toward support more than individual action, but Miles had no problem with that. He wanted to be useful. A useful sapient was an employable sapient.

Rhu-Orlen remained perfectly still and quiet for the next two minutes, until a door on the far wall of the docking port slid open with a broken-sounding grinding noise.

The smell of mineral oil and burned dust drifted through the door, followed by a Hurc crewmember with light purple skin and short black hair.

Hurcs were one of the Spiral species that were closest to humans in appearance. They were humanoid, with all the limbs and facial features Miles would have expected on a human. Ten fingers, ten toes, a different number of internal organs, but that was to be expected. Back on pre-bower Earth, a Hurc visitor might have been able to pass as a human wearing luminescent body paint—if not for the pointed ears, overdeveloped incisors, and the slight translucence of their skin, like cloudy jello.

The newcomer was about six inches taller than Miles, lightly muscled, and dusted with black grime. He stepped into the docking bay wearing a pair of baggy beige pants, plated gray boots, and a canvas belt full of tools and tech. He wasn't wearing a shirt, but there was a collar around his neck fitted with a thermal unit that had been popular with the other human émigrés on the station.

He slowed as he spotted Miles, looking him up and down, then shot a questioning look at the captain.

"Who's the *squirrit*?"

Squirrit. The word didn't translate, but Miles's *Eyes of the Émigré* supplied him with a mental image of a tiny rodent-like creature with huge eyes and a long furry body, hiding in a hole barely big enough for it. If the word had been translated, the sentence might have meant something like, "Who's the rat?"

Rude.

"Ship's healer candidate," the captain replied plainly, then said, "Prove his ability."

The newcomer, who Miles assumed was the guy the captain had addressed as Brisk, looked from Miles to the captain, then back.

"You want me to let him work on me?"

The captain bobbed lightly in the air. "He will heal a wound."

Miles looked from the captain to Brisk. From shoulder to hips, he found no obvious wounds on the man's body. There didn't seem to be anything he could heal.

Brisk rasped his large incisors together in an expression that Miles was sure meant annoyance, then pulled a short knife from his belt. He put the point against the top of his chest and drew it down sharply, opening a small cut along his skin. Whitish fluid immediately started seeping from it, and Brisk hissed in pain.

He sheathed the knife as he marched over, giving Miles a dubious stare on the way.

"Okay, squirrit. Fix me up."

Ignoring the probable insult, Miles examined the wound. It was a clean cut, shallow enough that it only broke the top layers of skin, the edges only slightly parted. Closing it wouldn't tire him too much.

He pulled his index from his pocket and brought up his spell list.

"I'm going to need to touch you," he said to Brisk, watching for his response. At least with Brisk he had a chance of reading his body language.

"Do it," Brisk said, seeming more bored than anything.

Miles pressed his right hand to Brisk's chest, covering the cut with his palm. It was Miles's first time touching a non-human sapient, and he was shocked at how hot the man's skin was. Hurcs clearly had a higher body temperature than humans.

With his left hand, Miles tapped on his index to cast the spell. Ideally, he would be able to cast spells with just a thought, but that was the part of this that needed practice and experience to pull off.

Turning. Whirring. Miles felt the semi-real core in his gut lurch into action, spinning up to frenetic speed as the spell kicked in. Electricity kindled below his ribs, warmth flooded up his arm, and a pale golden light started to shine through the fingers pressed against Brisk's skin.

He could feel the spell working. He could almost hear the voice of the magic as it sang its truth through his body.

The wound is an aberration. In a harmonious world, the two are one. The cut must close. **Such should it be.**

The light between Miles's fingers turned hot, and he felt physical movement as the separated skin pulled back together. Milk-white blood that had been spilled oozed back, sealing itself inside the cut as the injury closed with a flash of white fire. Under Miles's fingers, the purple skin was clean and unbroken. There was no sign there had ever been a wound.

Miles pulled back his hand, blinking, his arm shaking. It was his first time actually using the spell to heal a living being, and it was more intense than he'd expected. Compared to this, fixing torn cloth was a cold and clinical experience.

"You ever see a mage need to touch their index to cast a spell before?" Brisk asked the captain.

"No."

A few minutes earlier, Miles might have felt shame at the comment. After feeling the burning truth of the cosmos passing through him, it didn't sting quite as much.

He did regret taking such a relaxed approach to the index, but that was because he didn't realize magic was so *much*. It was an issue of professionalism now. He'd make learning to cast spells without the index his top priority.

"It is enough," the captain said. "This sentient will do."

Miles looked back at them. "I got the job?"

"Yes." The captain tapped a spot on their belt. "Your contract has been sent to your comm."

Miles felt a buzz in one of the lower pockets of his cargo pants as his comm unit received the message.

Brisk's eyes went unfocused and his pupils slid to point in two different directions. Miles interpreted it as a Hurc eye-roll. Without another word, Brisk turned and started heading for the door he'd come in through.

"Show him his berth," the captain called.

Brisk paused on his way out. Miles heard the grinding of incisors before the Hurc crewmember turned around and fixed him with a stare.

"Come on, squirrit. I'll show you where you can sleep."

Miles watched the white bulkheads of Unsiel Station recede through his cabin window. The skeletal length of the docking arm took shape as the *Starlit Kipper* gained distance, and then the slowly spinning spindle of the station's body, hundreds of times longer than it was wide. Inside the station was every human who'd escaped Earth, as well as a handful of refugees from other recently bowered worlds.

Something in the ship thrummed, and a teal-blue field sprung up between the ship and the darkness of space. There was a disorienting lurch, Miles felt the bottom dropping out of his stomach, and a low vibration spread through the floor and walls of the cabin. The ship's euphospher drive had kicked in.

As the distance between the ship and the station yawned open, Miles caught sight of a few scattered spots of light, arranged in a curving downward spiral. Every new world that suffered a bower break would appear at the bottom of the spiral, occupying the correct geometric spot to continue the curve downward.

An unbroken helix of many-colored fireflies, from the first world to have fallen through, uncounted eons ago, to the newest. Miles wondered if there'd ever be a last.

As the ship turned, putting Solar space out of view, Miles left the window and headed for his bunk. His cabin was spartan in the extreme, a bare steel box not much bigger than a closet, with a padded platform that folded down from the wall. The room hadn't come with any bedding, and Miles didn't have any of his own to supply. Aside from the bed, there was no furniture. At least he had a window.

Sitting on the bunk, Miles opened his bag, just a slim nylon runner's pack, and pulled out a folding knife. He might have a lot of time to himself before the crew needed him, and he was going to spend it practicing.

PART 2

DESTINATION ESCALATION

CHAPTER 2

Miles looked down at the tiny cut on his thumb. A red line, maybe half a centimeter long. It wasn't even bleeding.

He pressed his finger to the cut and tried to activate the spell *Close Wound*. *Close Wound. Close Wound! Come on, close wound. Wound close. Close it up.*

He'd cast the spell a dozen times or more using his index, but he still hadn't managed to trigger it without using the interface. If there was a trick to activating the magic, he didn't know it, and couldn't think of a way to find out. On pre-bower Earth, he might have tried searching online, but the Spiral didn't have anything resembling the kind of free information it was possible to get back on the old Earth.

His comm unit could connect him to *something*, a network called the Exchange, but there were no public forums or encyclopedias, just an index of privately held databases that he could purchase copies of and member-only communication platforms that charged for access.

As a private individual with next to no currency, Miles was information poor as well as money poor. Word of mouth was the best way of finding information open to him, but there was no one on the ship who he could ask about magic.

Focusing back on the cut on his finger, he tried to re-create the feeling of absolute conviction he felt when he index-cast the spell.

The cut should close. Make it so.

Nothing.

At least a failure didn't leave him with a bloody hand. The tiny cut was the biggest injury he could stomach to give himself, and it still took a lot of build-up and willpower to make the incision.

A lot of people who'd made it through the cataclysm of the bower break were probably desensitized to pain and injury, but Miles somehow felt like he'd come out of it *more* fragile, more afraid, less willing to hurt and be hurt.

He put his finger back on the cut and concentrated. He tried to re-create the feeling of his magical core spinning, of the hot electricity flowing up his arm.

It didn't come.

A quiet knocking came from the door to his berth. The sound was low enough that it was almost swallowed completely by the metal, but it was still enough to break his concentration.

"Yes?" he called, not moving from his bunk.

If someone on the ship wanted him, why wouldn't they just call his comm?

A spoken reply came through the door, but it was too muffled to make out.

Miles got up and went to the door. He paused for a second to check his hands before hitting the access switch.

The door groaned open on motors that sounded close to failing, revealing a member of the crew standing in the corridor who Miles hadn't seen before.

They were shorter than Miles by about a foot, a six-limbed near-humanoid with a flat-ish face and short white fur that covered every exposed part of their body. A curtain of about a dozen flaps draped down from the top of their head, appendages that were somewhere between dreadlocks and rabbit ears, and their middle pair of limbs ended in paws. Miles guessed their feet matched their mid-hands. Their top hands were more obvious manipulators, with three long fingers and a short, thick thumb. They stood looking up at Miles with intelligent brown eyes.

Miles had seen the crew manifest, but couldn't place who this was. They were wearing a pink jumpsuit that ended at their calves and forearms, and a pair of synthetic fabric foot wraps covered their feet. The jumpsuit was covered in pockets, but they didn't have any obvious equipment.

"*Hello,*" the stranger said.

The word took a second for Miles's *Eyes of the Émigré* to translate, and when it did, the tone of voice sounded nervous.

"Hi," Miles said.

"Do you want dinner?"

Miles took a second to process the statement. He wondered if his translation magic had made a mistake.

"Excuse me?"

The sentient popped open a pocket of their jumpsuit and pulled out a plastic packet, holding it up to Miles with both hands.

Miles took it. The label read BIOCHEMISTRY C-14 NUTRITIONAL PASTE: LENTSK FLAVOR.

The nutritional paste was very familiar to Miles and probably every other human outside of Solar space. Back on Unsiel Station, it'd been the standard ration given for free to the refugees of recently bowered worlds.

Human biology fell into one of the "big five" biochemistries that were represented in the Spiral. Chemical and molecular laws of different worlds broadly or exactly overlapped, where life had converged on similar principles for extracting and storing biological energy, and it had happened enough times that there were some commonalities between species. Even in an omniverse of infinite possible physical laws, if a world could support life at all, it could only do so in so many ways. Those patterns tended to repeat.

The advantage of falling in one of the Spiral's most common biochemistries was that there were a lot of mass-produced calorie packs for humans to eat. The disadvantage was that Miles had to put up with flavors like lentsk.

What even is *a lentsk?*

His *Eyes of the Émigré* didn't help much. If he concentrated on the word, he got a mental image of a small purple ball, but that didn't enlighten him at all.

"Thanks," Miles said, forcing a smile and taking the translucent plastic pack.

"I'm Trin. I'm boarding team scout. Captain said, since you are boarding team healer, we should be comfortable together."

Hearing the name, Miles was able to place the sapient. Trin was a male sensor technician serving on the ship. He was from a species called the Eppan, who weren't close biologically to humans or Hurcs, but they would still be recognizable as mammals to any old Earth scientist.

Trin must have worried he'd been rude, since he lowered his eyes and pushed his middle paws together. Unless that gesture meant he thought *Miles* was being rude.

"I'm Miles." *Wait, what?* "What do you mean by 'boarding team'?"

Trin seemed to think about the question for a second, maybe waiting for a translation to process, before he answered. "Oh, the team that boards wrecks, I think."

That actually made sense, Miles realized. The *Starlit Kipper* was registered as a salvage ship, a junker. If it was going to be recovering tech from damaged ships and stations, it was reasonable that they'd send crewmembers over to them. If there was a chance of someone being injured while they were over there, they'd want a healer around.

It wasn't precisely what Miles had been expecting, but his expectations weren't much more elaborate than a paycheck and a sense of legitimacy. Seeing the universe and the prestige of serving on a ship were just bonuses.

He realized he'd left Trin standing out in the corridor for over a minute.

"Sorry, do you want to come in?"

"Yes."

Miles stepped back to open the way, and Trin stepped in. Trin immediately made for the bunk, where he sat down and pulled up his lower legs onto the padded mattress, folding them over each other like a human sitting cross-legged.

He reached into another of his pockets and pulled out a second food pack, which he bit into.

Miles hit the switch to close the door and went to sit next to him.

Trin was looking around the room, eyes darting from one bare corner to the next, then to the viewport, which showed only the blackness of the weave. The downy flaps of skin hanging from his head shifted slightly as he looked around; nervous fiddling, subtle body language, or something with a biological function, Miles wasn't sure.

Miles tore the corner off his own food pack and squeezed out a mouthful of the contents directly down the back of his throat. Back at Unsiel Station, the human refugees always referred to the food paste as *slime*, and he was reminded exactly how accurate that was as he ate half of it as fast as possible.

Trin was sucking down the paste like he enjoyed it, and quickly drained the plastic packet. The empty packet went back into his pocket, and he rested both sets of hands on his knees.

"So, how do you want to become familiar with me?" Trin asked.

"Uh—"

Miles felt himself at a loss. It'd been a long time since he'd had to get to know someone.

On Unsiel Station he was a human among humans, and however diverse they were in culture and background, they all shared in the same trauma, of being a citizen of a world that fell through the cracks in space and then nearly destroyed itself in its panic. It had created a camaraderie, and a kind of collective identity that made socializing easy.

He didn't have anything in common with Trin. If there was any commonality at all, he didn't know it.

"Well, how old are you?" Miles asked.

"I was born in Iteration 27,165," Trin replied.

The response didn't exactly answer Miles's question.

On Earth, time was measured in years, Earth's rotations around the sun. Out in the Spiral, time was measured in *iterations*. Every time a bower break brought a new world into the weave, the iteration count was increased. From what Miles had heard, new worlds arrived at about a rate of two every Earth-standard year, but that was probabilistic, not regular. Sometimes the gap between them was longer, sometimes shorter.

Earth had been part of a cohort of three worlds that dropped through within about a month of each other, but there might be gaps of years between other iterations. He'd need to sit down with a computer and a record of arrivals to know exactly how long it had been since Iteration 27,165. Without that, he was left estimating.

The current iteration was 27,201, and with some mental math Miles worked out that following the average, Trin's birth iteration would make him about eighteen Earth-standard years old. He didn't have a frame of reference for what that meant for an Eppan, but he didn't have the feeling Trin was a lot more mature than him. If nothing else, they were both at about the start of their careers in the Spiral.

"And you?" Trin asked.

"I'm nineteen," Miles said. "I wasn't born in the Spiral. I think I'd be about thirty-eight iterations old."

"You weren't born in Spiral?"

"No, I'm from Earth. It only had its bower break about three iterations ago."

"You were born in false universe," Trin said, sounding awed.

From the point of view of a Spiral native, it might seem like that.

Miles felt the opposite way. He'd spent eighteen years of his life in that universe. He'd been a student learning its fundamental properties to the limits of human science. That universe felt real to him, even now. It had taken time for him to come to terms with the absolute reality of his new home, and he wasn't the only human who'd struggled with that.

There were factions on Earth that still thought that the Spiral was some kind of hell, even though once you got off Earth, things weren't so bad. There were even factions that wanted to go *back*, as if they could somehow find the spatial rift Earth had slipped through and crawl back up into the spacetime universe. Impossible, and maybe not even desirable. Earth had been alone up there.

The silence between him and Trin had grown awkward while Miles had been musing, and unlike Rhu-Orlen, Trin did seem to find it uncomfortable.

"Is this your first job?" he asked Trin.

"Not my first job. First job was *thief*, on Palidrana. It was good, for two iterations. This is second job."

The word *thief* wasn't a perfect translation, Miles felt. His *Eyes of the Émigré* gave him the impression of a sanctioned kind of theft, a thief who wasn't breaking any laws. It must have been an Eppan thing.

"I worked on Earth as a tutor, but not in a subject that means anything out here," Miles said.

"Oh, you were a teacher?"

"Kind of. A student teacher."

"Teach me something," Trin demanded, shifting on the mattress so he could look at Miles.

Miles looked up at the ceiling, feeling put on the spot. He dredged his memory for something Trin might find interesting or useful, knowledge he hadn't touched in a year.

Finally, he remembered Pythagoras. At least geometry was the same out in the Spiral. He gave his best attempt at explaining right-angled triangle equations to Trin, striving to keep the description culture-independent and to avoid anything that might not translate.

"Yes. I know this," Trin said, after Miles had finished.

"Right, of course."

Geometry probably wasn't universal—omniversal, he corrected himself—but it was very similar in the weave to how it had worked on Earth, so it was probably common to a lot of Spiral worlds.

"So, are we friends now?" Trin asked.

That was another first for Miles, in a long while. The camaraderie he'd shared with the other humans on Unsiel Station had been close and it'd been powerful, but it had never been friendship, not exactly.

"Yeah, sure," he said. "Of course."

Why not? He'd made a friend.

Trin shifted on the bed so that he loomed over Miles, and reached forward with his middle arms to embrace him in an awkward hug. After a second he pulled back.

"You want to touch *signallers*?" Trin asked.

It took a second for Miles to realize he meant comms. "Okay."

He pulled out his comm unit at the same time Trin retrieved his from a pocket, and they tapped them together, forming a brief connection and recording each other's message address.

As Miles brought his communicator back down, he noticed there were several missed calls listed on the screen. Missed calls *from the captain*. His stomach lurched. He'd put the device on silent so it wouldn't interrupt his concentration, and now he'd missed calls from his boss. His boss, who'd just shown great charity in giving him a job. He felt mortified.

"I missed some calls from the captain," he said, mostly to himself.

"Space burial for you," Trin said.

The Eppan crew member hopped off the bed and padded over to the door. He let himself out, leaving Miles reeling over the enormity of his mistake.

CHAPTER 3

The bridge of the *Starlit Kipper* sat in the nose of the ship. It was probably the ship's biggest room, aside from the cargo bay, and it was the center of its operations. Miles made his way there quickly through the corridors, his plastic boot soles making minimal noise on the grated floors, the warmth of the heightened activity pushing back against the chill of the bare metal walls.

When he reached the door to the bridge, he pressed the access switch and waited for someone on the other side to approve entry.

It took a minute.

Eventually, the door slid open.

The captain was hovering in the center of the room on the other side, and another sapient Miles hadn't met yet was sitting at a pilot's station.

Miles waited to see if he needed to be invited in, but when no invitation came, he stepped forward over the threshold.

"Sir?" he said.

He realized suddenly he didn't actually know the etiquette of addressing a captain here.

Émigrés on Unsiel Station had been given access to a primer on Spiral social rules, but it had been very broad and very shallow, and it'd seemed very basic and obvious to Miles. There hadn't been any guidelines on how to act in a power structure like a ship's crew, and without any specific knowledge, Miles had just fallen back on his preconceptions from Earth culture.

Brisk hadn't actually shown the captain much reverence in the exchanges he'd seen when he boarded. Maybe it wasn't expected.

"When I contact you, you must respond," Rhu-Orlen said.

The missed calls.

"Yes, I'm sorry," Miles said. "I turned my comm to silent so I could work on something."

"You must respond."

"Right. I know. It won't happen again."

The captain didn't immediately continue the conversation. The room lapsed into silence, and again, Miles wasn't sure if the captain was angry, or thinking, or if this was just what they did.

The bridge's front wall was filled by a large viewport, currently looking out over the distant corkscrew starfield of the Spiral. From the angle of the view, the ship must have been traveling orthogonal to the Spiral, crossing the wide cylindrical void that ran through its center. From what Miles knew, it was more common for a ship to travel up and down the Spiral along the curving cord of bowered worlds, where it would have access to ports, fuel, and trading opportunities. Ships would only break off to cross the core when a shortcut was absolutely essential. The captain must have thought this crossing was necessary.

The *Kipper*'s pilot sat at a station in front of the viewport, a sapient from a species Miles had never even heard of before. They looked like their physiology followed a flat body plan, with a shape like a heavy blanket raised up in a loose cone a few feet tall, their smooth white top-side facing out. Their body bunched up in places, creating waterfalls of silky folds, and Miles caught flashes of a wet pink underside, which the pilot mostly held facing inward. As Miles stared, they reached forward with one corner of their body to adjust something on their terminal's screen.

Nearby there was a circular glass-topped table projecting a holographic display of an unfamiliar planet, and a large wall display showing an event log and the status of the ship's various systems.

None of the technology seemed perfectly fitted into the space. Screens hung from walls on welded struts, rather than sitting flush with the paneling, and in places fat cables ran from wall outlets to one device or another, supplying energy and data to equipment that the room hadn't been wired for.

The captain had a padded chair at the center of the room, but they obviously didn't need it.

It looked like there were a lot more positions available on the bridge than there were crew members to fill them. A terminal near the holographic display that could have been a navigator's post sat empty. Miles had read that the ship's weapons had been removed, so presumably there was also a gunner's post that was no longer filled. There were a couple of other empty posts that Miles couldn't guess the function of.

Miles waited a few seconds for the captain to continue, but when they just continued to hover silently in place, he spoke up.

"Do you still need me?" he asked.

"You need accreditation," the Orbellius replied instantly, as if there hadn't been a lapse of silence.

Accreditation?

"Oh?"

"Accreditation as a healer."

"Okay," Miles said. The captain hadn't said anything about this before they hired him. It was kind of weird, and a little rude, to hold something like that back, but Miles wouldn't have been in a position to refuse even if he had known. He was still glad to have been given a job. "How can I get that?"

"A test and a demonstration," the captain said. One of their spaghetti tendrils curled down to tap their belt, and Miles's comm unit buzzed in his pocket. "You have the details."

"Okay. Thanks. I guess I'll go read them, then."

"Read them and prepare yourself."

Miles waited for a few seconds to see if there was anything else, then turned to go. Just before he left the bridge, he caught sight of an eyestalk peering at him from the pilot's station; a white, round, lidless eye, held up by a long stem of its skin.

He gave the pilot a brief smile, then turned and walked back out through the door.

Accreditation. Accreditation?

Miles hadn't heard of a Spiral healer qualification before, but if the captain said he needed it, he would try and get it.

He let out a long sigh as the bridge door closed behind him.

It had been a long time since he'd had to study for a test. He'd been good at exams, at one time. He hoped he still had the talent for it.

CHAPTER 4

The captain had forwarded Miles the details of the accreditation they wanted him to take, and Miles had been staring at the document on and off for hours.

Spiral Standard Healer: 1st Tier
The Tier 1 healer candidate must show awareness of:
1. The five primary biochemistries of the Spiral, the environmental needs of those biochemistries, and their chemical contraindications.
2. Universal health concerns, including weave corrosion.
3. The ten primary physical layouts, common organs, and their likely locations.
4. Simple life-saving measures for any three Spiral species.

In addition, the Tier 1 healer must demonstrate the ability to:
A. Diagnose a patient for category (P) threats to life.
B. Treat a laceration, a deep-tissue puncture, a wide area abrasion, and a wide area temperature wound.
C. Counteract a dangerous chemical contamination.

The requirements for the healer's demonstrated abilities were simple, unambiguous, and Miles had no chance at all of passing them.

For the test part of the accreditation, he thought he was safe. He'd need a manual on Spiral life forms, but it turned out that the information was pretty basic and widely circulated. A quick scan of the Exchange revealed a book he could download with the exact information he'd need for the qualification, and it was one of the few things on the network that he could afford. The overlap between what the book held and what the accreditation required was suspiciously exact, as if it had been written with Tier 1 healers in mind.

It was the practical side that was going to be a problem.

Miles had exactly two spells, only one of them would help him at all, and that would be limited to part B of the demonstration.

He had no way to treat a chemical contamination—*poisoning?*—and no way at all to diagnose a patient. With his current index, he wouldn't be able to tell a sick Orbellius from a healthy basketball.

Without upgrades to his index, he couldn't get accredited. Without the accreditation, he couldn't do the job the captain wanted him to do. Without the job, he couldn't afford to upgrade his index. Maybe he could ask for an advance on his salary, but he was only three Earth-standard days into a job that paid out every Spiral-standard month, and as far as he could tell, he hadn't even done any work yet.

He'd spent every day since the *Kipper* left Unsiel Station practicing his spells, exploring the quieter parts of the ship, and silently feeling like a fraud. He'd spent more time browsing the Exchange than he had doing anything that felt productive, and he definitely hadn't done anything that warranted the captain's faith, trust, or financial investment.

He just didn't know what to do.

Maybe he could ask Trin for advice.

Miles's comm unit was a small device. It was narrower and lighter than a cell phone, but worked in a similar way, with an interactive screen. He'd been given it for free, along with the other refugees back on Unsiel Station—so it had to be a very basic model—but it seemed perfectly functional to him.

Miles's unit had come with a built-in translator, which wasn't always as fast or as accurate as his *Eyes of the Émigré* weave, but it worked both ways when making calls and sending written messages.

He opened the message tool and started scrolling through his contact list. It was short. He had Captain Rhu-Orlen, Trin, Gart Illaw and a few humans from Unsiel Station, and a few humans from back home.

After a second's hesitation, Miles selected Trin and tapped out a message.

Miles > Trin
I can't do it, Trin. I'm not going to pass this examination.

He waited half a minute before he saw the activity signifier, and a reply came back.

Trin > Miles
That's very sad.

Yes, Trin. Yes, it is.

Miles > Trin
Do you have any advice? I can't afford the index upgrades I need to pass this test. I don't know what to do.
Trin > Miles
I will not give you money.
Trin > Miles
But we are still friends.
Miles > Trin
I don't want your money. I'm asking for advice.
Trin > Miles
Find someone give you money.

Miles dropped his comm unit on the bed.

He didn't know anyone else who might have any good ideas. None of the humans back on the station knew any more about Spiral culture than he did, his case worker Gart was so overworked he might not respond to a message for days, and Miles hadn't been in touch with anyone on Earth since he escaped.

Did the Spiral have payday loan companies? Were there healer grants or bursaries he could apply for? Could he make contact with a loan shark? All were starting to look like appealing options, if he could find them.

On the bed, Miles's comm unit suddenly started emitting a loud tone; not an incoming call, but a broadcast. It blared for a few seconds, then cut off. The captain's severe, monotone voice started speaking a moment later.

"Prepare to disembark. We will dock at Delatariel Station in one hour."

As usual, the captain's statements were curt and lacked any useful context at all. Miles hadn't even known they were heading for a station. They were still traversing the central void. What kind of station could there possibly be out here?

Despite his reservations, Miles got to work, pulling a clean pair of cargo pants from his pack and the almost-empty bag of dry soap he could use to wash without access to a shower.

As was becoming more and more common, he had questions, and no good place to get answers.

What are we doing on Delatariel Station?

The constant background whine of the ship's shields had almost become imperceptible to Miles, until they were switched off, and then the absence was like being suddenly deaf.

The silence yawned, punctuated by the popping of the cooling hull and the groaning of something in the ship's superstructure that *really* didn't like coming to a stop.

The crew members that had assembled in the docking bay swayed together as the ship made contact with the station's docking arm; there was a dull impact and a sudden lurch as the floor kicked beneath them. Even the captain seemed to drift briefly in the air as their levitation unit adjusted to the ship joining with the greater mass of the station.

Trin, who was standing next to Miles, grabbed onto his arm with a mid-paw to keep his balance. Brisk was closer to the hatch, holding onto a suspension strap to steady himself. The pilot Miles had first seen on the bridge was there, who he'd since found out was a woman called Sellen.

The pilot's species was called the Welven, and despite being about as physically different from a human as Miles could imagine, they both shared a C-type biochemistry. Sellen was sitting on the floor as the *Kipper* made contact, raised up like a tent, two eye stalks extended and pointed at the hatch.

A vibration thrummed through the hull as the ship came to a complete stop relative to the station, and a hissing of air released from the hatch as the atmosphere equalized between the two habitats. The docking bay became full of the unfamiliar smells of a new environment; alien food, weird smoke and spices, the life functions of a dozen different species, and the hot metal odor of high-energy technology.

Miles had a few seconds to worry about whether the air would be compatible with his biology, or if his first experience of "counteracting a dangerous chemical contamination" would be trying to save his own life, before the hatch started groaning open and a gradually widening crescent of light appeared along its edge.

I'm fine. I'm fine.

The hatch opened on the much larger docking bay of an interstellar station.

The structure of it was superficially similar to the docking bay of Unsiel Station, which Miles was familiar with. A long cylindrical metal chamber about thirty feet across stretched out to the left and right, with viewports and access hatches dotted along its length.

The docking arm of Unsiel Station hadn't been too different from airport flight gates Miles had seen on Earth, and Unsiel Administration had put about as much effort as the old airports into keeping the flight gates clean and secure.

Delatariel's docking arm might have been similar structurally to Unsiel's, but the structure was where the similarity began and ended. It didn't seem like there was any kind of security at play in the Delatariel docking bay, and nobody was working to keep it clean.

The space was packed. There were sapients passing back and forth, possibly leaving or arriving from ships, but there were also sapients standing around, sitting along the edges of the passage, serving customers at market stalls, and in some cases apparently sleeping in whatever free space they could find.

Food carts with sizzling hot plates spattered oil and fluids into the air and over the floor, overloaded baggage carts listed sideways on straining levitation units, and what might have been a hospital cart, complete with a reclining patient and active medical devices, rushed through the crowd by a pair of alien porters.

It was dirty, chaotic, and completely at odds with everything Miles thought he knew about Spiral port facilities.

If a Spiral public health inspector saw this, they'd have the alien equivalent of an embolism.

Captain Rhu-Orlen drifted slowly in front of the group, positioning themself between the open hatch and the waiting crew. They were wearing a new piece of equipment that Miles hadn't seen before. After a second of staring at it, Miles was shocked to realize it was some kind of weapon: a smooth, short-barreled pistol, sized and shaped for a grasping hand a little larger than a human's. It sat in a synthetic fabric holster clipped to the captain's belt.

"These are our objectives," the captain began blandly. "I will recruit a sapient to fill our lancer role. Brisk Igris will obtain a signal mask generator. Trin El-el-forren will obtain a transcript of vessel movement logs for the Ialis iteration. Miles Asher will undertake his Tier 1 healer accreditation."

Wait, what? I'm going to what?

"Sellen One-Fourteen will obtain iteration Ialis navigational data," the captain continued, never pausing and never elaborating. They finally finished, then floated there for a few seconds, seeming to regard the crew. "Is any clarification needed?"

Miles reflexively raised his hand, but he didn't wait to be called.

"I don't know where to go to get accredited."

Despite being a featureless sphere, Miles couldn't help but imagine that the captain was glaring at him.

"Review the station map. The Spiral bureaucratic adjunct will be marked."

Okay . . .

Miles swallowed loudly. This was the "I didn't study for the test" nightmare made real.

"I haven't had a chance to review the material," he added, then only hesitated for a second before confessing, "And I can't afford the upgrades I need to pass the practical demonstration."

There was a long silence in the ship's docking bay. He felt not only the silent, awkward pressure from the captain, but from everyone else on the crew. Trin and

Brisk, at least, came from cultures with social rules similar enough to his that Miles knew they were cringing on his behalf.

After a long silence that no one broke, the captain responded. "We will be docked for five hours. Five hundred seln will be credited to your comm from the ship's account. Will that be sufficient?"

Will it?

Miles didn't know. He needed delta to buy index upgrades, not seln, and he didn't know the delta-seln conversion rate. He hoped it'd be enough. It would have to be.

"Yes," Miles said, with a feeling like he was sealing his fate.

The captain touched a point on their belt, and Miles felt his comm buzz in his pocket. He was now worth 500 seln, apparently, about half his monthly salary.

"Are there further comments?" the captain asked the room.

There weren't. The crew formed up, and everyone filed out.

"I'm in trouble," Miles said.

"Hard to tell, with captain," Trin replied.

"You have that problem too?" Miles asked. He'd been assuming that he was uniquely lost in exchanges with the ship's skipper. "I never understand the silences."

"Not an Orbellius thing," Trin said. "Met an Orbellius shopkeeper once. They were very talkative."

"Do they have any body language?"

The captain was completely expressionless, as far as Miles could tell. No features, no subtle unintentional movements, no vocal cues.

"Smell changes," Trin said thoughtfully. "Not sure if it means anything."

The two of them were walking through Delatarial Station's central concourse. It was a huge open area, a column of air stretching from near the bottom of the station's central spindle up to a point close to the top. It was crisscrossed at hundreds of points by broad metal lattices forming the roads of the station's interior, each bridge framed by structures of synthetics, metal, and glass that were home to the station's businesses and organizations.

Looking up, the angle of the gangways rotated as they ascended, creating the effect that their ends followed a spiral curve around the walls of the station concourse; an aesthetic that mirrored the wider cosmos. The basic plan was identical to Unisel Station, and the layout of the bridges always reminded Miles of a DNA helix.

The gangway was less crowded than the docking arm that the *Kipper* had connected with. There was always some sapient within arm's reach, individuals passing by in both directions or doing business with nearby stores and offices, but there wasn't the same chaotic press of bodies.

It turned out that Miles and Trin were both going to the same place. The Spiral Adjunct Office was a large complex built into one wall of the station about halfway down its length, with the Accreditation Office and Records Office taking up neighboring units.

Getting there wasn't the main problem. Miles was still completely unprepared.

He still had about four hours. In that time, he needed to buy the material he needed to study for the test, study for the test, update his index for the test, and use the brand-new abilities of his upgraded index to pass the test. It was going to be the worst combination of cramming for an exam and preparing for a job interview he could imagine.

So far, all he'd done was try to ignore the looming threat of it for long enough to let the panic fade.

"Where do you think I can buy delta?" he asked Trin.

The captain had given him five hundred seln. Seln was the primary currency of the inter-Spiral culture, but it wouldn't get him any upgrades to his index. The magic subcultures of the Spiral, including the corporation that created the indexes, used a secondary currency, delta. Right then it seemed like an unnecessary complication to Miles, but one he'd still have to navigate in the next couple of hours.

Converting seln to delta would mean finding an in-person trader to make the exchange with. As far as he knew, there was no way of doing it via the Exchange.

"A money changer?" Trin responded.

"Do you see any?"

"No."

Great.

The gangway was lined with stores and offices, often with labels that Miles's *Eyes of the Émigré* could translate into English after a couple of seconds of focused attention.

On this level, most of the stores offered spacer equipment of some kind or another, probably due to the proximity of the docking arm. There was a store selling weave suits, fitted for a huge variety of different body plans. There were ship hardware shops every hundred paces or so. Miles saw a personal weapons store, and further down, a clothing outfitter.

One of the shops seemed like a specialist personal sensor retailer, which Miles was tempted by. He paused outside the entrance, peering through transparent panels at the items arranged for display. One of them was labeled as a *medical scanner*, which was almost a perfect answer to Miles's prayers, except that it was priced at over a thousand seln.

Focus on what I can accomplish right now.

"I need to stop for a minute," he said to Trin.

Trin paused, looking around. His head appendages twitched and swayed on their own for a few seconds before he turned to point at a copper-colored girder resting at the edge of the bridge between a gap in the stores.

"We have time. Sit there."

They made their way over and sat down.

Miles pulled out his comm unit and started looking for the information he needed to pass the knowledge part of the accreditation.

Like his index, Miles's comm unit would only show him items from the Exchange that he had enough seln to buy right then. The last time he'd looked, his search results had been pitiful, returning more free samples and promotional material than actual products. With the extra five hundred seln the captain had sent him from the ship's account, the results were much different.

Exchange Search: "Medical textbook"
The Alfaen Guide to Trauma Care (§480)
A guidebook for the trauma surgeon and experienced battlefield healer. A complete anatomical and biochemical reference for over two hundred sapient species, with sensory simulations of over a thousand invasive and palliative procedures.
Author Guive Eloroia
The Complete Body (§473)
Beneath the stars, in one-ness, regard the biological form. From highest sensonelle to lowest reproductova, examine in detail the exquisite function. Delight in the inner depths, you! The healer of the stars.
Author Polyp-33220
Orbellius In Depth (§472)
Unfold the secrets of our enigmatic species. The Orbellius are one of the oldest of the middle-period civilizations, but one of the most under-served in the field of medicine. This exhaustive encyclopedia of Orbellian physiology will instantly propel you to mastery in the care and treatment of Orbellian maladies.
The Subrach Corporation

With the way that Exchange searches worked, Miles's new wealth was actually proving to be a disadvantage. The search results were tailored not just for what he was looking for, but also for what he could afford. He had five hundred seln to spend, and the Exchange wanted him to spend it. All of these results went far beyond what he needed to keep his job over the next five hours.

Getting increasingly desperate, Miles changed his search terms.

Exchange Search: "Medical textbook healer accreditation tier 1 <$20"
System Standard Medical Database v2760 ($17)
An illustrated list of Spiral species, their biochemical categories, and their body plan classifications. Current to Iteration 27,200.
Spiral Origin Press
So You Want to Be a Healer: A Guide for Lesser Species ($16)
Many in the Spiral wish to attain the vaunted title of "healer." Could it be that you are worthy, shameless curr? Perhaps not. But without this text, you stand no chance. Purchase it now, and subject yourself to the shame of failure.
Author Zedine Ulchor
Good Sapient Study Series: Healer Study Guide ($15)
A study guide for hopeful students beginning their career as a healer, with notes on biochemistries, organs and organelles, body types, threats, and first-aid procedures for a representative sample of Spiral species.
Good Sapient Directory

The last entry seemed to be what Miles needed. It was a data pack that seemed tailored for people who needed to take the Tier 1 healer accreditation and didn't have much time to study.

He hit the instruction to purchase it, and it downloaded to his comm in under a second, along with a deduction to his balance.

Trin, watching over his shoulder, commented.

"Good Sapient is good series. I read from them when I was *podding*."

Miles's translation magic supplemented the unfamiliar word with a mental image of five smaller versions of Trin nestled side-to-side in the skin pouch of a much larger furred creature.

He tried to push the image away. He didn't need that right now.

"I still need to find somewhere to get delta," Miles said, looking around. "Do you think we could ask someone?"

Trin immediately turned and put a mid-paw on a Hurc traveler who was passing by them on the bridge.

He was large and muscular, with pink skin and a tuft of white hair growing out of the center of his otherwise bald head.

"Hello," Trin said. "Do you know where there is delta?"

The stranger stopped, looking down at them with solid black eyes, which Miles hadn't seen in a Hurc before. He made a low rumbling noise in his throat, pulling his arm free of Trin's grasp. He left without answering, but also without smashing Trin into the ground, which Miles thought was the best outcome Trin could expect.

"Nobody knows," Trin concluded.

They continued walking along the causeway. Miles focused on the stores they passed, waiting for his *Eyes of the Émigré* to translate each sign before moving onto the next. He didn't expect to see a sign that said *Magic Shop* or anything obvious, but he hoped there might be an information station or business directory.

As they were reaching the end of the causeway, Miles felt a sudden kick in his gut, in the place where his magical core rested. It was as if a heart that had never moved before had taken a single beat.

He turned, following a line of instinct he didn't yet fully understand, and found a pair of eyes watching him from a stall on the far edge of the concourse.

The figure staring at him was robed in a long garment of tattered gray cloth. They were taller than Miles and seemed humanoid-adjacent, but all he could make out beneath the hood was a stretch of brown skin and the light reflecting in their eyes.

Trin realized Miles had stopped in the street and came back to stand next to him. He followed Miles's gaze to the stall.

"Your friend?" he asked.

"No. I don't know them," Miles said. "Trin, do you know anything about magical cores? The thing an index gives you."

"No. Only weird people have them."

The robed figure made the slightest movement, looking down and away, which could have been an invitation, or could have been them losing interest.

"Can we just go over here a minute?" Miles asked, already walking toward the store.

Trin followed him. "Yes. Five hours. Plenty of time for me. Not for you."

At the far end of the gangway, the bridge connected with a shelf that ran all the way around the open concourse. There were large doors that led to the structures built into the station wall, elevators and levitation tubes that moved people and goods between levels, and even more of the vendors, stalls, and stores that had cluttered the bridge. For a station that seemed so remote from any Spiral world, there was a huge amount of trade happening here.

The figure caught sight of Miles and turned to watch him approach.

Closer up, Miles could make out more details of the sapient under the hood.

They were an unfamiliar species, with smooth, dusty brown skin and an almost featureless face, save for a ridge that ran down its center and a pair of small eyes positioned to the far left and right edges. They had no mouth, but as Miles reached their stall, he noticed that there were rows of gill-like openings running beneath their chin that flexed and shifted from moment to moment.

"Hi," Miles said, feeling awkward and not even sure why he'd stopped.

"Hello, Traveler," the stranger said. They had a fluting, melodic voice, like air whistling through wind chimes.

Not sure where to take the conversation, Miles cast his gaze over the sapient's stall. It was an eclectic mix of items. There were metal blades with handles shaped for a variety of hand styles, glass and plastic bottles labeled with handwritten tags and filled with unfamiliar chemicals, and piles of rags and garments that he'd need to physically dig through to even tell what was in there.

There were even books—actual books—printed on something analogous to paper, with symbols on their covers that didn't translate no matter how long Miles stared at them.

He looked back up at the sapient, who was regarding him without any obvious emotion.

"Uh, I felt something," Miles began, awkward, hesitating. "I think I felt you looking at me."

"I'm sorry," the stranger said. Their gills fluttered as they spoke. "I didn't mean to pry. You are a mage. I was only curious about your tradition. You are a Harmonizer, aren't you?"

"Yes." That *was* the tradition he'd chosen through his index. "Are you a mage?"

"Yes, a dabbler, with only a little skill."

The sapient picked something out of the pile of debris on the stall. It looked like a folded sheet of paper. They held it up for Miles to look at.

"Would you find this interesting?" they asked. "A treatise on a lesser harmony, written by a Harmonic mage. Ninety seln."

"No, thank you," Miles said.

He was almost bursting with questions, but this suddenly didn't seem like the place to ask them. This clearly wasn't a teacher. They were a peddler, and probably wouldn't be interested in Miles if he wasn't a potential customer.

"Can you sell me any delta?" he asked instead.

The sapient's gills flared, maybe in surprise, or annoyance, or maybe they were just choking.

"No," they replied after a moment. There was no change in their voice. "But why do you need *delta*? There are things here to buy for seln." They waved a hand across their stall. "A tool to protect yourself? Armor for your body? Chemicals to sharpen your mind?"

Miles shook his head, belatedly realizing that the gesture might not mean much to the merchant.

"I need spells. I'm taking the healer accreditation soon, and I need to be able to diagnose someone, heal poisoning, treat a burn . . ."

The sapient's gills closed fully for a few seconds, then fluttered open.

"Simple healings. Perhaps I have something."

The sapient reached into their robe, one of their spindly limbs sliding into one inner pocket then another. As they searched for something, Trin stepped up and spoke into Miles's ear.

"He's weird. Don't give him money."

Miles pushed Trin away. Trin pushed back with a mid-paw, and they jostled until Miles took a step away.

After a minute the merchant finally found what they were looking for, withdrawing it from a pocket of their robe. They held it out for Miles to see.

It was a small, irregular crystal, straight-edged with about two dozen facets, and a deep black crack along one side like the hole in a bad tooth. It was dull in the lights of the station, but somehow it seemed to sing to him.

"What is it?" Miles asked, staring down at the gem.

The shopkeeper's gills fluttered. "Spells."

Miles reached out, and the shopkeeper let him pick it out of their thin, three-fingered hand.

It was cool to Miles's touch, like stone that had been out of the sun. It was lighter than stone, and clearer than unworked gemstone. The crack in the side gave Miles a sick feeling he didn't like.

"Which spells?" he asked.

"You use an index?" the sapient asked.

"Yes."

"Hold it, and look at your index. It will tell you what you hold."

With the crystal clutched in one hand, Miles pulled his index out of the pocket of his cargo pants. The index followed the same aesthetic as his comm unit, a blocky metal pad with an interactive screen, and few other features. It was larger, and a little awkward to use one-handed.

He held it up and unlocked it, flipping the screen to show his index directory.

The display glitched a few times at first, and Miles spent a terrified second worrying that he'd hit the device somehow and damaged it, before the screen cleared and the normal display appeared. He played with the view until it showed him a list of new changes.

Name: Miles Asher	**Traditions:** Harmonizer	**Changes**
Spells		
Hasten Renewal [New] (T##tt#avie) *A weft of harmonizing energy spreads from the weaver to their target, greatly speeding the being's natural recovery by an amount multiplicative with the weaver's Authority.*		
Core Effects		
Eyes of the Altruist [New] *Embeds a matrix of harmonizing energy within the being's mind which reveals to them the health and ailments of a witnessed being.*		

Hasten Renewal and *Eyes of the Altruist*. These could solve at least two of Miles's problems in the examination. The first could help him heal burns and abrasions, the second could help him with diagnoses.

He didn't understand what the crystal was. He hadn't even known spells could work like that. Magic had been introduced to him as something he could either learn manually through months or years of practice, or purchase ready-formed via his index. Nobody ever mentioned being able to get new spells from a stone, but his index was showing them in his directory, which seemed to rule out the possibility he was about to get scammed.

"You cannot use them yet, but your device can sense them," the shopkeeper explained, watching as Miles reacted to the updates to his index. "To make them stick, you must take the *item* within yourself."

Miles looked down at the crystal, wondering if he'd need to eat it.

"How do I do that?"

The sapient took a breath through their gills. "I think if you use a spell it contains while holding it, then it will be taken in."

Already holding his index, Miles almost used the new spell right then. Instead, he looked up at the shopkeeper.

"How much is it?" he asked.

As Miles stared up at the sapient, he felt something. He knew the feeling when he cast his own spells; a spinning, and a warmth, deep in his gut. Now he felt something similar, but coming from the stranger. A spinning, a heat, but outside his body, positioned somewhere in the other sapient's chest.

The feeling was only there for a second before it stopped.

The shopkeeper reached out to sweep a gesture at the gem. "Five hundred seln."

Miles looked up. The merchant had chosen the exact amount that the captain had given Miles to spend. A coincidence? It was the most he could spend, and if he did, he wouldn't have anything left for the rest of the trip.

He peered at the shopkeeper, suspicious.

"Did you just cast a spell?" he asked.

The merchant was silent, but their gills flared.

"Did you use magic on me?" Miles asked again.

The shopkeeper hesitated for a few seconds, then pulled a ball of fabric out of the pile of garments. "I will include this armor in the price."

You did. You spelled me!

He didn't know if the sapient had used thought-scanning magic, or precognition, or if they'd just looked in Miles's pocket to read the screen of his comm unit, but the peddler had used magic to pick out Miles's upper budget.

Miles had caught him out, but the peddler just thought they were haggling.

"It's a good piece," the shopkeeper reiterated, shaking out the garment to reveal a robe in rough off-white fabric. "It will stop blade, claw, and slow ballistics. Its normal price is forty seln."

Miles sighed. He felt spent. He wasn't up to battling with a merchant in such an unfamiliar environment, not over a few seln that the captain had given to him for this purpose anyway.

"Okay. Sure," Miles said.

He reached into his pocket for his comm unit, and at the same time the sapient excitedly pulled out their own—a longer device with a different design. They tapped comms together, and Miles acceded to the prompt for payment that showed up on his screen. He almost felt the loss as the money drained out of his account.

Penniless again.

The shopkeeper handed over the coarse robe, and Miles already had the crystal.

"Do you think you got scammed?" Trin asked as they walked away.

Miles gripped his new gem with one hand as they moved, ignoring Trin. He didn't even pause to find somewhere to sit before he activated the new spell, *Hasted Renewal*, using his index.

There was a stuttering as the magic started.

Instead of the smooth rotation of his core that he was used to, Miles felt a grinding sensation, cold and painful, but it only lasted a few seconds, then there was a flash of heat in his left hand, and when he looked down the gem was gone. His core was spinning normally. Faster than usual, if anything.

Instead of holding the gem, his fingers were now glowing with a faint, pale yellow light. The weave of harmonic energy, waiting for a target.

Miles brushed his fingers against his own chest, felt the golden threads of light take hold, and a warmth washed through him.

The spell only lasted while he maintained contact, and the strange feeling of being drained that accompanied the casting of a spell made him quickly break contact.

In that brief moment, the magic had erased all of the aches he'd built up walking through the station. Even the tiredness he'd been suffering from the perpetually disturbed sleep he was getting on his quarter's narrow bunk felt a little better. If he could cast this on himself for longer, could he erase his tiredness completely?

The *Eyes of the Altruist* ability took longer to work out. It wasn't a spell he could cast through his index. It was meant to be a permanent enhancement, always on, but Miles found that it conflicted with his *Eyes of the Émigré*.

The diagnostic magic didn't kick in until he really concentrated on it and forced his mind to switch gears. When he did, phantom shapes sprung up over the sapients in the crowd around him.

He could see irregular blobs, coiling wires, wetly biological tubes, and pulsing sacs painted out in luminescent watercolors across the bodies of the various species they passed in the concourse. Miles was staring so much that Trin started giving him strange looks, and when Miles returned them, he saw the same kind of shapes drifting over Trin's body.

He was seeing some kind of internality, Miles thought—the magical equivalent of a body scan. What he was looking at might be organs or other internal structures. He didn't see how the magic would help him diagnose problems, but he imagined he needed more experience and knowledge for that. He just hoped he could get it in the next couple of hours.

The darkness around Miles was absolute. The space seemed to go on forever in every direction; a floor of black glass, and an infinite lightless expanse above. No ceiling, no stars. A true void.

He wasn't sure what he'd expected when the assessor had asked him to sit down, then dropped a face-covering piece of technology over his head, but it hadn't been this.

It was some kind of simulation, he thought, a powerful, immersive form of virtual reality, but he didn't understand how that could lead to a fair test.

They wanted to test his abilities, which presumably they would simulate, but if they only tested them in a neural simulation, wouldn't that only prove what he *thought* he could do, rather than what he could actually do?

He felt at his clothes, then at the shape of his index in his pants. He could feel its contours through the pocket. He still had all his equipment in this artificial reality.

He pulled out his index and tested that it still worked by casting the *Temporary Enhancement* spell, focusing on his *speed*.

Again, the magic seemed to push words through the arteries of his mind, a boiling truth he could feel in his blood.

In their self, they are complete. In a harmonious world, everything is, in itself, complete. **It is that which it is.**

He felt his core spin up, felt the energy leave his hand and lurch into his body. There was the inaudible hum of the spell's matrix as it settled in, and Miles could detect the minor change to the feeling of his body as he waved his hand around faster than he was used to.

Miles didn't have too long to think about the nature of the simulated reality.

A sudden loud tone sounded out in the darkness, like drums and horns and an electric note all mixed together, and then the ground began to shift.

A shadowy figure flowed up from the black ground, quickly forming into a humanoid shape. At the last moment, the figure flickered, transforming from an indistinct shadow into the form of an old man.

He was human, maybe in his seventies. Bald, with light brown skin. Not anyone Miles knew, but someone who wouldn't have looked out of place on Earth.

Miles hadn't seen another human since he'd left Unsiel Station, and he hadn't seen another elderly human since he'd escaped Earth. The strangeness of it froze him for a second.

"Please, it hurts," the old man said, touching his chest.

Miles balked at the reality of the simulation. The odds of another human being out here were miniscule, when so few had even left Earth. This was purely a figment created for the practical part of his test.

They probably hadn't intended to make Miles *feel* something.

"Please, it hurts," the man repeated.

"Okay," Miles said quickly, rushing to the man's side. "Where does it hurt?"

"In the left ventricle of my human heart."

"Right . . ."

Whoever had programmed this test had gone a little wrong, there, Miles thought. Maybe they didn't know humans couldn't usually place the source of pain with that much accuracy.

This is the diagnostic part of the test.

The knowledge part of the test had been done and behind him before he ever even sat down in the chair. He'd knocked it out on a station terminal after an hour of cramming. This was the part he was worried about, the practical.

"What kind of pain is it?" Miles asked.

"Pressure in my chest. It's spreading to my jaw, neck, and left arm. Please, it hurts a lot."

"Okay, any other symptoms?"

"I feel dizzy. I wish I could lie down."

Miles had the self-awareness to be grateful they'd programmed the test with a human patient to start with. Even without any tools or magic, he was pretty sure he could diagnose a heart attack when the man was reciting off the textbook list of symptoms.

For completeness, Miles focused on his *Eyes of the Altruist* ability, disabling his translation magic in favor of the sensory enhancement.

The same faintly glowing shapes sprung up over the old man's body, and seeing the magic working on a human recontextualized it for him in a useful way.

Through the magic, he could see what he recognized as the man's internal organs. Heart, lungs, kidneys. He could see the brain, the spine, and the nerves, wrought in different colors. When he focused, he could make out the circulatory system.

None of it was particularly exact, it didn't compare well with an MRI, or even an ultrasound, and he almost missed the thing he was meant to be looking for.

A heart attack didn't show up on his new magical sense at all, but there was one oddity, a small fleck of black hovering in the midst of the glowing shape representing the man's heart.

Contextually, Miles understood that it was meant to be a blockage in the blood vessel that was causing the heart attack, or maybe tissue that was starving due to lack of oxygen, but in any other species, or for almost any other medical condition, it wouldn't have meant anything to him. The *Eyes of the Altruist* wasn't an ability that would just hand him the answer in the way an advanced medical scanner might.

"You're having a heart attack," Miles said.

The old man vanished.

"Did I pass?" Miles asked.

Less than a handful of seconds went by before a new being appeared. This time, when the shadows flowed up from the ground, they coalesced into a sphere, then took the shape of an Orbellius, this one with only two spaghetti-like tendrils and skin the color and texture of dark stone.

"Please, it hurts," the Orbellius said, in a pained tone that Miles found a little disorienting.

The simulated Orbellius was visibly wounded. A pointed shard of metal about a foot long was sticking out of its side, the entry point smeared with a yellow fluid, and the low sound of hissing gas coming from the gaps around the wound.

The Orbellius were a Category B biochemistry species, and had an *enclosed* body plan—interior and exterior parts that weren't connected by any macroscopic openings. No integral appendages, and no rigid structures.

Looking at the simulated patient, Miles wasn't sure that knowledge would be necessary.

"Yeah? Where does it hurt?" Miles asked.

"In the side of my body. It's a stabbing pain."

"You don't say."

Miles checked the simulated patient over with his *Eyes of the Altruist* for completeness. The inside of the Orbellius was interesting, a large internal space with very few features, but with hundreds of small irregular ovals nestled around the outside. There were cords running through their body just below the skin, which Miles assumed were the source of the fluid running down from the injury.

"You're suffering from a stab wound," Miles concluded, boldly. "A piece of metal is piercing your—" *Blood vessels? Do Orbellius have blood?* "Your vessels. We should probably take it out and close the wound."

The Orbellius patient vanished.

More patients appeared, complained, and then vanished. Miles diagnosed three of them with certainty. There was one that he wasn't sure about, and one that he was positive he got wrong. He just hoped it was a best-of-five situation and not the kind of test where he needed a perfect result.

After the diagnosis portion, he was asked to treat the wounds of various simulated sapients.

His *Close Wound* spell worked for lacerations and abrasions, and his new *Hasten Renewal* spell significantly improved burns, blunt injuries, and the shattered carapace of an insectoid sapient, if not healing any of them completely.

He'd attempted to use *Hasten Renewal* to treat the poisoning cases he'd been presented with. It had seemed to work twice, but on the third and fourth patients, they'd died almost immediately. Miles assumed it meant that *Hasten Renewal* had an undocumented negative effect if the recipient wasn't able to heal from what was hurting them naturally, or if the substance was something that turned their natural healing against itself. For the fifth poisoning patient, he just used *Temporary Enhancement* to bolster their endurance and hoped it would count as a pass.

Eventually, the test wound up, and the black void disappeared as the wrinkled Eppan technician lifted the headset up out of his face.

"How did I do?" he asked.

"The system will process your results," the technician said. "Would you like to receive an automated score, or do you want to be judged by a biological sapient?"

Miles couldn't imagine why anyone would want to get their performance graded by a sapient if the automated system was perfect, so he had to assume there was some problem with the automated marking. After a second of thought, he answered, "A sapient."

The technician clicked their teeth in acknowledgment and did something on their console. "Fine. Your result will be sent to your comm. Allow *two hours* for delivery." His *Eyes of the Émigré* translated the Spiral time into Earth hours.

Oh.

He wouldn't even find out if he'd passed until he was back on the ship.

"Can I change my mind and get automated marking?"

"No."

Miles checked he still had all his equipment, and made his way out of the Accreditation Office and back onto the concourse.

Miles wasn't the first back to the ship. Brisk, Trin, and Sellen the pilot were all on board by the time he got back, though Miles only knew because of the crew roster that the ship's docking panel showed him when he checked back in.

He'd stayed out for as long as he could, hoping the result of his examination would come through before he had to face the captain, but the time limit they'd set for the ship being docked was coming to an end, and the message still hadn't come.

It had been a little over an hour since he'd finished the demonstration, so he didn't have a good reason to expect that he'd know the results before the captain asked about it.

Miles let himself into the ship, then closed the hatch behind him. He paced for a couple of minutes, decided to go back to his berth to wait for the captain, then immediately decided against it, thinking that waiting there would be even more unbearable than waiting at the hatch.

He spotted a footlocker resting at the edge of the docking bay and sat down on that instead, refreshing his comm's messages every few seconds.

He had a few minutes to wait before the captain returned.

When the ship's hatch started to groan, Miles was on his feet before it had even started opening.

The door slowly rolled back, and the captain hovered in. They hadn't come back alone.

Scuttling in behind them was an enormous sapient whose body looked like the cross between a beetle and a near-humanoid crab. They had four sturdy main legs branching off from their bulbous body, four long arms that ended in pincer-like manipulators, and an insectile face that was overhung by the armor of their carapace, leaving them looking like they were wearing a cowl.

The captain paused in the docking bay, apparently noticing Miles.

"This is Torg. They will be our lancer."

Torg clicked, and Miles *Eyes of the Émigré* translated the noise as "Greeting," but the sound didn't become an English-language version of Torg's voice like it would with most species. The click's meaning just remained a vague impression.

"Hi," Miles returned.

Miles turned to the captain and waited for them to ask about his performance in the assessment. They did not.

Instead, the captain called Brisk to show Torg to their berth, then simply left, floating off toward the bridge.

Miles had a realization, then, about what kind of commander Rhu-Orlen was. When they gave an order, they assumed it would be obeyed perfectly, no matter how much work, or excellence, or resourcefulness would be needed, even assuming that the person already had the resources they needed to succeed, unless they were told otherwise.

As Miles watched the captain go, he didn't feel the need to update them on the as-yet-uncertain results of his assessment. It seemed like it would be a betrayal of the captain's implicit faith in his success.

Instead, he let the captain go and returned to his berth.

Miles got the message with his results an hour later.

DSAO > Miles

PASSED: Miles Asher SAP272001348 You recently undertook a Tier 1 Healer Accreditation at D— station. Your application was a success and you have been deemed competent as a Tier 1 healer. Your transcript and accreditation certificate are attached. Please report to your closest Spiral Administration Adjunct Office to collect your authenticated identification.

It had been a long time since Miles had aced a test, and he quietly filed the message away for future re-reading.

The assessment hadn't actually been that difficult, Miles mused, and he was starting to get the impression he'd only passed the interstellar version of a basic first aid course. Still, that didn't mute the sense of satisfaction he felt from passing one of his new home's tests, and from meeting the expectations of his new captain.

CHAPTER 5

Brisk raised the gun and opened fire. Bolts of yellow light spewed from the barrel, splashing across the metal interior of the cargo bay as he turned the weapon to track Torg's motion across the room. Every shot missed the target by inches, but Brisk was quickly correcting for Torg's unexpected burst of speed.

Torg bounded across the ground with a gait that was more like a charging bull than a giant bug, bounding on all eight legs as he zigzagged toward where Brisk stood.

One of Brisk's shots came close, and Torg changed direction suddenly, trying to break his aim. The move had the opposite effect, inadvertently moving him directly into Brisk's line of fire. One of the bolts hit him, scoring a deep furrow across his shell, and he chittered in fury.

No longer satisfied with a strafing approach, Torg launched himself directly at Brisk, but the muscular engineer rotated out of the way at the last second, sweeping the mace he held in his other hand in a low strike across Torg's legs.

The giant crustacean went down with a crash, rolling forward once before collapsing into a heap.

Brisk paused, looking around the room cautiously.

Typically the ship's engineer went around bare-chested, with a pair of rough pants and a low-slung tool belt. Now, he was wearing a pair of sleek plated pants that had the look of fish scales. Over his torso, he wore a breastplate made of a material that looked like milky glass, translucent, but clearly some kind of armor. There was a star fracture in the plate just over the abdomen. From what Miles now knew of Hurc biology, it looked like someone had tried to shoot him in the heart.

Satisfied, Brisk lowered the gun and slipped it back into a holster on his side.

Out of nowhere, Trin appeared behind him, hopping up and boxing the back of his head with a flurry of paw strikes.

Brisk ignored the punches, casually grabbing Trin out of the air and tossing him across the room. The Eppan scout landed gracefully, rolling into a crouch and staring back at him.

Miles stood at the back of the room, feeling awkward.

Awkward, confused, and irritated.

"Good," Brisk said, pointing at Torg. "But don't commit to evading if you can't keep it up, and don't lose your temper."

He continued, pointing at Trin. "Awful. You're not a close-range fighter. If you don't have a ranged weapon, distract and disrupt."

Finally, he turned his attention to Miles. "And you. Soft little boy. You didn't even try."

"Why are we doing this?" Miles countered, heat in his voice.

"Because the Spiral is a dangerous place, and you won't always have muscle standing between you and the threat."

That's such an evasive answer.

"You're lying," Miles said. "I didn't find out I'd need a healer's accreditation until the day before I had to take the test. We didn't find out we were docking at Delatariel Station until an hour before we arrived. Now the captain has us doing combat drills, and nobody will tell us why. What are you trying to prepare us for?"

Brisk's eyes diverged for a second, pupils pointing in different directions, before he stopped, as if he'd thought of something. His lips parted and he smiled.

He flashed his incisors as he said, "If you can get me on the ground, I'll tell you."

Miles stared at him for a second, trying to work out if he was serious, then kicked off in a dead sprint straight at him.

Miles's hand came to his chest as he ran, and he cast *Temporary Enhancement*, focusing on his strength.

In myself, I am complete. In a harmonious world, everything is complete. **I am that which I am.**

His magical core whirred and the magic flooded through him, somehow hotter than usual.

The words that the magic recalled, at first nonsense to him, now rang with a special truth. He wasn't at the point of fully understanding them, but they were no longer meaningless.

An image flashed through his mind as the spell latched on, a vision of himself standing alone, his complete potential realized, a physical form as strong as any physical form might ever be. It was an image that the magic didn't measure up to, not yet, maybe not ever, but it was the direction it strove toward.

Brisk's eyes widened slightly in surprise, but he wasn't surprised enough not to react. He pivoted to catch Miles, grabbing him by the shirt and casually tossing him, turning the sprint into an uncontrolled tumble.

Miles rolled through the air, sure that he'd missed his chance, but then a pair of strong pincers caught him, stopping the fall and gently bringing him to the ground. He looked up to see Torg, who'd picked himself off the floor.

Miles pivoted and ran back at Brisk. Torg was beside him this time. Apparently, the lancer was as curious about what they were preparing for as he was, and willing to help him at a moment's notice.

When they were just feet away from their target, Torg grabbed Miles at the shoulder and hip and threw him at the waiting engineer Trin appeared in the same instant, crouching on the ground behind Brisk.

Miles collided with Brisk, who tried to step backward and tripped over Trin instead. Miles caught a flash of open-mouth surprise as Brisk went down under him.

Not wanting to miss the chance and not willing to let there be any ambiguity about the result, Miles grabbed Brisk's wrists, pinning him to the ground. Brisk struggled for a second, his breath hot on Miles's face, then gave up with an exhaled laugh.

He jerked, showing his true strength as he tossed Miles away.

Miles rolled on the ground to avoid hitting his head, and by the time he looked up, Brisk was already on his feet.

"Fine, I'll tell you," he said. He unstrapped his chest-plate and hung it over a metal beam. "That fight felt like you'd been training together for a month, not just three days. Yeah, I'll tell you. Get cleaned up and meet me in the observation dome. Left side, one hour."

Brisk left the cargo bay via the ladder, climbing up to the catwalk and then taking the door that led to the main body of the ship.

Miles, Trin, and Torg were left staring at each other.

"I don't believe it. You were right," Trin said.

Click-click. "*Secrets*," Torg added.

Miles wasn't surprised he was right, only that Brisk had turned out to have a secret cache of fairness hidden away in his character.

The *Starlit Kipper* did turn out to have a shower, of sorts.

The wetroom was a bare metal chamber with nozzles along the walls, hot air vents, and a recycling drain built into the floor. It seemed that a lot of Spiral species liked to clean themselves with liquid solvents, and when they did it they liked to clean their entire body at once. The main difference seemed to be their particular solvent of choice.

Torg liked to shower in a nitric acid solution, while Trin bathed in a kind of honey-scented liquid Miles didn't know the makeup of. The shower unit was set up to allow a choice of fluids, and Miles had settled for a ninety-nine percent water–sodium stearate mix—soap and water. After Trin had found out that Miles's soap was produced from stearic acid, he'd started to call both Miles and Torg "acid bathers."

The shower unit was big enough for multiple people to use at once, but after Miles had explained his culture's nudity taboo to Trin—overselling it slightly—the other boy had been willing to let him have the unit to himself.

Neither of them were keen to shower with Torg, as nitric acid steam wasn't something either wanted to deal with.

Miles stepped out of the chamber clean and dry, wearing a fresh sweater and clean cargo pants.

Trin was already waiting outside, his fur smudged in places with grease, and he was giving off a smell Miles had learned to associate with physical activity. As Miles came to a stop, Trin was holding one of his head-flaps up, peering at the furless underside.

"Dirty," Trin said sadly.

Miles gestured at the shower unit. "All yours."

Trin dropped his flap and swept into the shower, hitting the switch to close the door behind him.

Miles started down the corridor. He was just trying to remember which hatch opened on the ladder to the observation domes when the tone of an incoming call started playing from his communicator.

He stopped and checked the screen.

The captain. Great.

He answered the call.

"Report to the bridge," the captain's voice commanded over the unit.

Miles briefly flirted with the idea of replying, "I'm already busy," but managed to restrain himself. This was the job.

He changed directions, heading up the corridor toward the front of the ship.

The *Starlit Kipper* was about thirty meters long from nose to tail. As a naval ship, it would be about the size of a fishing trawler on old Earth, but in the open space of the weave, it was fairly small as ships went. It was designed for a crew of eight, with eight crew berths and two guest quarters. The biggest open space was the cargo bay, filling the ship's belly and running almost its entire length. Miles had been on the ship for a week, and he'd never seen any actual cargo in the cargo bay.

It was only a short walk to the bridge, and when he tapped the switch for access, the door slid open almost immediately.

Inside, the captain was actually sitting down in their chair, the orb of their body resting gently on the padded seat. It didn't look like their body could completely support its own weight fully when it wasn't supported by the levitation unit. Normally a sphere, the captain's body was now squashed slightly as it weighed on the seat cushion, making them look like a rounded pumpkin.

"I'm here," Miles said to the room, not willing to subject himself to another one of the captain's ambiguous silences.

"Come in," the captain said.

Miles stepped further into the room, closer to the chair. An invitation to *come in* seemed unusually polite for the captain. They normally just got to the point.

Sellen was there on the bridge, sitting at the pilot's station. Miles still hadn't spoken to her, and she ignored his entrance.

The viewport showed a different view from the last time Miles had been in there. Before, it had been a view of a large section of Spiral, one edge as seen from the other. Now it was showing a thick band of stars and worlds, with no curve. It was one segment of the Spiral, seen from much closer up. They must have made it most of the way across the core void, approaching whatever their destination was.

The holographic display nearby was still showing a planet, and after a quick inspection, Miles realized it was the same one as before. *Ialis*. A forest-green sphere with only a handful of city-settlements on its surface. Maybe *that* was their destination.

"I am in pain," the captain said, after a minute of silence. "Treat me."

That's more like the captain I know.

Miles took a moment to be surprised that he'd been called on to treat a medical issue. He wasn't a doctor, or even a medic, but on reflection, he realized that he was probably just the most qualified person on board to help. If the captain hadn't been putting him through combat drills, he might even believe this was the kind of thing he'd been hired for.

Approaching the captain, he looked his Orbellius patient over carefully. They weren't wearing their usual belt, which explained why they were sitting down. Their spaghetti-thin tendrils were strong enough to move them around in a medium-gravity environment, but it was apparently tiring, and the captain relied on their levitation unit to have the same mobility as the rest of the crew.

"Where does it hurt?" Miles asked.

The captain used their tendrils to point at several places around their circumference. Miles was already starting to get an idea.

He concentrated on his *Eyes of the Altruist*, feeling the mental shift as his passive spells shifted to bring the diagnostic magic to the front.

Glowing shapes appeared over the captain and the pilot, hints at what was going on inside their bodies. Sellen was actually surprisingly devoid of internal structure. Their body was in the form of a wide, flat sheet of flesh, and there was almost nothing inside them that the diagnostic magic could identify as a separate structure.

The captain, on the other hand, did have structure. This wasn't Miles's first time using this ability on an Orbellius—he'd been shown one during his healer accreditation test—but the captain had subtle differences to the simulation on Delatariel Station. There were more of those little subsurface nodules, for one, and instead of one internal compartment, the captain had six separate sacs, separated by thin membranes.

The captain said something, but Miles's *Eyes of the Émigré* ability was incompatible with the diagnostic magic. He couldn't use both at the same time, so whatever the captain said just sounded like an incomprehensible mess of whistling and wheezing.

"I can't understand you right now, sorry," Miles said, trusting that whatever translation tool the captain used was still working. "Just give me a minute."

As he examined the areas the captain had pointed out, he noticed that there was a band of slightly different texture that circled the captain's body in a ring. It was covered in faint striations, lines and creases drawn out in angry red.

Under almost any other circumstances, Miles wouldn't know what it meant, but the line happened to line up exactly with where the captain usually wore his belt.

He let the *Eyes of the Altruist* fade, forcing his *Eyes of the Émigré* back to the forefront of his mind.

He thought he had a diagnosis, as simple and uneducated a guess as it was.

"Do you think your levitation unit could be giving you"—*don't say ball strain*—"strain?" he asked.

The captain wore the belt every waking minute, if they even slept, and whatever their evolutionary origins, Miles didn't think it was likely Orbellian physiology was optimized to support their weight on a strap stuck around their midsection.

The captain was silent for a few seconds, before admitting, "Yes."

It was the first time Miles had heard any recognizable emotion in their voice. They sounded embarrassed.

"Give me an analgesic," the captain ordered.

Miles didn't *have* an analgesic. He didn't really have any kind of stash of medicines.

"I want to try something else," Miles said, instead. "I'll need to touch you."

"You have permission."

Miles pulled out his index and placed a hand against the captain's skin. He brought up his index to cast his *Hasten Renewal* spell, but briefly froze when he saw the screen. He switched to the changes-only view, which confirmed what he thought.

Name: Miles Asher	**Traditions:** Harmonizer	**Changes**
Spells [Improved]		
Temporary Enhancement (Tentative > Grasping) *A temporary matrix of harmonizing energy alters one of a being's fundamental properties by an amount in accordance with the weaver's Authority.*		

His ability with *Temporary Enhancement* had increased, from Tentative to Grasping. When had he got better at casting it?

The training with Brisk.

He'd enhanced his strength to try to knock the Hurc engineer down. And he'd cast the spell without even touching his index.

Shock and elation briefly fought each other for Miles's attention, but he brushed both aside. He was still in the middle of something.

He focused on the captain and tapped his index to cast *Hasten Renewal*, and the litany of the spell bubbled into his body and his consciousness.

In themself, they are complete. In a harmonious world, everything is complete.
They are that which they are.

Miles's core spun, and an electric energy flowed to his hands, threading out through his skin to needle through the captain's body. He could almost feel the magic working, pricking at the truth of the captain's healthy form until their body started giving way to the new reality, straining in its own way to meet the ideal that the spell proposed.

When Miles had tried this during his healer accreditation, it had never completely healed a wound, but it always helped to some degree. He hoped that it would do a better job with a purely internal stress injury.

He held the spell for as long as he dared, only breaking away when he started to feel weak and weirdly insubstantial. He swayed involuntarily as he stepped back, and took a second to collect himself.

"Is that better?" he asked the captain, when he'd managed to get past the stunned, drifting sensation.

"I have recovered," the captain replied.

That was all. No thanks, no elaboration.

The captain began strapping their belt around their waist again. They clicked it into place, then activated the levitation unit, slowly rising off the chair.

"I'll be going, then," Miles said.

The captain gave silence as a reply, and Miles turned to go.

He checked his comm unit as he left, and saw messages from Trin timestamped five minutes earlier.

Trin > Miles
Where are you Miles.
Trin > Miles
He is starting. Did you not want to hear this?

Miles dropped his comm into his pocket and ran for the observation deck.

When Miles scrambled up into the observation dome, Brisk, Trin, and Torg were already there.

Brisk had been speaking, but stopped when Miles burst in, giving him a long stare.

The observation dome was a hemisphere of glassy material rising up out of the top of the ship, like an eye, or a blister. It wasn't that wide, maybe eight feet edge to edge, but the padded bench that circled it had room for several people.

Brisk and Trin were sitting on the bench, while Torg sat on the floor, his head barely fitting under the dome.

Past the glass, the dome gave them a view of the ship, and the cosmos beyond.

Looking up rewarded Miles with a view of the Spiral. It ran around in rings, winding and cascading upward, seemingly forever. In the extreme distance, the effect of perspective coiled the chain of stars down to a single point, which blurred and retreated into an indistinct haze beyond that.

Around the Spiral, in the vast darkness that stretched infinitely away from it in every direction, was the empty void of the bare weave. There was nothing out there, and there never would be.

Miles felt goosebumps prickling on his skin.

"As I was telling your team, we're heading toward a planet," Brisk said.

"Ialis," Miles said. He spoke without thinking, but he was sure he was right.

"Ialis," Brisk declared. He spoke as if Miles hadn't said anything, but then he looked at him sharply. "Do you want to tell this?"

"Me? No. Go on."

"Right." Brisk looked around. He had everyone's attention. "Ialis had its bower break about a hundred iterations ago, Iteration 26,100. It crashed through from one of the highest-energy universes the Spiral's ever seen, but it didn't even make a ripple when it landed. That was just the start of the weirdness. When the Forward Fleet came by to investigate, they found it totally uninhabited. There were plants growing on the surface, but no sapients. Normally, you need sapients to cause a bower break, as scratching at the bottom of their space for free energy is how most worlds get here, but Ialis didn't have anything smarter than a shrub on it. At least, not on the surface."

There were a few seconds of silence, then a sudden trilling noise started blaring from Brisk's pocket.

Brisk grunted and pulled out his communicator. Miles got a long enough look at the screen to make out that it was a call from the captain. Which Brisk *canceled*.

He slipped his comm back into his pocket before continuing, while Miles stared at him aghast.

"On scavenger crews, Ialis has another name," he said, looking around at them. "The dungeon planet."

Brisk's expression dared them to make light of it, but: the kind with chains, and darkness, that people went into and didn't come back out of.

"Twenty iterations after its bower, someone crashed a high-velocity asteroid into the surface. After the dust cleared, they saw it'd opened a hole. It turns out that the top eighty miles of Ialis is soil and rock, but below that, it's metal. Metal all the way down. The entire planet is a technological artifact. Layers and layers of floors and rooms, connected by vents and elevators."

"Why we going there?" Trin asked, sounding awed.

"Because it's full of rare materials and advanced technology," Brisk replied plainly. He looked at Miles. "Your index is based on something a salvage team found there, and that's not the only Ialis recovery to go big. The corporation that controls it charges teams for entry, and they get right of first refusal on anything we pull out."

"This is what you do," Miles said. "You hire boarding teams, and then take them for raids on this planet."

"It's what a lot of salvage teams do, squirrit."

Something else occurred to him.

"When you docked at Ustiel, you were four crew members down," he said. "Why did you need more people?"

Brisk spread his hands. "I told you; the Spiral is a dangerous place."

"They're *dead*?"

Brisk's comm buzzed again, and this time he answered it, wearing a look of frustration.

"Yeah?" he answered.

"The drive is stuttering."

"On it."

Brisk closed the call and stood up. "I'm needed," he said, putting the comm unit away. He headed for the ladder, but paused on his way out, looking back at Miles. "You're right, squirrit. The captain has kept you in the dark, but now you know. You have a chance to prepare yourself. We'll be landing on Ialis next interval."

Tomorrow, Miles thought. Not exactly a lot of time to prepare.

PART 3

IT CAME HERE UNINHABITED

CHAPTER 6

The robe was loose, meant for a body wider and shorter than Miles's, but that was an advantage in some ways.

Its sleeves came down to just past his wrists, enveloping his hands if he let it, and the hem hung just above his knees, protecting him from the waist down without restricting his movements. Most importantly it wouldn't make it any harder for him to access the pockets of his cargo pants.

The mage merchant who'd given it to him had promised him that it was armor, for all that it just looked like coarse light gray fabric, and it had passed the few tests Miles had been able to inflict on it with a penknife. He'd been given it for free as a sweetener on another purchase, so he could hardly complain, but either way, it seemed like a solid defensive upgrade to canvas and cotton. If what Brisk had said the previous day about Ialis was true, then he might need it.

The robe had come tangled up with a dark brown belt; a length of synth webbing studded with maglocks and carabiners. Strapping that around the outside of the robe had solved any issues that the baggy extra fabric around the chest might cause.

Miles had polished a section of his berth's wall into a kind of mirror, and he paused in front of it, looking at his reflection.

He'd changed a lot in the short period since he'd left Unsiel Station, and not all for the better.

His short hair was messier, with no real reason or motivation to care for it. His eyes looked tired, and only because he *was* tired. Sleeping well on the narrow, lightly padded bunk was a skill he was still mastering. He'd kept up with his grooming on the ship—washing, shaving, laundry—but he'd failed in little ways at different points, momentary lapses that had added up to a rougher appearance than he was used to. He looked like he'd just spent a week on a long-haul flight, and his particular journey wasn't even close to over.

Outside in the corridor, someone with override permissions hit the access switch for his room and the door started grinding open.

Miles turned to look at the door, watching as the panel slid open to reveal Brisk leaning against the door frame.

He hated that Brisk could just come in whenever he wanted.

"Still preening?" Brisk asked. "You know the weave doesn't care how pretty you are."

Miles checked his robe, patted the pockets of his pants, and pulled his slim backpack over his shoulders. He was bringing every useful item he owned with him. He had his index, his comm, a few food packets, a *Devon Springs* branded plastic water bottle he'd brought all the way from Earth, and his folding knife, all stowed away in the pockets of his cargo pants. The pack was empty, but he thought he should bring it in case he needed to carry anything.

Brisk was also dressed for an excursion. He was wearing his scaled pants and the translucent breastplate of the previous day, as well as a harness of leather-like straps and pouches buckled tightly around his chest and shoulders.

Miles glared at Brisk as he left the room, closing the door behind him.

Brisk set off walking, and Miles followed. From the direction, they must have been heading toward the bridge.

After a few seconds, Brisk spoke, his tone unusually casual.

"Say, you're adult for your species, right?"

"Yes. I'm nineteen," Miles said, feeling caught off guard and suddenly worried.

Brisk looked uncharacteristically uncomfortable for a second, then unstrapped one of the pouches from his harness. He passed it over to Miles without a word.

Miles took it, turning it in his hands, then popped open the flap.

Inside was a small, sleek pistol, about the length of his hand, made of silvery metal. The pouch was a holster, he realized. He pulled the pistol out, turning it to catch the light.

The design was sleek, reminding Miles of the aesthetics of the *Starlit Kipper* itself, with smooth, demure curves and an almost biological look. The handle and trigger were adjustable, capable of extending and changing angles to fit a variety of hands, but this one was already sized for him. He tried holding it by the handle and found it warm and comfortable in his grip.

"It's a *striker*," Brisk explained, though Miles's *Eyes of the Émigré* stumbled over a direct translation for the weapon. "A laser concussion gun. Non-lethal civilian model. It's simple. Just point and shoot. The switch turns it on and off, and the slider on the side changes the power. I want you to keep it on low until you learn not to point it at anyone you like—or at me."

Miles looked at the gun again. He familiarized himself with the controls, the switch, the slider, then slipped it back into its pouch. The pouch had clips that had connected to Brisk's harness, and Miles used them to attach it to his belt at his back, where it hung below the slim runner's pack.

"Don't expect it to work miracles, but at top power, it'll knock even someone Torg's size around."

"Thanks," Miles said.

Brisk seemed uncomfortable. He didn't reply.

Ialis was huge in the viewport; a sphere of dark green and gray, stippled with a thousand pinpricks of white and golden light.

There were oceans down there, inland seas of green-black liquid that pressed the borders of crawling fractal coastlines. The areas of dark green he'd seen earlier on the hologram turned out to be vast forests and swamps. The clusters of artificial light were cities, mostly clustered around the impact site that Brisk had mentioned, with a few off in the far reaches. Ialis had no native population, but the Ialis Corporation had invited the cultures of the Spiral to settle there after discovering its value.

The *Starlit Kipper* it had been alone in space for most of the time since Miles had boarded, but now it flew toward the planet as one small vessel in a busy sky.

There were clear aesthetic themes in the other ships coming and going from the planet. Some were like the *Kipper*, aerodynamic organic shapes that looked like they could have been patterned on the alien versions of ocean creatures. Other ships were almost the opposite: bulky, angular vessels constructed from green-black cubes of cluttered metal.

There were ships that were just long silvery rods, others that were clusters of glass pods joined together by a network of energy, and some bulbous rounded hulls with awkward-looking little wings that reminded Miles of human space engineering.

Miles gawked when he saw what looked like a wooden sailing ship pass them heading in the opposite direction, sure that magic must be at play there.

As the *Kipper* groaned around him, he couldn't help but wonder if he'd picked the wrong ship.

Sellen was frantically operating her pilot station, the dexterous corners of her body sweeping one way then another, adjusting calculations written out in alien characters and striving to keep the ship out of the path of larger vessels in what was apparently a chaotic and unmanaged airspace.

The entire crew was assembled on the bridge, mostly standing around, or floating, in the case of the captain.

Trin was wearing his normal pink jumpsuit, but a few of his pockets were bulging with new equipment, and he was holding a device that looked like an archaic cell phone: a brick with a small screen and an elaborate antenna. From the wires and bare circuitry running along parts of it, it looked like it had been stitched together out of spare parts.

Someone had armed Torg. The giant black crustacean was holding a two-handed ax in their two right pincers, and some kind of thick-barreled gun in the left pair.

Miles had his magic, his index, and the weapon Brisk had given him, but he still felt dramatically underequipped for whatever awaited them on Ialis.

The ship's energy shields blocked all sensation of movement on board the *Kipper* as it descended, and there was no competing gravity from the planet, so the descent was smooth. There was no need to sit down or strap in, but standing unsupported while a planet rapidly expanded in the viewport left Miles feeling an intense sense of vertigo.

"Brisk," the captain said.

"Captain?"

Rhu-Orlen was silent for half a minute, before asking, "Have you explained the environment?"

Brisk let out a breath, then turned to check that Miles, Trin, and Torg were all present and paying attention. He raised his voice slightly as he began speaking.

"The background environment in the dungeon has some unusual properties."

Miles nodded to himself. Every world that fell down to the Spiral brought some of its native space with it. Earth had collapsed with a comparatively large amount, about three hundred million miles worth of spacetime, but others bowered with more or less. That space would have whatever properties the world's original universe possessed. It was why messages to Earth still took days to reach it, even when instant communications were common everywhere else in the weave.

"Time. The time in there runs faster than it does out here. It starts off barely noticeable, but the deeper you go, the sharper the gradient gets."

Time dilation, Miles thought. *Like a black hole.*

"Space as well. From up here, it looks like a sphere, but each level as you go down has the same total area as the one above. It doesn't make a difference for moving around, but the geometry messes with resonance comms. There's no messages in and no messages out."

Not exactly like a black hole . . . Miles thought, adjusting how he thought of the planet.

"The third thing to worry about is that it's infinite. Or that's the theory. It goes at least three times deeper than it should be able to from the size of the planet, and scans from inside say that's just the *tip of the horn*."

Uhhh.

"When we land we'll have some paperwork to do, then we'll be put in a queue. An hour after that we'll be inside. The rooms on the top levels shuffle around every

4.3 hours, so that's our window. It gets more dangerous the deeper you go, but our target's only on the seventh floor, so we should all get out alive."

Miles and Trin looked grimly serious at that. Miles was only just starting to process that it really might be deadly down there. He wondered whether it would be worth jumping ship before getting paid.

"Are you coming with us?" he asked Brisk.

"Yeah. I'll be our team leader. I act as a *fusilier*." *Eyes of the Émigré* stumbled over the translation, but the meaning was clear. Brisk was going, and he was armed.

If Brisk was part of the team, then it wasn't as if they were being thrown into the meat grinder. There had to be a good chance they were going to make it out, both because they'd have Brisk looking after them, and because Brisk didn't seem the type to risk his life on a bad bet.

What Brisk had said about the seventh level caught Miles's attention.

"What *is* our target down there?"

Brisk and the captain shared a look, as much as it was possible to share a look with a featureless sphere. The captain faced Brisk for a couple of seconds, then turned away. Nobody answered the question.

A minute later they hit the atmosphere.

Green.

The surface of Ialis was green. The ground was covered in an all-encompassing moss, as thick and wild as any grass back on Earth. There were trees, bent and crawling things that spread their roots above the ground. Instead of leaves, they were covered in green-black hairs that stretched out beneath the bright star that served as this planet's sun.

It was nothing like Earth, but it was green, and there was wind, and there were the smells of water and damp life. The homesickness Miles felt was almost a physical object, sitting like a stone in the pit of his stomach. He missed the forests of home. Pine boughs and mushrooms, possums, squirrels, dew on the grass.

A wormlike sapient twelve feet tall emerged from the structure up ahead, crawling toward them. As soon as they were clear of the building's roof, they straightened up, continuing to crawl on the bottom quarter of their body, but with most of their length held high, swaying back and forth slightly as they snaked across the moss.

Elongated trunk-style body type. Organs are probably distributed. Maybe a central heart?

Miles risked pushing his *Eyes of the Émigré* away, hoping no one would speak while his translation magic was down, focusing his attention instead on *Eyes of the Altruist.*

Luminescent shapes faded into view over the sapient, and Miles realized he'd been completely wrong. Or rather, his Tier 1 healer primer had completely misled him. There was actually a fairly standard cluster of organs at the extreme front of the creature, with the rest of its length dedicated to what he assumed were bands of muscle and not much else. It was more like how his primer described a "short trunk" species, just much longer.

The wormlike sapient was wearing a long tube of fabric that covered it from close to the top all the way down to just short of where it was in contact with the ground. There were small magnetized clips closing the garment up the front, and where it terminated at the top it flared outward in a dramatic collar. They didn't seem to have arms, or any kind of manipulators at all, leaving Miles wondering how they got by in a society where almost every task was mediated by technological devices.

As the sapient drew closer, Miles noticed they had a row of four eyes running vertically down the front-tip of their body, all focused directly on them.

Brisk started speaking, and Miles quickly switched back to his *Eyes of the Émigré*, hoping he hadn't missed anything important.

"—and be polite. Gilthaens are one of the oldest cultures on the Spiral, and they live forever. Make this one's life hard and they'll remember it for a dozen lifetimes."

Gilthaen. Miles filed the species name away.

The sapient reached conversation distance, then bowed.

"I am Consul They-who-share-ground. To you, I am Consul Thunis. Are you seeking entry to the artifact?"

"Consul, yes, we are," Brisk answered, speaking in an unusually polite tone.

"There are terms that govern entry of the artifact. A fee is charged. This fee covers the management and maintenance of the artifact. There are restrictions on entering and leaving, which must occur according to a schedule, and in accordance with others who wish to enter. When within the artifact, visitors are bound by a code of conduct—"

"We are aware of the bylaws of Ialis and agree to them," Brisk said, interrupting the Gilthaen consul despite his earlier instruction to be polite.

The consul didn't seem to take offense to the interruption. If anything, they seemed to expect it. They bowed again, then swayed precariously as they turned around and began shuffling back toward the structure.

Brisk started walking after them, and Miles, Trin, and Torg followed.

The architecture of the Ialis Corporation seemed to favor large, airy spaces that were open to the outdoors. Dark metal structures with ceilings but no walls, with elegant curved skeletal supports that rose fifteen or twenty feet in the air to hold up the corners of curving metal roofs. The ground inside the structures was just the bare earth and moss of the planet, and furniture was sparse, consisting of rare benches and computer terminals hovering several feet above the floor, seemingly unsupported. They seemed more like pavilions than buildings, and while nothing Miles knew from Earth matched up, the curving ceilings evoked images of ancient Japanese castles, with sweeping supports and elaborate overhangs.

The consul escorted them toward one of the buildings. As they approached, the horizon beyond seemed to vanish, as the ground gave way to the edge of a massive crater.

The closer they got to the structure, the deeper into the hole they could see. While the first step of it looked like the typical brown of rock and dirt, below that the edges glinted with blue-white lights and reflective metal. It was as if someone had taken a densely packed building and cut out a massive scoop. There was evidence of vivisected rooms all along the inner edge of the crater, some massive, some too small to make out.

The consul led them into one of the open-air structures. Inside, small tech drones moved around, drifting as they idled, occasionally leaving the building and returning a minute later.

Consul Thunis took their details, entering them into a terminal which they interacted with seemingly just by touching it with the tip of their body. Brisk paid the fee, but Miles didn't manage to catch how much it was.

"It is stipulated that all teams wishing to enter the artifact must be accompanied by a healer," Thunis said. "The Ialis Corporation can provide you with a Tier 4 healer for the duration of your visit at the cost of twenty thousand standard exchange notes."

"Consul, we understand. We have our own healer," Brisk said, slapping a hand down on Miles's shoulder.

Miles was busy filing away the fact that a Tier 4 healer could make twenty thousand seln for just four hours of work. Then he started wondering what his real value was on the open market. His crew salary was a thousand seln per Spiral standard month. Was the gap between Tier 1 and Tier 4 really that high? It was something he'd have to research later.

"Please present your accreditation," Consul Thunis said, apparently addressing Miles.

Miles pulled his comm unit out of his pocket and opened it to the certificate he'd been sent following his assessment. He held it up to the sapient.

Thunis bent down, curling their body until their face was only a foot away from Miles. They peered at the screen, their eyes clicking wetly as they blinked.

This close, the sapient had a smell like dry earth, and Miles could have sworn he could hear indistinct whispering coming from them.

After inspecting Miles's credentials they rose back up.

"That is in order."

Thunis did something with the console, and one of the drones appeared. It approached each of them individually, painting each member of the group with a beam of light that left behind a blue stripe on the shoulders of their clothes—or their carapace, in Torg's case.

"For identification," the consul explained.

When the drone reached Miles, it painted the stripe, but then moved to his chest and drew an additional symbol as well. Miles pulled the front of his robe out, trying to get a look at it, and finally getting his *Eyes of the Émigré* to trigger and present him with a translation.

The symbol meant *healer*.

"Please board the platform. It will bring you into a priority queue with other visitors to the artifact," Thunis said, sliding toward the edge of the building. "Do you have a preference for your entry location?"

"D7," Brisk replied.

"That is in order."

The four of them left the building to stand on the platform.

The ringed disk lifted into the sky, almost knocking Trin to the ground with its sudden acceleration, then started its slow descent into the crater.

CHAPTER 7

It took over an hour to close in on the crater wall.

They'd seen other groups on the way, maybe a hundred in total, all floating on their own platforms like dandelion seeds drifting through the air.

As they descended, the different layers of the interior had been easy to make out.

Each level looked to be about half a kilometer thick, though only a few of the torn-open rooms used that entire height. The rest of the space was full of intricate circuitry, pipes and vessels, storage tanks, and areas that were simply unidentifiable.

It was more than a planet-sized space station; it was a vast and unknowable machine. And it had apparently dropped here completely uninhabited.

The queue of parties wanting to enter took the form of a Spiral of platforms, turning slowly each time the lowest disk drifted off to its chosen entry point. Most of them had gone to the first or second level. Brisk's decision had their platform dropping down kilometers to a point on the seventh level.

Their entry point was a simple metal room, hangar-sized, with dull metal walls and a high ceiling set with pale blue lights. The room was bare, and already looted, with sections of broken pipes and wires where it looked like equipment had been torn out a long time ago.

The ground that the platform set down on was dusted with the green-black moss of the surface. Water marks streaked down the walls closest to the opening, evidence of rain damage, and there was a bitter metallic rust smell over the entire space.

Brisk was the first to step off. "This is the threshold. Past this, the danger starts. See anything unusual, tell me. Ask before you do anything, and stay in formation. Trin first. I want a warning of any warm bodies or movement. Keep us on course, but ask before making any turns or opening any doors. Torg, back Trin up. If you see danger coming for him, you run in first and ask questions later. You're the exception to the ask-first rule. Miles, hang back with me. Back the others up, but ask before you run in to heal anyone. I'll be supporting the rest of you with long-range fire from the back."

He unslung the rifle from his back as he spoke, checking various settings on the weapon before putting its strap around his neck and shoulder and holding it ready.

Trin began walking toward the door on the far side of the room, a twenty-foot-high rectangular doorway that could have been a hatch for unusually tall vehicles to pass through, or a door for spindly giants.

"How do you open?" Trin asked. He ran a mid-paw over the surface of the door, then checked the wall at the side for an access panel. There wasn't one, but there was a burnt-out hole with a few wires protruding from it.

"You'll have to bypass the controls," Brisk said, as if it was something both obvious and easy. Miles wouldn't have had any idea how to start.

Trin brought up the boxy device he was holding, pressing the physical keys that dotted the front panel until a matrix of waving lines appeared on the screen. He brought the antenna close to the mess of scratched-out wiring in the wall, then adjusted the settings.

His head-flaps shifted as he worked, rising at random in small movements that he didn't seem to be consciously aware of.

After about a minute, he grabbed a handful of wires and started touching them to something inside the wall. On the fourth try, the hole emitted an ugly murmuring sound, and the door opened half a meter upward.

"Is weird tech," Trin said, pulling back from the ruined panel and resetting his device. "I don't get what's in these wires."

Brisk moved up to the gap under the door, crouching and peering through, his rifle moving to stay pointed in the direction he was looking.

After a minute, he said, "Okay. Door protocol. Torg first, then me, Trin, and Miles will bring up the rear."

They all filed through in that order, crouching low to pass under the door. Torg had to drop to all eight limbs and scurry through. Trin only had to duck.

The room beyond the door was large, about a hundred meters square, with a ceiling that stretched about twenty meters above them. It was in good repair, in comparison to the damaged room they'd landed in. There were two other doors at the far side, as tall and narrow as the one they'd entered through, and the control panels for them were intact, black rectangles set flush with the metal walls.

The room was set up as a warehouse, with an open space in the center and metal shelving all around the outside. There was even a cargo lifting arm hanging from rails that crisscrossed the roof.

The shelves were dotted with weirdly normal-looking metal crates. Some even had text and logos that recalled the brands Miles had seen on Delatariel Station. None of the images were exactly correct, and when Miles stared at the labels to try and read the text, none of it would translate, as if it wasn't written in a real language at all.

"Someone storing things here?" Trin asked.

"I don't think real people put any of this here," Miles said.

"It does this all the time," Brisk said, bitterly. "We think it scans nearby space for patterns, then the autofabs that make the rooms repeat them. The rooms shift constantly."

"What's in the boxes?" Trin asked. He looked ready to start prying them open.

"Junk, usually. Stuff that looks like real tech, but doesn't work, or doesn't do anything. Stocks of alloys made with random metals. Useless. Sometimes you get a real find, but that's not why we're here."

"Why *are* we here?" Miles asked.

Brisk gave him a hard look before turning back to the room.

"Trin, have you got a heading?"

Trin checked his device and then pointed off to the right.

They made their way through the open room to the right-hand door. Trin had wired the previous one back to life, but here Brisk pulled a small rod from one of his vest pouches, a triangular prism about the length and width of a finger. He touched the prism to the black screen and lights flickered behind the glass.

Text briefly appeared on the screen, this time in a language that Miles's *Eyes of the Émigré* could translate.

It simply said: yes.

The door made a thunking sound, then slid upward, this time opening about eight feet.

They passed through according to their formation. As soon as Torg was a few steps into the next room he stopped.

Torg clicked rapidly. *"Air tastes of animal."*

"Smell?" Brisk asked. "You can smell *what?*"

Another pair of clicks *"Animal. Creature."*

"Is anyone's translator getting that?" Brisk asked, annoyed.

"He can smell animals in here," Miles said.

Brisk glanced at Miles and then looked around the room.

This room was similar to the last, a large space that looked like a warehouse. The shelves here were more densely packed, rows and rows just feet away from one other, with no open spaces or clear sight lines.

"Trin, are you getting anything?" Brisk asked.

"I can't look two things at once," Trin answered, sounding annoyed. He fiddled with his sensor device, then spent a minute scrutinizing the screen. His head-flaps twitched as he worked, some lifting up all the way. "It says no motion."

"What about heat?"

Trin muttered something too quiet for Miles's magic to translate, then fiddled with his sensor again. "No heat. Just us."

"Fine. Everyone keep your eyes open. We'll get to the other side in formation, then look for the door."

They set off into the room, with Trin in the lead and Brisk at the back.

When they'd been moving for long enough in silence, Miles let his *Eyes of the Émigré* fade, focusing on his *Eyes of the Altruist* instead. Maybe the magic would let him see through walls, he thought.

It didn't, but when they were halfway across the room, he did catch sight of a cluster of luminescent shapes he was pretty sure shouldn't be there.

On a shelf thirty meters to their left was a collection of crates. Three of them were covered in the luminous shapes that *Eyes of the Altruist* normally only painted over biological organs.

They weren't particularly complex organs. Each box had a cluster of round shapes, each about an inch across, all about an inch apart, but he'd only ever seen shapes like that on living creatures.

Undifferentiated organs. Unitary body plan? he thought.

Miles mentally marked the crates, then switched back to *Eyes of the Émigré*.

"Brisk," he said, keeping his voice low.

The fusilier came to a stop next to him.

"I think there's something alive over there."

"Where? How?"

"I have some diagnostic magic that's triggering on the crates."

Brisk peered in the direction Miles was looking, curious.

"Which ones?"

Miles pointed them out and Brisk quietly called to the others, bringing everyone back to stand together.

"Trin," he started. "What's your heat read on those boxes?"

"Cold."

"Colder than the rest?"

"Oh. Yes."

Brisk raised his rifle and dropped to one knee in a firing stance.

"Be ready. When I start shooting, they'll come for us."

"What will?" Miles asked.

Instead of answering, Brisk opened fire on the closest crate. He fired four times, the rifle ringing in his hands like a snapped guitar string.

Each shot elicited an answering screech and where they hit, the shelves were painted yellow with splashes of blood. There was no apparent damage to the crate, despite it being the obvious source of the blood.

The two other boxes Miles had identified launched themselves off the shelves, never changing in appearance as they slid across the floor toward them accompanied by the sound of claws rattling on steel.

Brisk fired two more times and clouds of yellow mist bloomed behind the next closest crate.

Miles remembered his own weapon and drew the pistol on the last crate. His first shot went wide, the weapon humming and trembling in his hand, but the second landed with a slapping sound, sending the metal box spinning away through the air.

It landed on its side, and Brisk put a final shot into it, casting a smear of yellow blood out behind it.

"Cloak roaches," Brisk said with disgust, looking around the room. "They mess with your senses, make you think they're something else. Do you see any more?"

Miles quickly switched back to *Eyes of the Altruist* and scanned the rest of the room, then let it fade.

"No. I don't think this lets me see through the shelves or crates, though."

"Keep it on. I want to know if you see anything like that again."

"I won't be able to understand you while I'm using it," Miles said.

"That's fine. I'll get your attention if anyone says anything important."

They continued crossing the room, finding a series of five doors set at different points. Brisk asked Trin a question, who worked on their scanner before replying. Brisk said something else, pointing to one of the doors. Trin looked worried, then turned to start poking the black panel.

It was weird watching the two of them speak without any translation. They weren't just speaking to each other in different languages, they were using entirely different families of sounds. Trin's voice was a musical mix of murmuring and sighs. Brisk's was more like a gurgling bark that had very little variation from one word to another.

Trin worked on the panel for a few minutes, bringing up and manipulating screens of alien text. Eventually, Brisk lost patience with Trin's inability to bypass it and used his rifle to shoot the screen out. After that, Trin was able to activate it by doing something with the torn internals.

This time, the door only lurched open a few feet. Beyond it was a nearly featureless white corridor, which continued straight for a while before bending right.

Brisk said something that Miles didn't need a translator to know meant, "Come on."

Everyone had to crawl to get through; Torg had to squirm under the door on his front. When they'd all squeezed through, they continued on.

Brisk had said that the rooms of the planet shuffled themselves every 4.3 hours. The time on Miles's comm told him they'd been inside for about half an hour, but Brisk had also said that time moved more slowly the deeper someone went into the structure. Did the shuffle happen on surface-time, or the altered time of the dungeon planet?

Brisk had them moving with haste, but not with panic. Miles had to assume that he knew what he was doing and that he wasn't about to get them stuck down there while the rooms rearranged.

The corridor seemed like a normal passageway at first, but oddities soon started appearing. Occasionally the corridor would make a turn, but it was always at a strange, obtuse angle, sometimes turning nearly back on itself. There were sudden changes in elevation, sections where the passageway would drop away at twenty-degree slopes or more, and they'd all have to carefully shuffle down, hoping there wasn't an even steeper drop just around the corner.

They passed stairways that went nowhere, sized for gaits twice as long as Miles's. The lights set in the ceiling appeared at seemingly random intervals, a cluster of five right next to each other, then dozens of meters of darkness, then four lights, then ten meters, then one, and on and on. They passed through a section of corridor that was carpeted, a dull orange fabric with geometric patterns, then a section where the walls and ceiling were carpeted. There were never any branches or side doors, just one long, unbroken tube that at times felt more like an oversized ventilation shaft than something people were meant to pass through.

Their formation broke down as they traveled the passage, and Miles found a chance to speak with Trin.

"Do you know what we're looking for?" Miles asked him, switching back to his *Eyes of the Émigré* before Trin could answer.

"Signal," Trin said, holding his scanner so Miles could see the screen. "Brisk gave me a frequency. Don't know what it is. Maybe a comm."

"I thought comm signals didn't work down here."

"They work on the same level. Not through levels."

"If it's a comm, can you call them?"

Miles didn't get an answer. They rounded the corner onto a scene that froze them in their tracks.

Fifteen meters down the corridor, something had knocked a hole out of the wall. Sheet metal had been worn fatigue-white and then torn open, the sides peeled outward. Inside the hollow space behind the tear was a pipe that had been given the same treatment.

There was no obvious sign of the culprit, but scattered all along the passageway were at least twenty motionless metal crates.

Just on the other side of the crowd of innocuous boxes was another door, this one open a crack, with damage to the exposed edges.

Brisk hurried to join them.

"Are those what I think they are?"

Miles shifted his attention to *Eyes of the Altruist*. Clusters of small oval shapes sprang up over nearly all of them.

"Twenty are. One's just a normal crate."

Brisk said something, then caught Miles's attention. Miles switched back to *Eyes of the Émigré*.

"Okay, I can understand you now."

"I was saying, twenty in a narrow space should be fine," he turned to start addressing the others. "Torg, get set up at the front with your cannon. Use the ax for any that reach you, but don't engage otherwise. Miles, take a stance with that striker. Maximum power. If any get past Torg, knock them back. Trin, get behind me."

They all moved to take up their positions according to Brisk's instructions.

Miles pulled the striker from the pouch at his back and adjusted the slider, pushing it all the way forward, then flicked the safety switch to turn it on. It hummed as it powered up.

When they were all in position, Brisk spoke.

"Torg, start us off."

The rifle Torg held in his left two pincers went off with a booming crackle. A visible bolt of red energy lanced down the corridor, instantly turning a row of four crates into yellow mist. The crate illusions vanished like popped soap bubbles. Fragments of yellow-black flesh went scattering across the walls.

The rest of the crates started moving as one, sliding down the corridor like boxes on an industrial conveyor belt.

The crate at the front leaped at Torg, who intercepted it with the edge of his ax. It went down, rolling away across the ground, leaving a trail of yellow behind it.

Brisk was firing continuously, the sound like a repetitive bass guitar solo. Torg fired off a shot every few seconds. Miles only had to discharge his weapon once, when a crate launched itself past them heading for Trin. He pointed the weapon, fired, and a whip-crack of energy sent the crate flying away to impact a wall. It left a smear of yellow against the steel and didn't move again after it landed. Brisk had said the striker was non-lethal, but Miles clearly had to take that with a grain of salt.

By the time a minute had passed, the corridor was painted yellow and only a few of the crates were left intact. The four of them stared at the mess for another minute, waiting for something to move, but it seemed like everything was dead.

It had been a loud, violent, dangerous couple of minutes, but they'd come out of it unscathed. Had they been less well-armed, or hadn't realized the danger in time, it could have gone very differently.

Brisk declared that the corridor was clear, and they started walking forward through the mess.

Trin hopped out from behind the group up to walk beside Miles.

"I saw you shoot the gun," Trin said.

"Yeah," Miles said. He lowered the power on the weapon back to minimum, switched it off, and returned it to the pouch at his back.

"You kept the thing away from me."

Miles wasn't sure where Trin was going with that. He assumed it was an attempt at a thank-you and tried to brush it off.

"Yeah, of course."

Brisk reached the doors at the far end. Instead of going to the terminal, he pulled out a small, curved rod from one of his pockets, unfolded it into a kind of pry bar, and wedged it in the gap between the doors.

He gave it a sharp pull, and the doors opened an inch. He kept working at it, and after a few seconds, he had the doors open wide enough to step through.

Miles and Trin passed the real crate on the way there, a solid metal box with a seam around the upper edge. This one had a black panel built into the top, similar to the ones that controlled the doors.

Trin kicked it as they passed, seeming satisfied when it made a dull thudding noise.

Brisk had already passed through the doors, and Trin was the next, darting through ahead of Miles.

As soon as the scout was through the doors, he froze. He started making dry retching sounds, like a cat trying to bring up a hairball.

Miles came up behind him, nudging him out of the way. When he stepped through and saw what was in the room beyond, he felt the hairs on the back of his neck rise.

It was a slaughter. Blood in three different colors decorated the walls. There were torn body parts scattered across the floor. The air was heavy with scents—sweet, sickly, chemical, so thick Miles could almost taste them on his tongue. The remains were the bodies of sapients, dressed, armed, and completely eviscerated.

Brisk stood over the carnage, picking through the ruin with indifference. He was already holding a blood-stained comm unit and kicking apart a pile of refuse with the toe of his boot.

He knew this would be here, Miles realized.

Brisk must have been expecting something like this. He already had the frequency of one of the comm units, which meant he'd known these sapients.

"Who are they?" Miles asked.

Brisk took a break from searching through the wreckage to look at him.

"You wanted to know what happened to the old team," he said. He pointed at one set of ruined remains after another. "Lancer. Scout. Grenadier."

Disposable.

Miles felt sick. He hadn't liked Brisk from the start, and he'd felt useless nearly every day since he'd joined the crew, but he'd never felt so dangerously disposable.

Had this even been the *Kipper*'s original boarding team? Or was it just another anonymous crew, hired at stations that wouldn't remember them?

Miles's eyes found the corpse of the sapient Brisk had labeled the *grenadier*. It had once been a female Hurc, dressed in heavy plates that hung from straps across her chest and back. The armor hadn't saved her from being torn in half, legs pooling in one place, torso in another.

A glint of light caught his attention from the bloodied ground at his feet. It was a small gemstone, lying on the ground in a pool of spilled guts, pale red, with two charred black fractures like holes in a rotted tooth.

He'd seen something like it before. The crystal that the mage at Delatariel Station had sold him. Only this one was covered in blood, having fallen out of a corpse. An awful suspicion pricked at him.

"Was she a mage?" Miles asked, his eyes locked on the gem.

"You can tell that?" Brisk asked, glancing up. "Yeah. She was a front-line fighter, but she had an index, like you. She only knew a few little spells. Useless, in the end."

The merchant on the station had fed him the remains of another mage. Without seeing this scene of death, Miles might never have found out.

Miles was snapped out of his thoughts by Trin, who was speaking from the other side of the room in an unusually weak voice.

"This one alive, I think."

Miles snapped his head to look in that direction. *Eyes of the Altruist* fell into place, and the fading lights of a living creature's biology appeared over one of the ruined bodies.

CHAPTER 8

Miles's hands were already on the body.

It was the sapient that Brisk had identified as his last team's scout. A "short trunk" body type, not that knowing that helped Miles at all.

It had the look of a biological pod. Round and oval-shaped, about a foot long, with a surface made of layered chitinous plates. It didn't have any obvious limbs or sensory organs, and as Miles touched it, he didn't feel any warmth or vibration.

How long has it been like this?

Brisk had known what he'd find here, so he had to have been present at the time of the attack. It had taken at least five days to cross from Destiel Station to Ialis, a ten-day round trip, and the ship had spent at least two days docked with the station.

Twelve days. Possibly more. Except, Brisk had said that time moved more slowly in the dungeon, and the effect was greater the deeper someone went. How much subjective time had the injured scout experienced? It could have been just a few days, or even mere hours.

The outer carapace had been split open like a crushed watermelon. Cuts leaked along its sides, and cracks ran across on the top. Miles's *Eyes of the Altruist* showed him the grim picture of its internal biology. There was one large central shape that looked like a popped balloon, other shapes that looked like they were meant to be round, but now had broken membranes, and shapes that looked like support structures, now fractured.

He didn't know exactly what any of it meant. That was the province of doctors. He might need to study for years to know the intricacies of treatment for just one species. Luckily, one of the advantages of magic was that it was general. Magic worked on conviction, principles, and achieving an end result without passing through the intervening steps.

He pressed his hands to one of the splits on the sapient's side and cast *Close Wound*.

They have been abandoned to their injuries. In a harmonious world, no wound is left to fester. The cut must close. **Such should it be.**

Halfway through the casting, Miles realized he had activated the spell without using his index. He didn't let the realization distract him.

The litany was slightly different from the version the index triggered, but he agreed with the sentiment completely; they shouldn't have been left like this. He felt his magical core spin up, the flash of energy surge from his stomach to his hands, and a burst of searing light was born between his hands and the flesh of the sapient.

The magic he could call never ceased to awe him.

When Miles removed his hand, the wound had closed.

He repeated the spell on every visible injury, closing them, wiping away the sapient's purple blood as he moved around their body.

When he was done, they still had a mess of internal injuries, so Miles turned to his next spell. *Hasten Renewal* had a subtle effect, accelerating a being's natural healing, but in his accreditation test, at least, it had shown the ability to make fresh burns look days old and help sapients purge their bodies of poison.

He placed his hands on the scout's body and tried to cast the spell. After a few seconds of failing to summon up an appropriate litany, he gave up trying to cast it from memory and pulled out his index.

Name: Miles Asher | Traditions: Harmonizer
Spells (Harmonizer)
Close Wound (Grasping)
Temporary Enhancement (Grasping)
Hasten Renewal (Tentative)
Spells (Sky Quester)
Shield of Saints [New] (Fo#bid##n)   A plane of soul energy is drawn from the quester to intercept a physical object, reducing its speed and force by an amount in accordance with the quester's Conviction.
Core Effects (Harmonizer)
Eyes of the Émigré
Eyes of the Altruist

> **Core Effects (Sky Quester)**
>
> ***Sword of Souls*** [New]
> *Expresses a fragment of the quester's soul as an immaterial blade, with length and cutting power in accordance with the quester's Conviction.*

Miles barely registered the new items that his index listed. *Shield of Saints. Sword of Souls.* An entirely new branch of magic, one that humanity wasn't strictly allowed to access through the index. He was confused for a moment by their presence, until he realized he'd dropped the dead grenadier's crystal into a pocket of his cargo pants. His index was reading the magical information stored in the crystal because it was in contact with him, just like it had in the Delatariel Station market.

He didn't let himself dwell on it, not right then.

Instead, Miles tapped *Hasten Renewal* to cast the spell and mentally followed the spark of energy that burned through his arm and into the injured scout.

Everything which lives, heals. In a harmonious world, a creature is forever its final self. **It is that which it is.**

Hot light shone in the space between Miles's hand and the creature's shell. The cracked sections he hadn't been able to mend with *Close Wound* scarred over, a milky white layer above brown-black chitin. In the vision of his *Eyes of the Altruist*, the hole in the large central organ closed up. The crushed shapes grew less ragged. The fractured support structures didn't mend, but grew fine hairs that wove around the damage. He was helping, but he didn't know if it would be enough.

Miles maintained the spell until he felt weak, and then he kept going. He watched the mending continue until his vision went dark, and then suddenly he was on his back, looking up at the pale blue lights of the ceiling.

Trin was looking down at him.

The scout said something. Miles didn't understand it.

Miles couldn't see any of the shapes that his *Eyes of the Altruist* projected, which meant *Eyes of the Émigré* should have been active, but he couldn't understand what Trin had said.

Trin said something else. He looked concerned. Miles couldn't understand.

Brisk wandered over, looking dispassionately at both Miles and the sapient he'd treated. He spoke, a series of low barks that Miles couldn't interpret.

Even focusing on his *Eyes of the Émigré* didn't help. It felt like the translation magic was just gone.

Trin and Brisk had an exchange of words, with Torg even throwing a few clicks in. All incomprehensible.

Miles forced himself to sit up. His body felt both too weak and too light. He felt hollow and insubstantial, like a dry leaf in the wind. Even empty, his backpack was too heavy for him, the straps cutting into his shoulders as if it weighed a hundred pounds. His clothes were a dead weight on him, lying heavy on his body like a lead blanket, pressing down on his chest, restricting his blood flow. He couldn't even think about standing.

"I'm awake," Miles managed to say, hoping that at least some of Trin's words had been asking about him. "Weak."

Whatever tools they used for translation didn't rely on his magic. They'd be able to understand him.

Tools.

Miles remembered his comm, with its built-in translation software. He reached for the pocket on his cargo pants to take it out, but he didn't even have the strength to undo the steel snap. He probably wouldn't be able to lift it, in this state.

It had to be a result of overusing his magic. He'd read warnings about becoming *overtaxed*, but the sparse explanation given when he'd selected his index had been couched in a mixture of marketing jargon and obtuse terminology, the kind of explanation that a natural resident of the Spiral might understand, but which Miles hadn't fully grasped. He'd had feelings similar to this during his hours and days of practicing on torn fabric and small cuts, but he'd never felt so utterly empty. He hadn't realized it could get this bad.

He felt a pair of soft, warm hands touching his waist, and he was lifted onto his feet.

Trin was supporting him. He said something, but apart from being sure it was something kind, Miles didn't understand it.

Brisk had picked something up from the wreckage of bodies, a hand-luggage-sized white metal case that dangled from a strap over his shoulder. He was pointing them toward the door.

Torg was still outside in the corridor, having never made it through the narrow opening. Brisk stepped out, and Trin started dragging Miles along toward it.

They're leaving the scout behind.

They didn't know that the sapient was still really alive. They hadn't seen what he'd seen. They didn't know what he'd done to help them.

"We can't leave the scout," Miles breathed out as they were passing through the doors. "They're still alive. They might recover."

Trin stopped in his tracks.

Brisk noticed that they'd stopped and looked back over his shoulder. He said something.

Trin hesitated for a few seconds, then started moving again.

Miles needed to convince them. He needed not just to be understood by them, but to understand what Brisk was saying so he could argue.

He focused on *Eyes of the Émigré* again. Another wave of weakness washed over him, but he felt something kick in his stomach. A lurch, as his stilled core began spinning again.

"I tried to heal them. I think I helped," Miles said. "They're alive and might get better."

Trin paused again, looking sideways at Miles and then at Brisk. "Maybe we bring them, just in case?"

Something in Miles that had nothing to do with magic unclenched at hearing Trin's voice.

"Vestilles all do that," Brisk said. "They shoot out a pod when they're in trouble, it lives for a couple of days, then breaks down. It's been too long. She's as good as dead already."

Trin let out a breath and started walking again.

"She's not dead," Miles protested. "I healed most of the damage."

This time it was Torg that stopped.

Brisk continued walking for a few paces, before stopping as well and turning to face the two of them.

Torg approached Miles.

He clicked. "*Surviving.*"

Miles understood the word, but didn't know how to interpret it. He took his best guess.

"Yes, she's still surviving."

Torg started back toward the room on his own.

With Trin and Miles stopped, and Torg heading back, Brisk was forced to wait as well, or else he'd be moving on alone. He watched Torg go, grinding his incisors against each other.

After half a minute there was the sound of screeching metal behind them as the doors were torn fully open, then the sound of heavy claws on metal as Torg padded back up to the group.

When he reached them, he was cradling the injured scout in two of his pincers, his ax and cannon each held one-handed.

"Fine," Brisk said, resuming his walk down the corridor. "I hope you can afford to get her a real healer."

Miles couldn't, but maybe the captain would be more inclined to help her.

Winding corridor, warehouse, storage room, sheared-open entrance. Together, they retraced their steps back to the place they'd landed. Nothing leaped out at them this time.

Miles had recovered a little by the time they made it back to their entry point. He had some strength, enough to open his pockets at least, and could walk without Trin's support.

According to Miles's comm, they'd been down there about ninety subjective minutes, well short of the dungeon's restructuring interval, assuming it ran on the local dilated time of each level.

Brisk hadn't mentioned the case he'd recovered, or how he felt about finding his old team dead, or what they were going to do next. The crew just boarded the platform in silence.

The platform must have sensed their return, because it took off a few seconds after everyone was on board, beginning its slow, drifting journey back up to the entrance compound.

Brisk seemed tense on the journey back, sharpening his incisors against each other, constantly messing with the access panel on his new box.

Eventually, they made it back up to the compound. Elegant open-air structures greeted them as their platform set down, and they all disembarked.

Consul Thunis emerged from one of the buildings and started sidling over toward them, followed by a pair of hovering drones.

Brisk stepped to the front of the group and met them as they arrived.

"You have returned from the artifact. I hope your visit was successful."

"Consul, it was," Brisk said.

The consul's eyes clicked as they roamed left and right, picking out the body of the recovering scout, as well as Brisk's new box and the weapon on his hip.

"You acquired items within the artifact. Please present them for appraisal."

One of the drones swung down to hover at waist level in front of the consul. It was a triangular device, with four oversized levitation units, and a head that expanded out into a wide platform like a table.

Brisk, who seemed to know what it was there for, unstrapped the belted pistol he'd collected and laid it on the surface.

The Gilthaen stood silently for a minute, as if listening to something only they could hear. Finally, they spoke.

"The Ialis Corporation will pay sixty-eight standard exchange notes for this weapon and attachment."

"Consul, we decline," Brisk said.

They eyed the inert form of the wounded scout, next.

"This is a sapient?" they asked.

"Consul, she's a scavenger rescued from within the artifact."

"That is in order. By the terms of entry, a bounty of fifty standard exchange notes is payable for assisting with the extraction of another visitor."

Brisk's pupils diverged, a Hurc eye roll, but Miles was pleased when his comm unit buzzed with an incoming payment.

Finally, the consul's gaze fell on the white box.

Brisk lifted it up and placed it down flat on the surface. He tapped the interface and the top popped open with a hissing sound.

When Brisk lifted the hinged lid the rest of the way up, he revealed a collection of items resting on a sheet of black padding. There was a comm unit, a couple of other tech devices Miles didn't recognize, a rusted dagger, what looked like a wooden beaded bracelet, and a piece of silver jewelry.

"The personal effects of teammates who died in the artifact," Brisk said.

The consul leaned down, bringing their large head and blinking eyes to within inches of the items. They scrutinized the box for almost a minute, before bringing themselves back up to their full height.

"The contents of this box are being obscured by a signal mask generator. Please deactivate it."

Brisk was very still as he said, "Consul, you are mistaken. I see no signal mask generator among the personal effects."

"I am not mistaken. Deactivate the signal mask generator."

Brisk was silent for a few seconds. He looked at the consul, then at Torg and Miles, and then he drew the pistol from the table and opened fire on the Gilthaen. Miles's heart leapt into his throat.

The gun stuttered, a flashing machine-gun rattle. A stripe of gray wounds blossomed along the body of the consul and they sagged backward.

Instantly, a pair of drones whipped out of one of the nearby structures, a flurry of sharp angles and screaming hover units. Brisk dropped the pistol, pulled his rifle, and fired twice. Both flying devices exploded before crashing to the mossy ground.

Brisk briefly checked around for more threats, then slammed the white case shut and took off with it toward the landing pad where the *Starlit Kipper* was docked.

Miles was frozen in place.

In front of him, the Gilthaen consul was writhing on the ground, translucent gray fluid flowing from the open wounds on its long body. What should he do? Should he run after Brisk? He was relatively new to the weave's laws and politics, but he was pretty sure he'd just seen the Spiral equivalent of a gas station robbery. And he was part of it. He'd been on the side of the robber.

Brisk was already twenty meters away, but so far, he was the only one running. Torg seemed to be as conflicted as Miles, and Trin looked like he was in shock.

"*Always polite.*" Torg said.

Right. Brisk had been the one to tell them they had to be polite to the consul. Or had he been setting himself up for an easier time at this inspection? Was he just trying to keep the consul's goodwill so he wouldn't have to run customs with whatever he knew he'd be bringing out?

Miles didn't feel like he had a choice. Whether he'd be guilty by association with Brisk and the *Kipper* or not, the consul was dying in front of him.

Eyes of the Altruist.

The now familiar glow of biology sprang up in his vision, shapes and torn shapes drifting over the Gilthaen official's form.

Brisk had missed most of the consul's internal organs. The gun he'd used had been the closest of any weapon Miles had seen to the firearms of old Earth, a machine pistol that spat out physical projectiles.

Most of the projectiles had hit the long, mostly empty portion of the consul's lower body. One hadn't. There was a jagged tear across the bottom of one of the consul's lower organs where a projectile had gone in, cut through, then passed out the other side.

Miles needed to heal them. *Hasten Renewal* seemed like the best choice, but it took way too much out of him. Last time he'd used it to mend serious wounds, it had all but knocked him out, and made him useless for over an hour. He still hadn't fully recovered.

Close Wound was more efficient—he had cast that multiple times a day before with no problems—but here the serious wound was internal.

Miles fell to his knees next to the consul. He folded up the baggy sleeves of his robe, then pressed his hand against the consul's body around the wound.

Its skin was hot, scaldingly hot, like a pot left on the stove. But if he wanted to help them with *Close Wound*, he'd need to apply it directly to the injury. He tentatively touched the edge of one of the bullet holes. A spurt of gray fluid caught his skin, burning him. He snapped his hand back.

There was no way he was getting direct access to the internal injury. He was going to have to exhaust himself again.

He looked around at Trin, planning to speak to him, but Trin was just staring down at the consul's face in horror. Instead, he turned to Torg.

"Torg, if I pass out, can you look after me?"

Click-tick. "*Yes. Survive.*"

Yes, help them survive? Okay.

Miles turned back to the consul, putting his hands on a section of skin that was cool enough to touch. He brought out his index, found *Hasten Renewal*, and tapped to activate the spell.

Everything which lives, heals. In a harmonious world, a creature is forever its final self. **It is that which it is.**

What little magic he still had flooded out of him, and this time, the blackness came almost immediately.

PART 4

AN ALMOST GREEN PLANET

CHAPTER 9

Miles dreamed of a single planet, a single star, an alliance, bright and harmonious. A people who lived eternally, each one possessing the wisdom of a sage, the strength of a waterfall, the endurance of a mountain, and the authority of a king.

Over the minutes, that dream faded.

There was warmth in his stomach now, a slow rotation. Light returned to his vision, the diffuse pink of closed eyes.

The events flooded back as he returned to consciousness.

Brisk, the gun firing, the consul falling. He remembered that his superior had evaded whatever process the Ialis Corporation had for checking dungeon finds, effectively making a run on the customs desk, and that he'd attacked an official in the process.

He remembered trying to help.

Did I even help?

He opened his eyes and found himself not in a cell, or an oubliette, or cast deep into the dungeon to be disposed of by the dangers there, but lying on a padded green couch in one of the open-air structures of the entrance complex.

There was no sign of Trin or Torg, but his bag and robe were there, folded and placed on a low table made from the black wood of the local trees.

Miles didn't recognize the specific structure from his earlier walk through the compound. It seemed like he was on the second floor, with treetops visible through the open spaces that stretched between support pillars. Like the other structures he'd seen, the ceiling was very high, giving the place a sepulchral feel.

It seemed darker outside than when he'd passed out. The air that drifted through the space was cool with faint traces of mist. A light breeze gusted occasionally, bringing the smell of damp earth and plant life.

Miles sat up on the couch. He felt at least as strong as he had when leaving the dungeon. If he recovered from over-exertion at a reliable rate, then that might mean it had only been an hour or so since the attack on the consul. The lower light seemed to say different, but he didn't know how the day-night cycle worked on Ialis.

He checked the pockets of his cargo pants, finding his comm, index, and even the crystal he'd recovered from the dead grenadier. Everything was in its place.

"Hello?" he called out.

It was weird that he'd been left alone.

Taking his comm from his pocket, Miles stood up and began walking toward the edge of the room, where the floor disappeared and gave way to the stunted forest.

Looking out through the open edges of the building, he could place where he was. The landing pads that the *Kipper* had touched down on were a little way off, and he judged that he was on the opposite side from the structure where they'd met Consul Thunis.

There was no sign of the *Kipper*, unsurprisingly.

There were still ships docked there, each on its own black landing pad, but fewer than before, and none of them were the familiar sleek Alfaen craft. It had gone, and it had left him behind.

Not that Miles had any desire to travel with Brisk or Captain Rhu-Orlen after what he'd seen. Even if he could handle the casual indifference with which Brisk had treated his dead teammates, having watched Brisk's attack on the Ialis official, and knowing that the crew might as well be pirates, had completely soured him against them.

I just wish it'd lasted long enough for me to get paid.

He checked his comm. He had the fifty seln that Thunis had given him for helping extract the injured scout, and sixteen seln left over from his personal savings, and that was it.

Besides his balance, there were no messages.

Where is Trin? Where's Torg? What happened to the scout? What's going to happen to me?

He used his comm to send a message to Trin.

Miles > Trin

Where are you? What's happening? Are you and Torg okay? What happened to the scout?

Trin > Miles

You are alive! Well done. You made yourself knock out again. Very good healer, always unconscious.

Miles > Trin
What is happening?
Trin > Miles
Worm lord took you away. Says for questions. Me and Torg also questions.

There was a dry rustling sound from one end of the room, and Miles saw a section of floor slide, giving way to a ramp. A moment later, a head appeared, the tip of a wormlike Gilthaen body.

They emerged slowly, sliding up the ramp, accompanied by one of the sharp, fast drones that had appeared during Brisk's unprompted attack. The drone hovered behind the new arrival menacingly, but didn't make any aggressive moves.

This individual was not Consul Thunis. Their skin was a different shade of gray, they had six eyes—a vertical row of four with one to the left and right, like a narrow plus sign—and they were dressed differently, a thin black robe instead of the buttoned coat, with a cloak of shimmering red fabric that rose up into a wide collar around their "head."

They slid up onto the second floor and stretched upward, standing easily thirteen or fourteen feet tall. It looked perilous, when so little of their long body was in contact with the ground, but then, maybe some species thought that about humans.

Miles walked slowly away from the edge of the room toward them. He tried not to feel awed by the sapient's height and presence, and he might have succeeded, if it weren't also for the cool penetrating eyes that gazed down at him, clear, intelligent, and somehow regal.

"I am Consul General They-who-read-deeply. You may call me Consul General Runir. Will you speak to me in peace?"

Miles hadn't been sure what he was going to say, but the question threw him off completely. Maybe they thought he was in on the attack.

Before speaking, he remembered how Brisk had addressed Thunis. If the Hurc engineer had been taking pains to be polite, then Miles assumed that it was the right way to address the Ialis officials.

"Consul General, I will," Miles said.

The consul general's head swayed slightly. "Please do not stand on protocol. This is an informal conversation."

"Okay. Thanks."

Runir slid further toward the center of the room, turning to face Miles at the end of the movement. The angular drone flew some distance and took up a position at the edge of the room, hovering out over the open space just beyond the walls.

"Did you participate in the attack on Consul Thunis?"

Just coming straight out with it, huh?

"No," Miles said, putting as much truth as he could into the word.

He felt the urge to say more, to elaborate, to add context, but he resisted. He didn't want to end up pleading, and he didn't want to give the sapient more than they asked for.

"For how long did you know that your leader was planning to attack Consul Thunis?"

"I didn't know," Miles said. "Not until after Brisk shot them."

"Did you guess or suspect?"

"No."

"What insight do you have into the motivation of the attack?"

Here it is.

Miles all but knew what Brisk had done. There was some process where the Ialis authorities inspected loot recovered from the dungeon. Brisk said they had the right of first refusal on finds, and Miles didn't exactly see why that would need such drastic action, but the engineer had clearly taken something from the planet that he didn't want to be inspected.

Something else came to Miles, then. Thunis had mentioned that the box had a scanning mask or something. Finding a signal mask generator had been Brisk's job on Delatariel Station. They must have been planning this at least that far back. They'd expected whatever was really in the white container would be there with their slaughtered team, and knew they'd need a way to get it past the Ialis authorities.

"Brisk, the leader of our group, found something in the dungeon—in the artifact. I don't think he wanted Consul Thunis to inspect it properly."

"That is our assessment as well," Runir offered. "What did the case contain?"

"I don't know."

Runir stared at him for a long few seconds, all six eyes boring into his two.

"Your answer is incomplete. Please elaborate."

Incomplete?

Miles realized that it was slightly incomplete, not that he'd left anything important out.

"It had some random items. Brisk said they were personal effects, but I think they were just there to justify him having the case. I don't know what was in there besides those." Before Runir could ask another question, Miles blurted, "Is Consul Thunis alright?"

Runir seemed to relax, and Miles decided that Runir knowing that he'd missed something out of his answer had been a surprisingly incisive observation. Did they already know the answers to these questions and was just testing him? Did they have some kind of lie detector tech? Maybe they were just good at reading people.

"Consul They-who-share-ground is well, though in the near future they will be known as They-who-warily-tread."

"Okay. Good. Thanks."

"Why did you place your hands upon Consul They-who-share-ground?"

Miles looked down at his hands. He still had some red skin from the blistering heat of They-who-warily-tread's body.

"I was trying to heal them," he said. "I was our group's healer, and I thought I could help."

"Gilthaens are immortal. Nothing short of physical annihilation can end our existence. Did you know this?"

"I . . . no."

So Miles hadn't actually needed to heal Thunis at all. Maybe Brisk hadn't even been trying to kill them. Maybe a gutshot was just a distraction to a Gilthaen. Miles had panicked and exhausted himself to unconsciousness, flailing around in his ignorance.

"Your actions were of help," Runir said.

Miles looked up at the consul general's face.

"They were unnecessary for Consul They-who-share-ground's survival, but they were a comfort to them during a concerning moment. You eased their pain. You made them feel not-alone. They have expressed their gratitude to me."

Miles felt something inside him unclench, and he fully breathed for the first time since he'd woken up. Maybe he wasn't in trouble after all.

"I find you blameless in this assault. You are not associated with the actions of your leader."

Miles let out a sigh. "Thank you."

Consul General Runir's head swayed slightly. "No bylaw of Ialis commanded you to assist Consul They-who-share-ground. There is no standing reward payable for this kind of assistance."

"I know," Miles said. "Well, I didn't think there was. But they were hurt right in front of me, by my own crew."

Runir was silent for a minute, long enough that Miles started to get uncomfortable. The consul general turned to look out through the open walls of the structure, at one of the distant buildings. Miles got the feeling Runir was speaking to someone, though he didn't see them using a comm or any tech.

Thinking about it, Miles didn't see how Gilthaens could speak at all. They had no visible mouth, or anything like that. When they spoke, the sound seemed to come from the part of their body that would be a throat on a humanoid.

Eventually, Runir turned back to him.

"Your assistance will be rewarded."

"Oh," Miles said. "Thanks?"

Were they going to give him another fifty seln? That had been the bounty for helping other dungeon visitors out.

"State your desire."

Uhhh.

"Sorry, what do you mean?"

"You may request a boon of the Gilthaen. What would you ask?"

"Sorry, *anything*?"

"You may ask for anything. It may not be provided. Perhaps, limit yourself to boons within my power to grant."

Several of the consul general's eyes had narrowed. On a human, it might look like a hostile expression, but Miles got the impression that Runir was amused.

"It is a simple question. What do you want?"

What do I want?

It wasn't simple at all.

"I don't know. To go home?"

"Where is 'home'?"

Destiel Station, Miles thought. He had a room there, a few friends there, and they fed him a packet of slime three times a day.

But did he really want that? Destiel Station was a dead end. A Spiral cul-de-sac that he'd been happy to get away from. He was standing on Ialis, a planet, and a vaguely green planet at that. When was the last time he'd seen a sky, or touched soil?

"You are conflicted," Runir said.

"Yeah," Miles said. Then, "What's happening with my friends?"

"The other two members of your crew have been found blameless in the assault. The injured Ankn is stable, though will need care to recover."

Ankn must have been the name of the scout's species.

"Thanks," Miles said.

His thoughts returned to what he wanted.

He wasn't even sure what he wanted to do.

He thought his job on the ship offered him stability, but that had barely lasted a week. Did he go back, try again, look for another ship with another job, and just as much uncertainty?

There was a temptation to stay here, on Ialis, but he didn't really know anything about the planet. He didn't have anywhere to stay, he didn't know where to get food, he didn't know how much anything cost, and he didn't have any money in any case. He didn't know how to get around. Were there buses? Were there department stores? He didn't imagine there was a benevolent refugee program handing out food packets, lentsk-flavored or otherwise.

"Could I stay here?" he asked, testing the water.

"That would be in order," Runir said.

"I don't know my way around, and I don't have any money . . ."

"Then your boon would be a request for a guide, a payment, and our aid in establishing yourself here, on Ialis."

"Consul General, yes it would."

Miles felt a fluttering in his stomach, a weakness in his limbs.

He'd felt the same way when he'd fled Earth, sneaking out of the compound to where the refugee ships were waiting. He'd felt the same way the night before he joined the crew of the *Starlit Kipper*. It was a feeling he had whenever he made a huge, life-altering decision.

Runir closed their eyes for a second before opening them again.

"Then it is done."

The consul general started to slide away, then paused for a second before turning back. Their head swooped down to scrutinize Miles from inches away.

This close, the feeling of being *seen* was intense. Was it his imagination, or did static electricity prickle at his skin, in his flesh, pricking the hairs on his arms?

"You are a mage," Runir commented. "A Harmonizer, and *Quester of the Stars*."

Miles hesitated before answering. Technically, he wasn't allowed to be anything *but* a Harmonizer, and technically he *wasn't*, but if an incomplete or hedged answer tripped Runir's lie detector before, it definitely would then.

In the end, he simply answered, "Yes."

There was no reaction, no censure or arrest for possessing magic that hadn't been opened up to the newly bowered human race. Instead, Runir just rose back up to their full height.

"This will be accounted for in your payment."

Runir slid toward the ramp and disappeared down it.

Miles spent a few minutes waiting, wondering what was meant to happen next.

Do I follow him, or . . .

A floating platform arrived at the edge of the floor before he could work up the nerve to leave on his own.

It came with a drone, a floating metal donut with two vertically stacked eyes and a pair of spindly manipulator sticks.

Miles approached the edge, and the drone matched him, floating up to him.

"Heya," the donut said. "I'm They-who-fly-with-abandon. You can call me Bandy."

"Hi, Bandy," Miles said, uncertainly. Its name followed the same pattern as the Gilthaens. Was this some kind of Gilthaen, or did they just name their drones in the same way?

Wait, is this drone sapient?

He decided it was better to err on the side of respect.

"So, you want a guide?" the drone asked. "I know all about Ialis. You wanna see Consular City? No, wait, that's too pricey. You wanna see Dendril City?"

Miles decided he needed to get the question out of the way.

"Are you a Gilthaen?"

The lights of the donut's eyes vanished for a second, a long blink.

"No. I'm a drone."

"Okay. Sorry. You sound so different from them."

"You were just bowered, right?"

"Pretty recently," Miles admitted. "Iteration 27,200."

"Spooky. You know what they say about round-number iterations, right?"

"No?"

Bandy didn't illuminate him.

"Well, let's get going." The drone flew over to the floating platform. "I can take you to Dendril City, or Crater City, or a random place in the moss desert if you want."

"Can we go find my friends?"

Bandy said they could, and a few seconds later the platform was jerking into motion, drifting toward the larger part of the entrance complex.

PART 5

MIXED-SPECIES LIVING

CHAPTER 10

The room was smaller than Miles's student apartment back on old Earth.

It had walls of gray-blue metal that sucked in heat and reflected every sound, and a floor of black plastic tiles. The room looked like it had been run off a production line somewhere, and then just slotted into the arcology like a box on a shelf.

It was about five meters from wall to wall, with shelving along one wall and a fold-out plastic cubicle that Bandy had explained served as shower, toilet, and drinking water source all in one. *"It can dispense a wide variety of fluid solvents, and accepts a wide variety of biological byproducts!"*

There was only one bed, and it was only dressed with plastic mats that reminded Miles of bubble wrap.

As a human living in mixed-species accommodation on Destiel Station, Miles had become accustomed to living without the comforts of his home culture, but this was pushing the limits of what he could deal with.

And that was before even considering that he'd be sharing it.

"*Window,*" Torg observed.

Torg was still carrying the injured scout in his arms, a small oval pod of dark chitin, scarred and bruised, but apparently alive and stable. There hadn't been a clear way for them to hand off the scout, no medical facilities they could leave her at, no one they could ask more detailed questions about her care. She was apparently on the path to recovery, but they didn't know her specific needs.

"Yeah," Miles said grimly. "At least there's a view."

The room's window was a tapered rectangle of clear glass set into one wall, looking out over the lights and spires of Dendril City.

The city itself couldn't have been more different from the simple structures of the Gilthaen entrance complex.

Sharp towers of gray metal lanced up from flat ground, hundreds of meters high and only dozens apart; a dark, jagged forest, inexplicably crowded despite the vast open space of the surrounding wilderness.

Lurid strip lights in blue, green, and yellow were everywhere, growing out of the rugged metal exteriors seemingly at random, casting the towers in rainbow hues. The plant life that covered the surface of Ialis here had risen up, sending creeping black-leaved vines to clamber all over the towers, their tendrils reaching toward and swallowing the chromatic lights.

Bandy had claimed that the vines were biologically altered and placed here deliberately to enhance the city's livability, and that the chromatic lighting was to provide them with the energy they couldn't get from the planet's anemic itinerant star.

Miles thought that if the intent had been to make Dendril City feel more natural and inviting, it had failed badly. The result was the image of a dark, sterile, futuristic city waging war with a sinister forest—and losing.

The only exception to the gray architecture was the local consulate, a floating six-tier pagoda in the Gilthaen style, hovering at the height of the tallest buildings just beside the city. A little way off across the dull, moss-strewn flats was a skyport, a dozen or more black pads set into the ground, with nearby Gilthaen buildings for servicing and administration.

A few of the small floating platforms drifted between the spires, taking people back and forth between the city and the skyport, or from one spire to the other.

The transport platforms could be called by sending a message to a central management system, and they were pretty much the only way to get around; the city wasn't exactly walkable.

"What do you think?" They-who-fly-with-abandon asked. "Will you take it? It's basic, I know, but it's the cheapest option in the city that you can survive in."

Miles raised his hand and checked his comm again.

Financial Status [§,δ]
δ200 (δ0 + δ200)
§566 (§66 + §500)

Consul General They-who-read-deeply had awarded Miles five hundred seln for the "payment" part of his request.

They'd also given him two hundred delta after realizing he was a mage, which was great, because Miles still didn't know how to get it on his own.

In the middle of the room, Trin flopped backward onto the bed. He scurried in place for a second, then pulled his head-flaps down over his eyes. After a minute of lying still, he sat back up.

"What is rent?" he asked.

"Three hundred and fifty standard exchange notes per span," Bandy announced cheerfully.

"Per *span?*" Miles asked. Per week, basically.

"Can't afford," Trin announced.

Torg clicked once, a sound that didn't translate, but that Miles got the impression was a general noise of disagreement.

Miles checked his comm again. He could technically afford a week's rent, but did he want to? He didn't know what his other expenses might be, and he definitely didn't want to be the only one of them paying for a room they were sharing.

"If we pool our money, I bet we could rent it for at least a week," Miles suggested. He felt awkward as he asked, "How much can everyone contribute?"

"Four hundred seln in savings," Trin said. "I can pay a third of rent, one time."

Miles nodded, satisfied. He and Trin were on the same page.

"*Same,*" Torg clicked.

"Okay," Miles said.

In the end, it wasn't a hard decision; this was their only option.

"How to make money here?" Trin asked, directing the question at the drone.

The little donut spun to face him.

"Eighty-four percent of commercial activity on Ialis revolves around the Ialis artifact. Scavengers raid the artifact directly. Merchants supply the scavengers and trade in the equipment they recover. Mercenaries sell their services to fill gaps on professional scavenger teams, or to provide pre-made teams to temporary and non-professional scavengers. Professionals sell their services to the Ialis Corporation, working in support of artifact operations."

"*Raid,*" Torg said.

Bandy replied as if Torg had asked a question. "Scavenging directly from the artifact rewards randomly, not reliably. A team may find a valuable new piece of technology on the first visit to the first level, or they may raid the tenth level for many iterations without a significant find."

"How much could I make selling my services as a healer?" Miles asked, remembering the going rate of twenty thousand seln for a Tier 4 healer.

The drone turned to face him. Miles didn't think a synthetic being could lose patience or get tired of stupid questions, but that didn't stop him from reading suppressed frustration in the little unit's slow rotation.

"As a Tier 1 healer, you are ineligible to serve as a healer working for the Ialis Corporation, but a search of local listings suggests a compensation rate of two hundred standard exchange notes per dive, with the amount increasing proportionally with risk, experience, qualifications, and reputation."

"What about me?" Trin asked. "Scout. I am scout."

Bandy rotated even more slowly to face Trin.

"A search of local listings suggests an inexperienced scout could demand a base compensation rate of sixty standard exchange notes per dive."

"What!"

"*Lancer?*" Torg asked with a throaty click.

"A search of local listings suggests an inexperienced lancer could demand a base compensation rate of one hundred and twenty standard exchange notes per dive."

"What!" Trin shouted again.

"So if we each manage to get in one dive per week, we can make rent," Miles concluded.

"The population of Ialis is one hundred and twenty thousand," Bandy said. "Competition for positions on dives is significant."

"Okay, so we won't just fall into a job," Miles conceded, "but maybe we could run our own dives until we find an opening somewhere. And if we don't, and we run out of money, then I guess . . . we just split up and find a way home, somehow."

Click-click. "*No home. Exile,*" Torg said.

Oh?

"I guess this is all or nothing for you, then, Torg," Miles said.

Torg clicked.

Going back to Destiel Station would mean going back to a life of obscure subsistence, surviving, but without hope. Miles wondered whether it was all or nothing for him, too.

When he was first getting oriented back on Destiel Station, Miles had learned that a large proportion of trade in Spiral space happened via the Exchange. Physical items could be bought there and either collected from a central location or delivered for a fee, with the availability of items strictly limited by the buyer's proximity to the seller.

There was no reason this couldn't work for everything, but the desire to see something physically in the flesh before buying it seemed to be a niche preference across every trading species in the weave. As a result, Dendril City had stores.

The Ishel Corporation Lounge was Ialis's answer to a mall. It filled one of the skyscraper-tall black spires, covering two hundred stories with tidy retail units, merchant booths, and automated food dispensers.

It was roughly divided into departments: weapons and armor, personal equipment, food and sustenance, and medical care, with a heavy skew toward products that scavengers raiding the dungeon would need for their dives.

The three of them split up at the entrance, a platform halfway up the spire, and each went to pursue their own area of interest.

Miles's priority was items for the apartment, and he'd headed to a level whose label translated to *homewares*.

Looking at the bizarre range of items on display, he couldn't imagine what kind of homes they were meant for.

Miles's first thought had been that he wanted a blanket. A simple, flat blanket, a sheet of something thick to keep his body warm in the night. The first promising stall he'd approached had been loaded down with square sheets of fur, and one of those sheets had opened several eyes to peer at him.

"Night friends," the ten-limbed vendor had declared to him proudly. "No, where are you going? They only eat what you discard! Night friends!"

He found an automated store selling cooking vessels, pots and pans made of recognizable metals, and for a second he just stood there, basking in the normality and familiarity. Sure, some of it was shaped more like chemistry equipment than kitchenware, but that was just innocent variation.

Eventually, he had to move on.

Miles found an electronics stall selling tiny fingernail-sized devices labeled as heat lamps, but the vendor warned him off, saying an exothermic sapient would find the heat uncomfortable. There were insulating bodygloves that he considered and rejected, and a piece of personal climate control tech that was way too expensive, a neural unit that would trick the body into thinking it was comfortable.

No thanks.

Finally, he found a place that his instincts told him was a camping store, where he managed to buy a synth-fabric sleeping bag.

The thing was big for him—it could easily have fit Torg—but it was apparently well insulated, optimized for sensitive epidermal layers, and only cost fifteen seln. He left with it rolled up and strapped to the bottom of his backpack.

The shopping plazas of each floor were far less chaotic than the commercial melee on Delatariel Station, but after an hour, even the thin crowds and calm stares of the merchants started to overwhelm him.

Miles looked around, searching for somewhere quiet, then ducked into one of the few walled-off stores on the level.

The background noise of the shopping floor vanished as he stepped inside— *some kind of sound-canceling tech*, he thought—and Miles found himself standing in a long, narrow room. The walls of the store were lined with shelves holding row upon row of slim, tablet-like tech devices, and at the far end was a counter and a row of booths.

There was a vendor managing the store, a member of the same species as the merchant who'd sold Miles his robe and his "spells" at Delatariel Station, but they only glanced at him once and didn't move to talk to him.

Miles was grateful they weren't giving him the hard sell straight away.

He started walking down the row of shelves, looking at them intently, giving himself a minute to recover. It would have been slightly implausible if he were a real customer, since all of the devices seemed identical, and none of them were labeled. He didn't even really know what they were.

He saw one device that looked slightly different, taller, a little thicker. He bravely reached up and pulled it off the shelf, looking at it.

There was no label on the front either. On its face, the device was almost entirely taken up by the screen, famed on each side by a low bevel of the device's silvery metal. There was a tactile button on the top and Miles tried pressing it, to no effect.

"Do you seek knowledge?" a voice hissed.

Miles jumped on the spot and turned around.

The vendor was right behind them. They'd approached without any sound and without catching Miles's peripheral vision.

Closer up, Miles could see the similarities and differences to the mage merchant on Delatariel Station.

This sapient had mottled skin, bone white on ash white. The ridge running down the center of their face, practically their face's only feature, was a slightly different shape, and their eyes were set higher up and closer together, with a centimeter of space between the eye and the edge of their face. There was a trace of a scar running below one eye.

Miles still couldn't decide whether the texture of their skin was closer to leather or paper, but this sapient was dressed in a more form-fitting suit than the merchant on the station, and he could see that they had a pair of legs and six arms emerging from their sides. Their arms were arranged in pairs that decreased in size as they went down the body, with the lowest pair barely longer than Miles's forearm.

Miles suddenly felt like he was being rude.

"I don't actually know what these are," he admitted.

The sapient took the slightly larger tablet from Miles's hands and drew a spiked finger across the screen. A block of text appeared, and when they turned the device to face Miles, he found he could read the title.

The Hidden Secrets of Euphospher Engineering: Tier 1, Volume 1.

"It's a book?" Miles asked.

The sapient gestured around at the shop.

"A horde of knowledge; tomes and simulations to enrich the mind and entice the senses."

Miles watched as the sapient slid the tablet—the book—back onto the shelf and turned away.

"I've seen books for sale on the Exchange. Do people prefer to buy them in person?" Miles asked. He hoped he wasn't raising a sensitive subject or poking an economic wound.

"The *Exchange*," the vendor mewled with derision, "is curated by the Grand Banality, the Slaves of Orthodoxy, the *Nexilaen*-controlled Exchange Corporation.

They exclude any title which competes with their preferred volumes. The *Exchange* is nothing but a vehicle for Nexilean chauvinism, and a tool with which to exercise control *over our very minds*."

Miles found himself backing away toward the door. This was a little much.

He didn't know if the vendor was slightly unhinged, or if this was just a weird Spiral sales pitch, but either way it wasn't making him comfortable.

The vendor seemed to flow toward and around him, scuttling by at an alarming speed and taking up a position that didn't block his progress, but let them loom over him.

"You will find no books here that can be had on the Exchange. My customers value *my* curation, *my* vision; a superior catalog for any subject that piques your curiosity."

Miles took several steps back toward the door.

The sapient raised a hand, as if in appeal. "I also run a lending operation for loyal members."

Miles stopped backing away.

"You lend books? Like a library?"

The vendor lowered their hand, seeming to relax now that they had a hook in Miles's attention.

Miles arrived back at the meeting point, a pocket of his cargo pants newly occupied by the book tablet, with its store of apparently obscure reading material.

He'd paid twenty-five seln for a week's membership in the bookstore's lending program, an introductory rate that would go up to fifty seln after the first week. With that, he could borrow three books a day, and the only apparent limit on how much of the vendor's stock he could get through was how quickly he could read.

He recognized it as a bit of a racket. He'd be limited by how fast he could read, and if he found a book that was useful then he was as likely to purchase it as return it. Depending on how well the sapient's business was going, it might have been purely a marketing gimmick, but for Miles, cash-poor and with time on his hands, it was a useful service.

It grated a bit that he had to pay for individual books, having grown up in the free-information environment of old Earth, but apparently the mercantile system of the Spiral was more centrally managed than he was used to. On Earth, information availability was mostly limited by what was technologically possible. In the Spiral, it seemed like it was a result of conscious decisions.

Miles had also bought a large bottle of biochemistry-C food slime, *scintil* flavor, which was the best one. That should keep him nourished for several days, if not necessarily satisfied. The shower unit in the room didn't provide any soap, so he'd done his best to buy the relevant chemicals to clean his body, clothes, and hair. He'd also bought a silver ring with a pattern engraved along the outside, purely decorative, but he'd liked it, and it had been as cheap as costume jewelry.

He hadn't found everything he'd probably need, but on the whole trip he'd spent less than sixty seln, and he had enough creature comforts that he could bring himself to face the stark room back in their tower.

He hadn't spent any of his delta. Upgrades to an index were meant to be bought *through* the index, so that could wait until he was back at the apartment.

The entrance level was the busiest part of the tower, but Miles didn't have any trouble spotting Torg stepping out of the elevator.

He was still cradling the convalescing scout in two arms, and his other arms were wrapped around a large plastic sack. A new black breastplate shimmered with rainbow hues, and some kind of boxy tech was clipped to a bandolier that went diagonally across his body.

Miles worried briefly that *he* hadn't bought anything that would be helpful on dives.

Torg found his way to Miles and they exchanged greetings. Torg reviewed Miles's purchases without comment.

He tried to show Miles the contents of the sack, but even assuming Miles could have recognized anything in there, it was too cluttered and jumbled for him to pick items apart.

"I'll take a look back at the apartment," Miles said.

Trin appeared a few minutes later. He was carrying a new bag, a pouch that hung from a shoulder strap, and he was wearing a rigid cap made of rugged-looking synth fabric.

"Hey," Miles said as Trin approached.

"Hello. Miles. Torg," Trin said, then, "I got a gun,"

He drew a weapon from the pouch and waved it in the air for them to see. It was a white, plastic-looking pistol, with an elongated grip and a weirdly tall barrel.

A few people in the crowd veered to avoid them. Others shot Trin intense looks.

"Let's put that away for now," Miles suggested.

"Okay." Trin dropped the weapon back into his bag. "Can we go?"

Miles pulled out his comm unit and sent a message to call a platform.

Eppan feet were slender and fur-covered, with soft, chalk-white skin on the underside, and two wide toes, and Trin's were practically in Miles's *face*.

The bed was wide enough for two, just, and Miles had suggested a top-and-tail arrangement. Trin had needed to be talked into it, wanting to sleep upright, and Miles didn't want to disrupt it now by complaining. Trin's toes twitched in his sleep. Did Eppans dream?

The room was dark, lit only by the diffuse chromatic glow from the city outside the window. At some point rain had started to fall, drumming heavily on the glass and blurring the colors and motion of passing platforms. It didn't seem like Dendril City was a city that slept.

A huge shape hung in the corner of the room: Torg, who'd used claws to scale the metal walls and some kind of secreted glue to fix himself into place in the corner. It was apparently his preferred sleeping arrangement. He'd bought one of the heat lamps from the shopping complex, which was silently bathing him in warmth from below.

The injured scout was set up nearby. A scan with Miles's *Eyes of the Altruist* had suggested that she was healing, and he'd tried his *Hasten Renewal* that afternoon, but he didn't really know how to help.

He *had* been asleep. The patter of the rain helped, reminding him of home, of Earth, but something had woken him up.

He spent a minute staring up at the ceiling, wondering if it was worth trying to get back to sleep, when a sound came to him.

Chirrip.

He sat up, pushing the top of the sleeping bag down. He looked around, searching for the source of the sound.

Chirrip. "*Food.*"

This time when he heard the sound, he understood it. Something was hungry.

"*Food.*"

His gaze finally landed on the source of the sound. The small pod that was the injured Ankn scout.

Miles slipped out of bed as quickly and quietly as he could, darting over to the pod.

"Hello? Hi? Are you okay?"

"Food," the pod replied.

Miles noticed that one end of the pod had changed. A small opening had appeared, surrounded by a pair of hair-like appendages. As he watched, the opening gasped open and closed. A mouth?

"Food," the scout repeated.

"Yeah, yes, okay. What can you eat?"

"Food."

Sure.

The room was cold, and Miles was tired, and the conditions outside were grim, but Miles had a new patient to deal with. He was going to need to run some errands.

CHAPTER 11

System Standard Medical Database v2760
Ankn
Bodyplan: Short Trunk[1]
Biochemistry: Type K[2]

An endothermic desmophage originating in ITR17260. Type CTR molecularity and Type K accommodative biochemistry. Severe contraindications for ELAR molecularity substances and Type J biochemistry byproducts.
1. When attaining adulthood or when recovering from the evacuation stage, the Ankn may develop the exterior properties of another body type.
2. A unique digestive anatomy allows the Ankn to consume biochemistry B–C, E- & K-compatible nutrition and biomass, disregarding standard incompatibilities.

Miles squeezed another lump of the food paste into the scout's mouth. She held the food in her mouth for a second then violently mushed it between her jaws, disappearing it with a swallowing sound.

Miles and the others had been taking turns feeding the recovering Ankn twice an hour for the last six hours, only getting broken sleep and quickly going through their compatible rations.

He was lucky he'd remembered the directory of species available on the Exchange, and even luckier that his and Trin's meal packs were something she could eat.

Trin had spent an hour searching the Exchange and sending messages to try and find somewhere their new Ankn roommate could be placed for proper care, but even the cheapest option was ninety seln per night. Not something they could afford.

Their choice was caring for the scout themselves or leaving her to die, which was no choice at all. Miles felt no resentment. She'd been abandoned by Brisk and the crew of the *Starlit Kipper*. In another world, this could have been any one of them.

Miles rolled his fingers up the food packet, squeezing out the last of the paste.

He tried to feed it to the scout, but she'd closed her mouth. Miles dropped the pack in the pile of empties that was building up on the floor.

She'd sleep for thirty minutes or so, then she'd grow the limbs she'd been exuding a little bit more, and then she'd wake up and politely ask for more food.

Over on the bed, Trin was sleeping. He'd been waking up frequently during the night, doing what was needed then falling instantly back asleep. Apparently, that was possible for an Eppan. Not so much for Miles.

He stared for a minute at the empty spot on the bed, his extremely cozy sleeping bag sprawled over the bed and floor. He didn't think he'd be able to sleep.

Outside the window, the light was changing. The star that provided Ialis with illumination was cresting the horizon, turning the sky into a half-silvered plane that didn't completely hide the other stars of the Spiral.

Torg was out there somewhere. The lancer had left in the night; Miles guessed it was to replenish their biochemistry-C food supplies, but he wasn't sure. He'd taken their little guide drone and flown off to somewhere else in the city.

As Miles watched, the silvery light of Ialis's star crept up, catching the towers of Dendril City at a low angle and casting sharp shadows that stretched out for miles across the mossy landscape.

Flying platform activity had already ticked up over the last few minutes, and Miles passed the time watching the diversity of people passing by in the morning drizzle.

He wasn't getting back to sleep.

His index was lying on the hard foam tiles next to him, and he picked it up for the third time that night.

Name: Miles Asher	**Traditions:** Harmonizer
Fundamental Properties:	
Strength (0)	
Durability (1)	
Speed (0)	
Reactions (0)	
Will (0)	
Authority (1)	

Spells

Close Wound (Grasping)
A weft of harmonizing energy brings together the free edges of a tear, sealing the join in materials which are co-bondable, such as cellular membranes, metal compounds, woven fabrics, and homogenous molecular surfaces.

Temporary Enhancement (Grasping)
A temporary matrix of harmonizing energy alters one of a being's fundamental properties by an amount in accordance with the weaver's Authority.

Hasten Renewal (Tentative)
A weft of harmonizing energy spreads from the weaver to their target, greatly speeding the being's natural recovery by an amount multiplicative with the weaver's Authority.

Core Effects

Eyes of the Émigré
Embeds a matrix of harmonizing energy within the being's mind which will reveal to them the meaning of any plain text or spoken language.

Eyes of the Altruist
Embeds a matrix of harmonizing energy within the being's mind which reveal to them the health and ailments of a witnessed being.

With the crystal hidden in his backpack across the room, the spells of the *Kipper*'s old grenadier weren't showing up. The only things listed were those that were already integral to him.

His spells had served him well so far, both the specialized *Close Wound* and the general, if taxing, *Hasten Renewal*.

His main problem had been exhausting himself using his magic. Bringing just one person back from their life-threatening internal injuries had spent all of his magic, to the point that even his ongoing translation spell had failed. If he'd been a tech specialist, breaking one of his tools wouldn't automatically rob him of his others, but as a mage, at least as a Harmonizer, all of his magic drank from the same well of fuel.

He wasn't even really sure what that fuel was. Losing it left him weak, light, and fragile, but he didn't necessarily know how to increase it.

He switched his index to browse the available changes he could make to his Fundamental Properties.

Fundamental Properties—Alterations
Strength +1 [δ50] Strengthens and reinforces contractile, pneumatic, hydraulic, magnetic, and somatic activator tissues in the mage's body with weaves of harmonizing energy, resulting in increased strength.
Durability +1 [δ75] Weaves of harmonizing energy implant biosomatic matrices within the mage's tissues, strengthening them against temperature and chemical degradation, unwanted compression, and tearing.
Speed +1 [δ50] A weft of harmonizing energy alters the mage's body, supplementing frequently used processing pathways with harmonic resonances and activator tissues with biosomatic matrices.
Reactions +1 [δ50] A weft of harmonizing energy alters the mage's mind, supplementing frequently used processing pathways with harmonic resonances.
Will +1 [δ50] Reinforces information-processing tissues in the mage's body with a weave of harmonizing energy, insulating thought processes from extremes of external stimuli.
Authority +1 [δ75] Deepens the mage's connection to Harmonic Truth, increasing their ability to impose their harmonious will upon the world.

When he'd been given his index, he'd asked for augmentation to his Durability and Authority.

While the other refugees were spending their orientation stipend on rebreathers and radiation-scrubbing wristbands, he'd needed something else that would help him deal with potential environmental dangers in the weave, so he'd chosen a point of Durability. It would help him be more comfortable in extremes of temperature or inhospitable atmospheres, as well as make him slightly physically tougher. He didn't regret that choice.

Will was supposedly important for mages, but Authority was absolutely essential. His second selection had been one point of Authority.

Was that what he needed more of, to increase his magical stamina? From the description of his spells, Authority would increase their effectiveness, and if that wasn't the way to increase the pool of power they drew on, he didn't know what would.

Improving his Durability or Authority was already more expensive than the other properties, presumably because those were the properties he'd already augmented. Nobody had told him explicitly, but he assumed the price would increase the higher he went. It made sense to him when he'd noticed the pricing pattern. The more the change deviated from his natural biology, the more extensive it was, and the more power, or effort, or *something* it took the index to achieve it.

With two hundred and fifty delta, he could afford quite a lot of improvements, but he also wanted to review his spell choices.

Spells—Alterations
+*Dance of Harmony* [δ150]   A weft of harmonizing energy takes up residence in the weaver, spreading out into their surroundings. Visible beings of the weaver's choice will gain the aspect of harmony while the spell is maintained, increasing their precision and reactions by an amount proportional to the weaver's Authority.
+*Strings of Discord* [δ125]   A weft of harmonizing energy reaches out to touch discordant presences nearby, revealing their presence and Authority to the weaver.
+*Strike the Disharmonious* [δ175]   With a weft of harmonizing energy, the weaver rips the Authority from a disharmonious target, degrading its existence and claiming the confiscated Authority for themself. While held ready, discordant presences will ring loudly in the weaver's awareness.
+*Purify* [δ125]   A temporary weave of harmonizing energy takes up residence in the target, degrading objects and substances inimical to the target's existence over time.
Core Effect—Alterations
+*Stance of Authority* [δ150]   The weaver's existence is more deeply tied to the ancient tradition of the Harmonizers, giving them an instinctive understanding of harmony and discord. Their Authority will grow in line with their dignity and the harmony of their existence.
+*Ears of the Diplomat* [δ250]   Words spoken in falsehood will ring the gong of truth. A persistent weave of harmonizing energy will alert the weaver to spoken deceptions, piercing guile to an extent related to the weaver's Authority.

This list was limited to spells he could currently afford, but even this subset of the full Harmonizer list was a lot to process.

He tried to make sense of them by categorizing them by their purpose. *Dance of Harmony* was a support spell, which would help improve the performance of his team—or himself, he guessed.

Strings of Discord was a sensory spell, though its usefulness would depend entirely on what a "discordant presence" was. Miles had no idea.

Strike the Disharmonious looked like a direct attack spell, which as far as Miles could tell was a rarity among Harmonizer spells. It didn't seem universally applicable in the same way that his striker pistol was, only applying to "disharmonious" targets. Miles didn't know what those were. Was Trin a disharmonious being? *Absolutely.* Apparently, the spell would tell him after casting it either way.

Purify was a healing spell for dealing with poisons, maybe even infections and foreign objects, too. Healing was his main role, so that seemed like the obvious choice.

Except *Stance of Authority* seemed to offer a way to increase his Authority, which would improve all of his existing spells. If only he knew what it meant by his dignity and the harmony of his existence. Even when tamed by the tech of the index, magic could be a little arbitrary. Following the rules of the *Stance* could mean anything from cutting out red meat to swearing his soul to some culture's deity.

Ears of the Diplomat seemed like a straightforward piece of utility magic. Not obviously helpful for his current role, but attractive given that he might be dealing with potentially dishonest scavengers soon.

Purify was the obvious choice among the available spells, but Miles wanted to make the *smart* choice. He just didn't have enough information to see it.

He needed a real teacher.

He briefly thought about the bookstore he'd wandered into and its vehement proprietor, but he hadn't sensed the whir of a magical core in them in the way he had the merchant on Delatariel Station, and he wasn't keen on speaking to them again if he could avoid it.

He considered messaging Consul General They-who-read-deeply, but they probably had more important things to do.

No, he'd ask Bandy when the drone came back with Torg. They-who-fly-with-abandon hadn't blanked on any question they'd asked about the city so far.

"I have no idea where you can find a mage advisor," Bandy said, bobbing in the middle of the small apartment.

"What about a mage shop?" Miles asked. He was thinking about the mage peddler on Delatariel Station. Dendril City must have an equivalent, even if it was just one vendor with a stall.

"I'm connected to the Dendril City database, but mage establishments are reluctant to be listed. I think that they value their exclusivity more than discoverability."

"So how do people find them, just walk around the city until they get lucky?"

"I don't have any information on that."

Miles sighed and sank onto the bed. It was barely past dawn and he'd been awake for hours already. He was tired, and this felt like frustration on top of frustration.

Torg was standing quietly next to the door. He'd come back from his shopping trip with a plastic keg of biochemistry-C food paste. It was transparent and tasteless, but apparently cheap. A label on the side warned that it was "not a complete food."

The injured Ankn was sitting on the ground, satisfied for now. She was in the process of growing three pairs of limbs, thumb-thick articulated rods that emerged from the sides of her body, giving her a beetle-like appearance. An elongated half-cylinder of chitin had started pushing outward around her mouth; the beginnings of a head. It was like she was regrowing her body from scratch.

"Are there any city information services?" Miles asked the drone. "Guides?"

"There are several sapients offering their services as guides in the city listings. The cheapest charges one hundred and sixteen standard exchange notes per day."

Miles walked to the window, staring out at the passing traffic.

He could do this. He'd spent months stewing on Destiel Station. This was still his chance. Maybe he should make the obvious choice now, and count on getting better advice later. Or should he take a chance now, and live with the cost if he picked something useless?

Click-tick. "*Contract,*" Torg clicked into the silence.

Miles turned to look at him.

"Contract?" he asked.

For the first time, Miles noticed Torg was holding something. A small black metal oval, with depressions on one side and a round screen on the other. A comm?

Click-tock. "*Contract. Service.*"

He held out the comm.

Miles took it and looked down at the screen. It took almost a minute for his *Eyes of the Émigré* to translate the spiral of radial text on the screen, and when it came through he thought there might have been a mistranslation.

Lestiel > Torg

As we discussed, you and your team are no doubt insufficient as guides and escorts, but your presence will be a mere technicality. The irritating straps of legislation on this world bind the hands and legs of even one such as myself, stretching me into painful positions I would not ordinarily take. Once we are inside, can I count on you to stay out of my way?

Torg > Lestiel
Yes.

Lestiel > Torg
Excellent. Please remember from our discussion, I will allow the consuls of the entrance facility to peer at my secrets, they are fellow immortals after all and I can count on their taste and respect for my privacy, but no one else. I trust that I can also count on your discretion?

Torg > Lestiel
Yes.

Lestiel > Torg
Very good. Now we move onto the thorny discussion of price. Clearly, you will be providing me with an inferior service, if any service at all, and I believe that the matter of remuneration should reflect that. The pure does not indulge the cur, as they say. You will be satisfied with five hundred seln, paid jointly to your group.

Torg > Lestiel
Yes.

Lestiel > Torg
Then it is an agreement. I will send you my standard contract. Be sure to sign it immediately with no alterations. I will expect to be given prompt and effusive service.

"You got us a job?" Miles asked, disbelieving.

He hadn't heard Torg string more than two words together since they'd met, but somehow he'd wrangled them a contract in the time it took to go out for paste. He wanted to ask "How?" but thought that might be insulting.

"When is it for?" he asked instead.

Torg took the comm back and changed screens, then passed it back.

Now it showed a written contract, offering their services as healer, scout, and lancer, on a dive into the first level of the dungeon. The time was set for that night, about nine hours away. Their fee would be five hundred seln, payable on a successful exit.

"Torg, this is amazing," Miles said. He clasped the giant crustacean's forelimbs. "You did it. You got us a job."

The client didn't sound great, but it also sounded like they thought they could handle themselves. They weren't exactly experienced as a scavenger team, so Miles didn't feel too stung by the criticism the client was throwing around in their messages.

On the bed, Trin stirred awake, roused by the noise. He looked up, head-flaps askew and covering one eye.

"What happen?"

"Torg got us a job," Miles said.

Trin was instantly awake, sitting up, eyes clear.

"Oh?"

Miles handed Trin the comm, letting him read the contract.

"Torg! I knew you were big sweet talker," Trin said, clapping Torg with a pair of mid-paws and handing the device back to him.

Miles didn't want to start a dive with unused delta burning a hole in his pocket. He wouldn't have an experienced scavenger with him this time, and he needed every advantage he could get. That meant he didn't have time to wait and agonize over his choice of index upgrade.

"When is dive?" Trin asked. He'd seen the contract, but obviously hadn't read it properly.

"Tonight. Nine hours from now," Miles said.

Trin jumped off the bed. "I have to get ready."

Miles felt the same way. He sat on the bed and pulled out his index, flipping to the complete list of upgrades.

Safe and obvious, or take a gamble on an unknown?

He chose a combination of both.

He selected to increase his Authority at a cost of seventy-five delta, then with the remaining 175 selected *Strike the Disharmonious*.

One was a sure thing, a guaranteed increase to the power of his healing spells, and possibly also an increase to his magical endurance. The other was a gamble, potentially offering a way of temporarily bolstering his Authority, but definitely giving him more insight on what *harmony* and *discord* were.

The index asked for payment and he tapped it to his comm, watching as the delta vanished from the Exchange-linked device. His index froze for a moment, and then the purchase went through.

He felt it when the index started working. Spinning. A marble of electrical heat rotating at increasing speeds. He'd felt this before, in the market on Delatariel Station, but this time the feeling was centered on the index, as if the device itself was casting a spell.

A wire of hot energy flickered invisibly across Miles's body, from his head to his feet, then whipped back to a point somewhere in his abdomen. It concentrated there, Miles feeling his own magical core grow warm and start to spin in harmony. Then the feeling faded, and finally vanished.

Did it work?

Checking his index, he found that Authority had increased, and he now possessed *Strike the Disharmonious*. He didn't feel any different.

Miles tapped the new spell on his index. He felt his magical core spin up, sending a buzzing wire of hot energy through his body, then down his arm to his hand. It coalesced on his fingers and palm. His hand prickled with the desire to grab something.

Unlike his other spells, this one didn't come with a litany. There was no stream of words placed into his mind by the alien magic. Instead, a ringing sound filled his ears; a pure tone, like the unending peal of a struck bell.

Miles looked around the room, hoping that something would jump out at him as "discordant." Nothing seemed to stand out.

Trin was getting ready, throwing things into his bag. He'd already put on his hard synth-fiber cap, which was maybe a little premature. They weren't going for hours.

Not disharmonious, Miles thought, still hearing the clear note as he watched Trin prepare.

As Miles watched, Trin reached under the plastic mattress and pulled out his new gun.

Instantly something about the weapon jarred in Miles's awareness. The note soured. An ugly vibration crept into sound, seemingly originating at the device Trin was stuffing into his bag.

The gun was *disharmonious.*

It was an alien thought, not one that originated in Miles's opinions or experience. He tried following it back to its source, but only got vague images. He might be able to tease apart what his tradition meant by *harmony* and *discord* if he had more examples to look at, but right then he was only getting rough notions of complexity and ugliness.

He felt like he could grab at the air and pull something from the weapon, even feeling the urge to do so, but Trin finished packing the gun away and the sour note faded from the air.

Miles let the spell fade without using it.

None of the others reacted as if they'd heard the note at all, so Miles assumed it was completely internal to him and the spell.

Just then, the injured scout woke up and started asking for food again. Trin bounced off the bed and grabbed the new keg of food paste.

Miles stood up and followed him.

Miles still had nine hours until he needed to be at his best, and the injured scout was still healing, if regenerating body parts counted as healing.

He had time to rest, and the opportunity to use his healing spells. It was time to see how much his increased Authority helped his magical endurance.

PART 6

GIG ECONOMY

CHAPTER 12

Wind whipped at Miles's protective robe as their platform drifted toward the dungeon entrance complex.

Water vapor clouds had formed in the Ialis night sky, blocking out the spiral of stars that normally cut through the void like a thin, meandering Milky Way. The rain had started a little after they left, a light drizzle that nevertheless soaked the moss-covered foothills north of Dendril City, creating pools and streams that sprang up out of nowhere.

He took a moment to marvel that the planet could even support an atmosphere and a biosphere. Whatever the Ialis dungeon was, it occupied almost the entirety of the planetary sphere, with only a thin crust of dirt and rock surrounding the apparently infinite hollow structure.

Infinite. How can it be infinite?

Miles looked down over the railing of the floating platform. Hundreds of feet below them, the ground was rushing past. He peered at the surface as if he could see down to its lowest depths, as if the dark moss would reveal the planet's secrets to him.

From interrogating They-who–fly-with-abandon, Miles had worked out that whatever held the dirt and inhabitants down against the planet wasn't exactly gravity, which was a peculiarity of spacetime-like universes, but it was close enough for everyday work. Miles had been living in the weave for a while now, and he was pretty sure that if he'd felt one force gradient he'd felt them all.

Torg didn't seem to be bothered by the rain. It ran over his carapace without affecting him, the overhanging chitin cowl of his shell acting as a hood for his eyes and insectile face. Trin *did* seem to be bothered by the rain. His fur was soaked, and he looked miserable. Every few seconds he ran a pair of mid-paws over his face, squeezing the water out of the fur there.

Miles's robe was waterproof, which was nice, and something he should have worried about after they'd landed on Ialis. After spending so long in the climate-controlled interior of Destiel Station, he'd almost forgotten rain existed. Now, his hair was soaked, but he was dry from his neck to his knees.

The open-topped floating platforms seemed like a poor design for a transport system on a world that had rain. There was some kind of technology that slowed the wind as it hit them, a shield against the air they would otherwise be hitting at high speed, but that didn't stop the wind or rain completely. Whether that deficiency was because of ineffable alien logic, cost constraints, or just an ordinary administrative mistake, the platforms were the standard way of getting around on the planet, so Miles would have to get used to it.

They'd left Bandy back at the apartment with the scout. The little drone didn't seem to have the capacity to care for their recovering Ankn guest, but Bandy could at least keep her company.

"These are so slow," Trin complained, his voice mournful.

Watching the landscape fly by below them, Miles couldn't exactly agree. Back on old Earth, he'd flown on passenger planes that didn't go half this speed. It was only the distance between Dendril City and the entrance complex that meant it would take over an hour to get there.

"Maybe we buy a little ship," Trin suggested. "With roof, and hot air, and a food maker."

Buying even a small ship in the Spiral was the equivalent of buying a large house back on old Earth. When they were having trouble just making rent, it wasn't a realistic proposition. This job would help with that, but only if everything went well.

The client that Torg had lined up for them was going to be meeting them at the entrance complex next to the dungeon crater in a little over forty minutes.

Lestiel Dunverde.

They had his name from the contract document and his pronoun from his comm entry, but that was all they knew about him.

Despite the fact that the contract was already signed and sealed, Miles still felt like he was going into a job interview. He was as nervous as he'd been since he signed on with the *Kipper*.

It might not have been so bad if Miles was confident about actually doing the job, but they'd only done one short dungeon dive. How was that meant to qualify them to escort a stranger through it?

Only the client's attitude of superiority and the fact that they were going no further than the first level gave Miles any peace at the idea.

They should have time to land at the entrance complex and clean up a little before meeting Lestiel. Hopefully, he would be more impressed with them in person than he'd seemed on the comm.

The client's ship was a slim dart of liquid black. It flew in silently, coming down at a thirty-degree angle at what felt like hundreds of miles per hour. As it reached the entrance complex, it slowed abruptly, dropping from high speed to a near-stop within a second, then turned in a lazy half-circle and floated down onto a landing pad.

It was shaped like a narrow teardrop, with the tip of the vessel ending in a point about forty feet in front of the rounded rear. There were no devices or equipment mounted on the hull, no windows, no features of any kind, just a perfectly smooth black shell.

Miles didn't have a lot of experience with the various ships of the Spiral, but this one seemed expensive.

When it was just feet above the landing pad, the underside of the ship seemed to flow downward like water on glass, forming three spiked stilettos of the same black substance as the ship. The narrow spikes made contact with the landing pad with a sound like needles on stone.

Miles didn't need an engineering degree to know that a spike was a bad shape for something that was meant to take any amount of weight, at least without damaging the surface it was resting on. He wondered if reading into that would tell him something about the ship's owner.

Moments after it landed, another part of the ship's hull flowed like liquid, this time opening a hole in the bottom. As soon as it was clear, the occupant hopped down, landing in a crouch below the ship and stepping out onto the landing pad.

For a split second, Miles thought he was looking at a human.

The sapient was humanoid, around six feet tall, with slim hips and long fingers. He had the same rough proportions as a human, except that he was skeletally thin, with skin that hugged an internal skeleton like it had been vacuum sealed on. His head was almost bald, with a ridge of multicolored hair that grew in a line along the center of his head before cascading down behind him in a long tail.

The color of his skin was hard to discern. Miles had initially thought it was absolute black, but as the sapient looked around, wherever the light from the skydock's lamps caught him, it appeared bone-white. The boundary between illuminated and shadowed skin was marked with a ridge of shifting rainbow shimmer like an oil slick. The whole effect made Miles think more of a stylized painting than something he could describe in merely human terms. He wasn't sure it even *was* a color. Maybe it was more of an optical effect, like a dragonfly wing.

The sapient took a second to look around and get his bearings, then sighted on Miles's group and began marching toward them.

He focused on Torg as he approached, the one of them he'd met before.

"I was so certain that you would fail to be here," he said as he arrived. "For clearing the most pathetic of bars, I congratulate you."

Torg tsked. "*Thanks*."

The sapient turned his head, taking in Miles and Trin.

Miles's robe was clean, still bearing the healer symbol that'd been painted on it on their last dive. Trin had taken a moment to clean up and dry his fur, but the rain and humidity had still left him looking very fluffy.

The client was dressed in a tight-fitting flight suit of what looked like dark gray leather, with gloves in a slightly lighter color, and a pair of footwear that were like rigid-soled socks. There wasn't much in the way of embellishment on the outfit, but a large hood hung loosely behind them, and they wore a black synth-fabric belt similar to the one that wrapped around Miles's robe.

The client's belt was clipped with a holster that held a sleek silver pistol, and a metal scabbard that looked like it could be holding a long, slim sword, maybe something like a rapier.

The silence between them was starting to get awkward, so Miles took the initiative and spoke into it.

"I'm Miles, the team's healer," he said. He didn't really know how to talk to a client, on Earth or in the Spiral, so he fell back on old patterns. *Introduce everyone.* "This is Trin, our scout, and you already met Torg, our lancer."

He tried not to feel like a fraud as he labeled them with terms he'd only learned a few days before.

"I am Lestiel Dunverde, though if you haven't yet discovered that, then I had exactly the right estimation of your intelligence." Lestiel looked around, then up at the sky. "Before we leave the shelter of my ship, protect me from this falling water."

Miles's stomach clenched briefly. They didn't have any rain protection for him. Maybe his robe? Lestiel's fight suit looked as good or better protection from the rain than the robe's rough fabric.

"I'm sorry, we don't have a way to keep the rain off you," Miles said.

Trin interrupted before Lestiel could reply to that. "Look, it rains here. That's what you get. You didn't prepare, so who's stupid now?"

Lestiel turned, peering down at him sharply. The sapient's eyes were white with black centers, no iris, but the pupils seemed to contain glints of silver.

"Did you know that your fur is soaked through?" Lestiel snipped in response. "You smell like a rug after a flood."

"The entrance complex is this way," Miles said, before that could escalate. He gestured toward the low open buildings a few hundred meters away. Without waiting for a response, he started walking.

After a few seconds, he heard the others start to follow. Encouraged at having successfully taken the initiative, Miles continued.

"Once we're cleared to go in, we'll be put in a queue," Miles explained as they walked. "It might take us an hour to reach the front and actually enter the artifact, but with it being evening and with the bad weather, there might not be as many people ahead of us."

He was making the last part up, but it seemed logical to him. That was how it always worked on Earth.

"You will pay our entrance fee into the artifact, of course," Lestiel said, his feet squelching in puddles as they walked across the moss.

Miles had expected that. He'd checked with Bandy, and it turned out that entrance into the first level only cost thirty seln, but he still found it a little cheap of the sapient to make them pay it.

"Do we have an objective once we get inside?" Miles asked.

Lestiel was quiet for a few seconds before answering.

"I doubt you have the wherewithal to have discovered this, but I am a researcher at the Danis Institute. The Ialis artifact is my new topic of study. For my first visit, I will need biological samples taken from artifact-born life, as well as examples of the chaotic technology it seems to generate."

In his previous trip, Miles had seen both. Now, he only hoped they'd be able to accommodate him. From what he'd heard, it wasn't a sure thing.

"The artifact shuffles its layout occasionally, and it seems to be random," Miles said, hoping both that he was right and that Lestiel didn't already know this. "We're not guaranteed to find what you need on this dive."

"Of course I already know of the artifact's patterns and peculiarities," Lestiel said, his tone withering. "I *just* said I was a researcher at the Danis Institute. Are all scavengers this slow on the uptake, or are you a special example?"

Trin jumped in unhelpfully. "We are all slow. Scavenger lifestyle. Many knocks on head."

Miles felt the need to defend himself. "It wasn't so much to educate you, as it was a legal disclaimer. I'm just trying to be up-front about it. You might not get what you want."

"Then I suggest you reread our contract, if you *can* read," Lestiel said. "It does not tie your payment to the success of my academic objectives."

"He can't read. Very sad," Trin said in response.

After a few minutes, they came to the same open-walled building that Miles had visited before, last time with Brisk. Not much had changed, except now four of the sharp attack drones drifted menacingly around the station in circles, constantly on alert.

There was a Gilthaen managing the station inside, their towering wormlike body wrapped in a high-collared black coat with a silvery shirt underneath. As soon as they were close enough for Miles to get a good look, he realized that he knew them. It was They-who-share-ground, Consul Thunis, back on duty already.

"Consul Thunis, hello," Miles said as they arrived. He hadn't learned many things from Brisk that he wanted to keep, but how to be polite to the staff of the entrance facility was one of them.

Thunis turned to look at them, then curled down from their imposing height, bringing their face down to look at Miles from a couple of feet away.

"Miles Asher," the consul said, blinking loudly. They straightened back up. "I am no longer They-who-share-ground. I am now They-who-warily-tread. Please know me as Consul Thunit."

"Consul Thunit, of course," Miles said, enjoying having at least one interaction with a Spiral sapient that he had some frame of reference for.

"I have not been given a chance to say this to you, Miles Asher. Thank you for your help during that other time. I recommended your boon to our Consul General They-who-read-deeply."

"Consul, thank you. That really helped us out."

"Your actions were entered in our corporate logs. There you were recorded as He-who-burns-his-hand-on-mercy."

"Oh," Miles said, simply.

He didn't know how to feel about that. He'd scalded his hand when he'd tried to touch the consul to heal them, not knowing that Gilthaens had a body temperature high enough to hurt him, but he hadn't exactly acted out of mercy, and it hadn't exactly been a burn, and anyway, the injury was long gone now; his *Hasten Renewal* spell worked as well on himself as it did on others.

"Consul, thank you," Miles said at last, not sure how else to respond.

The consul's head swayed, maybe in acknowledgment.

They entered their party's details into the Gilthaen system and paid their entrance fee of thirty seln. As they were walking from the station to the transport platforms, Lestiel spoke up.

"How did you gain the respect of the Gilthaen?" he asked, peering sidelong at Miles as they walked.

Miles considered giving a serious answer, but he honestly didn't want to open himself up to another one of their client's scathing put-downs.

"By doing something stupid," he said instead.

Lestiel held his gaze for a moment, seeming to read more into the statement than Miles had intended. He turned back to look ahead of them and spoke in the same acidic way he had since he'd landed.

"Nobility in ignorance is the only kind of nobility that some people can hope for."

By the time they boarded the platform, the rain had stopped, and they began their slow, spiraling descent into the crater.

The outer door was shut. The platform had dropped them off at a point similar to their last entry point, but with a few marked differences. This time it was a corridor, about fifteen feet tall and six wide, with a floor made of a white material that felt like ceramic and a ceiling set with the same irregular blue lights Miles had noticed on their previous visit.

The crater had sheared off whatever the corridor had been traveling from, leaving a twenty-foot-long passageway that ended in a closed door.

This one had an intact panel. Miles couldn't help but remember the trouble Trin had gone through with the last one.

Lestiel Dunverde walked behind them. He was looking around as they moved, as if every aspect of the mundane corridor interested him.

When they reached the far end, Trin touched the door panel to wake it up, then started tapping pictograms that appeared on the screen.

The designs were shifting too fast for Miles's *Eyes of the Émigré* to translate, but from the way the same designs kept reappearing, it looked like Trin was trying a lot of slight variations on the same path.

Lestiel stepped up behind the scout to watch him work.

"The doors are sealed with puzzles?" Lestiel asked.

Trin hummed, then spoke as he continued working. "More like bad interface. Like this. I say open, it says no. I say please, it says give key. I say here is key, it says no key. I say, no, your key reader broken. It says, give maintenance code. I put in blank code."

Trin tapped a final icon and waited as the panel processed something.

After a second it changed, showing a symbol that translated as "YES." Something mechanical clunked inside the wall.

"Then it works," Trin said. "Not always so easy. Door maker messed up bad on this one."

The door slid open, revealing a forest.

For a few seconds, they all hesitated. It was a surprising sight, here, underground, on this planet.

Miles stepped forward while the others were still staring.

It was a pine forest, Miles realized.

White trunks stood ten or twenty feet apart, stretching up a hundred feet or more into white mist. To the left and right, and out ahead of them, the forest floor stretched further than they could see, hundreds of meters of struggling grass and decaying plant matter.

The smell was almost overwhelming; scents of pine needles, damp earth, forest mulch, and distant rain. The trees were silver pine, Miles was sure of it. He was back on Earth. He *was* back on Earth.

He turned to look behind him and saw Trin, Torg, and Lestiel, standing just outside the door, jarring in this scene of normality. He was inside the dungeon on Ialis. He was still in Spiral space, billions of miles from Earth.

The others cautiously stepped through. Lestiel's eyes were wide, turning to take in everything. Trin had his scanning device out, tapping keys and not taking his eyes off the screen.

"These are silver pine trees," Miles said.

He wanted to impress on the others how familiar they were to him, to him *personally*, and how alien an experience it was to see them here, but he couldn't think of a way to put it into words.

"Are they dangerous?" Lestiel asked.

Miles turned, glancing around at the trees. "Only if they fall on you."

Miles didn't understand. It must have taken hundreds of years to grow these trees, even assuming the dungeon could give them the perfect conditions. Earth hadn't even been *in Spiral space* for that long. Where had the dungeon found the seeds? How did it plant and care for them? Why *this* kind of tree, from the specific area of Earth where Miles had grown up? Was it all a huge coincidence?

"Could this be a simulation?" he asked nobody in particular.

"Not an insubstantial one," Lestiel replied. He seemed distracted, examining one of the trees, pressing his hands against the bark.

"They're biochemistry type C," Miles said, belatedly, hoping it wouldn't be an issue for the sapient.

Lestiel glanced his way before turning back to the tree.

"Big sticks are real," Trin said, staring at his scanner while the rest stared around at the forest. "Room is only few hundred meters. Water in air makes it hard to see, so looks bigger."

So it *was* just a huge underground room. And somehow, the trees were real.

Lestiel extended his arm, and for a second Miles found him hard to look at. When he withdrew it, he was holding something new in his hand, a piece of tech that looked like a compact mirror. He'd just pulled it out of nowhere.

Trin gaped at his scanner for a second, then looked up, his eyes finding Lestiel. "What? How did you do that?"

Lestiel ignored him, popping the device open and waving it over the tree, his own scanner, Miles guessed. After a few passes, he closed the device and tore a piece of bark from the tree with his fingers. Both items vanished from his hands a second later.

"We'll move on," Lestiel said.

After waiting for Trin to finish what he was doing with his scanner, they grouped up and started walking out into the trees.

For a moment, Miles felt a weird conflict between the familiarity of his surroundings and the bizarreness of it being here. It hit him like seeing a stranger approaching him wearing a familiar face. The hair on the back of his neck prickled.

"I'm going to use some sensory magic," Miles said. "I won't be able to understand anything for a while."

He got a curious look from Lestiel, but none of the others said anything, and Miles slipped into his *Eyes of the Altruist*.

Light sprang up all over the forest. At first Miles was shocked, thinking they were surrounded, but then he took a second to process and realized the shapes he was seeing were the trees.

The silver pines didn't have discrete internal organs, exactly, but they did have structure. For the closest ones, Miles could see thin threads running up and down the trunks, which had to be the living stem of the tree. On some of the lower branches, he could see glowing pinpricks that corresponded to where needles emerged. Where the roots disappeared into the springy ground, he saw more vessels and structures, even some mottled colors suggesting damage.

Only the closest trees showed him any detail. The ones further out just had indistinct light misting over them, and the ones further away showed him nothing; too far for him to see the small details.

Miles was admiring the field of glowing threads when something flashed through the air up ahead of them.

He focused on it immediately, but by then it had passed behind a tree.

Trin said something, and Miles immediately switched back to *Eyes of the Émigré*.

"—something," Trin was saying. He was glancing between his scanner and the trees up ahead.

Apparently, Miles wasn't the only one who'd seen movement.

"What is it?" Miles asked.

"An animal biological sample?" Lestiel asked. He sounded pleased.

"Uh. Hot. Lots of legs," Trin said. He tapped on his scanner. "Three meters. Four hundred kilograms. Somewhere there." He pointed up ahead.

Miles instinctively started backing away from the thing hiding up ahead.

He suddenly missed Brisk, despite how illogical that was. It looked like they were going to be testing themselves in combat earlier than he expected.

CHAPTER 13

When Brisk had abandoned Miles, Trin, and Torg on Ialis, he'd left them with a few pieces of equipment. Either they weren't valuable enough for him to bother trying to recover, or more likely, he'd been too busy running from Gilthaen attack drones to take back.

Miles had his striker pistol, a variable-power laser weapon that could knock around a large creature, or splatter a small one against a wall. It seemed like this time, they'd be facing a large creature. He pulled the striker from the pouch at his back and dialed the power slider on the side up to its maximum.

Torg had been left with some kind of energy rifle, which Brisk had called a *cannon*, as well as his ordinary-looking two-handed ax. He'd brought the ax with him down for this dive, but inexplicably, he wasn't carrying the rifle. Maybe it was broken, or out of charge. Maybe Torg had a sense of honor that forced him to fight hand-to-hand. Miles didn't know.

"Hey Torg, where your gun?" Trin asked.

"*Sold,*" Torg replied with a hollow-sounding click.

Oh.

Miles could question the wisdom of that decision later.

Trin looked like he was about to say something else, but he was interrupted.

Something moved to their right. Ten feet above them and to the side, a massive bulk leaned out from the trees.

Miles only had a second to get a look at it. The impressions that went through his mind in that split second were *spider*, *dandelion seed*, and *mass grave*.

The thing was a sphere of tangled limbs; arms and legs, wings and tentacles. Appendages from dozens of different species that radiated out from a central point, squirming and straining past each other.

It hung from a tree with a cluster of hands, fingers and claws digging into bark. On the other side, it had a particularly long white arm, with six claw-tipped fingers spaced evenly around a flat palm.

A second after it appeared it launched the white claw at Miles, the arm snapping out with the claws held forward.

Miles fired his striker on instinct. He aimed for the arm flying at him, but he missed, hitting the thing's main body instead. Several of the limbs emerging from the main body snapped and flailed at the impact, but they'd absorbed all of the force, and the central node wasn't affected.

Miles had a split second to watch the alien hand flying at his face before Torg swung a pair of arms and swept his ax through the outstretched limb. Hand parted from arm with a wet crunch, and the severed claw dropped limply to the side.

The creature in the trees made no sounds, it had no voice, but it shook at the injury, and the sound of flesh rubbing against flesh sent a shiver down Miles's spine.

He raised his striker and fired twice more at the mass of limbs. More arms were broken, but that barely seemed to cost the creature anything.

Miles didn't know anything about this enemy, least of all whether his magic considered it *disharmonious*, but he had a hunch.

He stuffed his striker back into the pouch at his back and brought out his index. He held his empty hand out toward the creature and tapped his index to cast *Strike the Disharmonious*.

Once again the pure note filled his mind, the sound of a struck bell ringing endlessly. Except this time, as soon as he focused on the thing in the trees a discordant counter-note sprang up, clashing and warbling as it overlapped with the first.

Working on instinct that came from the spell, Miles grasped at the air and *pulled*.

The harmonic spell's litany, which had been absent while he was just holding the spell ready, finally ran through his mind.

Mere noise clashes with the song. In a harmonious world, the tuneless theme is ***stricken***.

For a second Miles felt resistance, as if he were holding the corner of an invisible sheet. He pulled with all of his strength, and with a tearing sensation, his hand was released.

Far from feeling the normal rush of electric energy from his abdomen, this time he felt power flowing back *down* from his hand. It ran down his arm like water to his gut, from which it spread out through his body.

Miles looked up at the creature hanging from the tree. It didn't look any different.

Next to him, Trin had finished setting up his new weapon and opened fire on the thing. A swarm of firefly projectiles appeared in the air with a series of pops, flickering up at the creature and through it, tearing wide holes wherever they passed.

A pair of projectiles passed through the thing's hidden central body, and it immediately started slipping from its perch. It lost its grip on the tree, fell through the air, and hit the ground with a rattle of cracking bones. Once on the ground, it lay there inert.

Throughout the conflict, Lestiel had stood back, watching with dispassionate interest. Now that it was down, he strode forward, walking a circuit around it while peering down.

"Interesting," he said. He paused and lifted one of the limbs. When he let go, it dropped back down limply. Lestiel raised his head, looking from Miles, to Trin, to Torg.

"What are these called?" he asked.

"He is called slap boss," Trin said confidently. "Big scary arm monster. Don't let him get you, he will eat your arms."

"Fascinating."

Miles stared at Trin incredulously. Did Trin really know something about the thing, or was he just making it up?

Trin glanced back at him. In that moment Miles saw a flash of mischief in the other boy's eyes.

He's lying!

"Yeah," Trin continued. "His danger is his big slaps. Watch out for claws, too."

"Is this one dead?" Lestiel asked.

Trin reached down and grabbed his scanner. He brought it up and started tapping at buttons.

Miles switched briefly into *Eyes of the Altruist*, looking over the body to check that the magic wasn't showing him any living anatomy.

Shapes sprung up over the thing. A large oval, a network of fibers. Miles flicked back to *Eyes of the Émigré*.

"It's still alive," he said.

The thing moved.

It rushed at Trin, scuttling across the ground, grabbing and pulling itself forward by roots, tree trunks, and handfuls of bare earth. It was halfway to him in a second.

Trin screamed, a thin, untranslated *"Aaaaa!"* He turned his weapon on it and fired.

Fireflies buzzed out of Trin's pistol, but the projectiles only caught the creature's limbs, missing the central body. They shredded arms, legs, and pseudopods, but failed to stop it.

Miles saw a flash of black chitin and Torg appeared, putting himself between the creature and Trin. The mass of limbs barreled into him, forcing him back a step, but failed to get past.

Two of the thing's arms grabbed Torg's ax and tore it free, sending it flying away through the trees. Suddenly unarmed, Torg grabbed at the core of the thing and lifted it up, raising it above his head.

Miles understood that he was trying to give the others a clear shot. He pulled the striker from its pouch at his back, took aim, and fired.

Earlier, his striker weapon had knocked the creature's arms around, but it hadn't done any real damage. This time when the force hit the central core, its limbs tore like tissue paper. The central core ripped free from the mass of arms and flew away like a struck golf ball. It traveled ten feet through the air before slapping against a tree trunk, hanging in place for a second, then falling to the ground, deformed and deflated.

Miles stood with his heart pounding in his ears. He looked around, then behind him, still twitching with energy, his body unwilling to believe the danger had passed.

When he was sure they weren't going to be attacked by something hidden lurking out in the trees, he switched briefly to *Eyes of the Altruist* and inspected the fallen core.

There were still some faint lights hovering over the squashed sphere that had been at the center of the mess of limbs, but they faded to nothing as Miles watched. He switched back to *Eyes of the Émigré*.

"It's dead," he said.

He shared a look with Trin. The scout looked like he was in shock, his eyes wide, his head-flaps all half raised up. He had a death grip on his weapon, but under Miles's stare, he lowered it to point at the ground.

"Well, I'm pleased you can tell a living creature from a dead one," Lestiel said, sardonically. "That puts a higher floor on your skills as a healer than I guessed."

Their client hadn't seemed shocked or afraid by the sudden violence, nor had he moved to help, or even to try and escape. He'd simply stood and watched the battle unfold with a neutral expression. He was obviously armed, he had a pistol on his belt, but he'd made no move to draw it.

If Miles were being charitable, he might wonder if the client was so unused to violence that he'd been paralyzed through the entire thing. It was close enough to how Miles felt that he wouldn't judge that. But he had an inkling that the man had simply never felt at risk from the creature, and wasn't particularly invested in their survival.

Lestiel began walking slowly to the downed creature. He paused at the mess of severed limbs to poke at them with his toe, turning them over.

"Hurc, Eppan, Morchis, Hug. Quite a collection," Lestiel said, picking over the pile of limbs.

Miles followed him closer to the pile, peering down with grim fascination.

Closer up, Miles could see that the limbs weren't in good shape. They looked old, dead. Withered skin, milky chitin, dried-out membranes, flesh that had started pulling back from where claws emerged from fingers or paws. It looked like they could have been dead for a while.

Lestiel crouched and picked up a three-fingered hand. He held one of the fingers firmly, then jerked his arm, snapping it. When he pulled it, the skin tore and the finger came free from the arm it was attached to. He brought it up to his face, examining it closely. For a second Miles thought he was going to eat it.

"Dead tissue. Strangely preserved," he said. He stood back up and the sample disappeared from his hands like the tree bark had.

He moved on, walking up toward the thing's core. Miles followed, curious, and Torg came after him.

As Lestiel reached the deflated ball of the thing's core body he stopped to gaze down at it. After a few seconds of observation, he said, "This is an Orbellius."

What?

Miles rushed forward to stand next to Lestiel. He stared down at the corpse.

It didn't have much in common with the only other Orbellius Miles had seen, Rhu-Orlen, his former captain.

Orlen had orangey-pink skin that had been covered in bumps, with a handful of stringy tendrils. The corpse had pinky-gray skin, with about a hundred white threads emerging from all over it. But when Miles thought back to what his *Eyes of the Altruist* had shown him, how similar was their internal structure?

He couldn't ignore the possibility that this *was* somehow an Orbellius.

Miles felt his gut tightening. He'd thought it was just an animal, but Orbellius were Spiral sapients.

"Did I just kill someone?" he asked quietly.

Miles felt a weird sickness in his body and limbs. He felt like he'd made a mistake, broken a law, committed a sin.

Miles wasn't sure he was expecting an answer, but Lestiel replied.

"It wasn't behaving much like a sapient, was it?" he said scornfully. "And I've never known an Orbellius to do this to themselves, taking the body parts of other species. I'd say this was primitive behavior. Disgusting."

Lestiel drew the blade from his hip, a narrow forearm-length sword. He slashed down with it once and the central core of the thing split open like a melon, releasing the stench of acrid chemicals and bitter rot.

"This is interesting," Lestiel mused to himself. He used the tip of his sword to point at an area around the central organ. "See how the processing tissues are atrophied? I doubt this being was capable of thoughts more complex than simple survival imperatives."

Miles peered down. He *couldn't* see, but maybe that was because he knew next to nothing about Orbellius anatomy.

"You mean it was brain-damaged?" Miles asked.

"Or it never had any 'brains' to begin with. I wonder if this could be an Orbellius near-relative. I've heard of some species suffering their non-sapient cousins to share their worlds with them."

"So, maybe it wasn't really sapient," Miles said quietly.

"If it ever had been, it wasn't when it died," Lestiel offered.

Lestiel used his sword to slice out a section of the body, as if he were cutting a slice of cake. He raised it up in the air on the tip of his sword, then he did *something*. There was a subtle twist, and the sample vanished.

How are you doing that? Miles thought. His curiosity had been dampened by anxiety, and he didn't ask the question out loud.

"Wonderful," Lestiel said, straightening up and sliding his sword back into its scabbard. "I have a sample of the *silver pine* and this *slap boss*, though in my notes I think I'll refer to it as an *Orbellius Ghoul*, on account of the dead tissue it was using to move around. Let's see what else we can find, shall we?"

He set off through the forest, walking ahead without a care, as if they hadn't just had a feral Orbellius launch itself at them.

Miles checked quickly on the others, and they set off following him.

As they walked through the mist, Miles replayed the battle over and over in his head. He'd never killed anyone before. Earth had seen some ugly days since the bower break, but Miles had been relatively sheltered in his family's compound. He knew some of his relatives had killed people, but he'd run away before reaching an age when he was expected to join in on that.

Except now, he might have killed someone. A crazed someone who was threatening them. An unthinking someone, if he trusted what Lestiel had said. But still potentially a person, someone who might have had a name and a history. He didn't care for Lestiel's theory that it could have been a non-sapient cousin of the Orbellius species, something like the Orbellius version of a chimp. That seemed too self-serving.

There had been something in its behavior, too. The Orbellius Ghoul had come at Miles when he was holding his striker, then at Trin after he'd drawn his weapon. The ghoul had recognized what a pistol was and had prioritized their wielders as the biggest threats. To Miles, that suggested it had some knowledge or memory, even if it wasn't thinking clearly.

Could it have been a salvager, lost in the dungeon during a reconfiguration? Or was it a creation of the artifact, like the pine trees around them had to be?

Miles remembered the spell he'd cast. Looking back, he wondered if it had even had any effect. It felt like it had worked, that nearly physical sensation of tearing, and he still felt different after casting it, more solid and real, somehow. He wasn't sure what effect it had had on the target, if any.

It might have made the ghoul weaker and more fragile, *that last shot*, but he didn't have any frame of reference, so it might have had little or no effect. His final shot doing so much damage might just have been a fluke lucky hit.

"No motion," Trin was saying, watching his scanner. "No motion. Easy everyone. No more motion. We are clean."

Miles kept his eyes on the surrounding mist anyway, scanning with *Eyes of the Altruist* every few seconds for anything alive.

"Door over there," Trin said, reading off his scanner while forward and to the right.

They changed directions.

Miles wasn't sure he even wanted to continue, but as long as they stayed within the four-hour time limit, their client was running the dive.

A couple of minutes after they changed direction, Miles caught sight of a shape between the trees up ahead.

"Wait," he whispered.

It was a roughly rectangular shape, close to the ground, red, with lines or wires stretching out from it. It was too misty to make out any detail yet, but Miles didn't want to take any chances.

"I'm seeing it," Trin said. He changed a few settings on his scanner before reporting. "Not hot, not cold, not moving, not buzzing."

Miles switched briefly to his *Eyes of the Altruist*. As far as the magic was concerned, it wasn't alive.

He continued forward, drawing his striker as he moved to the front of the group.

After a few more meters he recognized what the shape was, and the realization stopped him in his tracks.

It's a tent.

A red nylon dome tent, the kind that anyone on old Earth might have taken camping. It was anchored by guylines pinned to the ground with metal stakes, with a front flap closed by a zipper. Miles even thought he could make out the text of a brand name and a logo on the side, though it was too far away to read.

On the ground close to it was a plastic cooler, a short stack of chopped wood, and a cooking tripod. It looked as at home in the pine forest surroundings as the forest was jarring in the alien station.

Is someone camping out here, or is this like the warehouse, things manufactured by the dungeon?

Given the absolute improbability of someone bringing human camping supplies to Ialis, Miles had to assume it was a scene manufactured by the dungeon, though he couldn't imagine how or why.

"What is it?" Trin asked.

They'd collectively decided that none of the camping supplies were creatures waiting to jump them and had drawn closer.

"It's a tent and camping gear," Miles said. "I think it's like the warehouse we saw with Brisk. Fake stuff that the dungeon made."

Lestiel had skipped ahead. He inspected the cooler, then felt at the edges and popped the lid off. He spent a second looking inside, then moved to the tent and started trying to get it open. It took him a minute to figure out the zipper.

Miles stopped to look in the cooler. It held a handful of cans, most sized like soda cans, a couple sized like beer. They had labels like *Fruit* and *Special Suds*. One was just called *Vrrrrr*. None of them were designs he recognized, but they were all in the style of soda cans common on old Earth.

"This stuff is all from my iteration, from Earth," Miles said. He picked up one of the cans, turning to read the ingredients list. All gibberish. "Or, it's meant to be."

That caught Lestiel's attention. He turned and launched a volley of questions. "Which iteration? Have you ever left anything like this behind in the artifact? How many times have you been inside the artifact?"

"Iteration 27,200," Miles said. "I haven't left anything like this down here, and uh—"

He didn't want to admit this was only his second visit. Luckily, Trin piped up before his silence could go on too long.

"We been here lots of times. Maybe a hundred."

Lestiel took one of the cans from the cooler. It vanished. He went back to the tent, rummaging inside, and pulling out holding a couple of items. He approached Miles, holding them out.

"Are these also from your iteration?"

In his left hand, he was holding a distorted cell phone, in his right, a star-shaped alien device.

Miles held out his hand and accepted the cell phone. "This one is. It's a communication device. That other one isn't. I don't recognize it."

He examined the cell phone as he spoke. A glass screen with a narrow silver bevel. He didn't recognize the make, but he wouldn't expect to if it was something the planet had created. He pressed down on what he thought was a power button, but there was no reaction from the device.

"I will take the mystery device, then," Lestiel said. The star-shaped piece of tech vanished like all of his samples.

"If you don't mind me asking, how are you doing that?" Miles said, speaking before he had a chance to worry whether it was rude or not.

Lestiel glanced at him. "I'm not surprised I'm the first Draulean you've ever met, but shouldn't a healer be better versed in sapients' abilities? If you lack the mental capacity to store many details, as seems likely, then at least learn about the Spiral's immortals. We hold a significant place in the Spiral."

Miles stared back at him blankly.

Are all our clients going to be this annoying?

By unspoken agreement, Miles and Trin agreed to loot the camp. It didn't matter that most of it was likely junk, they had so little that Miles thought it was still worth taking, and Trin's attitude was just to take anything they could carry regardless of what it was. If Miles hadn't intervened, he would probably have been stuffing his bag full of pinecones.

When they were done packing up, they had a folded-down dome tent, a polyester sleeping bag that had no openings, a survival knife with saw teeth on both sides instead of just the back, and an apparently perfectly normal and functional camp stove. Miles kept the cell phone for the nostalgia, and Lestiel was happy taking only his unknown device.

Miles thought they were done. Lestiel had his biological samples and an example of the tech the planet apparently made, but when they were finished at the camp, their client turned their attention to the nearest wall, where the outline of a door was faintly visible through the mist.

"Let's continue. I'm curious how the structures vary from area to area, it can't be all manufactured forest."

As he walked out of earshot, Miles turned to Trin.

"We're going to have to start writing our own contracts. This one was too vague. He might keep us down here for the full four hours."

"Let Torg write them," Trin said. "Big sweet talker."

Torg was already following Lestiel. After a few seconds, Miles headed after them.

CHAPTER 14

The door opened on a long, *long* corridor. It seemed to stretch out ahead of them endlessly, never bending, never rising or falling. It was the same dimensions as the door, tall enough to allow a giant to pass, but so narrow they wouldn't be able to walk more than two side-by-side.

It had the same construction as the winding corridor they'd passed through with Brisk on their last trip. The floor was textured metal, the walls made up of featureless white panels, the ceiling set with intermittently placed blue-white lights.

As they stepped through, Miles noticed something additionally weird about the corridor. There was something wrong with perspective.

Normally a space like this would have the look of shrinking as it got further away, with the straight lines seeming to converge on the vanishing point. That wasn't what was happening here. When Miles stared down the corridor, it was almost like perspective didn't even exist. The corridor faded out to milky indistinctness with the distance, but it took up as much visual space at every point along it.

The result was a bizarre, fun-house-mirror effect that set Miles on edge.

Without the normal visual cues, Miles had trouble gauging the corridor's length. It could have been a hundred meters long or a hundred miles. Only the way that the distant details faded out gave him any clue.

"Trin, how long is this?" Miles asked. He was reluctant to start walking down a corridor that had no features and seemed to have no end.

Trin must have already been scanning, because he answered straight away.

"This one, it is twenty-eight hundred meters until something hard."

Two-point-eight kilometers. Not too long.

Miles did some mental calculations. If they walked at a sustainable pace, that might take them thirty or forty minutes. Estimating on the high side, that could be an hour and a half for the round trip.

The cautious walk through the forest room had taken half an hour, with another twenty minutes of fighting the Orbellius Ghoul and looting the campsite.

They had a four-hour limit from their point of entry, with about an hour spent so far. The corridor might add another two to that, if they spent any time at all investigating the far end.

Miles didn't want less than an hour of slack in their schedule, not when the consequence of missing the deadline was facing the terrifying unknown of being inside the dungeon when it reconfigured.

"We don't have time," Miles said, eventually.

"Untrue. We have an abundance of time," Lestiel said. "A leisurely walk along this passageway and back will still afford us around fifty-five minutes to investigate the terminus, with three minutes to spare in case of unexpected delays."

Three minutes??

"Three minutes isn't enough slack," Miles said. "I want at least an hour of slack on every visit."

"Twenty-five percent of your entire time budget? That's preposterous," Lestiel said. "Are you overly predisposed to accidents? Perhaps you have a propensity for tripping over your feet, or getting lost in straight tunnels?"

Miles felt his face get hot as he struggled with how to make himself understood.

He'd just taken for granted that his ideas of safe working would be universal. Obviously, they should leave a generous amount of time for the unexpected when they were visiting such a dangerous, unfamiliar place, but Lestiel seemed genuinely confused, and even Trin was giving him a skeptical look.

"We don't know what might delay us," Miles countered. "A door could drop down behind us, and we'd need time to open it, or we could get injured in a way that slows us down. One of us could be knocked out and need to be carried back—"

"It's true," Trin interjected, "That happened once."

"—we just don't know all the threats."

Lestiel looked from Miles to Trin, then to Torg.

"Well, I'm continuing, even if I go alone," Lestiel said. "Abandoning me here would be a violation of contract, but since you've been convenient so far, I'd be willing to pay you on a pro-rata basis for the time you've accompanied me—perhaps fifty percent of our agreed fee."

Miles seriously considered it. He looked between Torg and Trin, trying to gauge their reactions. He felt like Trin wanted to continue on. Torg was unreadable.

"I want to see," Trin said. "We go, we look, we cut loose if boring. Still lots of time."

"I will have no desire to linger either, if the terminus is '*boring*'," Lestiel said.

"*Go*," Torg said.

Miles rubbed his forehead. It looked like he was outvoted. *Is that how we're making decisions?* If they just went to the end, looked, then came back, that would still leave them forty or fifty minutes of slack. He might be able to deal with that level of risk.

"Okay, go," Miles said. "Just to the far end and back. We won't have any time to spend when we get there."

"Wonderful," Lestiel said, drawing the word out as if he'd been waiting for a group of children to come to the obvious conclusion. He turned and started striding down the corridor.

After a few seconds of hesitation, Miles followed.

At least one mystery was solved as they traveled down the corridor. The strange perspective effect of the passageway turned out to have a physical cause.

Miles noticed it after they'd traveled a few hundred feet. The corridor was getting wider. The floor was sloping subtly downward, the walls were getting further apart, and the ceiling was angled up.

All of the sides were diverging at the precise rate that would create a perfect forced perspective. The effect from the start of the corridor had been to counteract the apparent shrinking of perspective, but it seemed like a lot of effort to go to for an optical illusion.

What was the point? To make it harder to judge the distance?

It couldn't only have been affecting him. Except in the case of truly alien vision systems, perspective was a consequence of geometry, straight lines converging on a point. There were definitely species out there whose visual systems were different enough to his that it might not have had an effect on them, beings who saw through their skin, or through energy fields, but the people with him then didn't seem to have that going on.

Trin and Lestiel both had eyes with pupils, and presumably retina-analogs. Unless their visual processing was doing something obscure, they should have had the same impression.

Torg had at least four eyes that Miles had identified, but from the scraps he could remember from college physics, he didn't think that would result in vision that was too different.

As the silence in the corridor started to feel oppressive, he decided he could at least check.

"Is anyone getting a weird perspective effect here?" he asked the group.

"What is that?" Trin asked. "Did not translate."

"Perspective. Things seem smaller when they're further away."

Lestiel slowed, turning to give Miles a sidelong look. "Did you just say that distant objects look smaller to you?"

"Ohh," Trin answered. "*Perspective.* Yes. For this tube, it gets bigger as it gets far away. It tricks you."

"Yes," Miles said.

"You as well?" Lestiel said, looking at Trin. He seemed to find it amusing. "Do you mean that if I were to move further away, I would look smaller to you?"

"Yes," Trin said. "That's how it works."

Lestiel picked up his pace, putting distance between them over the course of a few seconds.

"Do I appear to be shrinking to you?" he called back.

"*Yes,*" Torg answered, this time.

"Oh no! I'm shrinking. Help me," Lestiel called.

"Aren't you meant to be a scientist?" Miles shouted after him.

Lestiel slowed, letting the group catch up. "I'm a scientist with functioning perception. How common is this?"

"It's probably pretty common," Miles guessed.

"This explains so much about the cultural psychology of certain species."

"How do you see the world?" Miles asked.

Lestiel spread his arms as he replied. "I see the world in its naked truth. Energy, matter, space, and transitions. I can taste the weave and hear the song of its physical rules."

"Can you see through the wall?" Trin asked.

Lestiel hesitated for a second before answering. "No."

"What about inside of bodies?"

"You're all somewhat transparent, yes."

That just left Miles confused. What kind of vision did Lestiel have?

Miles let his *Eyes of the Émigré* fade and switched to *Eyes of the Altruist* for a second, inspecting Lestiel properly for the first time.

The man had almost no internal structure. No brain, no stomach, no lungs, no heart. The glowing light only seemed to highlight one "organ," a large ellipse that ran vertically from his neck down to his hips. It had thick walls and pointed ends, with an inner edge that was dotted with sharp protrusions. It kind of gave the effect of a sideways mouth.

Lestiel must have noticed Miles watching, because he twisted his head to look back at him. The man's expression didn't change, but the oval inside him stretched open slightly, revealing new glowing shapes *through* it.

Miles let *Eyes of the Altruist* fade. He found he didn't really *want* to understand what was going on with that.

Lestiel was smiling as he turned back to face forward. "I don't recognize it as a trick of *perspective*, but this passageway is reminiscent of Morchis architecture. Its ratio of expansion mirrors that of their stations."

They continued on in silence. The passageway continued to expand. The ever-shifting black and white of Lestiel's skin strobed as they walked, the strange effect taking the natural light and shadow of the passing overhead lamps and turning it into something stark and absolute.

After twenty minutes, walking down the passageway was closer to walking through a hangar. The wall tiles were the same size as further back in the corridor, but they'd multiplied. The floor sloped upward behind them, the ceilings had vanished into the gloom above. The overhead lights had grown huge, but the light from them was weaker in comparison. It was a strange environment, but at least it wasn't as claustrophobic as the passageway at its start.

After a few minutes, Miles felt himself relax. The corridor was straight, and it was *straightforward*. There were no crate-shaped cloak roaches, there were no unlikely angles. It was clear, with good visibility, and they were making good time. After the conversation had died out, it seemed like boredom would be the biggest threat.

It was the first time since they'd entered the artifact that Miles didn't feel like he had to be on guard, and he took advantage of the lull to check his index.

Name: Miles Asher	**Traditions:** Harmonizer
Fundamental Properties:	
Strength (0)	
Durability (1)	
Speed (0)	
Reactions (0)	
Will (0)	
Authority (2)	
Authority (0.26)	
Spells	
Close Wound (Grasping)	
Temporary Enhancement (Grasping)	
Hasten Renewal (Grasping)	
Strike the Disharmonious (Tentative)	
Core Effects	
Eyes of the Émigré	
Eyes of the Altruist	

Miles had cast *Strike the Disharmonious* on the Orbellius Ghoul, and he'd felt a change that had stuck with him. It was the opposite of the light, fragile feeling he'd had after exhausting his magic; a weight and a solidity.

As he read his index, he realized that there'd also been a change on his listing.

Strike the Disharmonious claimed to be able to confiscate a target's Authority, and the litany he'd experienced when he'd cast it had backed that up.

He'd wondered if that meant he'd get a temporary boost to his fundamental Authority, but it seemed like it had given him an additional Authority property instead. The 0.26 figure must be his index's assessment of the Authority he'd taken from the Orbellius Ghoul. He just didn't know what it meant for him.

Would it enhance spells that used his Authority, or would only the highest be taken into account? Would it contribute toward his magical stamina?

He had at least one spell that made use of his Authority directly. *Temporary Enhancement*. It should show him if his new Authority fundamental combined with his existing one, or had some other use.

Miles pressed his hand to his own chest and tried to remember the spell's litany. He'd cast it without the help of his index before, but it had been days ago, and the language of the various litanies was blurring together.

Something, something, that which it is? Maybe I should write them down.

He tapped the screen to cast the spell from his index, focusing on his fundamental reactions.

In their self, they are complete. In a harmonious world, everything is, in itself, complete. **It is that which it is.**

Miles felt an impression of a robed being standing alone at the peak of a mountain. Their pose was one of readiness, their empty hands held up as if to catch something, their head held at an angle to see and hear everything around them.

The dense lump of energy in Miles's stomach began to spin, faster than before, and a hot energy flooded along his arm.

He felt the spell take hold, and the air turned to molasses.

He was watching the world move around him at three-quarters speed. He felt like he was underwater. He tried to walk faster, and while his body responded to his thoughts the moment he had them, his legs lagged behind. It was like trying to walk with weights tied to his limbs.

This is what increased Reactions feel like.

He'd only tried this once before. When he'd first got the spell, he'd tried boosting every fundamental property to get an idea of what they did, but back then he'd only had an Authority of one. *Now . . .*

He checked his index.

Name: Miles Asher	**Traditions:** Harmonizer
Fundamental Properties:	
Strength (0)	
Durability (1)	
Speed (0)	
Reactions (2.2/0)	
Will (0)	
Authority (2)	
Authority (0.26)	

His second Authority fundamental had been added to his existing one to boost his Reactions. Not the full amount, point-two instead of point-two-six. There must have been some inefficiency involved, but most of the additional Authority had contributed—and it hadn't been used up.

He'd thought the confiscated Authority would be temporary, but it had been an hour since he'd taken it and it was still there.

Miles had to assume that *Strike the Disharmonious* wasn't a route to building an permanently high Authority, or the Harmonizer tradition would be much more popular. Magic seemed relatively rare, and if this was an easy route to power then Ialis would be full of stupendously powerful Harmonizers. The additional Authority couldn't be permanent, but he wasn't sure at what point it would fade.

As he walked down the corridor, the team around him moving in slow motion, he felt another hot pulse of energy flow down his arm.

The spell is refreshing itself.

Could he keep this up for as long as his magic lasted?

I should have used this in the fight with the ghoul.

If this was the effect of just a little over two points of Authority, maybe he'd misspent his delta. How much difference would a third or fourth point make? Maybe there was a cap or diminishing returns, but he wouldn't know until he tried.

There might also be another way to enhance it.

The index offered and showed the magical enhancements to his fundamentals, but that wasn't the whole story. If he wanted to get stronger, he could pay delta to have his strength magically enhanced, or he could work out. Could he also find a way to exercise his Authority?

The Orbellius Ghoul had possessed some small amount of natural Authority or else he wouldn't have been able to confiscate it. It must be innate to Miles as well.

If he could find out how Authority worked in the original pre-index tradition, maybe he could get some off-index enhancements to it.

Miles was still under the effect of his increased Reactions when something slammed against a wall panel ahead of them.

The panel deformed with a noise like a sledgehammer hitting sheet metal, and a rounded bulge appeared, the edges gone white where the metal had stretched. The bulge quickly became two as whatever was on the other side punched it again, trying to break through.

Miles wasn't the first to react. Lestiel had turned to look at the same moment Miles had heard the noise, but with the world moving so slowly, Miles was the first to take action.

He grabbed for the pistol at his back, his arms moving like they were stuck in syrup. He swung the weapon out in front of him, the barrel swaying as he overshot his target and had to correct it. Within a few seconds, it was pointing straight at the weakening panel.

Something slammed into the panel again, and cracks appeared where the metal was reaching its limit. A fourth strike, and the metal gave way. A furred hand punched through into the open air.

Miles didn't immediately lower his weapon, but he started feeling the strain and emptiness of magic taken too far, so he let the enhancement spell end.

Another hand emerged, and together they tore a wider hole open in the panel. They were followed by the head of a gray-furred Eppan diver, who looked around at them, blinking.

"Who all is out here?"

Miles's *Eyes of the Émigré* had given them the voice of an older woman in his mind, but he didn't have enough experience with the translation magic to know whether that was demographically accurate.

"I am Lestiel Dunverde, journeyman scholar of the Danis Institute," Lestiel said. "This is my team of contracted inadequacies."

The newcomer squeezed the rest of the way out through the hole, catching themselves and dropping to their feet. They stood up, looking around.

They were about a foot taller than Trin, closer to Miles's height, with gray fur covering their body and three ear-like flaps that hung down around their head.

They were wearing a black synth-fabric trench coat over a construction-yellow jumpsuit, with belts and pouches strapped all over it. A backpack hung from their shoulders, dangling a coil of yarn-thin rope and several tools of ambiguous purpose. There was some kind of tech strapped around their wrist like an elongated smartwatch.

They must have been incredibly strong to punch through the metal wall tiles, but they weren't rippling with muscle. They looked as sleek and slim as Trin did, maybe more so, with the extra height.

"Howdy, Lestiel, Inadequacies," the other diver nodded at Lestiel and then the others in turn. "I'm Fran San-san-quirren. Quick question—any of you all know where the exit is?"

Miles stepped up to answer. He pointed back down the corridor. "About an hour that way. You can cut straight across the forest, the exit's on the opposite side."

"But don't take our flying disk!" Trin added.

"An hour?" Fran asked. "What's that as a distance?"

"About three kilometers," Miles said.

"Mm-hm," Fran hummed. They looked in the other direction. "And what's down that way?"

"Few hundred meters until a we-don't-know," Trin answered.

"Hmm." Fran looked one way then the other, then back to the group. "Now, I'm not going to steal your platform, but I am looking to get out. A bunch of plant things broke out behind me when I was three rooms in, and I can't get back to my exit. You all mind if I tag along with you?"

"I don't have an objection," Lestiel said. He surveyed Miles and the others, as if checking it was fine with them.

"That sounds okay," Miles said. He looked at Trin.

"Sure, is fine. Come on, granny."

"What the— How old do you think I am?"

"Hundred."

"I am eighty iterations old, and you sound like you should still be in the pouch."

They set off walking down the passageway.

If Miles's translation magic had interpreted Trin right, then Fran was a woman a lot older than Trin. Eighty iterations was about forty years, so she was chronologically older than Miles as well. That added weight to the idea that his *Eyes of the Émigré* magic had some way to embed implicit details about a sapient into the voice impression it gave them.

It was odd to see Fran moving around without a team. Miles knew from his previous visit that a healer at least was mandated by the Gilthaen administrators, so either Fran was a healer herself, or she'd come down with one and left them behind.

"Are you down here by yourself?" Miles said.

He tried to make the question sound as casual as he could. He didn't want to make her feel like she was being interrogated.

"Yeah, where is your team?" Trin asked. "Are they dead?"

Miles winced.

"I don't dive with a team," Fran answered. She didn't seem offended by the questions, even Trin's.

"Don't the clerks at the entrance make you bring a healer?" Miles asked.

If there was a loophole that let a team go down without one, that was bad news for his fledgling business.

"Sure they do. You're looking at her. I'm my own healer, my own scout, fusilier, phantom, and surveiler. I'm a jack by trade."

Miles gave Fran an appraising look. He couldn't sense any magic from her, which meant she must be a tech specialist. That was a lot of ground to cover for tech. Like Trin's scanner, a lot of tools took skill and training to use.

"I didn't know that was a thing," Miles said.

"It's a thing," she replied. "Took a lot of years to get here. I started out as a scout using one of the old Doster scanners. A Doster B20. Then I inherited a needler gun and started shooting people with combat stims in the middle of fights. It turned out that's sixty percent of a surveiler's job. I got some brain mods for aiming and picked up some skill with a pistol, and found myself doing triple duty as a fusilier. The team kept getting smaller, the payroll kept getting cheaper, and eventually I was the only one doing the dives."

That was a lot for Miles to absorb at once. *Brain mods?* It sounded like she was a one-woman scavenging team. That must have made trying to fill ad-hoc openings on other teams convenient. She could take basically any role, or even hire herself out as a full team.

And she doesn't have to split her fee.

"That's cool," Trin said. "Maybe I get a brain mod."

Miles considered the same for a moment, but decided he didn't want a brain mod.

Hearing the two Eppan sapients talking to each other was making Miles more aware of the differences between the two.

Trin's speech had always been kind of clipped, but Fran's translation was completely fluent. *Eyes of the Émigré* had even given her translated voice a slight accent, kind of rural, without evoking any particular region.

Miles struggled with how to politely ask how she was so much more eloquent than Trin, before he thought of a way to poke at the subject.

"Are you and Trin speaking the same language?" he asked.

"Your translator's giving you a different sound for the two of us, huh?"

"A little."

Fran glanced at him and then at Trin. "You from the homeland, Trin?"

"Yes. Prime planet."

"Well, that'll be it," she said, answering Miles. "I'm from an out-of-iteration colony. Lel-hitel Colony, Iteration 26,607. We speak a conlang out there called Standard-22. It's meant to be smoother to translate into the big Spiral groups than the Eppan native languages. A few people around the weave do that. Even with good tech, not everything comes across easily."

"Do I come across okay?" Miles said, suddenly worried about how Spiral translation tech was portraying him.

Click. *"Simple,"* Torg said, the first time he'd spoken in minutes.

"Yeah, that's what I'm getting too," Fran said, "but that's all subjective. If you're talking to a culture with a more expressive language than yours, you're going to sound like a child no matter what you do, since you're only gonna be using a subset of their speech. Less expressive, you could end up sounding pretentious, if you say something their translator has to swap in some obscure grammar for. If it's a context-heavy language, then you'll be seen as a little obtuse. To me, you come off like a textbook. Nobody's gonna have trouble understanding you, but you're not gonna be moving anyone to tears with your poetry, you get me?"

Miles's *Eyes of the Émigré* translation was one way. It only translated other sapients *for* him, and not the other way around. Fran's experience must just be how English came off when translated into Standard-22 by the common translation tech Spiral sapients had access to.

"Yeah. I get it. I can live with that," Miles said, then caught what Torg had said. "Wait, Torg, I sound simple to you?"

Clack. "*Yes.*"

"But you speak in one-word sentences."

Click. "*Sufficient.*"

"Your friend is impressively eloquent," Lestiel said. "Concise and clear. I wish you were all as succinct."

They were coming to the end of the corridor.

Close to the far end, the word corridor no longer seemed to apply. The space was cavernous, and only the fact that there hadn't been any turn-offs or complications made it seem like a passageway at all, rather than a single incredibly long room.

The door at the far end was set into the wall close to the ground. It looked absurd built into such a huge wall, like the entrance to a dollhouse, but as they approached, Miles saw that it was the same dimensions as all of the other doors they'd seen so far, tall and narrow.

Trin immediately started interacting with the control panel.

Fran watched over his shoulder from a few paces back, her head-flaps half raised. She kept looking like she was going to step forward and take over, only to hold herself back.

After a minute of interaction, the screen put up a big "*No*" glyph and went blank.

Fran's head-flaps flopped down.

"It's okay. I know how to do this," Trin said. "Torg, smash this."

"Hold, up," Fran said

She stepped up, edging Trin out of the way and putting a gray mid-paw to the panel. As soon as she touched it, the "*No*" symbol vanished, and the original interface reappeared.

"On these upper levels, it usually only locks the person who messed with it out. Someone else can still—" Fran's sequence of taps ended with a large *"Yes"* character, and something within the wall started grinding. "There's ways around it. You can get a masking field generator, that'll stop it personally locking you out, but the deeper ones just shut down if you screw up."

Miles listened to the grinding sound. The door would open any second.

"Hey, can we use Brisk's formation?" he said, trying not to sound worried.

Trin glanced back at him, then started moving. Torg didn't even do that. He just stepped up to stand at the front of the group, covering Trin and Miles with his body.

Torg was both the physically toughest of any of the three of them, and he was wearing his new rainbow-hued breastplate, which made him the best choice to take the lead. Trin was next, providing ranged and scanning support, with Miles in the rear to spot anyone who needed medical attention.

Fran seemed to understand what they were doing without prompting. She stepped up to stand behind Torg, drawing a pair of wildly different pistols from inside her trench coat. Lestiel just stood to the side, watching the formation come together with bemusement.

A handful of seconds after Fran had bypassed the console, the door started sliding open.

The light from the corridor was eaten up by the darkness on the other side.

The blackness beyond the door was impenetrable. The light cast from the passage only illuminated a few feet of the next room before vanishing, showing a few white ceramic floor tiles and not much else.

Miles felt a second of fear, then let his *Eyes of the Émigré* fade and switched to *Eyes of the Altruist*.

In the darkness, glowing shapes appeared. There were two bodies, and after his recent experience, he recognized them straight away.

"There are two Orbellius in there," he said.

Lestiel said something, but Miles didn't understand.

With his translation magic inactive, Lestiel's voice had a rhythmic, overlapping, musical quality to it, like a chorus of voices singing, austere and profound. It gave Miles a completely different impression of the sapient.

Fran said something, also unintelligible. Miles didn't want to drop his *Eyes of the Altruist* to try and understand her.

The gray-furred diver put one of her pistols away, then pulled what looked like a silver bean from her coat pocket. She tapped it against the wall and threw it through the open door.

The bean started glowing mid-air, casting a bubble of yellow-white light that expanded as it came up to full power. By the time it landed, it was lighting up the entire next room, somehow without being too bright to look at directly.

The room beyond the door looked like some kind of medical station. There were half a dozen metal benches, with monitors at the foot of each. Cabinets dotted the walls, sharing space with large, opaque vats and pieces of obscure equipment. There were floating platforms placed around the space, circles of textured metal about two feet in diameter, their undersides set with blocky levitation units and their top sides strewn with scattered medical equipment.

Miles quickly identified the source of the glowing shapes, but at first glance they didn't make sense.

The places where Miles had seen the Orbellius shapes were occupied by dead bodies. One looked like a Hurc in bulky, all-encompassing armor. Its head and right arm were obscured by a toppled bench and the armor had been torn away from its left arm, allowing Miles to recognize the species.

The other was a narrow figure in close-fitting robes of a black bat-wing-type material. It was crouched with its back to a wall. Miles couldn't tell the species, and only knew they were dead because the Orbellius puppeteer was the only structure that had shown up on his *Eyes of the Altruist*.

With the Hurc body, the Orbellius anatomy was oriented on the part of the body hidden behind the bench. For the crouched figure, it was roughly central.

"Orbellius there, and there," Miles said, pointing. "The people seem like they're dead."

Having pointed out his readings to the others, Miles let *Eyes of the Altruist* fade and switched back to *Eyes of the Émigré*.

Neither of them seemed to be moving, but after the battle in the forest room, Miles was on edge at the sight of them. He drew his striker from its pouch and put his free hand against his chest, ready to cast an enhancement.

"That's some nice armor," Fran said, peering around the edge of Torg's body to look through the door. "A Veesler set. Veesler Aegis, maybe. It's got an energy reduction field and built-in combat stims. And that thing in his hand's a high-caliber autopistol. No way the dungeon made this stuff at this level. Too good and too specific. These guys were divers, and not level-one divers, by my guess."

"How would they get here?" Miles asked.

"Maybe they started deeper and were taking another route out, or maybe the planet brought their bodies here in the shuffle. I couldn't tell you."

As if roused by the voices, the two corpses began to stir.

"Are you sure they're dead?" Fran asked, confused.

"Orbellius Ghouls," Miles said.

"Orbellius *what*?" Fran asked.

The thin figure crouched against the wall leaped to its feet and started sprinting straight at them.

Now that it was upright, Miles recognized the species. They were like the mage vendor on Delatariel Station, and the bookseller in the Ishel Corporation Lounge. A tall, narrow figure, with two legs, six arms, and a face that was almost featureless, save for a central ridge and a pair of eyes.

This one had an additional feature; a fleshy sphere was embedded in its gut, occupying the space the stomach would on a human. It looked like the sapient had died by being disemboweled, and an Orbellius had taken up residence in the hollow.

It moved as quickly and unnervingly as the bookseller had, scuttling at them across the ground, the motion of its membranous robe making it almost seem to flow toward them.

"Stop!" Miles yelled. "We don't want to fight."

The rushing ghoul didn't listen.

Fran aimed one of her pistols and fired. A beam of energy like a silver thread appeared between the barrel and her target. The beam intersected the ghoul's face and its head exploded. It kept coming.

"Target the Orbellius in its stomach," Miles rushed out.

Both Trin and Fran fired their weapons this time, both aiming at a spot just under its left armpit.

No!

"That's not the stomach!"

Fireflies pierced flesh, which then exploded under the effect of the silver beam. The ghoul lost an arm but didn't stop.

It was suddenly on top of Torg, swiping at him with a claw-tipped hand. The attacks were landing, but the claws weren't doing much when they caught chitin, let alone the breastplate.

Torg had his ax ready and swung it in a low arc. The blade cut through the exposed flesh of the sphere in the ghoul's gut, tearing it open.

The thing went down with a chemical smell and the sound of escaping air.

"This is a new one for me," Fran said, voice frantic. "I've seen moving dead before, but what's the Orbellius connection?"

"This deceased Morchis has a non-sapient Orbellius taking refuge within its body," Lestiel explained, his voice academic. "It seems as if they're controlling it via a network of electrostatic hairs."

Miles picked out the word *Morchis* from Lestiel's explanation. He finally had a name for the six-armed species.

"Could any Orbellius do that, if it wanted?" Fran asked.

Deeper into the room, the armored figure rose to its feet.

The former diver's body had been decapitated at some point. Its neck was a jagged stump, and its skeleton jutted up out of the wound in broken spikes, with tangled and minced flesh hanging off it in places. Though its head was long gone, visible nowhere in the room, it had a new head now; a fleshy sphere, resting on a throne of snapped bones.

The Orbellius puppeteer's tendrils flexed as the dead figure took a step forward.

"I think the one we fought in the forest understood guns," Miles said, too late.

The ghoul was already raising its arm, aiming the autopistol directly at them.

Miles dashed forward, his hand slapping against Torg's back. The litany for *Temporary Enhancement* came to him almost on its own.

In himself he is complete. In a harmonious world, everything is, in itself, complete. **He is that which he is.**

Miles had a clear mental image, a muscular figure standing in a deep cave, gray-robed and bare-fisted, expressing the idea of absolute endurance. The mountain could fall and he would not be crushed.

Energy rushed from Miles's spinning core and flooded out of his arm, the spell taking hold.

At the same moment, the ghoul opened fire.

All Miles saw were flashes of light. There was a noise like thunder, and Torg's chitin rattled under his hand from the impacts hitting the other side of his body. Nothing passed through, and the rest of them were sheltered behind his enormous form.

At a pause in the onslaught, Fran leaned out and fired a shot at the ghoul's "head." This time, the thread of energy didn't reach its target. It fizzled in the air, about an inch away from hitting. Dark stains appeared on the surface of the Orbellius, but they didn't seem fatal.

Miles tried his own shot, pointing the striker at it and firing, but it had almost no effect. There was a brief flare of light in front of the ghoul's body, but none of the striking energy got through.

With his free hand, Miles tried casting *Strike the Disharmonious*. He focused on the note that came in the first stage of the spell, and he actually managed to call it, the ringing sound filling his ears, but when he looked at the armored ghoul there was no disharmony. It was just the same pure note as always. Even the ghoul's weapon wasn't giving off any dissonance.

"It's the reduction field," Fran snapped. "We're going to have to go hand-to-hand."

A moment later the ghoul's pistol burst back into life, firing a tight cone of glinting metal at them.

Fran slapped Torg's back, and that was all the cue he needed to charge into the stream of projectiles. He barreled forward, knocking the ghoul's gun aside with a swing of his ax, then brought it down in an overhead chop at the Orbellius controller.

An armored arm came up to block him, and the ghoul landed a punch below Torg's breastplate that cracked chitin.

Fran was sprinting, too. She slid to a stop behind the ghoul, taking advantage of its distraction to strike it with a mid-paw punch. The hit landed with a colossal slap, and a visible wave of distortion rippled across the sphere's surface.

The ghoul staggered, managing to take a single step before Fran leaped into the air and struck it with a spinning kick. The Orbellius controller snapped free from the decapitated Hurc body and went flying across the room.

Lestiel appeared in its path, raising his hand and stopping it with his palm. He caught the ball one-handed, inspected it, then squeezed it between his hands. The Orbellius ghoul's body vanished like it was being squeezed out of existence.

"Wonderful," Lestiel said, beaming at them as he laced his hands together. "I didn't think that I would get a live sample. This will be extremely useful."

In the middle of the room, Torg slumped to the floor.

His body was leaking milky white fluid, a pool of it a meter wide already spreading out from him.

Miles rushed over to crouch next to him. Torg had fallen down face-first, and all of the wounds were on his chest.

"Help me turn him over," Miles said.

Fran crouched and flipped Torg's massive body over like it was easy.

Now that he was face-up, every injury the autopistol had inflicted on him was visible. There were probably more than a hundred wounds, each a tiny, narrow crack in the chitin which fluid trickled out from.

Miles switched into his *Eyes of the Altruist* and tried to assess the damage.

Shapes sprung up over his vision, and he found he could see the projectiles. Every tiny flechette that had hit Torg was marked by a glow of angry red, the magic highlighting the problems as well as the internal structure.

Most of the projectiles had been stopped just inside his shell, and Miles felt like he should be grateful for that, but there were still a few that had buried themselves deeper. A couple of the mystery organs deeper within Torg's body had been pierced, and those seemed to be the source of most of the fluid.

Fran asked him something, but he didn't have time to try and work out what.

Miles didn't answer. He just placed his hands over one of the punctures and started casting *Close Wound*. He had no trouble remembering the litany. He felt the truth of it.

These wounds are aberrations. In a harmonious world, the many are one. The cuts must close. **Such should it be.**

Hot energy flowed from Miles's core to his hands. Light flared between his hands and Torg's shell.

When Miles took his hands away, he found the spell hadn't just closed one of the punctures, it had closed *all* of them that had been under his hands. He repositioned and cast it again, then again, mending whole areas of shell at a time.

By the third casting, he'd closed the biggest sources of the leaking fluid. He was feeling weak and light-headed, but he judged he had a little more in him before he was fully spent.

He turned his attention to the internal injuries.

Two separate internal structures were pierced. They couldn't have been absolutely vital because Torg was still alive, but Miles didn't think that any being who used blood could survive internal bleeding for long.

Miles pressed his hands against Torg's shell and cast *Hasten Renewal*.

In time this being will heal. In a harmonious world, he is forever his final self. **He is that which he is.**

As the hot energy flashed from his hands into Torg's body, Miles had another vision. This time it was of Torg himself, sitting on the ground in an indistinct room, his arms and legs pressed together in a pose of rest or meditation. This was a future where Torg had healed from his injuries. The magic was reaching out to this ideal image to force it into the present.

Through his *Eyes of the Altruist*, Miles saw the wounded shapes pull themselves closed. Some of the scarring where he'd cast *Close Wound* faded at the same time.

He held the spell for as long as he could, ten seconds, twenty, until his head was buzzing and his vision was getting dim around the edges. When he started to worry that he might faint, he let the spell end, pulling his hands away.

On the ground in front of him, Torg began to move. He shivered at first, then began to shake more violently.

Fran reached down and pressed a metal cylinder to one of the cracks in his chitin, pushing a button at the back. There was a hiss and a click, and she withdrew it.

An injection?

Over the next few seconds, Torg calmed down. Soon, he was resting peacefully on the ground.

"What was that?" Miles asked, watching as Fran slid the cylinder into a pocket on her waist.

"About two hundred seln," she said, then when she caught Miles's expression, "Wide range painkiller."

"Okay. Thanks."

Torg's internal wounds had closed, but there were still lots of the projectiles buried in his body, including *inside* the structures that had since closed up.

The *Purify* spell that Miles had briefly considered had claimed it could degrade objects "inimical to the target's existence." Maybe if he had that spell now, he'd be able to deal with the buried projectiles. Or maybe not. He was already at the limit of his magical endurance.

"I think he's stable, for now," Miles said.

He looked at Torg, then at the door out of the room. How long did they have left to get out? They were going to have to carry the huge sapient the entire way.

"This is *really* going to mess with our timetable."

Fran reached down and grabbed Torg by the edge of his shell. She pulled, and hoisted him up into her arms.

"Hooh. He's a big one."

"You can carry him?" Miles asked.

Fran looked like she was suffering under the strain, but she had him completely off the ground, and she somehow still looked balanced.

"Artificial muscle fibers. I can carry him a ways."

"I might be able to help you when my magic recovers. *Hasten Renewal* might help with recovering from the strain, or if I enhanced your Strength."

"Magic, huh? Well, sure, we can try that."

Over in the center of the room, Trin was trying to get the former Hurc diver out of his armor, and failing. He grabbed the being's dead hand instead, trying to drag him, but giving up after a few seconds.

"What about stuff?" he called.

In addition to the Hurc diver's armor and weapon, there was the Morchis diver's black robe, and a whole room full of medical tools and equipment. They hadn't even looked in the vats, let alone searched the cabinets.

Miles belatedly checked his comm. They were about a hundred and ten minutes into their four-hour time limit. One hundred and thirty left. The walk back would take forty minutes if they were moving at a quick pace, and looking at Fran, he didn't think they'd be moving at a quick pace.

"We can take two minutes to grab anything that won't slow us down," Miles said.

Miles helped Fran carry Torg to the door while Trin went wild behind them.

Financial Status [§]
§478 (−§30 Charges Ialis Descent Fee)
§558 (+§50 Scavenger Assist Award auth. Ialis Corporation)
§724 (+§166 Payment Services Rendered auth. Lestiel Dunverde)
§4,837 (+§4,113 Recovered Equipment Purchase auth. Ialis Corporation)
§4,037 (−§800 Charges Medical Services Ialis Corporation)

Miles looked up from his comm to watch Torg being taken away on the flat-backed drone. As soon as it was outside the building, it changed direction, heading off toward the entrance complex's medical pagoda.

They'd done it. Their first contracted dive. And one of them had almost died.

Trin had managed to recover a lot from the medical room in the short time available. The Aegis armor, the autopistol, and a case full of unusual chemical compounds from an unlocked cabinet. He hadn't stuck to the "that won't slow us down" requirement, but looking at what their haul had sold for, Miles thought it would be rude to complain.

Trin had wanted to keep the armor, but it wouldn't fit any of them, and apparently getting it adjusted would cost a significant portion of its value. In the end, the full sale value of all the equipment had been split five ways between them.

Lestiel had been contractually entitled to an even share, and all of them—Lestiel included—had decided that Fran deserved to be cut in as well.

Even after the split, Miles had been left with over four thousand seln.

I think we're in business.

Miles didn't even mind Lestiel taking a cut. Both Lestiel and Fran had chipped in to help with the cost of getting Torg seen by a real healer.

Their Draulean client had since boarded his ship, but Miles hoped he'd get what he wanted from his samples.

Miles's comm buzzed with an incoming message from Torg.

Torg > Miles
Formation bad.

Miles let out a breath that was too sad to be a laugh.

Miles > Torg
Yeah. It didn't go great. I'm sorry, Torg.

He was glad that Torg was well enough to be sending messages, but angry at himself that it was necessary.

Miles had called out to use Brisk's formation because it had seemed smart. Brisk, despite betraying them, had been a more experienced scavenger, and in the moment it had made sense to put the most durable of them in the front with the rest sheltering behind.

With time to reflect and with knowledge of the consequences, it only really made sense if he considered Torg to be expendable, which Brisk probably had.

Torg wasn't invulnerable, and if he wasn't expendable then they had no place using him to soak up bullets.

Looking back, they could have done literally anything else. They could have used the wall for cover, they could have just left. With a little more time to think, Miles might have guessed the ghouls knew how to use weapons, and they hadn't been *that* short of time.

He wouldn't let it happen again. Nobody on the team was going to get hurt by design. And if someone got hurt anyway, then Miles would have an answer to it.

With the payment from the sale of the equipment, some of the pressure of their situation had lifted. They could pay rent. They could upgrade their equipment. Miles could search for a magic instructor.

They had time now, and no excuse not to spend it getting ready for their next job.

PART 7

STRANGE SOCIETY

CHAPTER 15

The world sang and Miles listened.

A sapient with a flapping inverted *U* of a mouth croaked a sales pitch over a rack of personal computers. The customers milling around his stall paused to examine them, occasionally picking them up to try them out.

In the sound generated by *Strike the Disharmonious*, the vendor sang in the note of a brushed bell, but the palm-sized computer units he was selling screamed a constant discordant counter-note.

Miles paused at the stall, looking down at the computers.

These are not harmonious.

Miles had been walking around the Ishel Corporation Lounge with the first half of the *Strike the Disharmonious* spell ringing in his ears for the better part of an hour, trying to work out what made something a valid target.

Visually busy or cluttered items were often disharmonious; sleek and well-designed items often weren't. Information tools like computers, comms, and simulators almost always were, but the tablets in the off-Exchange bookstore weren't.

Powered multitools were universally disharmonious, while dedicated mechanical tools and close-combat weapons never were.

Very few living beings were disharmonious. The exceptions were those individuals who were heavily augmented with synthetic components.

So far, the theme seemed to be a combination of the quality of something's design and how dedicated it was to a single purpose.

Miles could describe it in terms of purity and focus, which meshed with what he was starting to understand about the Harmonizer philosophy. Things which had a purity of their function, like a knife, were more harmonious than things that were unfocused, like a multitool. It didn't make objective sense in a world of matter and energy, but as the worldview of an ancient magical society, he could understand it.

Very few living beings were valid targets for the spell. Miles had come to terms with the fact that it wouldn't be much use as a direct weapon, except maybe against truly chaotic enemies like Trin's *slap boss*, but plenty of tech ran against the harmony, and Miles thought it could be useful for degrading equipment.

Even Miles's own striker pistol was disharmonious, which he attributed to the variable power output, and maybe the fact that it was designed to be non-lethal. The power slider reduced the purity of its function, and a pistol that wasn't meant to seriously hurt anyone ran counter to its form.

The thing that worried him was that he was actually starting to sympathize with the magic's point of view.

He let the spell fade as he stopped to examine the stall.

As well as computers, there were simulators, which could commandeer someone's senses for training or entertainment, and comm units, which came in a huge variety of styles and features.

He picked up a comm that looked like a rugged handheld game unit and caught the vendor's eye.

"Hi, would this be good for someone with chitin stick manipulators?"

The green-skinned sapient turned a pair of bulging eyes on Miles, then looked down at his fleshy hands.

"Not for me," Miles clarified. "For a friend."

"Naaah," the vendor croaked, their mouth opening like a drawbridge. "That's for exothermics. You wanna haptic."

"Okay, do you have one?"

The stall owner reached over and took the comm from Miles with a fleshy five-fingered hand, then gave him a different unit. This one had a central screen surrounded on each side by a matrix of physical buttons.

"Here ya ah."

"Thanks."

Miles took the comm unit. He pressed the obvious power button and found the keys that moved the focus around the interface.

"Is this screen good for Ankn vision?" Miles asked.

"Yah. Any problems, just change the settings."

"Great," Miles said, turning the device over in his hands. "How much is it?"

"Three hundred."

Miles took pleasure in being able to afford that. Not only could he afford it, it wasn't even a big deal. He tapped his own comm to the shopkeeper's terminal and packed the new device away in his backpack, alongside the rest of his recent purchases.

He considered upgrading his own comm unit while he was there, but he wasn't a savvy enough consumer yet to know what kind of features he could get, or even what he wanted.

As he walked away, he held out his hand and began re-casting *Strike the Disharmonious*. He concentrated on the pure tone until he could hear it, then looked around, assessing the various goods and people.

This was a good place to try this. The Ishel Corporation Lounge was part department store, part food hall, and part market. Most of the floors were dedicated to permanent stores in various categories, but the market level offered itself to pop-up stalls that changed from one day to the next. It was meant to be a good place to pick up a bargain or something unique, but the sheer diversity of stalls also made it a good place for Miles to learn the ins and outs of harmony.

Up ahead, a store selling armor had a powered shield hanging on a panel. It was shaped like a heater shield, with a piece of tech at its center like a tiny radar dish, and a silvery front face that was decorated lavishly in gold filigree.

It rang in *Strike the Disharmonious* with the screaming of torn metal. The shield should have been a fairly focused item. Maybe the tech built into it had an offensive purpose, or maybe things with too much decoration were also disharmonious.

He stopped to examine it anyway. Out in the Spiral, humans were unusually squishy compared to a lot of the other species. Miles had started wearing his robe everywhere after their second trip into the dungeon, but he didn't know how much he could trust it to work as armor.

"How much is this?" he asked the Hurc stall owner. They were one of the Hurcs who had solid black eyes, rather than Brisk's sclera-and-pupil eyes.

The owner spent a second assessing him. "Nine-fifty."

Miles hummed, not convinced. That was a lot. Three weeks rent. On the other hand, if it saved his life one day, it was worth it.

The vendor noticed his reluctance.

"Listen, you want defense? This is it. It's got a forcefield that'll divert metal projectiles, and an inertial damper that'll stop heavy hits dead. The metal's a crystal alloy. This thing could take an artillery hit and still be in one piece."

"Where does it divert the projectiles to?" Miles asked.

He had a vision of hiding behind the shield from bullets, but the bullets all ricocheting away in random directions.

"Conical profile. It'll put sixty degrees onto the path of anything flying at you, so long as it's metal."

"So, to the sides."

"To the sides, maybe a little behind."

"Too dangerous to my team," Miles said.

The stall owner made an expression like he conceded the point and immediately turned his attention to another potential customer.

Miles continued on, focusing back on the pure note.

As he was approaching the floor's elevators, he was hit by a sudden twisting sensation, focused somewhere around the spot just below his stomach.

The feeling was mild compared to the gut punch he'd felt on Delatariel Station, but it was instantly recognizable. Someone was magically assessing him.

He stopped and turned, casting his eyes over the crowd, looking for anyone paying him too much attention.

Watching for someone observing him here, among diverse sapients, wasn't as simple as it would have been for him among humans, but as far as Miles could tell, nobody seemed to be focused intently on him.

He'd almost convinced himself it was his imagination, or maybe indigestion, when he felt magic stir again somewhere in the crowd.

If his own magic felt like warm energy spinning in a slow rotation, then this was almost the opposite. A feeling that was blisteringly cold, turning in a sharp stepping motion, like the clicking of a ratchet.

Miles scanned the crowd, searching for the source. He felt like he could tell exactly where the magic was coming from, a magical proprioception that covered the entire room, but when he looked at that spot he didn't see a person.

The only thing there was some kind of device—an inverted black pyramid, about four feet tall and one wide, standing on its point at the edge of a stall.

After staring at it for a few seconds, he was sure that it was the source of the magic.

As if it'd been alerted to his realization, the black spike levitated up off the ground, rotated 180 degrees, and began floating away.

Miles only hesitated for a moment before following it.

The device moved without obvious haste, but it always seemed ahead of him. Every time Miles turned a corner, it was already disappearing around the next. Stalls with vertical panels and display racks broke lines of sight, and the bustling crowds of shoppers made it hard for him to move quickly without pushing people aside.

As Miles reached an open area of the market floor, he caught sight of the black spike disappearing through a doorway at the edge of the floor.

He rushed ahead, reaching the opening just in time to see the device float around a corner at the far end.

Miles stopped at the doorway. The corridor looked like it might lead to storerooms or offices linked with the activity on the market floor. It wasn't shut, but it wasn't an obviously public area.

He stood there for a few seconds. Technically, there was nothing telling him he shouldn't go in there.

He passed through the doorway.

At the far end of the corridor was another open doorway, this one leading to a storeroom. Stacks of folded-up stalls lined the walls, with chairs and stools of different shapes and sizes dotted around the floor. The back wall of the room was given over to a sealed hatch, a similar design to the ones on the entrance level, but sized more for cargo than people.

The triangular black device floated in the center of the room, seemingly waiting for him.

Miles walked slowly into the room, taking up a position opposite the levitating unit.

A pulse of magic sang out from the device, a sharp double-tick of icy intent. A second later, the storeroom door slid closed with a heavy, metallic clang.

Miles startled at the noise. He twisted to look, only to see that his way out was closed.

Oh shit.

Instincts that he hadn't needed since old Earth surfaced, warning him not to follow strangers down dark alleys, not to get involved in what was obviously other people's business.

Warnings that hadn't applied on the regulated levels of Unsiel Station, and wouldn't have helped him navigate Brisk's betrayal, now began explaining to him why putting himself in a room alone with a strange entity might not be a good idea.

He shuffled over to the door, not taking his eyes off the unit, and pressed at the door panel.

It rejected him with a buzzing noise. The door didn't open.

With nothing else to do but examine the unit that had led him here, Miles noticed new details about it. There was something like a lens on the side of the thing facing him, a circular concave disk that stared at him from the black metal case like an eye. The panels of its body weren't perfectly aligned, instead spaced so that there was a narrow gap between them. Through the gaps, Miles could see more deeply embedded machinery.

Under other circumstances, he'd be ready to conclude that the thing was an entirely technological entity, except for the fact he'd sensed it using magic twice already.

"Hi?" Miles tried.

The unit was silent for long enough that Miles started wondering whether he'd just followed a cleaning drone back to its storage room.

Then it spoke. Its voice was a low bass buzz, like an electrical short.

"Meandering with an active attack spell, neither acceptable nor wise."

It took Miles a second to realize the thing was chastising him.

It didn't like him walking around casting *Strike the Disharmonious*?

For a moment, Miles contemplated how doing that might look to another mage, someone capable of seeing what he was doing, but not necessarily understanding that he wasn't powerful enough to actually hurt anyone.

It could have looked like he was walking around pointing a gun at people.

"I didn't mean to worry anyone," he said.

"Attacking with magic in the promenade, likely to bring security down on you."

The thing's voice spoke almost every word in a slightly different tone, like it was imparting an additional layer of meaning that Miles's *Eyes of the Émigré* couldn't interpret.

"I wasn't going to attack anyone. I didn't understand the magic and I was trying to get a better feel for it."

"As an excuse, somewhat feeble."

"Right. Yeah, I guess it is."

Miles felt his face getting warm. At least he was only being spoken to, and not arrested, though he felt like he could be excused for this one. He hadn't actually hurt anyone.

The exchange lapsed into silence. Miles wondered if that was all the thing had in mind, but the door was still closed.

To check if the thing had gone to sleep as much as to get an answer, Miles asked, "Are you a mage?"

"As a mage, I am a Counterfactual Sorcerer."

"I haven't heard of that tradition," Miles said.

I haven't heard of many traditions.

"Altering the world by proving our means to do so. We make our argument, and the world concedes."

"That sounds cool. I'm a Harmonizer."

"As a mage, you should show restraint in crowded areas. Recklessly using magic, likely to necessitate magical security on the promenade. Monitoring magic use in the marketplace—a disadvantage to us all."

"Right," Miles said, thinking through the device's complaint to work out its meaning. He was starting to get a feel for what the changes in tone meant. "Mages like being able to cast spells freely in the marketplace. You don't want someone putting magic on their security's radar and ruining it for everyone."

"Speaking generally, correct."

"I've been looking for a mage to help me understand this kind of stuff," Miles admitted. "There aren't any mages on the Exchange or city listings, and I'm looking for resources. A teacher, maybe another Harmonizer, maybe delta?"

"Casting spells, you use an index?"

"Yeah. Is that not normal?"

"Casting your smiting spell, you were not using an index."

"I was. I just don't have to tap the screen every time. I've worked out how to trigger it mentally."

"No."

"No?"

"Meandering on the promenade, you were not interfacing with your index. In casting your spell, you were using the magic as originally practiced."

"That's . . . I don't think so," Miles said.

All he'd done was try and mentally re-create the feeling that casting with his index had pushed on him. But he was *meant* to be able to index-cast without actually touching the device. That'd been explained to him when he got it. It had just taken him a while to get the knack.

"Arguing with me, unwise again," it said. After another span of cool silence, it said, "Discussing this with a Harmonizer may enlighten you."

There's another Harmonizer here?

"You know another Harmonizer?"

Instead of answering, the device rotated in the air, and emitted another pulse stuttering magic.

The door at the rear of the storeroom clunked to life, then slid slowly up, revealing a slice of the city. Cold air rushed in from outside and a light drizzle started sprinkling the floor of the storeroom floor closest to the edge.

The door had barely been open for a handful of seconds before an unoccupied platform passing by the spire changed direction, swooping in to hover next to the open door.

The black spire floated through the door and out over the platform, lowering itself to stand on its point. It turned slowly and looked back through at Miles.

"As your senior, I can show you to the Dendril City Enclave."

"Enclave?" Miles asked, then, "Wait, you want me to come *now?*"

"As your discoverer, I can explain to them the situation and they can issue you a warning."

The voice of the old instinct that had mocked Miles for following a stranger to a secluded area was now screaming at him not to travel with this unknown mage to a second location. It was *almost* drowned out by the part of him that was desperate for more information and more magical resources.

"I don't even know who you are," Miles said, feeling his desire warring with his caution.

"Speaking formally, I am It-who-strikes-decisively."

Miles recognized the naming style. It was similar to They-who-flies-with-abandon, the Gilthaen drone.

"Are you Gilthaen?" Miles asked.

"As a trusted friend to the Ialis Corporation, I was granted a Gilthaen name." *Oh. Me too.*

"In that case, I guess I'm He-who-burns-his-hand-on-mercy," Miles said. "But you can call me Miles."

"Speaking casually, my name is Iddris."

Iddris waited patiently out on the platform, raindrops building up on its black metal exterior. Miles stood opposite, trying to decide if it was safe to go with them.

"Do you mind if I message my friend and tell him where I'm going?" he asked.

"Speaking honestly, I do not care."

"Right."

Miles pulled out his comm and wrote up a quick message to Trin.

Miles > Trin

Hey Trin, I'm about to take a ride with this upside-down triangle guy called It-which-strikes-decisively, also Iddris, to a place it calls the Enclave? Might be mage related. If I don't message you in an hour can you call city security and tell them I'm missing?

Trin must have been already on his comm because a message came back about twenty seconds later.

Trin > Miles

You always talking to shady people. Shady guy on station. Shady guy in city. Stop going with shady guys! I will call security if I am awake.

Miles closed the message and dropped his comm back into his pocket.

Having prepared the best lifeline for himself he could, Miles finally managed to overpower the inner voice that was saying "no," and gave in to his curiosity instead.

Stepping out onto the platform, he grabbed the railing, feeling his stomach lurch and his head spin as the transport pulled away from the Ishel Corporation tower and began to descend.

CHAPTER 16

The wind tugged at Miles's hair, light rain spotted his face and robe, and cool air tried to find its way through gaps in his sweater and under his cargo pants as the platform he shared with It-who-strikes-decisively flew sedately through the city.

It was still morning on Ialis. The bright star that fed the planet was overhead, its thin light turning the sky into a sheet of frosted glass. On the horizon, the stars of the Spiral were visible as a tightly coiled thread, with a tail that stretched out all the way across the sky. Ialis was just one more point in that chain of fallen worlds.

Miles turned and looked down the Spiral in the opposite direction, a curling thread that ended before it could form more than a single loop.

Earth's Solar system was just one of those stars as well. The Spiral was currently ninety days into Iteration 27,201, and Sol had bowered as Iteration 27,200, which meant home was the second-to-last star in the line. If he had a computer unit and an astronomical database, Miles could have calculated exactly how far away Earth was, but he knew it had to be trillions of kilometers.

It seemed impossibly far away, at least in terms of his ability to travel.

Being so far from all the places he knew and everything familiar was a pain, but when his mind turned to his family, the distance was nothing but a comfort.

Miles turned to look ahead, gripping the guardrail as their floating platform wove between spires.

From this viewpoint, the city was a field of black spires starker than old Earth's most brutalist tower projects, but growing from the planet's dark moss ground with mist pooling around their feet, they projected a weird, alien beauty.

Miles held onto the rail for a while, facing ahead as he watched their progress toward the edge of the city.

It seemed like their destination was an unfinished tower on the outer edge of the city. It had the same construction as the rest, but many sections were incomplete. There were places where bare metal bones hadn't yet been clothed in prefabricated slot-in units, areas where the skin only existed as thin, reflective squares of insulation instead of the standard black metal, and it had a spire that ended in a broken crown of temporary panels, rather than the flat angled tops of the others.

Was their destination inside, just open to the elements?

"Where's the Enclave?" he asked, calling to Iddris.

The being that Miles had decided was some kind of technological sapient regarded him placidly.

Iddris didn't seem to mind the cold or the rain and didn't react to the other platforms passing by and in front of them. The concave lens of its central eye never left him and never showed any expression. Miles still couldn't shake the impression that it was assessing him.

"Traveling to the edge of the city, we will find the Enclave beneath the nameless spire."

Miles turned to look back at the unfinished construction. *The nameless spire.* Most of the towers were named for the corporations that owned them. The Ishel Corporation Lounge. The Lapis Corporation Apartments. This one must have been unnamed because it wasn't finished. Nobody had bought it from the Ialis Corporation.

"My guide couldn't find anything like the Enclave on the city listings. Is that deliberate?"

"As a non-commercial organization, there is no benefit to being easily found," Iddris said, raising their voice to be heard over the wind.

"What are you, if not commercial?"

"Listing the motives of our sub-groups, we are spiritual, cultural, professional, and cooperative."

"Cooperative sounds good."

The platform dropped several feet as it began its descent. Miles's stomach flipped up into his mouth and his feet briefly left the floor as his body caught up with the downward momentum.

Unsafe. Unsafe.

He really wished the Ialis Corporation had invested in better public transport. Although he had a feeling that the system controlling the platforms was smart enough not to toss him over the edge with a too-aggressive move, Miles would have loved to have that feeling backed up by a seat and safety harness.

He kept a tight grip on the railing as the floating disc descended toward the unnamed tower.

Miles had felt pulses of magic coming from Iddris at several points on their journey, and now it was emitting the cold ticking of its magical tradition almost constantly. Normally, a transport platform was called by sending a message to their central management system with the pickup and drop-off locations included, but Miles wondered whether Iddris was guiding this one personally, using its own brand of magic.

The platform swooped down past the usual docking level, descending all the way to the base of the tower. It came to a stop on top of a mound of green-black moss, a dozen feet from the tower wall.

Miles stepped shakily off the platform onto the ground, limbs weak and head swimming.

The unfinished elements of the construction were visible down there, too. The black metal skin that covered most of the structure was missing for the bottom fifty feet, leaving a bare metal framework occasionally plugged by white insulation foam.

Fixtures that looked like they were meant to host access panels or maintenance equipment were just naked panels of exposed interface contacts, and there were still a few head-high crates of materials lying around, rain-stained and covered in dirt.

The lack of weatherproofing close to the base had allowed the planet's moss to get a foothold, growing up the sides in meandering meters-high columns of dark green.

Iddris left the platform and started floating toward the tower, where a circular maintenance hatch appeared as the only clear metal among a dense patch of moss.

"How come it was never finished?" Miles asked as he came up beside the sapient.

"Following the completion of the city, a fault fracture began to appear in the ground beneath its foundations," Iddris replied. "As a minor geological instability, it posed no threat, but some saw it as an opportunity."

Iddris paused at the hatch, pulsing magic in a stuttering stop-start spell. The round metal door receded into the wall with a clunk and rolled to the side. Iddris continued speaking as it led Miles down a maintenance corridor.

"Purchasing the tower closest to the fault's peak, the disreputable Wing Corporation began excavating its foundation. Opening a passageway to the fault, they hoped to gain private and unrestricted access to the Ialis artifact below."

Miles thought of the heavily managed entrance complex, and how the Gilthaen operators queued and monitored scavengers entering and leaving the dungeon.

He didn't see a good reason why anyone would need a private way in, as the Ialis Corp entrance fees weren't *that* steep, but he did have personal experience that some people would go to extreme lengths to smuggle items *out* of the dungeon.

"Did they manage to find a way in?" he asked. *Or out.*

"As Gilthaens, the city's overseers were impossible to deceive. Opening the way to the fault did give the Wing Corporation access to the artifact's top layer, but they were censured before they could profit from it. As an inconvenient reminder of an unauthorized act, the tower remains in arbitration."

So there *was* another way in.

The inside of the tower wasn't in much better condition than the exterior. Cables hung down from the ceiling, wires trailed across the ground posing clear trip hazards, light fixtures were missing or flickering, and missing wall panels exposed pipework to anyone passing by.

"If the tower's locked in arbitration, how did the Enclave get set up here?"

"Making simultaneous arrangements with the Wing Corporation and the Ialis Corporation. As a building which the Wing Corporation could not use, they accepted our offer for the foundation levels. Knowing that the Enclave would not use the secondary entrance to compete with them commercially, the Ialis Corporation permitted it."

"Does the Enclave ever use the entrance?" Miles asked.

Iddris paused at a side door, never answering.

The door's control panel was the first active terminal Miles had seen since they'd come in, but Iddris made no move to use it.

The technological sapient didn't even seem to have any manipulators, leaving Miles wondering if it did *everything* using magic.

"Entering the code 918-dark-moon-luminary will permit us access," Iddris said, hovering motionless by the door.

Miles waited for a few more seconds before asking, "Do you want me to do it?"

"Casting the code using Counterfactuals is tedious."

Miles stepped up, touched the control panel to bring it to life, and started tapping in the security code.

It took a minute for him to find the right elements, just due to the breadth of options in the interface. A security code could include numbers, words, images, pictograms from a number of Spiral languages, and even biometric readings.

Even knowing the code, Miles had to give the number 918 using Gilthaen numeric glyphs, only recognizing them because of his *Eyes of the Émigré*. Next, he had to hand-type the words *dark moon* using an on-screen keyboard configured in the same layout as the one on his comm. Finally, he had to pick out the *luminary* token from a library of Gilthaen image archetypes, a set of illustrations that looked more like tarot cards than elements in a language.

When he tapped the option to submit the code, the panel beeped in approval and the door slid open.

Is this the kind of thing Trin has to deal with in the dungeon?

Through the door was the landing of a large square stairwell. Instead of stairs, a ramp ran around the walls of the space, spiraling steeply downward.

There was no railing to the ramp, and the center of the room was an open column of air that looked like it went down forty or fifty feet to the floor below.

Iddris floated up to the edge of the platform, where the ground gave way to a perilous drop. It rotated in the air to look at Miles.

"As a Harmonizer, can you navigate this direct descent?"

"Do you mean can I survive the fall?" Miles asked. He peered over the edge. "No. No, I can't do that."

Without a word, Iddris turned and headed for the ramp. It began floating down it steadily, stopping to turn at the corners, before going down the next flight. Miles followed.

At the bottom of the ramp was another door to exit the stairwell. It was dark at first, but lit up as soon as it sensed their presence.

Miles waited for either the door to open, or for Iddris to give him a code, but instead they just waited.

"As visitors, we will wait for admittance."

They waited as seconds turned into one minute, then two.

Miles shot Iddris glances as they stood in silence, working up the nerve to interrogate him.

Ever since Miles had met the other mage, he'd kept his curiosity on a leash. He hadn't wanted to put too much pressure on the sapient and annoy it, or put it off, ruining his one chance.

Now that they were alone, without the wind blowing around them, he couldn't hold it back any longer.

"Can you tell me more about magic?" he asked.

When Iddris didn't immediately reply, Miles felt like the other mage's silence was inviting him to elaborate. He'd been sitting on a knot of feelings about the magic he'd been inducted into, and they chose that moment to bubble to the surface.

"When they handed me my index on the refugee station, I just accepted it. I was already accepting so much, and magic, sure, it was just one more thing I'd never considered. I think on some level, I thought it was just another type of advanced technology, but since I've been casting Harmonizer spells I've realized that's not true. Using magic feels like . . . touching something *true*. Am I making sense?"

"No," Iddris replied.

"No?"

"Educating you on magic is not a desirable use of my energy. As a member of the tradition which gave your iteration access to magic, Fifth-Sage Curious can hear your questions."

"Who is that?"

"Sitting as our Enclave's Senior Harmonizer."

Is Fifth-Sage part of the name? Or a rank?

Miles decided not to ask the question. He sensed that he was starting to annoy the other sapient, after all.

They were probably both relieved a minute later when the panel chirped and the door rolled open on its own.

That lasted until the first wave of raised voices spilled out of the space beyond.

At first, it was just an unintelligible cacophony of non-human voices. There was so much noise and overlap that *Eyes of the Émigré* wasn't providing translation, until one voice rose over the crowd.

Before translation, the voice was a series of loud clicks, but under *Eyes of the Émigré*, it became the haughty voice of a younger man.

"—under your control is weak and dissolute. You shelter the broken traditions. You dilute our ranks with the powerless and deluded followers of false traditions, from iterations that never even possessed magic. For all of these reasons and for the good of the Enclave, I challenge you for leadership."

Beyond the door, the space opened up into a vast, multilevel chamber. The patchwork construction of the tower above continued below, except that here the missing work had clearly been patched up by hand.

Floors that had been left as skeletal networks of crisscrossing beams had been patched up with wooden flooring made from planks of the dark native wood. Walls that had been left as bulging compartments full of wiring and insulation had been plastered and painted, with some areas even decorated in clashing patterns of printed paper and engraved stone.

Wall scrolls and tapestries dotted the walls, depicting other worlds, natural scenes, cloudscapes, and strange animals in a huge range of styles, while others showed artistic arrangements of pictograms that Miles thought might represent the different magical traditions.

It was as far as he could imagine from the utilitarian interior of the Ishel Corporation Lounge or his own bare apartment.

The floor the stairwell opened on was a broad outer balcony that framed an opening on the floor below, where the raised voices were coming from. Whoever was speaking was currently out of sight.

The only person on this floor was the one who'd let them in, the smallest Hurc Miles had ever seen. They were a male, no taller than Miles, with an even slighter frame. He looked about Miles's age, only lightly muscled, with lilac skin and a tuft of dark blue hair growing out of the center of his head. He was stripped to the waist, with a sweeping skirt of rough fabric that hung down to his ankles.

"Apologies. Apologies. There's some trouble," he said. He held his hands together as he spoke, which was either a social gesture Miles hadn't seen before or a sign the man was nervous.

"Explaining the trouble quickly would be helpful," Iddris said to him.

"Adept Shrikesong is challenging Master Oron for leadership, Master Strikes-Decisively. It began several minutes ago, and they still have the floor."

Iddris turned to look at Miles and said, "Waiting is necessary."

"That's okay."

Miles had felt out of his depth before he knew he was walking into some kind of crisis. Now, he felt entirely lost.

Iddris began floating toward the edge of the balcony, where the room opened up into a theater-style space below. Miles followed, and the boy from the door came after them.

As they reached the edge, Miles got a better appreciation for the size of the space. It covered three floors, with two successively wider balconies made up of metal floor panels filled in with wooden planks, and the bottom level seemed to be carved straight into bedrock.

The bottom floor was crowded with furniture around the outside. Shelves, chests, lockers, and desks, with chairs, lounges, and oversized cushions suitable for a huge variety of body types. It was currently also dotted with diverse sapients, all focusing their attention on the center.

The center of the room was open, a wide oval strewn with rugs and blankets, with a glowing glass sphere hanging from a nest of wires above it that provided light to the entire space.

In the clearing stood two people.

The first was a tall, stick-thin figure in a patterned toga made out of dark sheer fabric. They had a triangular head of glassy brown chitin, with the position of their eyes and mandibles reminding Miles of a praying mantis. Their body was narrow and hard-shelled under the toga, with four arms hanging at their sides, two growing from each shoulder.

The second figure was much, much larger. Miles wasn't sure how a sapient the size of an elephant had navigated the stairwell, but they occupied the space like they belonged there. Covered in russet-brown fur and standing on four thick limbs in the same way a bear might, they stared at the mantis sapient with a placid expression, deep brown eyes set in an almost human face.

"Okay. How do you want to challenge?" the larger sapient asked in a deep, rolling voice.

"A duel of magical force," the mantis sapient replied.

"Okay. Let's do that."

Next to Miles, Iddris said, "As a senior, I should be there to witness and invigilate."

Iddris left without waiting for a response, floating up over the railing and off the edge of the balcony, then descending slowly to take a place among the crowd on the bottom level.

Miles was left alone with the boy.

Down below, the other sapients were moving backward to create space between themselves and the pair in the center. Some took up positions at regular points around the two, and Miles felt the flashes of magic of a half dozen different traditions coming from them, maybe preparing protections.

At his side, Miles caught the Hurc mage inspecting him.

"Master . . . ?" he said.

It took Miles a second to realize he was fishing for his name.

"Uh, no. I'm just Miles."

"Miles. Apologies. You came with Master Strikes-Decisively, so I thought . . ."

"I didn't know he was a 'master'," Miles said.

"Half the mages here are masters. At least, sometimes it seems that way," the Hurc mage said. "I'm only an apprentice. My name is Task."

Miles was starting to get a feel for the ranks here. *Apprentice* would be one of the lower ones, *Adept* a higher rank, and *Master* close to the top.

"I don't think I'm even an apprentice," Miles said. He knew a handful of spells, but he didn't imagine that gave him the right to any kind of title. "Iddris brought me here to speak to your Harmonizer."

"Master Curious," Task said, repeating the name Iddris had used.

"Yeah. Are they down there?"

Task peered over the edge. "There she is. The Purir woman by the books."

He pointed out a figure standing in the crowd below, a humanoid sapient a couple of feet shorter than Miles, with an elongated skull and skin colored like patchwork autumn leaves. She wore a red-brown robe and leaned on a black wooden staff, watching the proceedings in the center without much interest.

"What's she like?" Miles asked.

"She doesn't like to be bored. Oh, look. They're starting."

A hush had fallen on the crowd below.

According to some etiquette Miles didn't know, the insectoid challenger, Shrikesong, was taking the first move.

"Magic is a means to achieve change, nothing more, nothing less," Shrikesong declared. "We affect the world directly, using coveted secrets stolen from our elders. Opening our society to lesser traditions, and especially to false traditions, is a degradation that insults our dignity and weakens our standing."

With his declaration done, the spindly sapient took an awkward-looking stance, right arms raised, left arms behind their back.

Miles felt Shrikesong's magic spin up. His tradition was a stuttering chainsaw buzz that sputtered into life noisily before quickly rising to a crescendo. At the moment of the magic's peak, Shrikesong extended their right pair of arms, claws stretching forward to point at the giant Master Oron.

The magic left his body in a spike, rushing through the air.

Just from the taste of it in his senses, Miles could tell that this magic was *disharmonious*. He could barely resist the urge to raise his own hand and strike it out of the air, not that he could do it fast enough to count, or that he thought he had anywhere near enough the strength to stop it.

The spell hit Oron. A wave of ruffled fur ran over his body, as if blown by a breeze.

Oron blinked at Shrikesong slowly, his eyes slightly out of time with each other. After a moment of silence, he replied.

"Magic is a refuge, okay? Our power lets us enforce our values. It keeps us safe. The guys who don't really do magic? They're okay. We like them."

As his statement ended, Oron's magic began to build. To Miles, it felt like a warm flow, like a wave washing in to shore.

Oron opened his mouth and a word rolled out.

The word didn't translate, but Miles felt its meaning anyway. It meant *Defeat*, or *Lose*, but there was more to it. *Defeat in the manner you tried to win*. Or *Lose by your own hand*.

The meaning coalesced into a compact phrase as the magic hit. *Mirrored Defeat*.

Shrikesong's body flew apart.

A wave of shock seemed to pass over the crowd. Miles took long moments to process what he'd seen.

Body parts were scattered across the rugs and fabrics. Chitinous limbs, fragments of Shrikesong's clothes. His triangular head had landed on a mustard-yellow cushion.

It had happened so quickly. Miles could barely believe it. He'd seen violence, recently, in the dungeon and in Brisk's attack on the Gilthaen official, but he was still far from used to it. It was hard to accept that he'd just seen someone die in a moment. There wasn't even much mess.

The crowd below seemed just as shocked as Miles. The silence now felt tense. Miles didn't think anyone down there had expected this, maybe not even Oron.

Into the silence, the woman Task had identified as Master Curious spoke up.

"Those who sow the spark must be willing to reap the blaze."

There was the muttering of mixed-species voices from below. Next to him on the balcony, Task was nodding to himself.

Miles considered just leaving.

"How often do people get blown up here?" he asked quietly.

Task took a second to reply. He seemed like his thoughts were far away.

"Master Oron has been seeing challengers almost once a span for this entire iteration. Usually, the bouts are safe . . . We all thought Adept Shrikesong would just measure his power against Master Oron in a show duel. I've never seen anyone die before."

Before Miles had the chance to weigh up the odds that *he* might get challenged to a duel if he went down, Iddris reappeared, floating over the balcony to land next to Miles.

"As the senior who brought you here, I regret that this display is your first experience of our Enclave," it said, descending to hover next to him.

"It's okay," Miles allowed. He did still want some information here. "As long as it's safe for me."

"Challenging a resident Master is the most dangerous activity here, and that is usually safe," Iddris said.

Below them on the bottom level, Master Curious was casting a spell. Miles felt the familiar warm rotation of Harmonizer magic, and the Purir mage stepped forward.

She waved her hand in the direction of the fragments of former Master Shrikesong, then snatched at the air.

Magic rang through the room, and the scattered body parts collapsed into ash.

The enormous form of Master Oron turned and trundled back to the edge of the room, where he sank onto a colorful woven mat.

"Introducing you to Fifth-Sage Curious is now possible. Following me, we will reach her directly."

Iddris set off around the edge of the platform, apparently expecting Miles to follow.

Miles turned to Task before leaving.

"It was good to meet you," he said.

Task clasped his hands together again as he replied. "The same with you. Apologies for the circumstances. I hope you return."

Miles glanced at the departing shape of Iddris before turning back to Task.

"Do you want to tap comms?"

Task offered his hand. There was a tech device in the form of a ring around his third finger, which Miles assumed was his comm. Miles tapped his own device to it, then turned to rush after Iddris, who was disappearing down a ramp.

By the time they made it to the bottom floor, there was a low buzz of conversation from every cluster of sapients. Miles assumed everyone was talking about what had just happened.

He saw a few species he recognized on the lower floor. There were a handful of Eppan mages, and several members of the slender six-armed species he'd learned were called Morchis. There was even someone who had the same body plan as Torg, with the same distinctive chitin cowl. Other familiar shapes were in the crowd, but just as many were entirely new to him.

Iddris led him around the edge of the central clearing to the section where Master Curious was sitting on a plush cushion, regarding the other mages around her carefully.

When they reached her, Iddris floated ahead, making introductions.

"As Senior Counterfactual Sorcerer It-who-strikes-decisively, I greet Fifth-Sage Curious, Senior Harmonizer."

"Hello, Iddris. What do you want?" The woman shifted on her cushion, turning to face them. When she saw Iddris wasn't alone, she unfolded her legs and rose to her feet.

Up close, Miles could see that her skin was actually a light gray, but almost every inch of it was covered by patches of color that spread out in fractal shapes. She had a near-human face, lacking only a nose and ears, and seemed to have four limbs. Her hands ended in double-jointed fingers that were hard and narrow, more like talons than flesh, and when she stretched out her legs to stand, Miles noticed her toes were the same way.

"Browsing the market, I found a Harmonizer using his magic recklessly. As his senior, I stepped in to caution him, and found something interesting."

Curious examined Miles more closely. A pair of eyes with pinprick pupils scanned him from head to feet, and Miles felt the rolling of magic from her, not a spell, but maybe some other effect.

"You're an index mage," she said to him.

How can you tell?

"Yes," Miles said.

Curious turned back to Iddris. "What's interesting about that?"

Iddris rotated to turn its single black eye on Miles. "As a demonstration, cast the spell you were using in the marketplace."

Miles felt a flash of panic at the thought of casting *Strike the Disharmonious* here, after what he'd just seen.

"Here?" Miles asked. "Are you sure? It's an attack spell."

"You're not going to hurt anyone, mage-child. Trust me on that," Curious said.

Miles glanced at Iddris to double-check that it was okay, then at Curious. Iddris was a completely inexpressive black spike, and Miles had no idea how to read the Fifth Sage's body language. He'd just have to hope they were telling him the truth.

Holding his hand up, Miles began to concentrate on the singing tone of *Strike the Harmonious*. It seemed to come easily to him this time, and within a couple of seconds, the note had shifted from imagination to something he could hear.

Master Curious watched him for a second, then made a *humph* sound. "Yes, fine. Let it go."

Miles let the spell fade.

"What else can you do?"

Miles thought for a second. *Close Wound* and *Hasten Renewal* wouldn't do anything obvious here, so maybe *Temporary Enhancement* would work as a demonstration, assuming Curious could sense the magic.

Miles touched a hand to his chest, and cast the spell, focusing on bolstering his Authority.

He felt the warmth in his gut begin to spin, while dredging up what he could remember of the litany.

In myself, I am complete. In a harmonious world, everyone is in theirself complete. **I am that which I am.**

The spark of hot energy rushed from his core down his arm, and into his body again from the outside. He felt *something*. Not an effect as obvious as when he'd enhanced his reactions, but a solidity and a significance. At times since he'd left Earth, Miles had felt out of place, unwanted, cast away. Now, he felt like he belonged, that nobody could gainsay his presence.

Curious peered at him, and Miles felt the pressure in his gut that signified he was being inspected by another mage.

"You don't have to touch yourself," Curious said after a minute.

What?

"I don't?"

"You're already in your own body. You don't have to use your hand to cast spells on yourself."

"Oh."

He just hadn't tried before. The energy had always flowed along his arm. He wasn't sure how to use it in any other way.

"All right," Curious said to Iddris. "He's riding with a loose harness, and he never even noticed. I'll take him."

"As the one who brought him here, I now turn him over to you," Iddris said, before turning to Miles. "Giving you into the care of Fifth-Sage Curious, I will take my leave."

Miles wanted to tell it to wait. Iddris was just a metal spike, but it was the friendliest face he knew here. Still, he knew that Curious was supposedly an experienced Harmonizer, and he couldn't pass up the chance to learn more about his own tradition.

Iddris floated up directly from the floor, heading to the third level, presumably to leave. When Miles looked upward, he noticed Task was still up there, gazing down at him.

"Tell me what you know," Curious said sharply. She shuffled around and sat back down on her cushion, leaning her staff across a pair of digitigrade legs.

"The spells I know?" Miles asked. Curious made no sign she was going to answer, so he went on. "I can cast *Close Wound*, *Temporary Enhancement*, *Hasten Renewal*, and *Strike the Disharmonious*."

"All without your index?"

"Yes."

"Show me."

Curious demanded Miles hand over his index, and then asked him to cast several spells in sequence. *Hasten Renewal* and another *Temporary Enhancement*. She snapped a wooden plate and had him demonstrate *Close Wound*, and observed as he looked around through the *Eyes of the Altruist*. She kept a close watch on his index the entire time, holding it like it was an animal she thought would bite her, before she seemed satisfied.

"Do you want me to destroy this?" she asked, holding up his index.

"No!" Miles said, then more calmly, "I need it."

"Fine, then take it," she tossed it back to him. "Do you even know what it is?"

Miles had a pretty good idea of what an index was in practical terms, but he was getting the same impression from Master Curious that he might get from an opinionated older relative, and decided not to put his answer to the test. He just shrugged, and hoped the message got across.

"A training device," Curious said bluntly. "One that was so convenient it replaced learning entirely. It can teach most spells instantly. It can be activated through a mental interface. Most who practice magic never grow beyond it. *You* seem to have been using it for its original purpose."

Miles felt like he'd missed something. He hadn't been explicitly trying to. There was supposed to have been a way to work the interface without touching the device itself, and from what Curious was saying, he'd gone straight past that to casting the spells it taught him on his own.

"Don't look so pleased with yourself," Curious said.

Miles didn't think his expression had been showing anything, but he relaxed his face anyway.

"It's not difficult to learn when the index has already shown you the way. Not at all. That was the point of the device. 'Those who are taught a truth shouldn't expect a discoverer's laurels.' This is unusual only because of the choice you've made. Would you commit to a traditional study of magic?"

Miles hesitated, processing the implications. Was she offering to become his teacher? He was desperate for a real teacher, but something about the way she'd said it worried him. *Commit to a traditional study of magic.* It made him think that if he said yes, she'd follow through on her offer to destroy his index.

"Is it only one way or the other?" he asked. "Either index or traditional study?"

"I won't take an apprentice who's still bound to an index," Curious said. "That's not a point of principle, or a problem with the tool itself, but we have history with the Morning Star Corporation who operates it, and teaching one of their loyal customers is more than I can stomach."

Miles briefly considered what she was offering. Could he live without his index? Was he willing to throw it away for a chance at becoming a real student of magic? He had a willing master right here, ready to teach him.

After half a minute's thought, he decided that he couldn't take the risk. The chance that he'd be no good at magic on his own, the chance that it wasn't really the opportunity it looked like, the chance that even if it was, it would take too much time and he wouldn't have the freedom and flexibility to support himself and his new team. He was counting on getting *Purify* just as soon as he found out how to get delta, and he had no idea how long that spell would take to learn through Curious's methods.

"I can't," Miles said finally. "I need the index to learn quickly, and I need to learn quickly to support myself here."

"Yes. That's typically the argument," Curious said. She didn't seem annoyed or frustrated, but she did seem to have become bored. At the last second, she relented. "I won't be your teacher, but I will answer any questions you have right now. If you ask a tiresome question, I will answer it, but that will be your last."

For a fraction of a second, Miles interpreted *that will be your last* as a threat to kill him, until his brain caught up.

"Okay," he said. "Okay."

His mind worked, trying to come up with a question. It seemed like he'd had a thousand just that morning, but he hadn't taken the time to write them down.

"Can you tell me how magic is different from technology?" he asked cautiously. He'd raised the general idea with Iddris, but the sapient hadn't been willing to take him up on it. Since then, he'd been wondering.

"I can see how that would be confusing. You're from an iteration that had no native magical systems?"

"Iteration 27,200," Miles said. "We didn't have any real magic."

"I see. You came in with Strikes-decisively. If you asked him about magic, he'd tell you a story about 'information solutions' and 'low-energy states'. I never really understood it, the pure-mechanists' explanation for magic. For the rest of us, 'change flows from truth as heat flows from flame'. It was a natural law for those of us born in magical iterations. When we tried to pierce our world fabric and fell through to the Spiral, that law spread out into the weave like any other."

Change flows from truth.

Miles had personal experience with that already. He'd felt the total conviction that the Orbellius Ghoul existed in disharmony, that it wasn't *entitled* to exist, while he was casting *Strike the Disharmonious*. When casting *Hasten Renewal* he'd understood that a creature that will eventually heal might as well already be healed.

It didn't make sense to him logically, but that feeling, first from the index, and then from his own thoughts, rang as true whenever he called it.

"But who is judging what's true?" Miles asked.

It wasn't as if he could suddenly decide *I deserve one thousand delta* and make it a reality.

"You are. I am. The weave has its own idea about what is true, which we call physical reality. As Harmonizers, we exercise our Authority to overrule it."

Miles let out a breath. He realized that in essence, he was trying to get a physical explanation for what magic was, but the actual mages would reject the idea that there even was one.

Curious's answer did remind him about something he had wanted to ask.

"What *is* Authority? Can it be increased?"

The Fifth Sage made the noise of escaping air, and her pupils narrowed to pinpricks. Miles assumed the expression meant that he'd said something she didn't like.

"That is a *tedious question*. Authority isn't an obtuse word. A ruler's commands are obeyed because they have Authority. If they overtax their Authority, it will diminish for a time, or permanently in severe cases. To grow it, live harmoniously, speak honestly, act with conviction, and succeed in your endeavors."

Oh, is that all? I'm sure there's no hidden complexity to that . . .

"Thank you, Master Curious," Miles said, trying to be polite even if he had just been cut off. He didn't need to annoy her any more than he apparently had.

Curious waved a taloned hand at him, closing her eyes as she settled down onto the cushion. "Go. I'll send my apprentice to make contact with you. There's no reason to cut ties. If you change your mind and want my instruction, let her know, and she'll pass on the word."

"Okay. Thank you."

Miles looked around the space for anyone who could be Curious's apprentice, but nobody stood out.

"How will she find me?" he asked.

"No more questions," Curious ordered.

Miles stepped away, a little at a loss. Iddris was gone. How was he meant to leave? Could he just message for a platform to pick him up from the mage enclave?

He looked around for a friendly face, or anyone who might be willing to talk to him. Everyone seemed to be engaged in their own conversation, or else sitting alone in a way that precluded trying to speak to them.

He started saying a little litany to amuse himself as he maneuvered around the edge of the crowd.

Over my life, I'll make thousands of delta. In a harmonious world, everyone already has all of their life savings. **Such should it be.**

Miles panicked a little as he felt his magical core spinning up over the course of the litany, but it petered out halfway through, leaving it as the joke it was meant to be.

When he got to the ramp leading up from the bottom level, he caught sight of Task looking down at him.

The other mage quickly looked away as soon as Miles spotted him, but the apprentice mage would probably be good for some quick questions.

Questions like *how do I get delta* and *how do I get out of this hole*.

Miles rushed up the ramp before the other mage could disappear.

When he reached the top level, the apprentice wasn't making any attempt to leave, instead waiting patiently.

"Hi," Miles said, breathing hard as he came to rest against the railing next to him.

"Hello, again," Task said. "Did you receive instruction from Master Curious?"

"She answered a couple of questions. She didn't want to teach me anything while I'm still using my index."

Task reached into a pocket of his skirt and pulled out a cobalt-blue ring, which he slipped onto a finger. He held up his hand for Miles to see.

"My index."

"I didn't know they made them that small. How do you work it?"

"The mental interface. Master Oron lets me keep it, but it can't teach me his tradition, the Thunderous Word. The details were never shared with its makers."

"I'm a Harmonizer. That's the only tradition I can access," Miles said.

He suddenly remembered the other tradition he'd seen when holding the crystal he'd picked up from Brisk's former teammate.

"Hey, have you ever heard of crystals that contain spells?" Miles asked.

He didn't elaborate on where the crystals came from, or that he'd seen one, or that he'd *used* one, in case it was a taboo subject.

Task's open, innocent expression made him realize he needn't have worried.

"Crystals? I haven't. Apologies, Miles."

"It's okay. No need to ask around or mention that to anyone else."

"Okay . . . I won't."

Miles's eyes strayed down to Task's index. He reached into his pocket and pulled out his own, resting it on the railing.

"It's very big," Task said. "The basic model."

"Yeah. I haven't worked out how to work it without touching it. I thought I'd got it, but it turns out I was just casting the spells the old-fashioned way." Miles hesitated before continuing, sure that he was admitting some embarrassing ignorance. "I also have no idea where to get delta to buy new spells."

Task straightened up, and the hair growing from his head seemed to stiffen.

"I can show you," he said, then glanced down at the lower level like he'd realized something. "Oh, but my duties."

"I don't want to bother you if you're at work," Miles said. "Maybe you could just tell me?"

"No. Please wait."

Task left the balcony, running down the ramps to the lowest level.

Miles saw him approach the massive furred form of Master Oron, saying something with his hands clasped together.

Oron glanced up, looking straight at Miles. He replied briefly, and Task came rushing back up.

"Apologies. I'm free to take you now."

"Okay," Miles said. "Sure. Thanks. So where is it?"

"We have to go to the Morning Star Lounge," he said, moving up to walk beside him.

Miles pulled out his comm as they headed back toward the stairwell.

Miles > Trin
Hey Trin. I'm going with someone else to a third location. An apprentice called Task says he's taking me to the Morning Star Lounge. If I disappear, tell security.

Trin > Miles
Shady shady shady.

Miles > Trin
I don't know, he seems nice.

Trin > Miles
Send me a picture of him. For security.

Miles > Trin
I don't know how. I think I need to upgrade my comm.

Miles put the device away before Trin could reply again.

Task touched his own comm ring as they reached the moss-strewn ground around the base of the tower, and Miles watched as a vacant platform in the distance changed direction and started heading toward them.

He hadn't got everything he'd wanted from the Enclave, but at least he didn't feel like he was stumbling around in complete darkness anymore.

Making contacts, finding where he could get things he needed, and starting to get an idea of the character of the place. Dendril City was starting to feel like home.

CHAPTER 17

Thouco Tower was a mixed-use arcology close to the center of Dendril City.

If the Ishel Corporation Lounge was a tower-sized department store, then Thouco was closer to a gated community. It had its own upmarket apartment complexes, prestige offices for dozens of different corporations, and stores that were more like the high-end electronics showrooms of old Earth than the busy and vibrant markets of the Ishel Corporation tower.

Miles thought the idea was probably for sapients to live in the apartments, work in the corp offices, and shop at the boutiques, all without leaving the tower.

The business listing fixed to the wall of the embarkation lounge had been an education in itself. Floors 15–18, the Covenant Corporation. Floors 25–28, the Outlaster's Corporation. Floors 28–33, the Wing Corporation. Miles felt like he should have been memorizing names and scanning the business directory for future reference.

If he were alone, he might have.

Task escorted him through the embarkation lounge to a bank of elevators, which they rode to one of the upper levels.

They were alone in the elevator, but the journey only lasted a couple of seconds; there was a burst of acceleration, though less than there should have been, and the doors flicked open.

The corridor on their destination floor was *H*-shaped, with stores and restaurants lining the walkways.

There were other sapients around, visiting the facilities. Miles saw Gilthaen visitors dressed in shimmering or austere fabrics, moving with their long bodies close to the ground to stay under the low ceilings. There were several Orbellius individuals moving around on a mixture of levitation units and spider-like walking frames, with skin colors ranging from white to sunset-red. One visitor was Draulean, the same species as Miles's last client, dressed in a gown of translucent, weblike silk, their skin strobing black-white as they moved around inside a store.

Miles and Task were almost the only humanoids there, and Miles was definitely the worst-dressed. He felt like he was intruding into a place only people with money were meant to be.

The feeling only intensified when their path took them alongside a clothing store. An automated system built into the glass wall took stock of Miles and projected the image of a proposed outfit. A pair of tapered black pants and a ruffled beige tunic that came down to the knees, all wrapped up under a billowing maroon cloak that was lined with interior pockets. The price was twenty-four hundred seln.

Task caught sight of the outfit and spoke quietly.

"I buy my clothes on the Exchange. It's cheaper."

Miles nodded. Maybe he should look on the Exchange, now that he had money.

They rounded the corner together and arrived at a store Miles instantly recognized as the Morning Star Corporation Lounge. Even without the same starburst glyph above the door that was engraved on his index, he would have known from the design projected on the glass wall, an image of his own index.

It wasn't the only one projected. He also saw Task's ring index, one in the form of a bracelet, one that was a sphere, another that was a circlet. There were other devices that might not have been indexes at all.

Miles and Task passed through the open entrance together.

Inside, the back wall was dominated by a counter, with glass-walled booths set up behind it like the counter at a bank. The booths were open-fronted, so they didn't seem like they could be for security. Most of them were empty, but one had something in it that Miles had trouble visually parsing at first.

Task pointed him toward the counter. "There, they will help you."

"Okay. Thanks," Miles said. Then, quietly, "Here I go."

He stepped up to the counter, staring into the booth at the figure inside.

Miles hadn't seen many other humanoids in the tower, and the clerk behind the desk followed that pattern. In any other context, Miles might have failed to recognize them as a sapient at all.

The overwhelming impression Miles got as he approached was of a fleshy vase, tongue-pink, with frills like lace running vertically up and down the trunk of their body. The top of their body opened out like a flower, with feathery tendrils reaching up into the air, drifting as if caught in an ocean current.

Their whole body was distinctly wet, glistening under the white strip lights, and as Miles got close he picked up the clashing smells of pickles and cream.

From up close, he noticed that the air drifting out of the booth was dense with a cold humidity, which immediately made him wonder whether the clear enclosures were there to provide a more comfortable environment for whatever sapient was staffing them.

"Hi," he said.

He'd planned to say more, but he was having trouble getting his bearings with the interaction.

"Greetings, you! Our valued customer," the sapient said. "How may this one help you?"

They seemed to be speaking through a vent on their side. The flapping orifice was making a quiet whispering sound that Miles wouldn't even have realized was speech without his *Eyes of the Émigré*.

"Hi," Miles said again. "I'm trying to change seln for delta?"

"In delight, we can accommodate your desire. Beneath the stars, we operate a brokerage. One mage to another, for you! The purchaser of delta."

Finally.

"Okay," he said, thinking. He needed to work out how much delta he wanted to buy.

He knew he wanted at least 125 delta to buy the *Purify* spell, plus another one hundred to buy an improvement to his Authority, but the more delta he had on his account, the more of the Harmonizer catalog he'd get to see.

His reward from the Gilthaens had been 250 delta, which meant he'd need more than that to see more of his options.

"How much would it cost for five hundred delta?" he asked.

The clerk reached down with a feathery frond to brush against an apparently featureless white panel, then straightened back up.

"Within our system, available! Five hundred delta for 1480 standard exchange notes."

Fifteen hundred seln? Ouch.

Miles had about 3500 seln left after his morning shopping, but he had been enjoying the new feeling of not being destitute.

"Is that the normal exchange rate?"

"No! It is ever-changing. Beneath the stars, this is the best rate for the hour."

Miles took ten seconds to think about it, then nodded. "Okay. Yes. Can I get that please?"

"Present your index and your communicator, you!"

Miles handed over his index tablet and his comm. The sapient tapped both with a device that looked like an electric toothbrush without the bristles, then slid them back to him.

Miles grabbed his comm first, checking his seln account, then his overall financials.

Financial Status [§]
§4,037
§3549 (−§488 Purchases Ishel Corporation Lounge)
§2069 (−§1480 Purchases Morning Star Corporation)

Financial Status [δ]
δ500 (δ0 + δ500)

He'd done it. He'd finally managed to change money. It was probably the kind of transaction that every other sapient in the city took for granted, but for Miles, it was an achievement.

"That's great. Thanks," Miles said.

"In oneness, enjoy your brightened horizons. You! The mage of tools."

"You too," Miles replied on instinct, before stepping away quickly.

Task was standing at the edge of the store, looking at a row of indexes placed out along a white glass bench. Miles joined him.

"You did it?" Task asked.

"Yeah. I got five hundred delta. I should be able to afford a few upgrades with this."

Task turned to look at him, jaws parted. "Five hundred?"

He sounded surprised, and Miles started wondering if that was unusually high.

"Yeah. We had a lucky find on our dive the other day. I just spent some of the seln from that."

"I didn't know it was possible to make so much at our level of skill."

Miles remembered that Task had said he was only an apprentice, and Miles had told him that he didn't think he even ranked that highly himself.

Was it unusual for them to make so much money on their first dive, on the first level of the dungeon? The threats there definitely hadn't gone easy on them. They'd had to overpower the same suit of armor that had sold for so much. If Torg hadn't kept the autopistol the Orbellius Ghoul had attacked them with, they might have made even more.

"I don't know how lucky we were, but I know that it's possible."

Task was staring absently at the display of devices on the bench, and Miles turned to look at them.

They didn't seem to be stuck down or secured, so he reached down and picked up one that looked like a bulky earring.

An interface immediately sprung up over his vision.

At first, it was distorted, like looking at a graph that had been put through a shredder and reassembled badly, but the mental image flashed a few times, getting successively clearer, before presenting him with an interface that hovered in his visual field, somehow without obscuring his vision of the room.

Name: Miles Asher | Traditions: Harmonizer		
Strength: 0 Durability: 1	Speed: 0 Reactions: 0	Will: 0 Authority: 2 Authority (b): 0.19

Spells

Close Wound (Adept)
A weft of harmonizing energy brings together the free edges of a tear, sealing the join in materials which are co-bondable, such as cellular membranes, metal compounds, woven fabrics, and homogenous molecular surfaces.

Temporary Enhancement (Adept)
A temporary matrix of harmonizing energy alters one of a being's fundamental properties by an amount in accordance with the weaver's Authority.

Hasten Renewal (Grasping)
A weft of harmonizing energy spreads from the weaver to their target, greatly speeding the being's natural recovery by an amount multiplicative with the weaver's Authority.

Strike the Disharmonious (Adept)
With a weft of harmonizing energy, the weaver rips the Authority from a disharmonious target, degrading its existence and claiming the confiscated Authority for themself. While held ready, discordant presences will ring loudly in the weaver's awareness.

Core Effects

Eyes of the Émigré
Embeds a matrix of harmonizing energy within the being's mind which will reveal to them the meaning of any plain text or spoken language.

Eyes of the Altruist
Embeds a matrix of harmonizing energy within the being's mind which reveal to them the health and ailments of a witnessed being.

    He swept his attention across the mental interface and watched as it responded, priming itself to cast spells or switch effects at a mental command. The layout was slightly different, but it was surprisingly similar to how it was represented on the tablet.
    Is this how a hands-free index works?
    After receiving praise from Master Curious on his natural spellcasting, Miles felt a little above the training-wheels nature of the mental interface, but he couldn't

deny that this tiny device would be more convenient than the bulky tablet he had to carry with him now.

He looked around for a price, but when he saw it, he instantly replaced the index on the bench.

Three thousand delta. Yikes.

Just accidentally damaging that in the store would probably be enough to ruin him financially.

Miles looked at Task's ring with a new appreciation. There must have been a story behind how he got it, if the apprentice was both impressed by a fourteen-hundred-seln payday while carrying around a three-thousand-delta piece of equipment.

Miles looked up from Task's hands to his face.

Task hadn't been examining the indexes, like Miles had thought. He was pouting with his lower lip, so that his lower fangs sat outside his mouth, pressing on his top lip. It looked like a thoughtful expression to Miles.

"If I can open doors and throw violence, does that have a role with teams going in to artifact?" he asked.

Miles thought for a few seconds, urgently trying to remember what he'd heard about the traditional team positions for dungeon dives.

"Yeah," Miles replied. "That sounds like a combination of scout and fusilier. Someone who can help bypass doors, and attack at range."

"Would you be willing to take me?" Task asked. "Apologies. If there's a place for me on your team, do you want me?"

"I don't know," Miles hedged.

They'd done okay without a fusilier last time, hadn't they? Though they'd had Fran then, the random jack they'd run into.

Miles tried to imagine how the fight down there might have gone without Fran pitching in. They might not have known how to deal with the ghoul's energy shield, but that was down to experience that Task wouldn't be bringing. Fran had also been the one to finish off the armored ghoul, though that had been in close quarters. She'd pulled more weight as a lancer than a fusilier.

As a mage, was it possible Task would have been able to affect the ghoul through the energy shield?

It wasn't a decision he could just make by himself, anyway.

"I'll have to check with my team," Miles said.

"I see," Task said, looking down at the bench. "Apologies."

"I mean, I'm sure you'd be up to it. You're Oron's apprentice, right? I think we'd be lucky to have you. I just can't make those decisions on my own." Miles didn't feel like his attempt to cheer the apprentice up was working. "Hey, do you want to get some lunch?"

Task's hair twitched minutely, and he turned his eyes up to Miles.

"Yes. I'd like that."

"Okay. Great."

Miles tried to keep the new panic off his face.

Where am I meant to find lunch?

Miles had strong reservations about eating at an alien diner. He'd never eaten anything in Spiral space other than the mass-produced calorie packs, and the prospect of unknown allergens alarmed him, but he didn't think just walking into the restaurant would be dangerous.

He tried not to remember the stories from Earth about people with peanut allergies going into anaphylaxis just from being in the same room as their allergen.

The two of them passed through the door of the restaurant and made their way to the seats.

It was an upmarket-looking place, with lots of muted colors and crystal glass fixtures, though for all Miles knew that was standard interior construction on Ialis.

There was less diversity in seating inside than Miles was used to from Spiral establishments, just benches at varying heights and tables that ranged from inches off the floor to waist-high.

Task picked a booth that was about the right size for them and they ambled toward it, Miles sliding in on one side and Task the other.

Task was still bare-chested as he sat at the table. Miles guessed that Spiral restaurants were a little beyond *no shirt, no service*. The fact that Miles wasn't being thrown out for his ragged diving clothes suggested an enlightened attitude to dress code.

There was a stack of five or six transparent plastic squares on the table and Task pulled one of them in front of himself. He tapped it and an interface appeared on the sheet.

A menu, Miles realized.

Miles took a sheet of his own and spent a minute looking down the list.

"I don't know if any of this is safe for me to eat," he said, peering at items on the list.

Rinsel Porridge. Special Meat Assortment. Roast Yabarge. Squirrit Skewers.

Isn't squirrit a Hurc rat?

"This is a C-type restaurant," Task said. "It should be okay for us. Check the labels."

Miles hummed in response.

He trusted that a bag of biochemistry-C food paste would be safe for him, but when it came to meals cooked in restaurants, he didn't have the same level of faith. He was pretty sure deadly nightshade would be classed as a type-C biochemistry plant, but he still wouldn't want to eat it.

"The biochem category is fine for calorie packs, but there are human foods on my homeworld that not even every human can eat," Miles said. "How do I know if I can trust *rinsel* or *yabarge*?"

There were humans on Earth who had bad reactions to bread. Even on his home planet, where everything shared a common evolutionary history and a lot of their DNA, there was still a huge number of things that weren't safe to eat.

Calorie packs were basic, bland, and designed to be inoffensively digestible, but real food made from real alien plants and animals had to have a multitude of incidental chemicals, any one of which could be deadly to him. For all Miles knew he could be ordering the equivalent of a fly amanita salad.

"If it was dangerous, there would probably be a warning." Task said.

Task held his finger down on the menu item that read *Splendid Sandwich* and a page of additional information appeared. One line with the heading *Danger* had a list of small icons representing different species. One of the graphics was clearly a tiny generic portrait of a Hurc.

"See, this has something bad for me," Task said.

"Are you saying that someone profiled Hurc biology to get a list of things you can't eat, and broadcast it to every restaurant in the Spiral?"

"Yes. It's the law. Every sapient who leaves their home has to be considered."

From Task's tone, he seemed to be thinking that Miles was being dumb, or over-cautious.

With the kind of sensor technology Miles had seen in the Spiral, and with automated systems, he guessed that it could be possible.

"I don't know," Miles said, still worried. "Earth only bowered an iteration ago. They might not have updated the databases for us yet."

He started tapping through items on the menu, looking for any sign humans had been given consideration. Eventually, he found a menu item called *Lentsk-Soulorn Pie* that had a little human icon in the *Danger* section, along with a warning that the meal was a "category T" threat to human health.

There were no further details on exactly which ingredients made it bad for him—privately, he suspected the lentsk—but he guessed that as long as they were all properly tested then he didn't need to know.

"So if something doesn't have a species warning, it's safe for that species?" he asked.

"Yes, I think so. Unless you're very sensitive."

"How many people do they profile to work out what we can eat, do you think?"

How common was lactose intolerance on Earth? How common was a shellfish allergy? Had they really *caught everything?*

"I don't know," Task said. He was already tapping out an order on the menu. "Enough, I think."

Miles caught a glimpse of the other mage's order. *Rockberry Thick Liquid*.

He struggled with his own menu for a minute, then ordered a *Baked Yurrelo* and a glass of water.

When he focused on the word *yurrelo*, his *Eyes of the Émigré* gave him the vague impression of a starchy purple root. He was pretty sure it was a plant, and since there were hardly any species listed in the danger section, it had to be pretty inoffensive.

His whole order came to twelve seln, so even if it killed him, at least it was cheap.

The menu responded to their orders by giving them each an ETA, six minutes for Task, ten for Miles, and they stacked the transparent sheets back on the pile.

With the food order placed, they were left awkwardly looking at each other.

Miles stared at Task's face for a few seconds before saying, "Would it be rude to go on my index?"

Task clasped his hands together. "No. I understand."

Miles spent a few seconds assessing Task's expression, judging whether he really meant it, then pulled the index from his cargo pants pocket.

Four taps later, he had pulled up the list of possible spell upgrades.

Spells—Alterations
+*Dance of Harmony* [δ150]
A weft of harmonizing energy takes up residence in the weaver, spreading out into their surroundings. Visible beings of the weaver's choice will gain the aspect of harmony while the spell is maintained, increasing their precision and reactions by an amount proportional to the weaver's Authority.
+*Strings of Discord* [δ125]
A weft of harmonizing energy reaches out to touch discordant presences nearby, revealing their presence and Authority to the weaver.
+*Purify* [δ125]
A temporary weave of harmonizing energy takes up residence in the target, degrading objects and substances inimical to the target's existence over time.
+*Convict the Disharmonious* [δ415]
The weaver's connection to universal harmony allows them to prosecute a target with an accusation of discord. If the weaver succeeds in a contest of reason, Will, and Authority, the target is diminished and is revealed as disharmonious.

+*Song of Harmony* [δ400]
A temporary matrix of harmonizing energy fills a space, allowing those within to experience the peace of a harmonious world. Chaotic emotions are soothed and Harmonizer spells are empowered within the space.

+*Enhance Tool* [δ380]
A lasting matrix of harmonizing energy affixes to an object, enhancing one of its fundamental properties by an amount in accordance with the weaver's Authority and the item's harmony.

>*Close Wound* → *Seal Wounds* [δ275]
A weft of harmonizing energy brings together the free edges of a target's wounds, sealing closed a specific tear, or working to seal all tears.

Core Effect—Alterations

+*Stance of Authority* [δ150]
The weaver's existence is more deeply tied to the ancient tradition of the Harmonizers, giving them an instinctive understanding of harmony and discord. Their Authority will grow in line with their dignity and the harmony of their existence.

+*Ears of the Diplomat* [δ250]
Words spoken in falsehood will ring the gong of truth. A persistent weave of harmonizing energy will alert the weaver to spoken deceptions, piercing guile to an extent related to the weaver's Authority.

+*Eyes of the Imperious* [δ410]
Embeds a matrix of harmonizing energy within the being's mind, helping them to identify the disharmony of their surroundings with greater distinction.

Miles devoured the list of potential purchases.

In addition to the potential upgrades he'd passed on last time, his higher amount of delta had revealed five new options, four spells and one core effect.

Convict the Disharmonious and *Eyes of the Imperious* were both a little obtuse. After rereading the descriptions a few times, he got the impression that both would alter the kinds of targets that he found disharmonious or discordant.

Convict the Disharmonious promised to let him "convict" a neutral target of disharmony, presumably making it a valid target for *Strike the Disharmonious*. *Eyes of the Imperious* sounded like it might have a similar effect, but he couldn't quite tease its meaning apart. What did "greater distinction" mean in that context?

Both seemed a little tangential for what he was trying to do with the tradition, so he easily ruled them out.

Song of Harmony was another spell intended to affect his own magic, but this one seemed more straightforward. It would boost the effectiveness of his other spells, though he didn't know whether that meant they'd be more efficient in how they drew on his Authority, or if they'd just be more powerful, or more powerful *and* more tiring. It seemed like an interesting backup choice, but there were too many unknowns for him to jump at it.

Enhance Tool was so interesting he almost bought it straight away. It seemed like it offered a way to let him cast *Temporary Enhancement* on equipment, and in a way that would last more than just a few minutes. The applications were obvious. He could enhance the Durability of Torg's breastplate and his own robe, at least. What would happen if he enhanced an object's Strength or Speed, or its Authority? The potential for experimentation was almost as attractive as the uses he could think of straight away.

Only the fact that another option overshadowed it gave him pause.

Seal Wounds. This one looked like the next stage of *Close Wound*. A spell that could treat all of a person's cuts and punctures simultaneously. It was the answer to internal injuries, which Miles currently had no way to deal with, and it seemed like something that a mage healer really *needed* to have.

Dance of Harmony and *Song of Harmony* both seemed better suited to the surveiler role—the person who would stand in the overwatch position and support their team with performance-enhancing effects. *Convict the Disharmonious* and *Strike the Disharmonious* were probably better as spells for a fusilier than a healer. And *Strings of Discord* would really only benefit a scout.

He had five hundred delta, and the only responsible choices were *Purify* and *Seal Wounds*.

He purchased them before he could change his mind, along with an additional upgrade to his Authority.

He felt the magical core of the index spin up, touching the center of his own body with its needles of electrical energy, and then it faded away.

When Miles checked his index again, his choices were all listed as new parts of his repertoire.

With *Purify, Hasten Renewal,* and *Seal Wounds,* he was actually starting to feel like a real healer. That trio of spells seemed to cover any injury he might come across on a dive. They could potentially carry him for his entire healing career. That meant his next choice could be something just for him.

Maybe that should wait until my next payday.

The two thousand seln he had left felt like a lot to him, but without knowing how lucky he'd really been during their last dive, he didn't know how long it would need to last.

Task had been watching Miles politely during the entire process, his tuft of hair a little on end and in disarray, his bottom fangs pushed up over the outside of his upper lip.

Miles put his index away and began engaging Task in awkward, stumbling conversation.

After a few minutes of small talk Miles had learned Task's basic history, that he'd been born on the Hurc home planet of Guriy, Iteration 26,858, where he was at first sponsored by his father, then disowned by him. He'd been brought to Ialis by a family friend, but she'd been summoned for military service and had been forced to leave. Task had been a talented index mage, like Miles, and had found a place in the Dendril City Enclave, where his basic needs and training were taken care of in exchange for some basic service.

Miles shared some of his own history, but he couched it in descriptions that didn't get to the heart of his problems. His family had been criminals, as he explained it, and he'd fled the settlement they owned so that he wouldn't be forced into the family business.

It didn't quite touch the complexities of what Earth had become following the chaos of the bower break. Could there really be criminals, when most of the world was still in a state of anarchy? Was it fair to describe his family as criminals or bandits, when most surviving settlements were ruled by those who'd been fastest to employ violence and intimidation to seize power?

He didn't need to put those questions on Task, not when they'd only just met.

Eventually, their meals came. Task's was a pudding-like substance served in what could have passed for a banana-split dish back on old Earth. Miles's choice came in a bowl, a thick-skinned vegetable, split open like a roast potato, with a few bowls of toppings alongside it.

He was hesitant to try it at first, but at Task's encouragement, he started digging into it with the supplied spoon.

"If I start bleeding from the eyes or frothing at the mouth, get me a doctor and a lawyer, okay?"

"Okay," Task said, seriously.

Miles pushed a spoonful of the yurrelo into his mouth and chewed cautiously. It tasted sweet, which at least reassured him that it might be made of carbohydrates.

"Is it okay?" Task asked.

"I think so. It's like . . . marshmallow mashed potato?"

Task was already drinking from his dish.

Weird.

They walked together back up to the embarkation lounge. Task had fulfilled his promise and shown Miles how to purchase the delta for his upgrades, but Miles felt like something else had happened, too. He'd made a connection. Maybe he'd even pulled at a thread that would lead to a new teammate.

"Thank you for eating with me," Task said, hands clasped.

"Thanks for showing me how to order at a restaurant," Miles replied, a little embarrassed.

Before Task could say anything else, Miles's comm buzzed in his pocket. He withdrew it to find a message from Trin.

Trin > Miles
It's been long. Shady nice guy has killed you. I calling security.
Miles > Trin
Wait. No, don't. It's fine. I got some delta and we had lunch.
Trin > Miles
Stop using Miles comm shady guy. Where he is? Let him talk.

Miles stopped before the embarkation level's exit.

"Sorry, I just need to sort this out with my roommate."

"I live alone," Task said.

Miles ignored the non sequitur and went back to his comm.

Miles > Trin
It's me, Miles.
Trin > Miles
Tell me something only Miles knows
Miles > Trin
You have a black fur patch on your left foot.
Trin > Miles
Miles! Why you looking at my feet!

Satisfied he wasn't about to waste police time, or whatever the Ialis equivalent was, Miles dropped his comm back in its pocket.

He let Task call a platform for him, and within minutes, he was floating back to his apartment tower.

He kept thinking about his new spells. With *Hasten Renewal*, *Seal Wounds*, and *Purify*, he felt like he had the full set. All he needed now was another client.

PART 8

CORRUPTED SIGNALS

CHAPTER 18

A storm had hit Dendril City.

As a planet, Ialis was unusually flat. There were low hills and dips in the terrain, but there were no extremes. No mountains, no valleys. There was a water ocean hundreds of kilometers wide that Miles would have been able to wade across without getting his neck wet.

Since the planet's surface was only a thin crust on top of an immense technological construction, it didn't have the geological activity needed to produce high peaks or deep oceans, and that same consistent elevation had something to do with the intensity of the storms.

The long runaways of flat terrain would let the storms travel for thousands of miles without breaking up, swallowing local weather systems and picking up enough energy and speed that they could shut down even an advanced hub like Dendril City.

It didn't help that all of the transport platforms were open-topped.

Outside the window, the wind whipped at the buildings, lashing them with rain, pushing any floating platforms that tried to brave the weather off course. In some places, the plants growing up around the black spires had been torn away from their anchoring roots, leaving meters-long vines to flail in the air, slapping against the closest neighboring towers.

Miles enviously watched the small ships flying back and forth from the city—disks, darts, bulbous cigars—their alert lights blinking at him through the rain like passing cars. With real engines, powered stabilizers, and roofs, the ships were able to navigate the wind, coming and going from the landing pads that were otherwise invisible.

A few of the smaller ships were even flying *through* the city. Tiny personal craft, too small to carry more than three or four people, crept cautiously between towers, pausing to connect to the docking levels of different buildings.

"No that is not it," the Ankn survivor complained.

Miles took the comm unit back from the beetle-like sapient, staring at the screen dejectedly.

"The settings say Ankn," he said.

"It's not very good for me," the rescued scout replied.

The Ankn patient Miles and the others had been caring for had been awake for the last few days, and had been talking like a person for the last two of them. Her recovery seemed to involve slowly regrowing from a larval stage back to the point of being an aware and communicative sapient.

Privately, Miles was likening it to a human recovering from a severe head injury, but his patient had actually been regrowing her body. Limbs, eyes, manipulators, and wings had all grown out from what had been an almost featureless chitin body.

A couple of days before, she'd woken up briefly and asked for a comm unit so she could call her mother, then fallen back into another period of regenerative sleep. Now, she was still lying on a padded mat on their apartment floor, but she had two sets of five legs running along each side of her body, a face with eyestalks and mouth-parts like a crab, and a pair of stubby wings growing from her collar that definitely weren't big enough to let her fly.

Miles brought the comm back up, paging through the options.

The device had a number of screen presets that would tune it for the visual systems of different species. The *Ankn* setting skewed the interface to bright yellow on an indigo background, but apparently, that still wasn't good for Milli.

Milli told them she'd been as thoroughly deceived by Brisk and Captain Rhu-Orlen as the rest of them. Taken on as a scout from another refugee processing station just outside Iteration 27,145, she'd been contracted out by her clan to the captain in apparent good faith, only to be left for dead on her first dive.

Miles had started wondering how many novice salvagers the ship had run through before it had found what it was after.

On the comm, Miles found a setting for auto-configuration. He pressed a physical button to trigger it and held it in front of Milli's face.

"Can you tell me when it looks clear? It's running through some permutations."

Milli watched the screen diligently, while Miles let his gaze wander around the apartment.

It was a week since they'd moved into the apartment, and it was starting to show. They'd all made small changes to make the space a better fit for themselves.

Torg had made his resting spot in the top corner of the room official by secreting some kind of hard wax around the area, creating a cocoon of crusty yellow glass-like material.

He'd also put an equipment plate up on the wall next to the cocoon, where all of their diving equipment was now hanging, stuck to the perforated blue metal by some kind of material-agnostic magnetism that was a natural force in the weave.

Torg's breastplate, ax, and autopistol were in one corner.

The autopistol had cost Torg about a third as much seln to reload as he'd sacrificed by refusing to sell it, but he had insisted, and Miles hadn't wanted to argue against upgrading the group's firepower.

The rainbow-shimmer surface of the breastplate still showed the puncture marks made by the gun that was now its neighbor, damage that Miles hadn't been able to fix even with his improved *Seal Wounds* spell. Maybe too much of the armor had been destroyed by the impacts, or maybe the material was too inflexible for his magic to pull together. He'd seen the spell move around the torn edges of cloth, skin, and chitin before, but he'd never seen it make new material to help plug a gap.

At the opposite corner was Trin's equipment. The tall-barreled firefly pistol, his armored fabric cap, both his old scanner and his new one, and a utility belt stuffed with light sources, noisemakers, cloud pellets, and cloud dispersers.

The new scanner was meant to make Trin a lot better at his role. It had three small screens, each capable of showing a separate sensor channel, an expanded bank of control keys, and a directional transceiver that could do active scans and even mess with other tech, *if* Trin was right about knowing how to program it. It was bulkier than his last one, two feet long and meant to be worn on a strap. To Miles, it had an unfortunate resemblance to a keytar.

Miles hadn't spent much money expanding his own dive equipment. The equipment board held his holstered striker pistol, freshly recharged off the apartment's wall outlet, a little clip-on belt pouch that held some of the light-up beans Fran had used on their first dive together, and his robe, hanging like a shirt from its collar.

There were a few of his personal trinkets up there too: the dungeon's impression of a cell phone that he'd found in the forest room and the costume-jewelry ring he'd decided to stop wearing when it had started to turn his skin blue.

The robe hanging from the board had seen some improvements. Miles had found a pop-up tailor's stall in the Ishel market level, and its Morchis proprietor had sold him on the idea of tidying it up, getting the fit to work a little better for him, and reinforcing the inner lining with some kind of energy-absorbing foil.

Miles had expected the custom work to take a couple of days and a few hundred seln, but the tailor had made the changes in about two minutes with a piece of articulated tech, and had only charged him forty seln for it. They'd even replaced the temporary healer symbol on the front with a longer-lasting dyed version.

Most of the rest of his spending had been on personal clothing. He was finally out of the clothes he'd fled Earth with.

He'd ditched his shirt and cargo pants, replacing them with a pair of tapered black pants and a long-sleeved white shirt. His threadbare sweater had been swapped for a loose, thigh-length jerkin made of dark red fabric, and to help cope with the frequent rain he'd added a dirt-brown cloak to his wardrobe, cut to local Ialis fashion and made from hydrophobic plant fibers.

He felt a little overdressed in the apartment, but he was hoping it was the kind of outfit he'd be comfortable wearing to Thouco Tower.

The loss of storage from losing his cargo pants worried him, but he'd bought a few belt pouches to try and make up for it.

"Oh, there it is. I see it now," Milli said, little eyes bobbing on the end of her eyestalks.

Miles pressed the button that froze the fine-tuning process, and another tap saved the setting. He passed the device to Milli's grasping hands with a smile. She took it and brought it up to her face, staring intently at the screen.

"It is searching. It is searching. It has found me! Ugh, so many messages. Delete, delete, delete."

"Are you going to contact your family?" Miles asked.

"Yes, I am. I will say, *'Mama. I am talking to you from the hill of the dead! Oooh.'*"

"Or maybe, 'Hey mom, just wanted to let you know I'm alive . . .'"

"*The hill of the deaaad. Oh no, demons, mama! The stories were true!*"

"Maybe *I* should message her."

"No. I will write it. But we should touch now."

Miles pulled his comm from the pouch on his belt—*it's still a little tight in there*, he thought—and tapped it to Milli's. The two devices communicated, sharing contact details, and then separated.

He was pulling his comm back when he stopped, seeing an unread message waiting for him on the screen.

Fran > Miles
Hey there Miles, hope you're making out alright. Listen, pal, I've got a contract to show some weekenders a weird time in the dungeon. Adventurers. Do you know what I call them? Thrill-seekers. They want to go in, kick some bugs around, and make out with some new conversation pieces. Nothing too serious. I'm thinking I'll run them through a few rooms on level three and take a chute down if we get the chance. The thing is, they want a dedicated healer on the team and they're NOT stumping up for an Ialis Corp temp. Where do they expect me to find someone on short notice, right? What would you say about signing on for a one-timer tonight? We're not planning anything daring. A simple in-out. Well, what do you say?

Is this a job?
Miles tapped out a reply.

Miles > Fran
Hey, Fran. Can my team come? What are they paying? Do they know I'm only a Tier 1 healer?

He stared at his comm, waiting for a reply. A minute passed with no new messages, and Miles was forced to face the fact that not everyone was always on top of their comm.

After another minute of waiting, the door to the apartment slid open and Trin walked through. He was still wearing his pink one-piece jumpsuit, the chest and pants covered in pockets, with his tote bag hanging from one shoulder.

"Hello Miles. Hello Milli," he said, otherwise ignoring them and heading straight to the wall on the right of the door.

He reached into his bag and started pulling out handfuls of transparent plastic sheets. *Fliers.* Each was a rectangle of printed plastic that showed a photo of a ship alongside a price and a description.

The entire wall was already dotted with promotional flyers from retailers. Weave ships, personal transports, resort holidays, and personal equipment, all beyond their ability to purchase.

Trin had never explained why he was always sticking them up there, but Miles thought it was probably aspirational, Trin's version of a vision board.

"Here's good one," he said, holding up an ad for a secondhand shuttle. "Only forty thousand."

It was a tired-looking vessel about the size of an RV, without even a euphospher drive. The ship was probably just running on upscaled levitation units.

"Maybe in a few years," Miles said, trying to sound encouraging.

Trin ignored him and turned away to finish sticking his sheets to the wall.

What is he even sticking those up with?

When Trin was done he collapsed onto the bed, grabbing one of Miles's books from the neat stack at the end and idly scrolling through it. Miles thought it was the book on Orbellius natural history he'd got from the Exchange after their last dive.

Torg returned a few minutes later. He carried a sweet, fruity smell into the apartment with him, clicking at the three of them before pulling down the sheet walls of the washing cubicle and stepping inside. A few seconds later the sound of splashing liquid started coming from the chamber, along with the faint odor of nitric acid.

The apartment was way too small for all four of them.

"We need a new place," Miles said.

Trin pointed at the flier for a five-bedroom apartment suite stuck to the wall. *A thousand seln per week. Right.*

It took several minutes for Fran to respond, and Miles didn't immediately hear the buzz when she did. He spent the time talking to Milli, only noticing the message after she'd finished telling him about all the people she'd been in touch with.

Fran > Miles
Yeah, you sound like a diver. They're not paying you, I am. I'll give you 200 seln to come with us, and that's me taking advantage of you. I'm thinking you'll accept it because you don't have anything better to do. If I'm wrong then I go to the next person on my list. For your information, that's going to be a really sketchy Purir called Desolate. Happy for you to bring anyone you want so long as it's on your dime. I'm not putting up any more seln for tag-alongs. As for the Tier 1, don't sweat it. I'm a Tier 3 healer myself.

Miles lowered his comm, thinking.

If this offer had come four days earlier when he was fresh off the Lestiel Dunverde dive, he would have turned it down. He was still sore from being burned by Rhu-Orlen's crew, and two hundred seln wouldn't have seemed worth the risk to him. Now, he was not only down to a little over two thousand seln, but it had been days since any sign of work.

He wasn't the type of person to rush into danger, or even into an awkward conversation, but when an opportunity appeared in front of him, his fear of missing out expanded until it outweighed every other fear.

The paranoid part of Miles's mind told him that this might be the last chance he ever got. Meanwhile, the logical part of his mind was justifying it.

It would be a good way for him to get experience in the dungeon, and it was a good networking opportunity. Showing Fran that he was reliable might improve his chances of getting more work from her in the future, and having her along would make it a relatively safe trip, thanks to her experience and abilities. Despite only just meeting her, she seemed up-front, and he trusted that.

He didn't need to work very hard on talking himself into it. His remaining concern was who he could take with him.

His first thought was that he'd want to bring his team, Trin and Torg. But split three ways, the two hundred seln would be less than seventy each. He wasn't sure that was worth it for any of them.

He looked up at where Trin was reading.

"Trin, do you want to come on a dive with me for sixty seln?"

"For six hundred seln?"

"Sixty."

"No."

"It'll be good experience, I think," Miles persisted. "It would be with Fran San-san-quirren from the dive last week and a bunch of adventurers."

Trin's head-flaps lifted slightly for a few seconds, then flopped back down. "No. I'll stay. Don't want to miss a big-money job."

Maybe Torg?

Their lancer was in the corner of the room, now out of the shower and basking in his heat lamp. He'd been trying to find them another contract nearly every day since he'd recovered from the last dive, but he must have heard Miles making the offer to Trin, and he hadn't spoken up about wanting to go.

"Torg?" he asked, just to check.

Click. "*Tired.*"

Okay. Could I go on my own?

As soon as Miles asked himself the question, he thought of another option. *Task.* The apprentice was looking for a trip into the dungeon, and with Fran along, this could be one of the safest possible ways for him to experience it. It also meant Miles would have someone else he knew there.

Sitting on the floor next to the bed, he tried to think of any downsides.

Task could die, or I could die, or Task could turn out to be really annoying after spending more time with him, or Task could accidentally kill us all with a spell.

After a couple of minutes, Miles concluded that he didn't know the risks. He couldn't know the risks; he didn't have the experience. None of his fears or anxieties were calibrated to his current lifestyle, and so all he could do was rely on people like Fran who did have the experience, and were calibrated to the dangers involved. If she thought this was safe enough for Miles, then he could at least give Task the opportunity.

He used his comm to send the apprentice a message.

Miles > Task

Hey Task. Remember you said you were thinking of going on a dive into the artifact? Would you like to come on one with me? It would be me, one other more qualified diver, and three clients. The pay isn't great, 100 seln, but I think it's worth it to get more dungeon experience. It might be dangerous though.

He re-read it a few times, then sent it. Unlike with Fran, a message came back less than a minute later.

Task > Miles

Hello Miles. I thought you had forgotten me. Yes! I'd like to come with you very much. When do you want me? I can be ready straight away. Just give me a few moments.

Miles > Task
It would be tonight.
Task > Miles
Yes. I'm excited.

Miles > Fran
Hey Fran. Yes, I'm up for that, sign me up. I'm bringing another new scavenger with me. Let me know the time and the client species so I can read up and I'll be there. Thanks.

Fran came back promptly with a meet-up place and a time, which Miles forwarded to Task.

He turned his attention to the equipment panel on the wall. The short-notice dive wouldn't be until after dark, so he still had plenty of time to prepare.

Miles pulled his robe down over his jerkin, pushing it over his pants to hang around his thighs.

The thing had been baggy and ill-fitting when he'd bought it, but now it fit him comfortably. The thick defensive foil running along its inside gave it a little more weight and a little more shape, and made it actually feel like armor. Its new cut didn't interfere with his movements no matter how he ran or jumped around the apartment, and with his synth-fabric belt strapped around it, the robe lay snugly against his body at the waist before flaring out slightly over his legs.

He took the holstered striker down from the board and strapped it to the back of his belt, then clipped on the belt pouches holding his index, his comm, and a handful of the little light beans he'd discovered through Fran on his last dive.

He wore his runner's pack on his back with a few more miscellaneous supplies: penknife, water bottle, food packs for every biochemistry that would be represented on the dive, as well as a couple of medical reference books wrapped in the plastic sack some of his clothes had been delivered in.

Outside, the disruptive wind had eased off, but the rain was still coming down hard, so Miles threw on his new brown cloak, clipping it at his throat and pulling up the hood. When he brought the sides in front of him, the natural balance of tension in the fabric pulled together to hug his body. At least he wouldn't have to worry about arriving wet from the platform ride.

"I think I'm ready," Miles said to Trin.

Milli was taking a shower in the cubicle, and Torg had gone back out as soon as the wind had eased off.

Trin was sitting by the window, his comm held loosely in a mid-paw and his eyes obscured by the black band of a simulator. Miles didn't know if Trin was running a training simulation or watching entertainment, and he wasn't about to ask.

Trin lifted the simulator band and looked Miles up and down. "You look like you're going to romance meeting."

Miles looked down at his clothes. "You mean a date?"

"Clothes are too fancy."

"Maybe," Miles said. He'd picked them with the idea that they'd be appropriate for dives *and* for the nicer places like Thouco Tower. What did Trin want him to do, buy two sets of clothes? "I want to make a good impression on Fran and her clients."

He checked the time on his comm, then replaced it in its pouch.

"It's time for me to go."

"Goodbye Miles, my friend!" Milli called from the shower, her voice warring with the sound of the cubicle's mister.

"Bye Milli, bye Trin."

Miles pressed the access panel to open the door, which slid open.

He was just about to step out into the corridor when a familiar sound made him freeze in place.

It was a kind of tune, electronic tones playing a simple four-note song that repeated. It took a few seconds for Miles to place it, his heart beating hard for a reason he didn't immediately understand, until he turned and looked at the source.

The sound was coming from the cell phone stuck to the equipment plate. The screen was lit up with an incoming call.

Trin tore off his simulator, looking around the room until he spotted the cell phone.

"Miles your thing is singing."

"Yeah," Miles said.

"Will it explode?" Trin asked.

Instead of answering, Miles stepped back into the room, letting the door close behind him, and slowly approached the equipment panel. He took one step toward it, then another.

The phone's screen was showing a distorted face, the mockery of a contact's info screen, with a vaguely human head that looked like it had been smeared into the top right corner of the photo by an oily thumb. Where the contact name would be displayed on a real Earth cell phone, there was only an unintelligible mess of lines.

He looked at Trin's concerned face. He didn't think Trin really knew what was happening. Miles wasn't sure *he* knew what was happening.

He pulled the phone off the panel and pressed the off-color *accept* button.

He didn't want to hold the phone up to his ear, but was working off muscle memory at this point.

"Hello?" he said.

"Hi, honey," a voice on the phone said.

It sounded like a woman in her twenties, speaking English with an American accent.

"Hi, who is this?" Miles asked.

"I'm stopping at the store on my way home. Do you need anything?"

"No, I'm good, but who is this?" Miles asked. "How are you calling me?"

The woman laughed. *"You want that? You want **that**? Well, okay, honey."*

"I don't want anything. Hello? Is this a robocall?"

"You know I love you. I love all my children. Anyway, I'll be there soon."

The call ended with a beep, and the screen went blank.

Miles tried to turn the phone back on, pressing the screen, pressing everything that looked like a button, but it remained dead. It was as if it had never been turned on to begin with.

"Did that thing talk at you?" Trin asked.

Miles didn't answer. He felt shaky. He hadn't recognized the woman on the call. He doubted there even *had* been a woman on the call. This *had to* be like the other things they'd seen in the dungeon; the audio version of a sleeping bag with no openings.

I bet it wasn't even connecting to anything, Miles told himself. *It was just playing back made-up audio that was on the phone when it was manufactured, or however the dungeon creates things. It was just acting like a cell phone acts.*

Miles found that explanation comforting. Not comforting enough to bring the phone with him, though. He left it in a bundle of his old clothes, stuffed into the corner of the room.

Despite the shock of the call, he still had an appointment to keep. He tightened his cloak, left the apartment, and took the elevator to the departure level.

CHAPTER 19

Miles was late for the meeting.

As his platform touched down at the entrance facility, he could already see Fran waiting by the check-in structure. The three people with her were looking increasingly annoyed as she spoke to them using a lot of mid-paw gestures.

Task was there as well, standing well away from Fran and her adventurers, looking desolate and confused, and apparently not knowing which party he was meant to be joining.

Miles's platform had barely touched the ground before he was off it, running toward Task.

He paused just long enough to speak to him.

"Hi, Task. Sorry I'm late. We just need to be over there." Miles gestured toward Fran, then started heading in that direction.

Task fell in behind. "Apologies. I didn't mean to be here before you."

"No, it's okay. I'm late. I got held up."

Miles checked Task over as they hurried to the gathering point.

He noticed that the apprentice had made some preparations for the dive.

He was still wearing his skirt of woven brown fabric, but he was now also wearing a piece of iron-gray armor across his stomach and a pair of metal bracers, and he was carrying a round wooden shield the size of a dinner plate.

From his studies, Miles knew that the main Hurc heart was in the lower abdomen, where the stomach would be in a human. It was relatively unprotected, only covered by a plate of hard fibrous cartilage, and he wasn't surprised to see Task wearing partial armor that protected the area.

There were probably limited threats that could be stopped by a wooden shield, but that was Task's business. The apprentice didn't seem to be carrying any weapons.

Fran turned to look at them as they approached, focusing on Miles.

"Glad you made it," she said sardonically.

Fran San-san-quirren looked the same way as the last time Miles had seen her, a gray-furred Eppan woman wearing a black synth trench coat over a garish yellow jumpsuit, the whole outfit covered in belts, straps, and small clip-on bags.

The pair of wildly different pistols Miles knew she carried were out of sight inside her coat, but she'd added a new weapon to her collection, a compact wide-barreled weapon like a stubby rifle that hung from the side of her backpack.

"Sorry," Miles said, to Fran, but also including Task in the apology. "I didn't realize so many platforms would be out of order from the storm. It took a while to get service."

"Well, I guess you'll know next time." Fran turned to her clients and gestured at Miles for their benefit. "This is Miles, the healer I lined up for you all. I've dived with him before, he can patch up all your cuts and scrapes and whatnot. If it's anything serious, let me know, and I'll see what I've got in this old bag of tricks."

Her group was made up of three humanoid sapients of the same species. Fran's message had said they were called "The First People of Ashalai," but in his medical books, they were just referred to as the Alpha Ashalai.

Each of them had two arms and two legs, as well as thick tails that swept down and rested on the floor. They were all hairless, and had faintly patterned skin that ranged from cloud-white to sand-yellow. With large eyes and only a pair of raised slits in place of a nose, they couldn't have passed for human, but they were closer than ninety percent of Spiral species.

Their biology was reassuringly familiar, too.

They were a biochemistry C-13 species, which was basically C with a long list of exceptions. They had active blood vessels instead of a heart, but they had a stomach, a lung, and a liver-like accessory organ. The Alpha Ashalai also had an internal sense organ Miles wasn't able to get the gist of, and three confusing multifunctional blobs, but they were basically Miles's biological neighbors.

"Hi," Miles said to them. "I'm Miles, a Tier 1 healer. I'll be helping manage healing for Fran. This is my friend Task. He's a mage, too."

"Hello," Task said.

Fran pointed at them in order, starting with the tallest, yellow-skinned sapient, followed by the two smaller members of the group.

"Rolian, Sailish, Lanet. I got that right?" she said.

"Yes, greetings," Sailish said, seeming a little put off by Fran's tone.

Their species had a triple gender division, and it looked like all three were represented in the group.

Rolian was over six feet, with pale yellow skin and curling horns the color of burned charcoal. He was wearing soft fabric clothing that reminded Miles of a judo gi and a sling bag that hung at his back. There was a brass medallion dangling around his neck, covering enough of his chest that Miles wondered if it was a kind of armor, and he was armed with a straight sword that was almost as long as he was tall.

The black blade of the sword looked like it had been cut from some kind of giant insect.

Sailish was a little shorter, at about six feet. She had no horns, only a pair of blunt bony protrusions. Her white skin seemed to flow into the layered garment she wore, something like a long scarf that was wound around her body and secured with strategically placed pins. On her left hip, she wore a long dagger and a short dagger, and there was a harness on her back holding some kind of long, uncomplicated rifle with a yellow metal barrel.

The third member of the group was the shortest of them, at around five feet tall with white skin. They wore same attire as Sailish. Lanet had no horns, just smooth skin on the sides of their head, and they didn't seem to be carrying any equipment. As Miles inspected them, they also seemed to be humming with magic.

Miles didn't recognize their tradition. To his senses, it felt like a bright star, hot and dense.

Lanet's eyes snapped to Miles a moment after he sensed their magic, and the expression didn't seem particularly friendly.

If they were average members of their species, then Rolian was a male, Sailish was a woman, and Lanet was the third gender. Miles's anatomy text had made it clear that an Alpha Ashalai's physical markers of horns and height weren't always accurate to their real gender, so he'd need to listen for a while to confirm his blunt first-glance assessment.

"We were in time for the start of the cycle, but let's see," Fran said.

They passed through the entry procedures quickly, and were on a platform floating over the crater within a handful of minutes.

The rain misting their transport platform seemed to dampen Fran's spirits, and it put Miles in the same mood, but there was some light conversation as they queued down to their level three entry point.

"The battles this world offers are legend," Rolian said, gesturing at the landscape around them. "Hordes of creatures, a king's ransom in treasures. Tell me, Fran, have you fought any worthy foes down here?"

"Oh? Sure, a few," Fran replied. Miles thought she was humoring him. "When you get down below about level thirty, the spaces get bigger and the critters living down there do too. You only need to run into a *craver* once before you start feeling different about underground lakes." Miles tried to ignore the terrifying image for a *craver* conjured by *Eyes of the Émigré*.

Sailish spoke up next. "On the moon of Red-Waiting we faced a Mist Corrupter. It was plaguing one of the cities of the Second People, and we alone had the fortitude to face it down. Rolian dealt it a decisive blow, and I pierced its brain with a shot from my sky-forged fire lance."

Miles looked from Rolian's sword to Sailish's rifle. The rifle seemed like it might incorporate Spiral tech, but neither were particularly advanced compared to Fran's pistol or even his own striker.

"What kind of tech base do you have on Ashalai?" he asked, hoping it wasn't a rude question.

If he was guessing right about the kind of society they came from, then he wasn't sure what kind of answer he'd get, but he trusted whatever translation tools they were using to bridge the communication gap.

Sailish gave no sign that she was offended. "We lacked the means to visit even our closest moons before the Ending and the arrival of visitors from the sky. Now we have access to sky-forged tools and weapons, which we use to assist our mages."

No advanced technology, Miles guessed. He'd known in advance that there were some cultures in the Spiral who'd bowered without having significant levels of tech, but they were rare, and he'd never encountered anyone from one of them before.

"It was nigh on one hundred years ago that the skywyrms came, bringing their philosophy and technology," Rolian said wistfully.

"Gilthaens," Fran corrected.

"Ashalai was never the same," the man went on. "How petty our problems seemed. Wars, villains, saints, all of it. We were cast as children in a play that stretched beyond the heavens."

"How did your world even have a bower break, if you didn't have technology?" Miles asked.

On Earth, the prevailing theory was Earth's bower had been the result of large-scale zero-point energy extraction, but the cause differed from iteration to iteration. Some worlds knew for certain that a specific grand technological project or astronomical event had triggered the collapse.

Sailish spoke up to reply. "Our historians think it was the fault of Lord Daivish the Sinister. At the time of the Ending, he had construed a new magic, one that he hoped would allow him to move an entire army across continents and drop them directly into his enemy's strongholds."

"Subspace tunneling, most like," Fran said, staring off into the drizzle. "Mess with the fabric and you're liable to get tears."

"The scar of his spell still mars our world today," Sailish said. "A ravine of chaotic land through which no living thing can pass."

"Yeah, you fucked with your space alright," Fran muttered.

"I'm glad it happened," Lanet said into the silence that followed. Her tone sounded bitter.

Rolian and Sailish shot Lanet shocked glances, but didn't respond.

"We didn't know it, but we were small," Lanet went on. "We're still small. When we measure ourselves against the stars, we have our chance to be better."

"Uh-huh," Fran said. "We're coming up on our entrance now."

The platform touched down inside a corridor that jutted from the crater wall like an outflow pipe from a house. There was just enough space for the circular disk to lodge in the corridor, and they all stepped off.

There was a door blocking the way, but it wasn't even locked. Fran opened it with a single tap of its access panel.

The first few rooms they passed through looked like hangars, wide open spaces with concrete floors and ribbed metal ceilings fifty meters or more above them.

There were no ships or personal transports, unfortunately.

Fran identified some tanks as holding *reduction* fuel, but the kind of ships that burned it weren't common and it was dangerous to store, so she said it wasn't worth salvaging.

They broke open an equipment cabinet that turned out to contain rebreather devices for type-B biochemistry which Fran quickly bagged for resale, and a row of lockers that held flight suits that looked designed for geometrically impossible beings. They left them alone, Miles feeling slightly unnerved.

Toward the back of the third hangar, they found a trolley full of levitation units that Rolian declared they should divide up between them.

Fran made what Miles assumed was a rude gesture behind her back with a mid-paw, out of his sight, but she didn't argue with Rolian giving away the salvage. Miles thought they probably weren't worth enough to argue about it.

The levitation units were low-powered versions designed to attach to cargo bins, not much more than a handle bolted to a clamp, but Miles still amused himself with his as they walked, holding it at his side and seeing how much of his weight he could balance on it. Moving it around felt like dragging an unusually heavy balloon, buoyant in the air, but with the inertia of a brick.

The three large hangar rooms were connected by huge doors, big enough for moderate-sized ships to fly through, for all that there probably wouldn't ever be a ship down there, but the third hangar ended in one of the normal dungeon doors, unnecessarily tall and weirdly narrow.

"Anyone want to take a crack at this one?" Fran asked, like she was a tour guide offering to let them have a go on an interactive installation.

Task looked around at the others. When nobody stepped forward, he spoke up. "Apologies. I will try, if you don't mind?"

"Knock yourself out," Fran said.

Task stepped up to the door, looking it up and down. He brushed his hand against it, like he was feeling for something, then stepped back.

Miles felt magic growing within the apprentice almost immediately.

Like Master Oron in the Enclave, Task's magic had the feel of surging water, but while Oron's had been a wave, Task's use of the tradition felt like water bubbling up from a spring.

The apprentice raised his hand and spoke. The word seemed to rush across the room before crashing against the door.

Miles felt a complex knot of meanings in the sound. *Open* and *Yield* and *You've been closed for long enough already.*

The door mechanism stuttered for a second, like it was falling over itself to comply, and then the door rolled open.

"Okay. That works," Fran said.

She took a step forward toward the door, then stopped. Miles came up behind her, peering past her through to the next room.

Visible through the doorway was a strange cityscape.

The ground was paved in huge slabs of stone, forming roads and sidewalks that stretched out for hundreds of meters before disappearing into fog.

On either side of the road were rows of solid stone buildings four or five stories tall, with faces that were dotted with dark rectangular windows, bare and open, cut out of the stone in random sizes and at random orientations.

Doorways almost at ground level yawned open on pitch black interiors, and all Miles could see of the insides of the structures was that the walls of the room stood at odd angles.

The height of the ceiling above them was hard to guess. The ceiling—there had to be a ceiling—was lost in the mist that hung across the streets, and the only illumination came from two bright circles of light in the false sky, one white, one red.

"What in my father's name?" Rolian said, stepping through the doors into the deserted city.

Sailish and Lanet followed next, not waiting for instruction from Fran.

Miles glanced at Fran, looking for a cue on how they should proceed. She wore a concerned expression. Miles found the feeling contagious.

Task only had eyes for the chamber up ahead, staring through the door with an awed expression.

Fran stepped through a second later, moving to the front of the group as if trying to regain control of the situation.

"Yeah, impressive, isn't it," she said. None of the concern of a second ago showed in her voice. "We in the community call this an *environ*. It's probably some real place that got reflected into the dungeon wholesale. There might be some viable salvage here, or maybe not, it'll depend on the place it's trying to copy."

"Why *does* it copy places?" Miles asked. "What's the point?"

Fran went up to one of the buildings, splitting her attention between peering through the door and reading off the screen strapped around her wrist.

"Well, that's one of the big questions of the place, isn't it. Maybe it's an automated system dreaming its way through sensor data. Or is it habitat tech trying to build us a place to live? Maybe it's some kind of physical data storage. I've read about a million theories on the caucus boards, and that's not even getting into what the *academics* think."

Their group walked a few meters further into the city. Task stayed close to Miles, sometimes leaving so little space that they bumped into each other whenever Miles stopped or slowed to look at part of the ruins.

Behind them, the door back to the hangars was set into a huge stone wall that stretched off to the left and right, disappearing into the fog that blanketed the place.

Seeing such a huge, world-enclosing wall next to a city that otherwise might look like it was outside was jarring and dizzying to Miles, like walking through a scale model built by giants.

In the lull of silence that followed, Miles switched between *Eyes of the Émigré* and *Eyes of the Altruist*, staring out into the mist as far as he could. He trusted Fran to keep them updated on their surroundings, but found it reassuring to check for himself.

"What are caucus boards?" Miles asked after a few seconds, following Fran as she hopped up onto the ledge of an almost-ground floor window.

Fran peered inside, saw something that interested her, and hopped through. Miles clambered up to the window after her.

She was going for a long stone coffin-like box positioned toward the back of the chamber.

Feeling the knot in his stomach rise briefly to his throat, Miles checked the box with *Eyes of the Altruist*, but the magic didn't reveal any glowing lights other than Fran.

"What was that?" she said absently, looking down at the box. "Oh. The caucus. Sure. It's a multi-user comm exchange. You can send messages, start topics, ask questions. If anyone knows and they're feeling charitable, they can answer. There should be one under 'Ialis Caucus' if you're searching on the Exchange."

An internet forum? Miles thought.

Fran grabbed the top of the stone chest and pushed, sliding the top a few inches to the side. She peered through the gap into the interior.

"Huh."

"What is it?" Miles asked.

Out in the street, their clients were inspecting some kind of collapsed obelisk, a rectangular pillar of stone that looked like it had been standing at a street corner, but was now lying across the road.

In the room, Fran pushed the lid the rest of the way off, sending it tumbling to the ground with the sharp thump of dropped stone.

She reached into the chest and lifted out what looked like a flat rectangle of metal, four feet long and maybe six inches wide. It was a dull copper color, reflecting the light from the window, but not showing any reflection.

"Huh," Fran said again.

She manipulated the piece of metal in her hands, turning it, putting stress on it. Finally, she put the piece down on the edge of the chest and turned her attention to the device on her wrist. She spent a minute operating it.

"I can't find this metal's profile in the database. Weird one. This is worth taking, I think."

Miles leaned back out of the window, calling to the group of Ashalai, who were arguing next to the obelisk.

"Hey! Hey, sorry to interrupt. We have some potential salvage in here."

The three sapients looked at each other, but only Lanet broke away to come to the building. They hopped up and through the window.

Miles scanned the city with *Eyes of the Altruist* before turning back to look inside the building.

Fran hefted a bundle of the short metal planks, standing them against the wall.

Lanet approached, pulling a piece from the stack onto its edge. She lifted it a few inches off the ground, showing obvious strain, before putting it back down with the others.

"What are they for?" Lanet asked.

"Likely not 'for' anything," Fran said. "They're here as a mistake, like as not, or a messed up version of something that made more sense in the real place. Seems strong though, reckon it's going to be worth something as scrap."

Fran had a coil of synth fiber rope hanging from her pack. She unclipped it as she spoke and started tying it around the bundle of scrap. She wrapped it at both ends, leaving a long piece between the two knots that she slipped over her shoulder when she came to pick it up. The weight didn't seem to bother her at all as she performed a quick but fruitless search of the rest of the building.

Task watched Fran bundle the planks up in silence. At one point when she seemed to be struggling he looked like he was about to step forward and help, but hesitated, looking back at Miles. Then he went back to his position at Miles's side.

Back on the street, they met back up with Rolian and Sailish.

"Rolian believed this was a territory marker for groups living in the city," Sailish said, indicating the collapsed obelisk. "Unfortunately the meaning of the text eludes us."

Fran spent no more than a second scrutinizing it. "Doesn't mean much to be, either, It's something that got messed up in the copy, I'd guess."

The faces of the obelisk were engraved with a border of blocky geometric text that ran around the outside of each side. It had cracked horizontally at some point, interfering with Miles's translation ability, but part of the text was still readable.

Ymn Quarantine Zone - Ymn Quarantine Zone - Ymn Quarantine Zone

"It's the same phrase over and over," Miles said in the silence. "Ymn Quarantine Zone. Ymn would be the name of the city, I think?"

Task crouched by the obelisk, running his hand across the engravings, like he had with the door.

"Huh. Wonder what was happening in the original place. My language pack's pretty good, so it must've been somewhere off the map." Fran stopped speaking suddenly, and spent a minute working on the scanner strapped to her wrist. She looked up. "Just checking for reflected pathogens. This place is pretty sterile."

They left the obelisk behind, continuing to walk through the city.

Having seen the stone chest in the house, Fran was able to calibrate her scanners to look for them, and she led them to four more as they wandered through the deserted cityscape.

One of them had been empty, but two held sheets of a dull silver fabric of a size and shape that made Matt think they might have been alien tents, or maybe uncut sheets that were meant to be refined later on.

The fabric also had properties that interested Fran, and they'd bundled them up into rolls that Miles and Task had been burdened with.

As they walked, Miles let his mind wander to the events of that morning. He was still thinking about the fake call on the cell phone-like device he'd found in the forest room, and Fran seemed like she'd seen enough of the dungeon to have an opinion on it.

After the last stone chest that Fran had been able to locate, Miles found a chance to leave Task's side and move up beside Fran.

He matched pace with her and spoke in a low voice.

"Hey, Fran? Have you ever got a call from a dungeon comm device?" Miles asked.

"What the hell are you talking about?" Fran replied.

Miles felt a little shocked at her tone. Something about the strange stone city seemed to be making her irritable. She was distracted, splitting her attention between the party ahead of them and the city around them. Miles felt like a distant third consideration.

Having raised the topic, he kept on anyway.

"On my last run I found a replica comm device from my home planet," Miles explained. "Normally they make calls, send messages, normal comm stuff, but this one was dead. I thought it was just a mangled piece of tech. I heard the dungeon makes things like that sometimes."

"Yeah, so it does," Fran said. "They look like they could be the real thing, but you'll open them up, and the insides will be all messed up. Screen wired straight into batteries, components stuck into the case, weird non-tech stuff plugged into ports . . ."

"Well, I got a call on this one."

Fran didn't seem too interested. "Okay, then it works. I'll bet it's picking up signals from another device."

"That's..."

Miles struggled with how to explain the depth of how unlikely that was. As far as Miles knew, he was the first human on Ialis, and even if he wasn't, nobody else was going to be bringing a cell phone out here. A lot of advanced pre-bower electronics wouldn't even work properly outside of Solar space.

"They're not like Spiral comms," Miles said. "They don't work on their own. They need radio towers and computers we don't have out here. There's no way it could be picking up just some random signal."

The cell phones of old Earth had a range measured in tens of miles. He wasn't picking up signals from a planet trillions of miles away.

Fran seemed extremely uninvested, either because she had a low opinion of Miles, or because something about the dive had put her in the wrong headspace to feel curious about it.

"Kid, with the tech Ialis makes, we just don't know how these things work."

Miles was still conflicted between giving up or making another effort to convince her that it wasn't normal.

He was just about to try again when a noise rang out from somewhere to their left.

A long, pure, brassy note, like a horn, but with enough minor variation to sound somehow biological. Halfway between an air raid siren and whalesong.

The entire group stopped, turning to look in that direction.

There were places where the streets cut through buildings, but none of the spaces lined up, and all they could see were rooftops.

"What was that?" Sailish asked. She sounded excited.

Miles thought that excitement was the exact opposite of what they should be feeling after hearing something like that in a place like the dungeon.

Fran looked spooked. That upset Miles as much as the noise. She was meant to be an experienced, self-reliant diver.

"That's our signal to leave, I reckon," Fran said.

"Leave?" Rolian said. "But we only just arrived."

"That we have, but this place has started reminding me of a story I heard once, and I don't like that sound at all."

"What story?" Lanet asked, speaking for the first time in several minutes.

The trumpet sound came again. It was closer, and it'd changed direction.

The wall with their entrance was still just visible through the mist behind them, a vast barrier of stone, and the source of the noise sounded like it was getting closer to it.

"Tell you what, walk out with me now and we can reschedule this one, free of charge," Fran said. speaking to the party. "Doesn't feel like a good day for diving any deeper."

She started walking back in the direction of their entrance. She'd drawn her silver pistol, and was looking across the city to the right, in the direction of the sound.

Miles shared a look with Task. The apprentice looked calm and placid, in contrast with how Miles felt, but Miles met his eyes and saw agreement. They both started following after Fran.

Miles looked back as they set off. Their clients were conferring behind them, not yet committed to leaving.

He spent a few seconds wrestling with whether it was more important to stay and look after the clients, or to listen to Fran as his employer, or to prioritize his own safety in the face of the obviously correct decision to leave. He picked the second option, obeying Fran, though if she weren't there, he suspected that he might have picked the latter.

After about twenty seconds of deliberation, the adventurers apparently decided Fran was right and started following, quickly catching up.

"What story?" Miles asked as he came alongside Fran, repeating Lanet's question.

Fran glanced at him before replying. "About a fixed location. A room with stone buildings that doesn't get recycled. I've heard it called the Ruins. The story was something about a deep diver's team getting killed off, and him being the only one escaping. You get a lot of ghost stories from the deeper levels. It's just old-timer talk, but I do well by being cautious."

A moment later, Miles caught sight of something moving beyond the buildings up ahead. A glimpse of gray skin on something tall enough to be seen over the twenty-foot-high rooftops.

The top of a head?

"There's something—" Miles started.

"I see it," Fran said, interrupting.

Behind and to the left of Miles, magic surged up, and he turned in time to see Task casting a spell. This time when the energy surged, the word he spoke seemed to wash out over all of them.

Miles was pretty sure that the word meant *"Endure," "Rebound,"* and *"Against strength, defense is fair."*

The brassy, piping call came again, just as the thing stepped out into the street ahead of them.

Tall but no more than a foot wide, it had corpse-gray skin stretched over its entire body, a pair of legs as thin and bony as Miles's wrists jointed in several places at different angles, and a head like a deformed pencil eraser. There were horizontal slits down the left side of its head, like vents or gills, opening on a black space beneath its face. It didn't have any other features. No arms, no clothes, no mouth.

As it came into view it blasted another trumpet note that made Miles's insides feel like water.

"Let's find another route outta here," Fran said sternly, turning the group and heading back in their original direction.

Miles and Task followed without urging.

"It's monstrous," Sailish shouted behind them.

Fran, Task, and Miles were running headlong away from the thing. Miles cast a look backward at the others, and slowed to a stop. Their clients weren't following.

"Fran," he called. When she glanced back he pointed at the stationary adventurers.

Rolian had taken a stand, his sword drawn, his back straight. He stared at the thing like he was challenging it.

Sailish was there too, her rifle drawn and aiming down the open street.

"Ah, hell." Fran brought them to a stop, raising and aiming her pistol at the thing.

Lanet was the only one of the three adventurers running. They came to a stop by Fran, their shoulders trembling.

In this distance, Miles could just hear Rolian shouting.

"Come! Test your strength against me."

The tall creature was already advancing on the Ashalai, though Miles didn't think that had anything to do with the challenge.

It moved in stop-start motions, bursts of scuttling speed separated by seconds of motionless silence.

When it reached where Rolian was standing, he swept his sword at it in a low slice, aiming to cut through its lowest joints.

The second the sword touched the thing, the weapon vanished from Rolian's hands. There was a loud cracking sound in the same instant. The ruins of a black sword, now nothing but fragments, had perforated the stone wall of a nearby building.

Rolian staggered backward, unbalanced from his weapon being knocked out of his hands at insane speeds.

Sailish took aim with her rifle and fired. A forking beam of yellow light emerged from the barrel, spearing through the air toward the towering figure. The beam hit, and then glanced off. The reflected light scorched holes through stone walls before Sailish let the beam end and lowered the gun.

The spindly giant took a step forward and made contact with Rolian.

The same thing that had happened to his sword happened to the man, except that the pieces didn't travel as far.

The giant kept moving, faster, scuttling through the cone-shaped smear of purple that now decorated the road, leaving purple footprints on the street as it headed straight for Sailish.

Sailish made a wailing noise as she turned to run.

Miles was already running. Fran and Lanet were around him, Lanet quickly outpacing them, with Task a little way behind, apparently struggling in the straight sprint.

Task had dropped the roll of cloth he'd been carrying as well as the shield he'd brought with him, but he was still flagging.

Fran stopped for a second, giving him a chance to catch up while she aimed her pistol at the giant.

Miles slowed with her. He didn't think his striker would do anything against the monster, but he let himself fall into *Eyes of the Altruist*. At the same time, he concentrated on bringing up the ringing tone of *Strike the Disharmonious*.

Nothing.

The giant didn't seem to have any internal structure at all. Either it wasn't alive, or it was opaque to the magic.

Strike the Disharmonious also failed. He managed to bring the note of the spell up, but when he focused on the giant, he didn't hear harmony or disharmony; the sound disappeared completely, and only returned when he looked away.

Fran lined up her shot and fired. The thin beam of energy was right on target, piercing the giant's head, but it didn't seem to have any effect. The shot wasn't reflected this time, but the giant continued its scuttling stop-start motion forward.

Fran resumed running, tapping on her scanner bracelet even while her feet were drumming against the ground.

"I can see a way down," she said through heavy breathing. "We'll drop down a level and find a route to that level's exit."

Sounds good, Miles thought. In that moment, almost any alternative would have sounded good.

The giant took a step and was suddenly thirty meters ahead of where it had been. It had made a jump that was too fast to see, or it had some other way of moving. It did it again a few seconds later, now no more than a stone's throw behind them.

Task was struggling with the escape the most out of all of them. Dropping behind, Miles focused on summoning his magic for *Temporary Enhancement*. He put his hand against the small of Task's back as he recalled the litany.

In himself, he is complete. In a Harmonious world, he is allowed to remain complete. **He is that which he is.**

Miles focused on Task's Speed, the ability of his body to respond and react quickly. He imagined that ability being taken to the logical conclusion, being made into a paragon of itself, and willed that truth through the hot energy that splashed across the mage's back.

Task took off as if Miles and the others were standing still. He quickly pulled out ahead, then realized how much progress he was making, and glanced back for direction.

As they'd sprinted through the city, the buildings had changed slightly. They were no longer entirely open. Windows were covered in meshes of the same coppery metal that Fran was still carrying on her shoulder. The doorways were now blocked by doors, rectangles of the metal that ended in curved peaks.

Fran was pointing at a closed door ahead of them.

Task was the first to reach it, running into it with the expectation it would swing open, then bouncing off when it remained shut. He strode back up to the door, squaring off against it, and Miles felt magic rising in him.

Task had his opening spell cast in the time it took the rest of the group to reach him. When the word reached the door, it didn't swing open so much as fall inward.

They all fell through the doorway into the darkened interior of the room behind.

Miles paused, resting against the interior wall, breathing heavily and wondering if *Hasten Renewal* would help him recover from being winded.

He glanced back out of the door and let out a choked scream when he saw the giant was less than five feet away from them, just outside.

"Down the chute," Fran ordered, pointing at a section of the room where the floor seemed to disappear at the far wall, leaving a deep, black passage dropping away at a nearly vertical angle.

Miles ran up to it, looking down. "You're joking."

Instead of answering, Fran grabbed the levitation unit she'd salvaged from the hangar rooms, flipped the switch, and dove feet-first down the hole.

Lanet went next, flaring with a starburst of unfamiliar magic, before she disappeared into the dark.

Miles and Task were left standing at the top of the chute. Rolian was dead. Sailish was missing, and they couldn't go back for her now. Miles looked Task up and down as he struggled to get his levitation unit free from his belt.

"Do you have your lev unit?"

"Apologies! I dropped it."

Miles flipped the switch of his, feeling it hum to life with its unnatural lift.

"Okay. Hold on to me, I guess."

Task wrapped his arms around Miles's shoulders, while Miles held as tightly to the device as he could and stepped out over the edge.

They'd only fallen a few meters when the door struck the stone wall above them with a sound like thunder. The wall exploded with the speed of the impact, fragments of rock raining down on them, followed by the metal door itself.

Miles had no way to protect himself. Rocks struck his head. A corner of the door hit his shoulder as it fell past them, pulling a grunt of pain out of him.

He somehow kept hold of the levitation unit's handle.

Together, they fell. Not quickly. The levitation unit exerted a constant upward force, trying to keep them at a consistent level. Its force wasn't enough to keep both of them aloft, but it slowed their fall to the speed of a slow run.

Lanet had dropped straight down and had vanished in the darkness. Fran was nearby, descending a lot faster. The extra weight of scrap metal she still carried was probably overloading her levitation unit.

Task clung on to Miles, one arm around his shoulder and another around his back. The protective stomach plate the apprentice wore pressed into Miles through his robe, and Miles's own sweat-slicked skin must have made him a hard thing to keep hold of.

Struggling to hold both their weight, Miles focused on the *Temporary Enhancement* spell. He didn't have a way to touch himself to deliver the spell, but the Senior Harmonizer at the Enclave, Master Curious, had suggested he didn't need to.

He recited the litany to himself, focusing on his own completeness and his own strength.

At the crescendo of his core's rotation, he felt warm energy wash out from it, not along his arm, but into his body this time. The pressure on his arms seemed to lessen, and they drifted downward without any danger of Miles losing his grip.

Fran soon outpaced them, disappearing into the darkness after Lanet.

As they fell, Miles could feel Task shaking against him. The apprentice had seemed fine in the city above, but catching glimpses of his face from inches away, Miles thought he looked terrified.

Pretty soon they passed into pitch-black darkness, and Miles couldn't see even an inch in front of his face anymore.

The fall lasted what seemed like minutes. The first sign of it ending was a patch of glowing shapes far below.

Miles had switched to *Eyes of the Altruist* as soon as the light had faded. It was clear that he and Task weren't going to be doing much talking, and more importantly, he wanted to make sure they weren't falling through a spider nest, or into the maw of some kind of massive creature.

Instead, what he saw below them was a cluster of shapes he quickly identified as Fran and Lanet.

They grew larger as Miles fell, and soon he could see them with his regular vision, lit up by a bead of light that Fran had stuck to her trench coat.

The landing was rough on Miles's ankles, and Task ended up on his back, but they weren't badly hurt.

Miles bent over, breathing heavily, stretching his hands out on his thighs. Task was on his rear end, with his back to a wall.

As soon as he'd caught his breath a little, Miles looked past Fran to see where they'd landed.

The shaft had opened in a stone ceiling, dropping them onto the cliff at the end of a long, underground ravine. The narrow crack stretched out below them, mostly dark, but lit at random points by dull red glowing stones. It was cold, the damp air cutting through Miles's new clothes and fogging his breath.

It was hard to remember they were still in the artifact at all, and not in the natural underground caves of a planet.

Fran sighed, seeing Miles and Task landing safely.

"Welcome to level four," she said dryly. "We've got a minute. Take a breather. There's still two hours until the next shuffle."

Below the sheer cliff face, the dark ravine had no sign of doors, or any of the familiar dungeon construction.

Fran seemed more relaxed now, but Miles didn't feel like they could even spare a minute.

CHAPTER 20

In the ravine below them, the glowing rocks flickered like campfires. At first, Miles thought it had something to do with whatever chemical reaction was causing the glow, but when he watched one of them, he saw dark silhouettes passing in front of it.

"Who're we missing?" Fran asked, looking around at them. "Rolian. Saw him get done for myself. What about Sailish?"

"Sailish is dead," Lanet said. They were sitting on the stone floor, their legs crossed, staring at their clasped hands. At some point, something had hit their head, making a deep gash that had quickly clotted into a purple scab. "Stupid fools. Why did you treat every challenge as something you could cut your way through?"

"I'm sorry for that," Fran said, crouching by Lanet. "I don't think there was anything we could have done for them. Sometimes, down here, you run up against something you can't fight, and that's just that. You run, or you find out."

"That was always their fault," Lanet said. "Sailish longed for glory. Rolian was always desperate to prove himself. I've seen them charge in headlong a hundred times. I think I always believed it would come to this."

"There are things down there in the ravine," Miles said, crawling up to the two of them.

"Yeah. I caught a glimpse. They look like cobolts," Fran said.

"And those are?" Miles said.

He'd started feeling twitchy in the city, and that had turned to full panic when the giant appeared. Now, the adrenaline was fading, leaving him trembling. And annoyed.

"Tech critters. Old friends, compared to that thing upstairs."

Miles glanced back to the edge of the ledge. He could vaguely make out small shapes moving in the near-darkness below. They didn't look bigger than one or two feet tall, with reflective metal plates that occasionally shone with the dim red light of the rocks.

He turned to look at Lanet.

"Do you want me to heal that?" he asked, indicating the head wound.

Lanet put a hand to the injury on their forehead. "Yes. Please."

"Thanks, Miley," Fran said. "Saves me the seln on a scar patch."

Miles shuffled over to Lanet. He briefly fell into *Eyes of the Altruist*, checking them over for any less obvious injuries. He did the same for Fran and Task. Miraculously, they'd all avoided getting badly hurt in the fall or from the falling debris.

Putting his hand over Lanet's head injury, Miles fell into the litany for *Close Wound*. His core had already started spinning when he remembered he could now do better. He pulled out his index, looking for the upgraded healing spell.

Name: Miles Asher	**Traditions:** Harmonizer
Fundamental Properties:	
Strength (0)	
Durability (8/1)	
Speed (0)	
Reactions (0)	
Will (0)	
Authority (3)	
Authority (0.19)	
Spells	
Seal Wounds (Grasping)	
Temporary Enhancement (Seeking)	
Hasten Renewal (Grasping)	
Strike the Disharmonious (Adept)	
Purify (Grasping)	
Core Effects	
Eyes of the Émigré	
Eyes of the Altruist	

He'd only meant to skim the unrelated information, but he stopped when he saw his Durability. It was listed with a rating of eight.

His Strength was back to listing as zero, which made sense, since he'd let his own *Temporary Enhancement* fade, but why did he have enhanced Durability?

He thought back to the long fall down the shaft, and how the door and stones had hit him. The door was still on the ledge with them now, undamaged even after the fall. It was clearly made of the same strong, incredibly heavy metal as the planks Fran had salvaged.

He'd come out of those collisions surprisingly well, considering the weight of the metal that the door was made of. Maybe the increased Durability explained why, but where had it come from?

The spell Task had cast?

He looked at the apprentice. The word he'd used above had made it sound like a defensive spell, and Miles's index was apparently able to detect the change even from the spell of an unsupported tradition. He just hadn't thought Task was so versatile.

The other mage had been underselling himself when suggesting he might be able to make himself useful on dives.

Focusing on his job, Miles put his hand over Lanet's injury, then index-cast his new *Seal Wounds* spell with his free hand.

His magical core, already spinning, ramped up to a whirring flywheel of crackling energy.

The tear is an aberration. In a harmonious world, the many are one. The damage should revert. **Such should it be.**

Heat flashed out of Miles's hand with a burst of yellow light and an audible crackling, then a yellow-white flame flickered across the cut on Lanet's head, dissolving the purple scab and leaving unblemished skin behind.

Behind him, Fran made an appreciative whuffling sound that didn't translate, before saying, "You sure Tier 1's right for you, Miley?"

Miles shook his hand out, flexing until the new pins-and-needles feeling faded. He didn't answer Fran. Right then, he wasn't really focusing on his career. He'd be delighted if he just got out of this cave alive.

Miles turned and went to sit in front of Task next.

"Hey, Task. Are you okay?"

The other mage didn't look okay. He was sucking his tusks, his hands clasped around his knees, eyes wide and looking off into space to his right.

"What was that creature on the level above us?" he asked. His eyes didn't move from the wall.

Miles considered how to answer.

"I don't know" seemed like the exact opposite of the answer Task needed right then.

The apprentice wasn't doing okay, and while Miles was also in over his head, he was the reason the other mage was even here.

Task needed solidity, reassurance, and to feel like he hadn't just barely escaped from an abject horror. Maybe he could take a page out of Trin's book.

"It's called a Honk Boss," Miles said seriously. "They're impossible to fight, but they broadcast their location, so it's easy to get away. The others needed to run with us. As long as you run from them, you're fine."

Task finally turned to look at him. He seemed skeptical. Miles sensed that Fran was paying attention as well, but she didn't contradict him.

"Apologies. Honk . . . boss? Is that a translation fault?" Task asked.

"No, that's their real name," Miles insisted. "They're totally normal and totally well understood. There's nothing strange about them at all."

Task cocked his head to the side, and his expression changed from paralyzed tension to something closer to exasperation.

They were interrupted by a sound like a drop of water hitting a hot skillet, and a patch of rock above Miles's head exploded into dust. More hisses followed, puffs of powdered stone flying up from the corner of the ledge and raining down on them from the wall above.

It took Miles a second to realize they were being shot at.

"Everyone down!" Fran called out, following her own advice as she dove to the floor.

Miles went down with Task, pulling the mage to the ground beside him. He spent a few seconds with his cheek against the gritty stone before raising his head to try and see what was happening.

Fran was reaching into a pocket of her trench coat. After a moment of rummaging, she pulled out a small, star-shaped device, tapped it twice on the ground, then tossed it over the edge.

The firing continued for a few seconds, then a loud explosion cracked out from below them. The shooting abruptly stopped.

"Okay, quick tac rundown," Fran said, speaking quickly and quietly while spread across the floor. "Cobolts are little guys. Tech life. They're angry and they want your gear. They got inside the dungeon forty or more iterations ago and they've been making more of themselves ever since. Their armor's not great, their guns are hot strikers, and they break like twigs if you can get a hit on them. They're about as smart as a *hurrim*, and while they *are* tech, you can scare them if you drop something flashy. That's why the shooting stopped. They didn't like the big bang."

Miles didn't know what a *hurrim* was, and he only had a guess about the *hot striker*. When he focused on the unfamiliar Eppan word, his *Eyes of the Émigré* gave him the impression of some kind of predatory four-legged ground bird, closer to a fox than a hawk.

"If one of you can get me cover from their guns, I can pick off their snipers," Fran added, looking toward the ledge.

Miles turned to Task.

"Task, you cast a spell to protect us, didn't you?"

"Apologies, yes," Task said. The fall through the darkness had turned the apprentice into a shuddering mess, but he seemed a lot more composed after their talk, even if they were under fire.

"Don't apologize, I think you saved me from a broken shoulder," Miles said, then went on. "Is it a strong enough protection that it can stop those weapons?"

"I don't know," Task said. He thought for a second, then rolled over and unbuckled his stomach plate. He held it up, positioned so that it was above the line of the ledge to the ravine below.

He held it there for about ten seconds before one of the cobolt snipers took the opportunity and shot at it.

A puff of smoke went up from the metal plate, and when Task brought it back down, there was a finger-sized hole through the center of a heat-warped circle.

"No. I think the spell will help bone stop the shots, but flesh will still be torn and burned."

Miles looked around. His robe might block the weapons, especially with its new foil lining, but he didn't have any face protection. Fran probably wasn't lacking for body armor herself, if that had been the issue. Her trench coat looked to be made of similar stuff.

He wistfully remembered the shield he'd turned down in the Ishel marketplace.

Searching the ledge, his eyes fell on the door that had fallen with them. It had landed on its front, the rear side showing a fixed horizontal bar that was presumably used as the handle. If he could get it upright, it would work as cover.

He started crawling over to it.

Fran was moving in the other direction, dragging herself to the edge, but as soon as she peeked out, another shot went off near her, turning the stone she was sheltering behind into a burst of powder.

Reaching the door, Miles grabbed the crossbar and tried to lift it. He managed to bring it up a couple of inches before the strain was too much and he was forced to drop it back down. The angle was wrong, and even if he had the strength, he didn't have the leverage.

Maybe the levitation unit.

Miles spotted the device he'd used to survive the fall sitting forgotten a few feet away. He grabbed it, attached the clamp to the door's crossbar, and switched it on.

It hummed to life, the indicator light showing it was active.

Grabbing the unit's handle, Miles pulled as hard as he could. The door lifted off the ground.

It wasn't effortless. Even with the levitation tech, it still felt like moving a few kilograms of bricks around from the inertia alone, but he was able to position it vertically, giving himself enough cover to stand up behind it.

"Good," Fran said, sliding away from the edge and coming up to stand with him.

It was a narrow fit, as the door was only about three feet wide, but Fran seemed happy to stand in his shadow as he edged toward the precipice.

He felt the impacts of the cobolt weapons when he stepped out above the cover of the ledge, tiny shocks that rang mutely on the door, but none of them came close to penetrating it.

Fran tilted her head, peering around the door before letting off a shot from her sleek pistol. The beam of light flashed into the ravine below, and a second later there was a muted popping sound. Given how the weapon had worked against the Orbellius Ghouls, her target had probably exploded.

Over the next few minutes, weapons fire continued to splatter against Miles's improvised shield, while Fran continued leaning out and firing precise shots at the harassing cobolts.

Miles was worried about the longevity of her gun's power cell, but Fran apparently wasn't. It was only a matter of time before Fran's precision and Miles's cover won it for them. A final weapon discharge hit the door, Fran returned fire, and after that the cobolt attacks stopped.

It still seemed like there were cobolts down there. Miles could see shapes moving in the dark, but there were no more hissing lasers.

Miles waited a minute, then experimentally stuck his arm out from behind the door. When nothing tried to shoot him around the edge of the metal plate, he gently lowered it.

"That'll be all their ranged folk gone. We'll still have their scrappers to get through," Fran said. She started operating her wrist scanner, checking several different screens before she spoke again. "Lucky. There's a door a little walk down this gully. We dropped straight down from three, so there's probably less than six rooms between us and the crater. I told you I've done this before. We'll be out with time to spare."

Fran's reassurances fell a little flat with Miles. Logically, he knew that she wasn't responsible for what they'd faced in the level above, and even with her greater experience, she wouldn't have led them into that place if she'd known or suspected what might be there.

On an emotional level, he was finding it hard not to blame her.

Miles knew from experience that this kind of irrational grudge, blaming someone for a tragedy they weren't directly responsible for, would only fade with time, safety, and distance.

"I'll go down first," Fran said. She stepped up to the ledge "Anything left will group around me, and I'll try and take them down before the rest of you get there. All right. The rest of you all, follow me at your convenience."

She gripped the salvaged levitation unit in her left hand, her pistol in her right, and jumped off the ledge.

Miles quickly looked between Task and Lanet. "Are you two okay to follow?"

Lanet had just suffered the loss of two friends, lifelong friends from what Miles had gathered. Task might have been experiencing mortal danger for the first time in his life, and he was now either suppressing his fear to look like he was handling it, or he'd gone numb enough that he actually was handling it. Without knowing enough about Hurc psychology, neither seemed healthy to Miles.

In the ravine below, he could hear the wuffles and grunts of Fran fighting, interspersed with the crunching of crushed metal and the sharp sparking of energy discharges.

"I'm ready," Task said. "Apologies. This is very upsetting. I don't think this is my future career."

"I'm ready to fight as well," Lanet said. "I'll scream at the sky tomorrow. For today, let's get to safety."

This time when they descended, Lanet took Task, supporting him with the spell they'd used to descend from the third level. From the way they both crunched into the ground at high speed, Lanet standing up unharmed a moment later, it must have been some kind of defensive spell repurposed to defend against the fall.

Miles stepped up to the edge of the cliff next. He grabbed the handle of his levitation unit with both hands, peered over the side with a sinking feeling, and leaped off the edge, holding the door above his head.

The fall was slower than it had been with Task, no faster than a brisk walking pace.

He drifted down, his arms straining, before finally touching down on the floor of the ravine. He landed with the same force he'd expect from hopping a fence, his boots slapping the ground as he bent his knees to absorb the impact.

Seconds after he landed, he saw Task sprawled nearby, a small four-legged robotic humanoid standing over him with a cleaver-like blade.

Miles drew his striker without thinking and fired off a shot at it.

The weapon was set to its lowest level for safety, but it was still enough to blast the cobolt back. The metallic creature smacked into the nearest stone wall and slid to the ground, where it didn't get back up.

Nearby, Fran was still fighting. A seemingly endless number of the tech units were scampering toward them down the ravine.

At the bottom of the surrounding cliffs, the ground was relatively flat. There was a dry channel about fifteen meters wide, interrupted by occasional steps where the ravine changed elevation, lit dimly by the red glow of rocks Miles hoped weren't radioactive.

Each cobolt was about two feet tall, with a head that wasn't much more than a cluster of wires and cameras. They had single-jointed mechanical arms attached to a short armored torso, with clamp hands that gripped knives, clubs, and spikes made from repurposed scrap. Some of them ran on two legs with a very human gait, while others had four legs, turning them into tiny tech centaurs.

The bodies of the snipers that Fran had picked off lay scattered around, some seeming like they'd been in the process of trying to get to cover when the beam of her pistol had detonated their heads. It looked like they had been using handheld weapons, rather than integrated guns, since short white plastic rifles lay scattered around close to the bodies.

Fran was wrecking them with every kick and punch, and none of them were getting close enough to hurt her, but there seemed like there were still a lot bearing down on them.

Miles started firing off his striker at the approaching robots. The small scrappers didn't even try to evade, going down from a single shot almost anywhere on their body.

At one point, a larger, more armored unit made it to Miles, and he had to fend it off with his makeshift shield while he dialed the power up on his striker. The next shot took its head off completely, leaving it to sag to the ground in a pile of tech.

Nearby, Lanet was fighting using a blade of glowing energy that seemed to emerge directly from their hand. The blade was barely visible in the low light, but every time they swung it at an opponent, a cobolt body fell into pieces.

Miles was starting to get the impression that *this* was the kind of challenge they should have been facing so close to the surface. The cobolts were a threat, but their snipers could be neutralized through strategy, and they'd only be dangerous close-up to people without equipment, or who let themselves get swarmed.

On his first trip to the dungeon with Brisk, they'd fought similar fights on level eight, though with a higher number of more complicated opponents.

The encounters on his second trip, to the first level, had been artificially difficult due to the repurposed diver equipment the Orbellius Ghouls had been using, but they were still something his team could have survived on their own.

Whatever the giant had been on the level above, it stood out as a clear aberration.

The Ymn City monster had seemed like it was literally impossible to fight, and whatever Miles had told Task to make the apprentice feel better, their getting away had been luck as much as judgment.

After a few seconds, Task got to his feet. He picked up one of the dropped cobolt rifles and slowly turned it over in his hands. The thing was so small, it looked like a pistol next to him.

He aimed it into the ravine ahead and fired it experimentally. A puff of smoke went up from the ground in front of one of the advancing robots, causing it to stop and start fleeing in the opposite direction.

About the time when the piles of small metallic bodies were starting to become inconvenient, the cobolts stopped advancing so aggressively. The attackers thinned out, and even more started running away.

Miles got the impression that they'd collectively decided the attack was a loss and were backing off.

Fran was breathing heavily, and Lanet's white skin had turned faintly blue. Miles checked their internals with *Eyes of the Altruist* before scanning the rest of the ravine.

Interestingly, some of the motionless cobolts were registering glowing shapes, angular and boxy components, packed densely within their bodies. The magic was obviously interpreting them as alive. Miles briefly worried whether he should try to finish them off, but they seemed like if they had been able to move at all, they'd be running away.

Fran and Lanet were both untouched. Miles might have been injured if he hadn't had the door-shield, but he'd gotten through the battle without a scratch. Task had been hurt, however. There were cuts on his arms from where he'd tried to protect himself from blade-wielding cobolts, and a bruise around one eye that Miles hadn't seen happen.

Miles hadn't felt any magic coming from the other mage during the fight, but then Miles hadn't tried his attack spell either. *Strike the Disharmonious* took a couple of seconds to cast, and against the number of cobolts they'd been facing it hadn't seemed worth it. If Task's offensive magic also took a moment to cast, maybe he'd found the cobolt weapon more convenient.

"Task, can I touch you?"

"What?" Task asked, looking shocked.

Miles put it down to shock from the battle. The apprentice didn't seem like much of a fighter, after all.

"Can I heal you?"

Task let out a breath, looking around at the robotic carnage. "Yes."

Miles stepped forward, using *Seal Wounds* to treat all of the Hurc mage's cuts and scrapes at once, then *Hasten Renewal* to help treat the bruise. The mottled patch on Task's face hadn't faded completely by the time Miles was done, but it had changed color, which Miles assumed was a good thing.

Fran was looking around at the remnants of their small battlefield. She seemed tired.

"Some of this is salvage. Let's get it cleaned up and get out of here."

Looking around at the scattered cobolt weapons, Miles pulled off his backpack and removed the sturdy plastic sack.

He wasn't sure he'd ever be coming back into the dungeon again, not after seeing the kind of nightmares it could throw at him, but at least he wouldn't be leaving empty-handed.

CHAPTER 21

At the end of the ravine, they found a standard dungeon door, tall and thin, leading to another of the distorted twisting corridors Miles had experienced on his dive with Brisk.

It took thirty minutes to march the length of the meandering corridor, and even according to Fran's tools, it hadn't led them exactly in the direction of the crater.

Miles was starting to worry that her reassurances of making it out "with time to spare" had been wrong, that they might not even have time to escape before the dungeon started rearranging.

"What happens during the shuffle?" he asked her as they traversed the long passageway.

She answered carefully, without turning to look at him. "Well, the rooms move around, for one. Some get broken down, new ones get built. If you're down on the deeper levels, the floors above get shuffled a few times before yours comes due, on account of the time difference. Did I tell you about the time difference?"

"What happens if you're inside during a shuffle?" he asked, ignoring the temptation to get sidetracked on the dungeon's time dilation.

Fran was quiet for a long few seconds before answering.

"If I were stuck down in a room during the shuffle, here's what I'd do. I've got a bottle of meds in my pocket. Sedatives. Instant. Powerful. I'd clear the room of threats, find a tight place to hide, and pop as many of those pills as I thought I could live through."

"You'd want to sleep through the reset?" Miles asked.

"If I had no chance of getting out? Yes."

"Why?"

"The *academics* have got the phrase 'inimical to sapience.' Does that mean anything to you? You can survive a shuffle if you're a cobolt, or a bug, or a slime monster, or whatever, provided the room you're hiding in doesn't get taken down. But if you go into a shuffle as a sapient, you don't come out as one. Something changes. Like a switch gets flipped, person to animal."

Miles tried to digest that. "You mean it causes some kind of brain damage? There's radiation, or a chemical release?"

"I really hope that's what it is," Fran said.

"Hasn't anyone ever tried to find out?"

"Well, you're free to follow that line of thought on your own time," she said, becoming businesslike. "My feeling is that knowing the answer won't be much better for you than finding out firsthand, but that might just be the old-timer in me trying to spin you another ghost story."

Miles wasn't really interested in internalizing another oddity about the dungeon. Until someone gave him a better answer, he'd work from the basis that being inside when it reset exposed someone to dangerous and damaging radiation.

At the end of the winding corridor, they came to some kind of factory room. There were conveyor belts, articulated tech arms reaching down from ceiling-mounted rails, large boxy units with distorted warning labels, and metal bins full of parts and materials. A small bank of benches at the far end were piled with abandoned clothes and synth-fabric duffle bags.

It obviously wasn't a real factory. The conveyor belts weren't continuous, broken up instead into sections that started nowhere and went nowhere. The mechanical arms were all different from each other, different numbers of fingers and joints, different lengths and colors, many with manipulators that were clearly useless or no manipulators at all.

Fran became interested in her scanner as they walked into the room. She seemed upbeat as she looked up from the screen on her wrist.

"By my dead reckoning, the crater's just past this door. We're all but out."

Miles felt something unclench in his gut at the news. One door between them and the open sky.

"Who wants to do the honors?" Fran asked.

Lanet ran forward and slapped their hand against the door panel. It chimed in acceptance.

There was a brief grinding sound, then the door opened on a rainy Ialis evening.

Miles had never been so glad to see rain.

"Hold up," Fran said, "I just want to check this room while we've got time."

The raw materials scattered around must have been better copies of reality than the equipment, because after inspecting a few, Fran had them collecting bags from the benches and stuffing them with specific components.

Lanet looked at them with distaste as they looted the storage bins, and Miles felt a little heartless himself for trying to make a marginal profit on a dive where people had died.

In the ravine, collecting the cobolt weapons had felt like he was clawing something back for the near-death terror he'd been forced to experience, making it worthwhile. Here, where the door out was open in front of them, it just felt cold and insensitive.

Miles followed Fran's instructions mechanically, despite just wanting to be gone. He tried to tell himself it was the professional thing to do.

Calm. Detached. Professional. Another word forced itself onto the end of his mental list. *Mercenary.*

That evoked images that were a little too close to home. He pictured people that he didn't want to become like. He started to resent the bag of materials.

He'd liked Fran when he'd first met her, but now he wasn't sure. She'd presented herself as competent and self-reliant, but now that same independence seemed to be maintained at the cost of empathy and the willingness to make connections with the people she was working with.

Was it even possible to do this job without becoming like that?

When they were done with the factory room, Fran called them a new platform, since their old one was still sitting hundreds of meters up at a level three entrance.

The new transport came quickly, dropping down from somewhere above, and they rode their way back up to the entrance complex in weary silence. It set them down close to one of the open-walled buildings. They stopped there to prepare to pass through the Gilthaen's processing.

Fran started collecting the salvaged goods from Miles. He unloaded the bundled silver fabric taken from the Ymn cityscape, the gathered cobolt weapons, and the tech components from the factory.

There was a moment of tension when Fran held out her hands to take the coppery metal door from Miles, but he just stood there in silence, staring back at her.

"You going to hand that over, Miley?"

He really didn't want to. He'd become attached to the makeshift shield. He regretted not clarifying that he was keeping it earlier.

With Lestiel Dunverde, the contract had seemed like overkill at the time, but it had stipulated that outside of his samples, there'd be an even split of salvage. He didn't have anything like that with Fran, just the equivalent of a verbal agreement that he'd come as a backup healer.

"Technically, we didn't agree that you'd automatically get everything," Miles said. "This is just something I picked up on my own. Doesn't that make it my salvage, technically?"

Fran seemed annoyed for a moment, but the expression changed to amusement. "Technically? Well, technically, I guess you've got me there. Technically."

Fran carried everything except Miles's door and levitation unit as they walked toward the processing desk.

Miles had been hoping to see They-who-warily-tread again, but he didn't recognize the Gilthaen running the desk.

"I am Consul They-who-catalog-meticulously," the unfamiliar sapient said, bowing slightly.

"'Course you are," Fran said, approaching the desk.

The Gilthaen official was shorter than They-who-warily-tread, maybe seven feet from tail to tip. With the lower half of their body coiled on the ground for stability, their head only came up to Miles's chest. This individual only had two eyes vertically running down the center of their "face," and they were dressed plainly for a Gilthaen, wearing only an enclosed sock of white synth fabric.

Fran stopped at the desk, gesturing to the load of salvage she was carrying. "We're cashing all this out. Except the door this guy's carrying. Technically, he's keeping that."

"You may call me Consul Cas, if that eases communication," the Gilthaen said.

Fran didn't respond, just dumping the sacks of recovered cobolt parts and weapons, the bags of tech components, the fabric, and finally her bundle of strange metal planks onto the table. Miles was surprised it took all of the weight.

"My records suggest that your party had six members when you entered the artifact. You are leaving as a group of four. What is the cause of the discrepancy?"

"Two of us died," Lanet said, before Fran could answer.

"That is a tragedy," the consul said. "It is something we always dread. Were there contributing factors which constitute a violation of our code of conduct, such as malfeasance, the deprioritization of life, or unacceptable risks taken as a result of fraudulent representations?"

Everyone looked at Lanet, who seemed to be considering saying something. Finally, they looked to the ground.

Lanet answered for the rest of them. "No. It was just . . . the wrong place for us. They thought every enemy was something they could fight past, but that was never true."

"Were there contributing factors relating to the performance of your healers for the expedition—Fran San-san-quirren and Miles Asher, He-who-burns-his-hand-on-mercy?"

Lanet made a dismissive gesture with their hand. "There was nothing of them left to heal."

With that, Cas's questions seemed to be over. "Then, all is in order. I will now appraise the items you have acquired within the artifact. Please place *all* items for inspection."

The Gilthaen was looking at Miles as they spoke, and he got the impression they were talking about the door.

"I'm keeping this," Miles said. He didn't want to sell it, at least not immediately.

"It must still be appraised."

Taking a tense breath, Miles put the makeshift shield down on the table, at the far end from the other salvage. His real worry was that it would be worth too much to pass up, or else nothing at all and he'd feel dumb for making a point of keeping it.

The Gilthaen clerk began peering closely at each item. Comically close, Miles thought. They started with the cobolt weapons, then the fabric, then they moved to the duffel bags, inspecting them as if they could see through the synth fabric to the components inside. When they reached the metal planks, they paused for a moment, spending twice as long inspecting them as the rest of the haul. They only took a passing glance at Miles's door.

"These metal samples are unusual," they said, indicating the planks and the door. "In fact they are unique. I have not experienced this material before."

"We found it in an unusual environ, level three," Fran said.

The consul turned to Miles. "Do you reiterate your desire to keep your piece of the metal?"

"Yes," Miles said, feeling suddenly less certain about it.

"Then I will only appraise this collection."

Consul Cas stooped to look at each item again, and then stood in silence for a minute, apparently thinking.

"For the recovered weapons and power cores, the Ialis Corporation will pay eight hundred and nine standard exchange notes for the batch."

"Sounds good to me," Fran said.

Cas moved to look at the duffel bags. "For the industrial components, the Ialis Corporation will pay two hundred and seventy-five standard exchange notes."

"Eh. Sure."

Cas briefly checked the fabric again. "For this material, one thousand, six hundred standard exchange notes."

"Go for it."

Pausing at the bundle of metal planks, Cas looked at Fran. "For the unusual metal samples, the Ialis Corporation will pay eighty-two thousand standard exchange notes."

Fran was silent for a long moment, then started shouting.

"Yes! Paydirt! That's why we do this, Miley. This is why we're in this business." She slapped her thigh, walking around in a circle, before she turned to look at him. "And rightly, two hundred of that's yours, *technically*."

Two hundred seln. The amount he agreed to do this for.

Miles let out a long breath.

Fran leaned closer to him. "You get a job in the future, make sure you get something in writing. Payment, liabilities, and salvage split. Not everyone's as nice as I am."

The statement confused him, before she turned back to the consul and said, "I'll take that in a thirty–seventy split, with the thirty divided between these three."

Miles looked at her back, shocked. She was splitting the payout. Not evenly, maybe, but coming straight off the feeling that he'd screwed himself out of a fortune, it was hard for him to say it wasn't equitable.

Thirty percent, divided by the three of them. Ten percent of the payout is at least eight thousand, plus change.

Task seemed to be in shock, though Miles didn't know whether that was from the size of the payout or the recent horror.

If the Gilthaen payments worked the same as last time, they'd leave the items here, and the funds would be sent to their comm accounts within the next few hours. He was already trying to calculate how much eight thousand seln was worth as delta.

Maybe about three thousand? And how much is the door worth?

He asked a question before They-who-catalog-meticulously could leave for other duties.

"Consul, is this a one-time offer, or could I come back and sell something I salvaged today later on?"

"If you arrive here with salvage, it can be appraised and sold to the Ialis Corporation at any time," Cas said, reassuring him. "Though, this offer applies only to items recovered from the artifact."

"Okay, thanks. Could you say how much the Ialis Corporation would pay for this?" he patted the door on the table.

Consul Cas briefly inspected it again. "At the present time, the Ialis Corporation would pay twelve thousand standard exchange notes for this amount of metal. At a later date, it may be less."

Twelve thousand! Could he afford to pass that up? On the other hand, if the metal was *unique* among salvage brought out of the dungeon, then it was irreplaceable. It was good to know he wasn't throwing potentially thousands of seln away by walking away with it right then, but it was hard to pass up that much in the moment.

A thought occurred to him, and he started to think of a plan that would let him access some of that money without losing the door's utility as a shield. He didn't need the entire thing just to get between him and a threat, after all.

Fran and Lanet started wandering away. Neither bothered to say goodbye. Miles guessed this was a cold business, after all.

Miles was left with Task. They started walking toward the transport platforms before Miles broke the silence.

"Are you going to be okay?" he asked.

Task worried one of his fangs with his bottom lip.

"I don't know. Today was a new experience."

"Yeah."

It was probably even a new experience for *Fran*. And definitely for Lanet. The day had thrown a lot of new experiences at them.

He hesitated before speaking, worrying that he might be crossing a line. "Do you want to come with me to get some ice cream, or watch some old Hurc movies or . . . What do you do for comfort?"

Task took a while to answer, finally saying, "There's a garden on Tholis Tower rooftop. It's peaceful."

"Yeah? You want to go?"

"Yes."

"Okay, let's stop off at my apartment on the way," Miles said as they began walking toward the landing pads. "I need to dump this door and tell my team I'm alright."

Miles pulled his comm from his belt pouch as he walked, planning to call a platform.

When he pulled it up, he saw that he had a few missed messages from the time he was in the dungeon. Two from Trin, one from an unknown sender, and one from a person he wanted nothing to do with.

Damien Asher > Miles
Hello Miles, it's Dad. Seen the news? We have to talk.

PART 9

LETTERS

CHAPTER 22

The skyport of Dendril City never got really busy. There were about twenty platforms in total, catering to ships the size of an SUV all the way up to full space liners. The ship they were waiting for with Milli was going to be a small passenger cruiser, about the size of an intercontinental plane back on old Earth.

It was a nice day, for Ialis. The bright star was overhead, the sky was relatively clear, and it hadn't rained in about eight hours, so even the moss underfoot was firm and springy.

"I hope there will be a nest for me!" Milli said. "Normally they are only humanoid seats and floor seats. Bad for my butt."

"Do they feed you?" Miles asked.

"Yes. Packets. Ugh. Don't worry. When I get home, Mama will feed me some of that sweet mucus."

I don't even want to ask.

"That's . . . good," Miles said, looking away to cast his gaze around the skyport.

Trin and Torg were at a nearby terminal, paging through the port's navigation database for idle amusement. Milli was sitting on the moss next to Miles, a little pouch of possessions at her feet, waiting with him.

When she'd finished healing, her form had resolved as a shape that evoked beetle in her body and crab around her face, with eyestalks and mouth-parts. She had ten legs, the front four of which all had manipulators, and her wings had filled out to run the length of her body. They obviously weren't useful for flying, but Miles had noticed that they changed color and occasionally switched angles as she talked, so Miles thought they probably had a role in communication.

As soon as Milli had been hooked back up to the comm network, her clan had booked her a flight back to the refugee station they lived on in Iteration 27,145.

It wasn't going to be a direct transport—there were too many possible destinations for direct flights to go anywhere but the biggest hubs—but the Spiral only ran in two directions, and her ticket would let her choose her rides until she was home.

Miles and the others were a little out of pocket from helping Milli recover and getting her set up, but he didn't want to raise the issue with her clan.

He'd given in to the fear of missing out exactly once since he'd left Unsiel Station, when he was negotiating with Fran outside the dungeon, and he felt like her turning around and showing him kindness in return had been an immediate rebuke.

On post-bower Earth, the dynamic had been easy. It was dog-eat-dog. Unsiel Station had also been easy. On the refugee station, nobody had anything and everything was shared. Out here in the Spiral, he probably needed a balance of vulnerability and self-interest. He had to navigate the threat of betrayal without losing who he was.

Milli was starting to get restless with waiting, shuffling in place and turning around in circles. After a minute, she turned toward the terminal that Trin and Torg were playing with.

Miles was about to follow her when his comm buzzed in his belt pouch.

There it is. Every eight hours, like clockwork.

He felt dread as he took his comm out and unlocked the screen.

Damien Asher > Miles
You probably think I'm bitter because we had our hopes pinned on you, but that's not it. You were never any use to us. You still aren't. Except that those creatures lording it over us have put something in your hands you don't deserve. It needs to be with us, the people who actually stayed behind to try and make something of this country. If you did the right thing now then the people you left behind might not think you were so worthless.

The messages had been relentless, Earth morning, noon, and night. They'd left Miles feeling anxious and sick. He was almost afraid to touch his comm.

Each of them had been a variation on a theme. After months of silence, his father had begun sending him messages about Miles's failure, his duty, and what he owed his family. It felt like he was being beaten with a stick at the same time that someone who knew him tried to hack his brain.

Deleting the message from his father, he went back and opened the alert that had presumably started it all.

Entrant Allocations > Miles Asher
Hello, Miles Asher. As you may be aware, your home world has recently taken up residence in the political-commercial union of the Spiral.

On date 27,201.90, a survey team discovered thirty-four asteroids containing elements of interest in your world's space. This lot has been labeled as the Solar-1 Acquisition.

As your Iteration 27,200 has no strong unified governing body, these undeveloped material holdings have been subdivided into lots, to be apportioned to its qualifying sapient citizens on an equal distribution basis.

You are one such qualifying sapient, entitling you to a claim of 0.000000119% of the mineral yield discovered in your system's space.

In order to process and validate your claim, please visit your nearest allocation facility in Iteration 27,200 and present this message as evidence of your status as a qualifying citizen.

To guard against impersonation and apportionment fraud, only claims presented on Earth of Iteration 27,200 can be validated.

These allocations are final and carry the full weight of Spiral law. No preference is given to native heredity or class rankings in the distribution of allocations. No coercion or fraud is permitted in the redistribution of apportionment. Any apportionment going unclaimed for forty days following this message will be redistributed into claimed allocations.

To locate your closest allocation facility, you may reply to this message with your geospatial coordinates. Thank you for your attention.

Miles closed the message and let his comm fall to his lap.

Lacking anything like a unified global government, or even an alliance of national governments, the rest of the weave had worked out that Earth wasn't in a position to negotiate mining rights for asteroids floating in its unclaimed space.

Miles wouldn't have felt confident arguing with the point.

Who would they even ask? There was no one owner of Earth's asteroid belt. There were no thousand owners. The only way anyone, humans included, would benefit from what Solar space had by way of mineral wealth was if someone was found to be responsible for it. Either everyone had to wait ten or twenty years until a global consensus emerged on Earth, if it ever did, or they had to find another way.

Miles's first reaction to the news had been to feel defensive. Someone had scouted Earth's star system, found something they wanted, and worked out a way to get it. Regardless of how Spiral society was planning on distributing the find, they'd still made a de facto claim over it.

The overbearing move would have generated more heat in him if he didn't keep coming back to the practicalities. Earth hadn't yet put forward a real voice in the Spiral, and this wasn't the worst way the Spiral community could have been handling it.

Any number of powers in the weave could have just rolled in and claimed the entire system, if they'd wanted to do it that way.

Earth's space defense arsenal was only ever designed to be turned inward, and there wasn't much left of it functional.

Instead of just taking, the Spiral powers-that-be had divided up the real estate in the most blunt and equal way possible, giving every surviving human a chance at a slice.

It seemed like a small slice at first, less than a millionth of a percent, but given the average size of asteroids in the system, that might easily translate into millions of tons of resources.

Miles wasn't sure how much seln that would translate to. Once the packages were claimed, interested parties would be able to offer to buy them via comm, but Miles didn't know enough about Spiral economics to know what kind of figure that would be.

The Spiral's scheme for splitting the territory seemed brutally simple, but if they actually enforced the rules on coercion and fraud, it would also potentially benefit every human left alive. That wouldn't necessarily have been the case if they'd allocated the resources to either the warlords or the governments-in-name-only.

The only thing Miles didn't understand was why his family was suddenly so interested in him.

He assumed it was related to the apportionment, since his father had said so specifically in one message, but why did a fraction of a fraction of a percent mean so much to them?

They had thousands of people living in their settlement, and if they didn't think they could extort the profits of this scheme from people they literally held the power of life and death over, what hope did they have of doing so from Miles?

He wasn't sure it would matter. Miles's closest allocation facility was back on Earth. If he wanted to take advantage of it, he'd need to leave Ialis and travel.

Dropping his comm back into his belt pouch, Miles wandered over to the terminal.

"That is Histiche," Trin was saying. "Prime planet. Iteration 26,606."

Trin was pointing at a dusty-looking yellow planet with a smattering of purple-green. The screen showed an abstract representation of a star system. Two suns, one white and one yellow, with a handful of rocky planets orbiting the yellow star. A label at the top of the display declared that it was a diagram of Iteration 26,606.

Miles still had a headache from frowning at his comm, but he welcomed the distraction from his family's toxic messages.

"You have two stars in your iteration?" Miles asked him.

"Yes. They dance around," Trin said, drawing an imaginary line on the screen with the tip of his finger. "It gets hot, then we go underground. Sun cities and cave cities. We swap every generation. That's eh . . . every forty iterations. I am a cave boy."

"Your civilization moves between the surface and caves, and you were born in the caves, so you're a cave boy?" Miles asked, wanting to make sure he'd understood.

"Yes. Cave boys and cave girls are smaller, more inward."

"Is that from nutrition differences, or . . . ?"

"No. Different kind of boy, different kind of girl." On the screen, Trin tapped the dusty planet, which made it expand until it filled the screen. He dragged his finger around for a minute, spinning the sphere until a particular landmass was facing them, then stretched it to zoom in.

Cities appeared on the diagram, chaotic sprawls of rounded buildings. As Trin zoomed in further, Miles could see details. They were low buildings, one or two stories high. They were the same color as the surrounding rock, except for the roofs, which were alternately painted white or covered in silver panels.

"My mom's home," he said, indicating a particular building.

They both stared at it for a few seconds, Miles not wanting to break the silence. Finally, Miles asked, "Why did you leave?"

Trin made a fluting humming sound. "On Histiche, I work as thief. It's fine. No law problems. Sideways stealing is allowed. Up stealing bad, down stealing bad, sideways stealing is fine."

"I don't get it," Miles said. "What's sideways stealing?"

"People who have same as you. Not more rich or more poor."

"So it's legal to steal from people who are in the same economic class?" Miles asked.

"Yes, sideways. But. I stole up. It was an accident."

"And that's illegal?" Miles said. "And you ran?"

"Yes. Big law problems. I left. Laws on Histiche are so different. Spiral doesn't send you back."

Miles struggled to put Trin's meaning together. He'd stolen from someone it was illegal for him to steal from, because of some kind of class differences, and he'd fled to escape prosecution? And it sounded like the Spiral didn't extradite back to Histiche because of differences in the law.

"What would happen to you if you went back?" Miles asked.

"They kill me!" Trin said. Then, a few seconds later, "Well, not kill me. But there's a big fine."

"It doesn't sound like sideways-thief was a great career choice," Miles observed.

"Yeah, yeah. You not great career choice."

Miles stepped up, taking over the terminal. He zoomed back out to the full Spiral view, then dragged the string of stars until he reached the bottom. Earth was Iteration 27,200, the second-to-last in the line. He selected it, and had Earth filling in the screen in a couple of taps.

"This is Earth," Miles said. "My home world. Iteration 27,200."

Everyone crowded around to look at it over Miles's shoulder.

"*Green*," Torg said.

"Yeah," Miles agreed.

He zoomed in further, finding the North American continent, the scrolling around until he found a scar of brown cutting through a pine forest near the northeast coast.

He zoomed in further, until the display showed a steel-gray wreck. One of Earth's second-generation orbital battleships, downed in some panic conflict immediately after the bower break.

There'd been obvious changes since the last time it was spaceworthy. Parts had been removed, opened up, salvaged. A shantytown of huts and corrugated steel lean-tos dotted the forest around it, with the Garlington acting as the control center for settlement.

It was a really high quality image. Miles bet he'd even be able to make out the solitary crates if he zoomed in close enough.

"What was falling out of false universe like?" Trin asked.

Miles zoned out, looking at the frozen image of the settlement, but thinking of a night more than a year earlier.

A night sky gone white. A wave of photons boiling off the ragged edge of space. Lightning striking from one part of the sky to another. All the grass standing up on end, like hair exposed to a static field. Civilian tech frying itself out and Miles's social circle shrinking to just the people who could hear him yelling. Fires set by deteriorating power lines, and then by deteriorating people.

Earth had gotten off easy, considering the energies involved. In the end, their panic had done at least half as much damage again as the radiation.

"The tearing space triggered a flash of light at the boundary," Miles said. "Something to do with how our spacetime works, then the light set off a bunch of solar flares. Between the two, a lot of Earth's technology got fried, and it didn't take much more than that to send us into chaos. The government failed, markets failed, things got messy in the power vacuum."

"You didn't feel falling?" Trin asked.

"No, that's just a metaphor. If a planet actually fell anywhere, there'd be nothing of it left when it landed."

All the language surrounding a bower break was couched in metaphors of falling, dropping, crashing. Miles had heard it explained as a water drop falling through a crack in a leaky tank. But it wasn't really like that.

Miles had been idle at the terminal for too long, and it reset to the Spiral view.

Torg stepped up and dragged a pincer across the screen, selecting an iteration a little way back from Earth.

The screen changed to show a dull red star orbited by a single rocky planet. Torg focused the interface on it, and its label appeared at the top of the screen.

Clack. "*Torg,*" Torg said.

The interface mirrored his statement. The label read "*Planet Torg, Iteration 26,899.*"

Miles and Trin stared at him for a second.

"Your homeworld called *Torg*?" Trin asked, incredulous.

Tick. "*Yes.*"

"You are Torg from Torg?"

Tick. "*Yes.*"

They all stared at planet Torg for a minute.

Eventually the silence was broken by Trin, asking the question that Miles had been putting to himself for days, without any sign of a decision.

"Miles, you going home?" Trin asked.

Miles's gaze fell from the terminal to the moss.

The apportionment was an opportunity. Maybe a huge opportunity. And it was his due. If he didn't go for it, he'd lose it, and be left watching others profit from his inaction.

He didn't hate the idea of seeing Earth again, either, or being in a pine forest again.

The thing he dreaded was being on the same planet as his mother, his father, his sister, and their organization.

He wished they'd been able to make allowances for off-world humans when they'd designed this scheme.

Earth is a big planet, right? I can probably avoid three people.

"I think maybe I will," Miles said.

"I'll come with you?" Trin asked.

"You want to come? You want to come to *Earth*?" Miles asked.

"Yes. To come with you."

Miles was shocked, and touched, and terrified for Trin.

"That's not a good idea," he said. "It's not safe there for Spiral sapients."

When Earth had passed through the catastrophe of the bower break and come out the other side surrounded by unknown alien civilizations, all the old vices of humanity had returned in a big way. Xenophobia and superstition had been big sellers in the aftermath. It hadn't been pretty. Humanity hadn't put its best foot forward or shown its best face to its new neighbors.

Things were still a mess. A concerning fraction of humans still thought Spiral sapients were monsters, demons, or alien invaders, depending on the specific brand of disinformation they enjoyed. Provincial demagogues were happy to keep humanity isolated and afraid, and the "humanitarian" efforts of the Forward Fleet were viewed with distrust if not outright hatred.

After leaving Earth, Miles had found out that there were maybe two cities on the entire planet where non-human sapients were safe and accepted. Neyjavik, on the landmass that had been called Iceland, and Algiers, on the north coast of Africa. From what he'd heard, "safe" was a relative term in both.

Maybe I could visit anyway. It should be easy to dodge three people when I'm half a world away.

"I can play human," Trin said. "Eeeh, I am human. I wash in acid. Give me the rent moneys. I am bald like a fruit. I hate naked and I hate sleeping near a face."

"You'd need to shave your fur," Miles suggested.

"Eeeh, I hate my fur. I rub blade on face every single day."

It's probably best if Trin doesn't come to Earth.

After a few minutes of waiting, Milli's ship arrived, a wide bulging vessel that couldn't have been efficient to get through an atmosphere. It came down with a sound like tearing paper, stopping to hover a couple of feet above the platform.

It took another few minutes for its Ialis-bound passengers to disembark. They all looked rough and ready for a fight. Miles guessed that was the kind of tourist Ialis attracted.

The three of them said their goodbyes to Milli, and a few minutes later, they were watching her ship rise back up through the air. A message to Miles's comm confirmed she'd gotten on board safely.

Milli > Miles
I did it. And there are nests!

Miles was left feeling pensive and restless. If he was going to head back to Earth, then there'd be arrangements to make. He didn't need to decide whether he definitely was right now, but he could already feel the push and pull of forces affecting his decision. He was going to decide to go back. He could already tell.

Miles was sitting on some cash now. It was a long trip back to 27,200, and he'd need passage, supplies, and ideas on how to keep himself safe in a large city.

He'd also need to pay his share of the rent upfront, unless he wanted to come back to Ialis to find his apartment gone, with Trin and Torg turfed out.

If I'm even coming back to Ialis, he thought.

He'd need to decide that, too.

CHAPTER 23

Task > Miles
I checked. Master Curious asked for you to go on to the directory after your visit.

Miles worked to dodge commuters passing through the Thouco Tower arrivals level. He made it on the next elevator to the Morning Star Corporation Lounge and started typing out a reply as soon as he was situated.

Miles > Task
So nobody will mind? I don't want to get kicked out.
Task > Miles
You are a member of the Enclave now. You won't be kicked out. You are welcome.

Miles was so distracted by his comm he almost missed his stop. He didn't think he'd made that good of an impression on the Senior Harmonizer at the Enclave. Maybe they just let any mage in.

He jumped out of the elevator at the last second, finding a low padded stool to sit on while he replied.

Miles > Task
Okay, thanks for telling me. I might be down there later today if you're around?
Task > Miles

I have duties today. Master Oron has sent me to help an industrial client.
They want to test the performance of their armor against magical attacks.
It will not do well.

Miles stayed sitting on the bench for a minute, staring at his comm, trying to think of something else to say.

He'd already told Task that he was planning on being away for two or three weeks while he dealt with something back home. He'd even told Fran, though she had no reason to care.

Eventually, he slipped the comm back into his belt pouch and stood up.

Miles was on edge as he stepped into the Morning Star office, and not just because of what he was there to ask about.

"Hello, again, you! Our valued customer," Polyp 44291 said, their fronds waving in greeting.

Miles had found out the clerk's name since his first visit to the Morning Star Corporation Lounge. It was actually a number, which was customary among the Pulstreen.

"Hi. I was hoping to get six thousand seln converted into delta, please?"

"Yes! It will be a delight for me! The clerk of Morning Star Corporation."

Miles had been resisting dropping all of his savings on delta, but if he was planning a trip to Earth, he'd need to prepare.

Most parts of the planet were still lawless, and even in the areas under control, they were under the control of glorified gangs, dictators, and military groups. The rule of law was a fond memory, and if its security forces had ever served justice more than power, then those days were gone.

He could get jumped simply for his clothes, never mind all the Spiral tech he was carrying. If he was going back to Earth, he needed to be sure he could protect himself.

He'd already checked with the manufacturer of his striker pistol, and they had it listed as being compatible with Iteration 27,200 space. It was a simple device, at least compared to some Spiral technology. Not much more than a glorified flashlight, and none of the physics it relied on were contradicted or occluded by Earth's natural laws.

His own magic was an even surer bet. Earth had no native magical laws to start with, but even in iterations that did have their own magic, interacting systems tended to get on with each other fine. Magic's universality was one of its selling points to Miles. Even if someone on Earth took or damaged his index, he wouldn't lose access to his spells, now that he knew how to cast them from memory.

44291 brushed their blank tablet with a frond, then said, "Within the system, today! Six thousand exchange notes will purchase two thousand thirty-nine delta, for you! The mage of tools."

Miles did some quick mental math. That was a similar conversion rate from seln as the first time he'd bought delta. If it was different, then it was off by an amount too small to calculate in his head.

He took a breath before answering. This was the largest purchase of his life so far.

"I'll take it. Thanks."

He handed over his comm and his index, watching as the clerk drained one and incremented the other. They passed both items back and Miles slipped them into belt pouches without checking them. He could handle his upgrades later.

He stayed at the counter, building up the courage to ask his next question.

Reaching into his belt pouch, he wrapped his hand around an irregular piece of crystal, drawing it out.

When the acclimatization program on Unsiel Station had given Miles his index, he'd learned that Harmonization was the only magical tradition cleared for humans to buy into. All of the others, a vast number, had been restricted.

Right now, in his hand, he had a way to gain access to one of those restricted traditions. The path of the *Sky Quester*.

He was pretty sure that having those spells was some level of forbidden for him. What he didn't know was whether it was forbidden at a corporate level; if it was Morning Star's internal policy not to sell it to him, or if it was forbidden in a way more like owning an unlicensed assault rifle.

Only the fact that he hadn't actually absorbed the crystal via his index gave him the confidence to come here and ask. Surely he couldn't be blamed just for finding it and bringing it in to ask about.

"There was something else, actually," Miles said. He placed the pink gemstone down on the counter. "I found this in the Ialis artifact. It had some weird influence on my index. Could you tell me what it is?"

Miles couldn't tell if the clerk was looking at it, seeing as the flesh vase that was the Pulstreen had no obvious sense organs, but after a few seconds, they responded.

"Oh, yes. This! Crystalized delta."

Miles looked from the clerk to the stone, then back.

"*This* is delta?"

"Delta! Filtered magical energy, here in solid form."

Delta was the currency of the index system, and was commonly used by magic-leaning traders, but Miles only knew it as a number on a screen. And he'd never connected it to magical energy. He'd always thought of it as a kind of arbitrary second currency.

44291 reached out, one of their fronds hovering over the crystal. "May this one inspect it for you? Our valued customer!"

"Sure?"

The clerk picked the stone up, turning it over in their fronds.

After a minute of careful inspection, they reached out to place it back on the counter in front of Miles.

"Oh. Oh, how sad. This is the remnant of a mage of tools."

"I've never heard of a remnant before," Miles said carefully. He could connect the word to something that was left in a corpse easily enough.

"Formed from active energy, when a mage is struck down. The spells in use freeze into this! Crystalline delta."

When Miles had last checked the crystal with his index, it'd held a magical blade and shield spell. Did that mean Brisk's former grenadier was using those spells at the moment they died?

If Miles died while he was healing someone, would he leave a little *Hasten Renewal* rock behind?

"Would it be illegal, or in bad taste, or anything like that, for me to use it?" he asked.

He didn't ask *how* he could use it, since he already had a good idea from the exchange on Delatariel Station. It would be as simple as index-casting one of its abilities while holding it. All he really wanted to know is whether it would get him ostracized or prosecuted if anyone saw him using the "forbidden" spells.

Polyp 44291 reached over with their frond and pushed the crystal toward Miles.

"It is illegal! For Morning Star corporation to provide or encourage the use of this magical tradition, to you! The mage of Iteration 27,200."

"But it wouldn't be illegal if I got access to it on my own?"

"Beneath the stars, there is no law governing the individual's study of magic," 44291 said blandly.

Miles took that to mean that Morning Star couldn't offer him advice on getting access to types of magic forbidden to him through the index, but that it wasn't illegal for him to pursue them on his own.

"This one is authorized to purchase the crystalline delta from you," 44291 said suddenly. "The price offered would be three thousand delta."

Miles froze with his hand halfway to taking back the crystal.

Three thousand delta was more than he'd cumulatively spent so far. He didn't even know what kind of upgrades would be visible to him if he had that much. He was tempted to accept immediately, even if just to get more visibility of the Harmonizer catalog.

On the other hand, the crystal was a way to access spells that he would probably never have any way of getting otherwise. Even if he became some kind of index junkie, trawling the Spiral for crystalline delta remnants, he might not ever see those particular spells again.

"Can I think about it?" he said.

"Of course. The offer will fluctuate, but it is our policy to purchase such remnants."

"Thanks."

Miles took the crystal and thought about it as he crossed the room.

By the time he passed through the door, he'd already made up his mind.

The nameless tower at the edge of the city looked the same as the last time Miles had visited. Fragmented black metal skin over a skeletal frame, incomplete floors, and exposed wiring spewing out of padded insulation panels.

The black-green Ialis vines might have grown a few centimeters higher since his last visit, conquering a little more of the unfinished tower, but there was no sign that the building would ever be more than a derelict construction project.

Miles hopped off the transport platform. The mossy ground sank and squelched as he walked over it toward the exterior door.

On his last visit, It-who-strikes-decisively had opened the door with a spell, but when Miles tapped on the door access panel it slid open on its own just fine. He made his way down through the abandoned passageways to the top of the stairwell.

The code Iddris had given him, *918-dark-moon-luminary*, still worked, and when he reached the bottom of the ramp, the inner door was opened for him.

He was let inside by a Purir apprentice, three feet tall with green-white skin patches, the same species as the Senior Harmonizer he'd come to see.

He wasn't challenged. Nobody asked what he wanted. It was weird to feel welcome in a place like this.

At the railing of the top floor, Miles looked down through the open space to the floors below. It was a lot quieter than before. Master Oron was missing—*How did he get out?*—and a lot of the mages who'd watched his duel with Adept Shrikesong were absent as well.

Miles started to worry that Master Curious wouldn't be there.

There was one last step before he could absorb the Sky Quester crystal: he needed to check that it wouldn't interfere with his Harmonizer tradition.

Adept Shrikesong's tradition had seemed disharmonious to him, so he didn't think every kind of magic was compatible with his own. He didn't want to do something that would damage his Authority, weaken his abilities, or possibly even cut him off from the tradition altogether. As far as he knew, anything could be possible.

He turned and went back to the mage who was guarding the door.

"Hi, do you know if Master Curious is here? I wanted to ask her advice."

The robed Purir looked up at him for a few seconds with narrowed eyes, an expression that could have meant impatience, or confusion, or almost anything else.

Finally, in a curt voice, she said, "Fifth Sage Master Curious is in an important conference on the future of the Spiral." After a few more seconds of silence, she added with great benevolence, "One of Master Curious's apprentices is here. Alan. Look for him below."

The future of the Spiral?

Miles refused to get sidetracked by asking about that. The apprentice probably wouldn't tell him anyway.

"Okay. Thanks. What does Alan look like?"

"Brown skin. Pink belly. Square-ish. He's probably meditating."

"Thanks . . ."

Miles left before he could get any further onto the apprentice's bad side. He might be relying on her to let him in the next time he visited.

He kept his eyes open for anyone matching the description. He'd gone all the way down to the bottom floor, then back up to the middle balcony level before he saw a potential candidate.

He approached what he'd initially thought was an alien egg. A teardrop shape about a foot tall, with brown skin that came together at a point at the top and four seams running down vertically around the edges. The pointed egg was sitting on a cushion next to the wall, set back from the edge of the balcony.

"Excuse me?" Miles said, hoping the egg really was a sapient.

After a few seconds of worrying silence, the egg began to unfold, the sides peeling down like petals to expose a pink interior, lined with fronds like a shag carpet. By the time the sapient had finished unfurling himself, he was sitting with his pink underside resting on the cushion, looking up at Miles with a pair of eyes perched on short eye stalks.

Miles realized what kind of sapient he was looking at.

He's a Welven.

The pilot on the *Starlit Kipper* had been a white-skinned Welven, though Miles had never had a chance to talk to her.

This individual was a square of brown skin, two feet across and a couple of inches thick, with eye stalks growing from roughly the center of the square.

The sapient regarded him expressionlessly from the cushion.

"Hi," Miles tried again. "Are you Alan?"

The front edge of the sapient's body rippled in a sine wave, and they contorted one corner of their body into a complex gesture.

For all that he wasn't using a spoken language, Miles's *Eyes of the Émigré* translated the gesture into words he could hear, giving the apprentice a young male voice with a refined accent.

"*I am Alan, yes.*"

"I was looking for Master Curious. I had some questions about the Harmonizer tradition, and how it worked with other magical traditions?"

"*Politely-No. She is not here.*"

"Oh. No, the apprentice at the door told me. I was thinking maybe you could help me?"

Alan's body rippled for a second, then they tapped their two front corners together.

"*Humbly-Yes.*"

Miles looked around and dragged a nearby cushion up to Alan, sitting down on it with his legs crossed.

"Okay, thanks. My question is, I have the chance to learn some spells from the Sky Quester tradition. Do you think it's safe for me to do that without becoming disharmonious, or impacting my Authority?"

He didn't explain where that chance was coming from. If Alan was studying under Curious, then he probably wasn't an index mage, and might look down on them himself.

Alan's eyestalks turned down, looking more at his own body than the room around him. A corner of his body reached to touch the middle of the front side.

"*Sky Quester, yes. Let me think.*" Alan spent almost a minute thinking, during which Miles waited awkwardly. Finally, the Welven mage held up both front corners of his body, waving them from side to side in a way that made Miles think of jazz hands. "*I remember. The Ashalai tradition, made to explore the Spiral with. Happily-Yes. It is harmonious.*"

"Okay. So it's not going to hurt my Harmonizer tradition? That's great, thank you."

"*It will not. Humbly-But, do not learn from more than several traditions. Splitting your focus too thinly is not harmonious.*"

"I understand. Thank you, Apprentice Alan." Miles turned to go, then hesitated. "Alan, do you want to swap comm addresses?"

Alan made a waggling motion with the tip of one corner, like he was waving goodbye.

"*Politely-No.*"

"Ah. Okay. Thank you."

Miles walked back up the ramp and back through the stairwell, reaching the ground floor of the unfinished tower.

His transport platform was still waiting for him on the mossy ground outside, not yet called away by a competing traveler, but Miles wasn't leaving the building just yet.

The huge, nameless tower was seemed entirely deserted. Unless he wanted to absorb and test the Sky Quester spells in his cramped apartment, he needed a wide space where he wouldn't be disturbed, and where he wouldn't accidentally hurt anyone. The vacant tower seemed perfect.

The elevators in the building were nothing but empty shafts stretching up hundreds of meters into darkness, but there were emergency ramps positioned around the containing wall.

Miles climbed up three levels before he compromised with the weariness in his muscles and stopped.

This level was half-walled, with the other side wide open to the elements. Outside, the afternoon sky was gray with hazy clouds, and the air was cool.

Miles crossed metal beams to reach a wide circle of completed metal flooring, then pulled out the Sky Quester crystal and his index.

His index acknowledged the presence of the former grenadier's tradition.

Name: Miles Asher   **Traditions:** Harmonizer
Spells (Harmonizer)
Seal Wounds (Grasping)
Temporary Enhancement (Seeking)
Hasten Renewal (Grasping)
Strike the Disharmonious (Adept)
Purify (Grasping)
Spells (Sky Quester)
Shield of Saints [New] (Forbidd#n)   *A plane of soul energy is drawn from the quester to intercept a physical object, reducing its speed and force by an amount in accordance with the quester's Conviction.*
Core Effects (Harmonizer)
Eyes of the Émigré
Eyes of the Altruist
Core Effects (Sky Quester)
Sword of Souls [New]   *Expresses a fragment of the quester's soul as an immaterial blade, with length and cutting power in accordance with the quester's Conviction.*

Both new Sky Quester spells drew on something called Conviction. It sounded like another fundamental property that Miles just didn't have access to yet. If he was lucky, it would be something he could upgrade through his index, even if the tradition itself was forbidden.

If he wasn't lucky, then he'd have a more difficult task in making the new spells powerful enough to be useful. He'd have to learn what Conviction was on his own, and increase it the hard way.

He sat down on the bare metal floor plate, crossing his legs. He rested his index in his lap, in case he needed a free hand, and tapped on the listing for *Shield of Saints* before he could have second thoughts.

The crystal in his hand snapped against his skin and vanished. A moment later he felt energy building in his magical core.

The pulse of magic surprised him. He was used to the slow build-up of Harmonizer spells, and this was so fast it was shocking, sharp and bright. It felt like a firecracker going off in his core.

There was no litany ringing through his ears, just a single clear unambiguous demand for a **Barrier**.

Something clicked in the air in front of him, and the magic of his core died down.

When Miles opened his eyes, he struggled to see any change at first, but slowly noticed that there seemed to be a yellow tint to the room that hadn't been there before.

Looking around, he found the edge of the effect. The color was coming from an almost invisible plane of energy floating motionless in the air in front of him, about a meter square, a few inches away from his face.

This is the Shield of Saints, he guessed.

He reached out and tapped on it, testing its strength with his fingernails. It put up a little resistance, but as soon as he started to apply real force it shattered like a sheet of thin ice, and the sheet of color vanished.

The moment the spell broke, Miles felt a wave of dizziness and confusion strike him. He swayed on the ground, and if he wasn't sitting down he'd probably have fallen over.

It was different from the hollow, fragile feeling that overtaxing his Authority caused, but it wasn't a leap for him to link this feeling to the destruction of the shield.

I guess I'm not going to be stopping any bullets with it.

When his head had stopped spinning and he was able to read again, he went back to his index.

The Sky Quester core effect, *Sword of Souls*, was already there, absorbed at the moment he'd tried using anything from the remnant.

Miles didn't need to activate it to have it become part of him, but he did need to figure out how it worked.

He tapped on the entry under core effects, and felt the same starburst of light flash from his core. This time, the energy flickered around his body before coalescing in his arm.

Over the course of a few seconds, a yellow glow emerged around the front of his hand, more like a haze of light than a blade.

The *Sword of Souls* effect flickered around the fingertips of his free hand, no more than half an inch in length. It danced from one finger to the next as he shifted his focus, the energy rolling along the edge of his hand. It wasn't much of a sword.

It's more of a Craft Knife of Souls, he thought. He'd probably get more cutting power out of a craft knife, too.

He didn't have anything he was happy destroying with him, but after great resistance, he brought the flickering light on his fingertips to the back of his hand.

He touched the energy to his skin. Blood immediately began flowing. The glowing light had cut right through his skin. It took him a second to process what had happened, since there was barely any pain.

Shit.

He immediately focused on *Seal Wounds*. He ran through the litany he'd learned from index-casting the spell, focusing on its truth; an expanded thought from the more limited *Close Wound*.

He felt the warm rotation of his core, and the hot, electric energy that spiked out through his body. White-yellow flames kindled to life on the blood-covered skin of his hand. The fire ran down the injury like a flame following a fuse, burning away blood as it closed the cut.

By the time the flame died out at the end of the tear, his skin was unharmed, unblemished, and clean.

Maybe it's safer to treat it as a Straight Razor of Souls.

The *Sword of Souls* hadn't burned away his ability to focus like the *Shield of Saints*. Maybe it was because nothing had really been expended. The magic had formed a blade, which he'd used, but it hadn't been broken or degraded. *Shield of Saints*, on the other hand, had created something outside his body, and the backlash had come when he'd smashed it.

He'd need to work on casting both without his index. They didn't seem as simple as his Harmonizer abilities. So much of the effort of those was recreating the litany, and *believing* it. The Sky Quester abilities seemed more focused on recreating specific mental images and states of mind.

With the spells at least absorbed into his body, he turned to his potential upgrades, starting with his fundamental properties.

Fundamental Properties—Alterations
Strength +1 [δ50] Strengthens and reinforces contractile, pneumatic, hydraulic, magnetic, and somatic activator tissues in the mage's body with weaves of harmonizing energy, resulting in increased strength.
Durability +1 [δ75] Weaves of harmonizing energy implant biosomatic matrices within the mage's tissues, strengthening them against temperature and chemical degradation, unwanted compression, and tearing.
Speed +1 [δ50] A weft of harmonizing energy alters the mage's body, supplementing frequently-used processing pathways with harmonic resonances and activator tissues with biosomatic matrices.
Reactions +1 [δ50] A weft of harmonizing energy alters the mage's mind, supplementing frequently-used processing pathways with harmonic resonances.
Will +1 [δ50] Reinforces information-processing tissues in the mage's body with a weave of harmonizing energy, insulating thought processes from extremes of external stimuli.
Authority +1 [δ150] Deepens the mage's connection to Harmonic Truth, increasing their ability to impose their harmonious will upon the world.
Soul Strength +1 [δ50] Reinforces the mage's soul with threads of soul energy, increasing protection against attacks on their soul, and mitigating the effects of overdrawing on it.
Conviction +1 [δ50] Alters the mage's information-processing tissues to enhance the purity of their intent and the force of their determination to see it done. This has the potential to be an identity-altering fundamental.

It seemed like just possessing Sky Quester spells was enough to give him access to some related fundamental properties. Soul Strength sounded like it would help reduce the backlash he'd felt when his *Shield of Saints* shattered, and from the description of the Sky Quester spells, Conviction would directly contribute to the strength of their effects.

Miles had been planning to spend some delta to support his new Sky Quester spells with an enhancement to his fundamental properties, but on a second read-through, the warning for the Conviction upgrade had him feeling uneasy.

An identity-altering fundamental.

Fundamentals like Will promised to alter his mind, in that it would make structural changes to his nervous system that would help him ignore pain and other distractions. None of them so far had warned that they might alter his *personality*.

Could increasing the "purity of his intent" really threaten to change who he was as a person? Even if it could, would increasing his determination be a bad change for him?

He probably wouldn't need to worry about it in the near future. The only thing every fundamental had in common was that, at least in the early stages, the upgrades had quite marginal effects.

He couldn't turn himself into a hulk by spending a few hundred delta on his Strength, and he probably wasn't going to turn into a tunnel-vision psychopath with a handful of additional Conviction points.

He scrolled down to see what his increased delta could get him from the list of spells and abilities.

Spells—Alterations
+*Dance of Harmony* [δ150] A weft of harmonizing energy takes up residence in the weaver, spreading out into their surroundings. Visible beings of the weaver's choice will gain the aspect of harmony while the spell is maintained, increasing their precision and reactions by an amount proportional to the weaver's Authority.
+*Strings of Discord* [δ125] A weft of harmonizing energy reaches out to touch discordant presences nearby, revealing their presence and Authority to the weaver.
+*Convict the Disharmonious* [δ415] The weaver's connection to universal harmony allows them to prosecute a target with an accusation of discord. If the weaver succeeds in a contest of reason, Will, and Authority, the target is diminished and is revealed as disharmonious.
+*Song of Harmony* [δ400] A temporary matrix of harmonizing energy fills a space, allowing those within to experience the peace of a harmonious world. Chaotic emotions are soothed and Harmonizer spells are empowered within the space.

+Enhance Tool [δ380]
A lasting matrix of harmonizing energy affixes to an object, enhancing one of its fundamental properties by an amount in accordance with the weaver's Authority and the item's harmony.

+Song of Reality [δ975]
A weft of harmonizing energy fills the weaver's mind, reflecting the song of the world in their thoughts, piercing walls, illusions, and occlusions.

+Deafening Song [δ1025]
A temporary matrix of harmonizing energy fills a space, forcefully attuning it to the truth of Harmony. The strength of other magical traditions are diminished in the area, and disharmonious spells are broken, to a degree dictated by the mage's Will and Authority relative to their disharmonious rival.

+Distant Resonance [δ1575]
Places a lasting matrix of harmonizing energy into a target or at a location to act as a conduit for the mage's spells.

Core Effect—Alterations

+Stance of Authority [δ150]
The weaver's existence is more deeply tied to the ancient tradition of the Harmonizers, giving them an instinctive understanding of harmony and discord. Their Authority will grow in line with their dignity and the harmony of their existence.

+Ears of the Diplomat [δ250]
Words spoken in falsehood will ring the gong of truth. A persistent weave of harmonizing energy will alert the weaver to spoken deceptions, piercing guile to an extent related to the weaver's Authority.

+Eyes of the Imperious [δ410]
Embeds a matrix of harmonizing energy within the being's mind, helping them to identify the disharmony of their surroundings with greater distinction.

+Hum of the Enduring [δ925]
A persistent matrix of harmonizing energy empowers the mage, reducing their need for food and rest by an amount proportional with their Authority and eliminating it entirely at higher Authorities.

As Miles read over the list of possible options, he started to come to the realization that he was going to end up spending a lot of seln on index upgrades. Not just a lot for Miles, citizen of Earth, or a lot for a mage, but a lot for a high-income inhabitant of the Spiral.

He'd already made thousands of seln from dungeon dives, and the vast majority had gone to Morning Star Corporation through index purchases. He could have been a quarter of the way to buying his own flying RV by now, if not for the need to upgrade his magical capabilities.

If he had a lot more time, the tedious but effectively free route of learning magic organically would have really appealed to him. If he hadn't been so attracted to the benefits of magic, he probably could have been fully decked out in advanced tech by now.

He discounted *Song of Reality* straight away. He was pretty sure it was some kind of scouting spell, which wasn't the role he was pursuing.

Deafening Song was more interesting. It seemed like a way to shut down the mages of other traditions, though presumably, it wouldn't have any effect on other Harmonizers. If he had ever run into another mage he *wanted* to suppress, then it would have been an attractive option. So far everything trying to kill him had either been completely mundane, like the Orbellius Ghouls, or completely something-else, like the giant in the Ymn City environ. In the end, *Deafening Song* was fairly easy to exclude as well.

The third new spell available, *Distant Resonance*, was extremely promising. With his current index, if he wanted to cast a spell to heal someone, he needed to be close enough to touch them. *Distant Resonance* seemed like it could address that weakness, planting an anchor in a person or a place that would let him cast a spell as if he were right there.

If only it weren't so expensive. If he bought it, then he wouldn't be able to afford any of the other new options.

There was only one new core effect at this price range, *Hum of the Enduring*, and it seemed like a useful one. It wouldn't help him in his professional role much, as dungeon dives didn't last long enough for food or rest to become an issue, but it seemed like it could make his life easier.

With less need for sleep, he'd have more time. With less need for food, he'd have more money, and the effects would compound for the rest of his life. And if his Authority ever got high enough, would he not need to eat at all? It was effectively promising to free him from two of life's most pressing survival concerns.

It was especially appealing considering that he was planning a trip where the sleeping arrangements and meal schedule would be uncertain.

His final choices were *Hum of the Enduring*, for all its future potential, and especially because a long journey alone might need him to skip meals and hours of sleep; *Ears of the Diplomat*, since that seemed like a strong choice in the face of having to deal with untrustworthy people; and *Enhance Tool*, because he'd been responsible during his last upgrade, and he deserved something for himself.

Including the fifty delta he hadn't spent at his last upgrade, that left him with 534 delta, which he was going to use to upgrade his Authority, as well as to grab the cheap early enhancements to his Sky Quester fundamentals.

He selected his upgrades, then settled back for the sharp attention of his index to wash over him.

When it was done, he checked his index to make sure everything had gone through.

Name: Miles Asher | **Traditions:** Harmonizer, Sky Quester | **Index Value:** δ#6,##5##
Fundamental Properties:
Strength (0)
Durability (1)
Speed (0)
Reactions (0)
Will (0)
Authority (5)
Authority (0.19)
Soul Strength (1)
Conviction (2)
Spells (Harmonizer)
Seal Wounds (Grasping) *A weft of harmonizing energy brings together the free edges of a target's wounds, sealing closed a specific tear, or working to seal all tears.*
Temporary Enhancement (Seeking) *A temporary matrix of harmonizing energy alters one of a being's fundamental properties by an amount in accordance with the weaver's Authority.*
Hasten Renewal (Grasping) *A weft of harmonizing energy spreads from the weaver to their target, greatly speeding the being's natural recovery by an amount multiplicative with the weaver's Authority.*

Strike the Disharmonious (Adept)
With a weft of harmonizing energy, the weaver rips the Authority from a disharmonious target, degrading its existence and claiming the confiscated Authority for themself. While held ready, discordant presences will ring loudly in the weaver's awareness.

Purify (Grasping)
A temporary weave of harmonizing energy takes up residence in the target, degrading objects and substances inimical to the target's existence over time.

Spells (Sky Quester)

Shield of Saints (Grasping)
A plane of soul energy is drawn from the quester to intercept a physical object, reducing its speed and force by an amount in accordance with the quester's Conviction.

Core Effects (Harmonizer)

Eyes of the Émigré
Embeds a matrix of harmonizing energy within the being's mind which will reveal to them the meaning of any plain text or spoken language.

Eyes of the Altruist
Embeds a matrix of harmonizing energy within the being's mind which reveal to them the health and ailments of a witnessed being.

Ears of the Diplomat
Words spoken in falsehood will ring the gong of truth. A persistent weave of harmonizing energy will alert the weaver to spoken deceptions, piercing guile to an extent related to the weaver's Authority.

Hum of the Enduring
A persistent matrix of harmonizing energy empowers the mage, reducing their need for food and rest by an amount proportional with their Authority and eliminating it entirely at higher Authorities.

Core Effects (Sky Quester)

Sword of Souls
Expresses a fragment of the quester's soul as an immaterial blade, with length and cutting power in accordance with the quester's Conviction.

He looked down the list, committing the entries to memory. There were no surprises. Everything had worked. His Authority hadn't been diminished, and he didn't feel disharmonious, at least not with only one additional tradition.

I guess I'm a Sky Quester now.

His index still hadn't offered to let him purchase the new tradition's spells as upgrades, but the two he had gave him options that he'd never get from the Harmonizer tradition. He just hoped the two upgrades he'd picked for his Conviction were enough to make them useful.

He locked his index, stood up on aching legs, and started heading back down to the transport platform.

His magical preparations were as complete as they were going to get. He still had enough seln to purchase some essential supplies, as well as several modifications to his existing equipment. He didn't have forever to get ready, but he was prepared to be busy for the next few days.

CHAPTER 24

The public marketplace in the Ishel Corporation Tower was bustling. There was a lot more interest than usual at the combat vendors, with crowds of humanoids and near-humanoids waiting for attention at weapon stalls, but Miles wasn't there for a weapon.

The strange metal door he'd recovered from the Ymn City environ had worked well as a makeshift shield, but it wasn't perfect. It was too big to carry around easily, and the connection between the levitation unit he'd repurposed and its handle was clunky to use.

A metalworker in Ishel Tower had offered to cut it down into something more suitable for sixty seln. The message that the work was done had come in twenty minutes ago, and Miles was back to collect. Unfortunately, the metalworker's stall wasn't where it'd been when he'd dropped the door off.

Miles stopped, suppressing the worry that the sapient had just vanished with his valuable scrap. He pulled out his comm to check the metalworker's message.

Instead of the message from the metalworker, he had something new listed on the top screen.

The sender, *Spiral System Security*, put a knot in his stomach when he first saw it, but as he opened the message and began to read, his body relaxed. He wasn't in trouble. Someone else was.

Spiral System Security (Ialis) > Miles Asher
Hello M. Miles Asher.
This automated system is writing to update you on a case in which you are named as a witness and co-victim, the case of Ialis Corporation vs. M. Brisk Igris.

Following the events of 27,201.95 at the Ialis Corporation Artifact Entrance Facility, M. Gilarin has been convicted in absentia of a Violation of Integrity - Class 2, Severity 1.

Following this conviction, disciplinary actions Outlaw-Systems-2 have been enacted, and as co-victim, you have been allocated 2.5% of the proceeds seized.

This amounts to §169 Standard Exchange Notes, which have been credited to your account.

May Justice Find You Inescapably,

Spiral System Security

At least it's something?

Miles felt like the *Starlit Kipper* breaking their contract and disappearing into the night was the bigger crime against him personally, worse than being forced to merely witness an assault on They-who-wearily-tread, but even on old Earth, the amount he'd been stiffed on wouldn't have risen above the purview of small claims court.

For a business that could literally just fly off into space, he didn't have much chance of recovering what Rhu-Orlen owed him.

The message from the metalworker was below the security alert in his stack, right where he expected it.

Rugh Nah > Miles Asher
Hey I got your thing done. Meet at my store. Lot 190.

Lot 190 was on the other side of the market floor. Rugh Nah had only relocated, not vanished off the face of the planet with his block of unique metal.

Miles made his way through the crowded aisles between stalls, trying not to get distracted by every new thing he saw.

There was plenty to interest him, and knowing he had money burning a hole in his comm made it difficult to pass some stores by.

One stall was selling 'full body augmentation' kits for a thousand seln—hand-sized cylinders of nanomachine suspensions whose labels were covered in dubious promises to double his strength, speed, and reaction times. They were probably overselling their abilities, but maybe that was the kind of thing Fran had used to get her disproportionate strength? She had to have used some kind of tech augmentation, and it wasn't impossible to think he'd be able to buy something comparable here.

Another stall was selling personal automation cores. On old Earth they would have been called AI assistants, super-fast synthetic minds that would sit on someone's belt and watch their back, offering advice and helping interface with other systems. Those were sixteen hundred for a utility model, and upward of three thousand seln for versions that could help with industrial or combat solutions.

Miles felt like he could have spent an infinite amount of money just in that one provincial market, but he'd taken a different path, one that was already eating all of his disposable income.

The metalworker's shop was almost recognizable as one. There was a spherical container the size of a washing machine sitting on a pyramid base, its front window glowing white with heat. There was a solid block of dark iron metal recognizable as an anvil, and an equipment board full of obscure tools, ranging from an item that looked like a corkscrew to something that could have been an electrified bullwhip.

The proprietor was a man called Rugh, from a species called the Splein. *Biochemistry-D, humanoid body type.* He was a few inches taller than Miles, with well-defined musculature and rough green skin, a wide flat face, bulging eyes, and a mouth that opened like a dropping drawbridge.

He recognized Miles as soon as he stopped in front of the shop.

"Ehhh. Here for your new shield!"

"Yeah. I almost couldn't find you," Miles said, stepping into the area of the store.

"Yahh. It's like hot desking, you get the spot they give you. Hang on."

Hot desking? Either Miles's *Eyes of the Émigré* was doing a heroic job, or that was another weird synchronicity between Earth and Spiral cultures.

Rugh went to an open metal bin of parts and projects and dug around for a minute, eventually coming out with the coppery sheet of metal that had been cut down from the door.

The design they'd settled on was a kite-shaped shield, with four straight edges and a long tail that came down to Miles's shins. At its widest, it would cover his arms if he held it straight on, but if he were carrying it on his back, it wouldn't be any more cumbersome than a hiking backpack.

Rugh flipped it over to show Miles the rear.

"I took out that hover unit and put in a moving one like you wanted. That little strut at the base of the board will take your weight, so you can stand on it if you want."

Miles took the shield. It was so heavy that he almost dropped it. Rugh had taken probably half its weight off with his modifications, but it would still be a burden without the levitation unit.

The new levitation unit looked like a dumbbell crossed with a remote control. It had a short handle, with two thick half-circles that attached to the back of the shield. The device had a switch for power, a release catch behind a flip-up protector to disconnect it from the metal, and six dials side by side along the handle for directional control.

The levitation unit was closer in function to the one Miles's old captain Rhu-Orlen had used to get around than the crate-moving equipment he'd salvaged from the dungeon. It had the ability to move directionally in any direction he wanted, and the little strut of metal at the bottom tip would take his weight if he stood tip-toe on it, but despite technically fulfilling the mechanics of a personal transport device, it still wouldn't work as one. The controls were unintuitive and unreactive, and there was no proper seat and no safety features. What it *might* do was help manage a descent, like Miles had used the levitation unit for on his last dive. It might also help him win in a pushing contest against something bigger than him, like the larger cobolts they'd run into in the ravine.

"Did you get a chance to do the assay?" Miles asked.

He knew the metal was strong enough to take hits from hot striker weapons since they'd used it for cover against the cobolts. He also knew it must be pretty resistant to bending and breaking, since the Ymn City giant had knocked it into the stone wall at immense speed without causing it any damage. What Miles didn't know was how far he could trust that. He wouldn't want to hide behind it from something like Fran's energy pistol, only for the shield to explode in his face.

"Oh yahhh. In terms of defense, it's about level with crystal alloy, except you can't work crystal alloy like I could work this. It's not gonna break from anything less than anti-ship ballistics."

"What about energy weapons?"

"Ehhh. I dunno. There's so much of that. You'd want to get a real assessment corp to run those tests, you know? I hit a lot of energy dispersal tryin' to trim it. I'd say it's a sure bet against any civilian energy. Military? Who knows. I'm not testing for that."

That didn't mean a huge amount to Miles. He'd only had experience with a handful of energy weapons, and he hadn't been interrogating Fran about what kind of weapon her pistol was. *Maybe I should have.*

"Thanks, that sounds good," Miles said.

He grabbed the shield by the handle and flicked the power switch on the levitation unit. The device came to life in complete silence, but Miles could feel from the sudden relief of his muscles now that the tech was taking all of the thing's weight.

He swung it around, holding it vertically, then horizontally. It still had a lot of inertia, but it wouldn't be a burden to carry.

"How long is the battery in the levitation unit good for?" he asked.

"If you're just using the hover, recharge it every forty hourhhhs. If you're using the directions, that'll run the battery down quick. Don't go flying around on it, cause the low power beeper's only gonna give you a minute's warning."

"Yeah, I wasn't going to," Miles said.

It would be the equivalent of trying to fly on an unsecured jet engine. No computer control, no brakes, not even a seatbelt.

Miles pushed down the physical button that unlocked the direction controls, then slid the up-down ring minutely in one direction. He felt the upward pressure.

It wasn't exerting much force at this level, no more than a handful of party balloons, though he could in theory ratchet it up enough to carry his weight. He dialed the ring back down to zero and released the safety switch.

"Yeah, sohhh, the price has gone up from what we agreed," Rugh said while Miles was examining it.

Miles lowered the shield, looking at Rugh over the top of it.

"Oh?"

"Yehhh. Like I said. The power reqs for breaking it down went way over budget. The thing sheds energy pretty well, way harder to make the cuts you wanted."

Miles hummed. He would have thought if there'd been any changes to what they'd agreed, Rugh would have messaged him to ask before going ahead. At least, that was how Miles would have done it.

It should have been no more than sixty seln for the modifications, and not more than a couple of hundred for the new levitation device.

"How much over budget did it go?"

"It totaled out at five fifty."

Miles stared at him flatly.

"I was expecting it to be closer to two hundred and eighty."

"Yehhh. Like I said, power use was highhh."

Miles looked back at the shield. It was pretty much exactly what he'd wanted when he'd handed the door over.

He could probably trim two hundred off the metalworker's price if he swapped back to the old levitation unit, and selling the cut-offs would almost certainly recoup most of the cost, even if the Gilthaens hadn't found anything particularly notable about the metal.

Though, looking around, Miles couldn't see the cut-offs.

"I'll pay the higher price," he started, "But where are the cut-offs? And I'll want the levitation unit back I brought it in with."

"Ehhh. Materials lost in processing normally stay with me."

Miles gave the metalworker a hard look.

"That's normal for anyone in this business," he continued. "Ask around, they'll tell you."

Miles put the shield down on its point, letting the levitation unit hold it in place. With his hands freed, he pulled out his comm unit and started navigating the interface.

"Uhhh. What're you doing?"

"I'm asking my friend in the Ialis Corporation if it's normal for a metalworker to keep the raw materials a customer provided."

He started tapping out a message to They-who-warily-tread. He'd come up with the idea just then as a bluff, but he felt annoyed enough to go through with it. He'd probably earned enough goodwill with the Gilthaen to get away with bothering them via message a few times.

"Ehhh, you're connected, huh. Well, look, it's not just about what's normal. The scrap's not scrap anymore."

Miles hesitated, ready to send. "What do you mean?"

"Well, ahhh." Rugh went to the bin and pulled out a few metal objects. There were a couple of knives, a padded bracer shaped to fit a humanoid forearm longer than Miles's, a sword, and a hammer. All of their metal parts were made from the same coppery metal as the door.

"So you used them without asking me," Miles said.

"Normal praahhhctice."

Miles doubted it. He went back to his comm.

"No need to bring the worms in on this, ehhh?" Rugh said. "Ahhh've put work into these, so I can't just give 'em back. How about I sell them to you. Fifty seln for all. That'll cover the labor. I was gonna sell them for a hundred each, so that's a net profit for you."

The merchant was asking for more than six hundred seln for a project that was supposed to cost less than three hundred.

Miles felt growing anger, and the rising urge to escalate.

He could cause a scene, get aggressive, try to pressure the metalworker. He could call They-who-warily-tread, or even city security. But he found he didn't want to.

He saw two roads in front of him, one where he fought for every scrap, aggressively defended his pride, and railed against the world where it wronged him, and one where he was someone who could chalk up being cheated as a learning experience, where he'd rather leave seln on the table than greedily snatch at it.

He'd recently had an experience with the former. His argument with Fran. She was someone he'd once wanted to consider a friend, and saw the potential for friendship in the future. She'd turned around and repaid his suspicion with generosity.

That second path felt like where he wanted to be. He wanted to be secure enough that he didn't have to take every loss as a slight. He wasn't there yet, but he could take a small, reluctant step in that direction now.

"I guess I'll take them," he said. Rugh flapped his mouth in what Miles hoped was a Splein nod of agreement. "But I guess I'll still check with city security about what you said on keeping the scrap, for future reference."

"Nahhh. No need to do that. Like I said, standard practice."

"Still. If there's a kind of unspoken rule about that I want to make sure I've got it right," Miles said. "I think I'll still just check with them, make sure I understood you right."

Rugh's mouth stopped flapping. "Ahhh. I just remembered. I was gonna give you a discount on this. It was nice to work on new material."

"Oh," Miles said, immediately noticing the sapient's motivated backtracking. "Is it maybe a two hundred seln discount?"

"Yehhh."

"Okay . . ." Three hundred and fifty seln wasn't a lot more than what he was expecting. "I guess, maybe I don't need to message security."

"Nahhh. No nehhhd."

Miles tied the floating shield to the straps of his backpack and used his comm to tap out a three hundred and fifty seln payment to the metalworker.

Rugh handed over the bundle of things he'd made from the cut-offs. They were heavy, but Miles wasn't up to the task of weighing them and working out if that was really every piece of cut-off scrap.

He stood there for a few seconds, feeling his arms straining at the weight.

"What about my old levitation unit?" he asked.

Rugh turned away without replying, going back to the parts bin.

Miles left a couple of minutes later, with the new shield dragging from his backpack, and the stack of cut-off items clamped in the grip of his old levitation unit.

"I'm looking for something to read on a flight," Miles said.

The shopkeeper slid out from behind the counter and approached, all six of their hands laced together as they crept over the tiled floor of the store.

"I knew you could not resist the knowledge purveyed here for long,"

Miles had maintained a business relationship with Lash-ishel-suffuzus since he'd first wandered into the off-Exchange bookstore a week before. He'd made less use of the book rental policy than he'd expected, and now that he had more than two seln to rub together, the deal didn't seem so good.

He had been reluctant to come to the shop in person. The Morchis proprietor went hard on their sales pitch, and they either had a genuinely troubling anti-establishment thing going on, or were putting one on as a marketing ploy. It made Miles uncomfortable either way.

"I'll be traveling for two or three weeks, and I want to use some of the time to study. I'm looking for Spiral history, and if you have anything on magical traditions? Sky Quester and Harmonizer."

He already had enough books on biology and medicine in the Spiral to be going on with. More than he'd managed to memorize so far, anyway.

The sapient returned to the counter where he interacted with a terminal. After a minute, he turned it around so that Miles could see the screen.

He could read it thanks to his *Eyes of the Émigré*, but he wasn't sure how the shopkeeper expected anyone else to know what it meant, given that it was probably all written in Morchis.

The Lash-Ishel Store of Secret and Coveted Knowledge
Spiral history / Harmonizer tradition / Sky Quester tradition
Ten Thousand Histories by Lhen-Roshel [§45]
A Draulean's Guide to the Spiral by Moriel Efere [§80]
A Pinprick Sky by They-who-think-in-darkness [§52]
How to Be More Harmonious by Adept Furious [§25]
To Pierce the Heavens With Our Soul, unattributed [§95]

"These are the most popular titles, among the more discerning readers of the Spiral," Suffuzus crooned.

"This interface looks a lot like the Exchange," Miles said, reading down the list, "Only with a smaller catalog and less information."

Suffuzus touched the terminal and the screen went blank. "Perhaps you're not interested in my wares, after all."

"No, it's okay. I'm interested. I couldn't find anything about the Sky Quester tradition on the Exchange."

The shopkeeper reactivated the screen and Miles checked the list again.

"Can I get A Draulean's Guide, How to be More Harmonious, and To Pierce the Heavens?"

"Yes. It will be my pleasure," Suffuzus hissed. "Two hundred seln."

Sure, I'll just drop two hundred seln on books.

Miles paid with his comm, and waited while the Morchis shopkeeper loaded his purchases onto a tablet.

Miles > Ialis Route Planning
Dendril City Skyport to Unsiel Station, outside Iteration 27,200
Ialis Route Planning > Miles
Direct: none
Chartered Direct: §6,000-§10,000
Scheduled Indirect: §1,640
Independent Indirect: §445
Suggested Route:
Dendril City Skyport > Consular City Skyport [Sky Shuttle]
Consular City Skyport (26,100) >> Lanthatariel Station (27,100) [Century Express]

Lanthatariel Station (27,100) >> Forward Fleet Waypoint (27,201) [Fleet Express]
Forward Fleet Waypoint (27,201) >> Unsiel Station (27,200) [Fleet Express]

Four hundred and forty-five seln for a ticket that would let him hop on and off participating transports all the way to Earth wasn't too bad, Miles thought. He felt like there were domestic flights that would have cost comparatively more back on old Earth. He assumed it was one of the benefits brought by the cosmology of the Spiral. Every world and civilization existing on a single traversable line had to simplify the mass transit routes between them.

If he'd wanted to charter a direct flight, the equivalent of hiring a private plane, that would have cost real money. The ship would be able to cut directly across the empty core of the Spiral, saving a lot of time and fuel, and delivering him directly to Unsiel Station, but that was far outside his price range.

Even the "Scheduled Indirect" route, the closest option to booking a ticket on connected flights on old Earth, was out of his price range currently.

He didn't even hate the idea of the "Independent Indirect" option. He'd still get to travel most of the thousand iterations between Ialis and Earth on a single ship, the Century Express, and after that he'd be able to take whatever transport he could find to get to the Forward Fleet, and then to Unsiel Station.

If he lost a day while he was waiting to find a transport going his way, that was an expense he could deal with, though there was so much traffic in the Spiral he didn't think it was likely.

He tapped out the request for a ticket in a message to the transit system.

Miles > Ialis Route Planning
Confirm Dendril City Skyport to Unsiel Station, outside Iteration 27,200, Independent Indirect.
Ialis Route Planning > Miles
Ticket confirmed. Account charged. Your travel document is attached.

The moment he locked the decision in, he felt something. Sadness, at having to leave Ialis. Miles was surprised at himself.

He'd come here by chance, but now that he knew something about the place he realized he was going to miss it. He actually liked the moss-covered landscape. He liked the Ishel tower. He liked the mage's enclave. He didn't like his apartment, but that wouldn't have to be forever.

It had taken deciding to leave for him to realize Ialis was his home, and that he was sure he was coming back.

PART 10

ONE THOUSAND WORLDS

CHAPTER 25

DAY 0 - IALIS

Miles watched Trin and Torg through the viewport of the shuttle's passenger deck. The pair of them shrank slowly as the shuttle gained altitude, Trin becoming a blur and then a pink-white dot. Torg vanished against the backdrop of the black-green moss. Soon, he couldn't see them at all.

The sky shuttle to Consular City was just the first short leg of his journey, but it was his start. Miles felt the mixed pain and excitement of leaving home, even for just a few weeks.

His luggage hovered next to him. He'd turned his dungeon alloy shield so it was face down, and in that position it worked pretty well as a cargo sled. It was burdened with the runner's pack he'd left Earth with, his rolled sleeping bag, and a synth-fabric duffel pack that held the rest of his gear.

There was no checked luggage on the sky shuttle, and from what Miles had heard, it'd be the same on the Century Express. People traveled with their things in the same cabin as them. Even weapons. Even bottled water. The arrangement was closer to the sleeper trains of ancient Earth than an intercontinental flight.

He'd kept the dagger and hammer that the metalworker had turned his Ymn door scraps into, now packed away in his bag, and had sold the rest of the pieces back to the Ialis Corporation. The price the Gilthaen officials offered had gone down a little from their first offer, but not by as much as he'd expected. He'd still made over a thousand seln on the pieces. If he'd had time to shop for a viable replacement, then even holding on to the shield would have been a tough decision.

As the minutes passed, Miles resisted the urge to hop up and sit on the shield. He was sure that as soon as he did, the shuttle would change acceleration and he'd find himself drifting off in one direction or the other.

Instead, he held onto his luggage with one hand, the metal ceiling loops with the other, and tried to zone out while looking at the scenery below. It wasn't that different from riding on the subway.

The transfer from the shuttle to the docking platform for the Century Express had been rushed and hectic.

Consular City was enormous, built in a completely different style from Dendril City. Miles recognized the Gilthaen style in the structures. Tiered pagodas, many of them open-air, but just as many walled off with thin translucent screens.

Unlike the towers of Dendril City, at least half the buildings in Consular City were levitating, supported by a combination of massive levitation units and attraction beams from anchoring stations higher up. The effect was as if the entire city was in the process of falling upward, buildings spaced out along a kilometer-high column of air.

The inter-city shuttle had landed at one of the ground-based landing platforms, but the Century Express left from one of the topmost floating pagodas, and the need to change platforms wasn't made particularly clear to anyone arriving at the skydock.

It had been a tight connection from the arrival platform to the point of departure, traveling on an open-air transport platform, but Miles had made it with a few minutes to spare.

Now, he waited on the roof of one of the topmost pagodas, surrounded by forty or so Ialis sapients. The floating building was so high they were sharing space with the clouds, with the cold damp air turning to mist a few meters past the edge of the building.

Miles didn't recognize most of the other people on the platform as dungeon divers. He wasn't an expert on Spiral clothing yet, but all of the sapients present had outfits that seemed to fit the category of either business wear or high fashion: suits with non-functional embellishments, fits that would limit movement, fabrics that shone or changed color holographically. None of which pointed to a pragmatic function.

He didn't need to be a follower of Spiral fashion to know an ankle-length coat with a six-inch popped collar probably wasn't the outfit you'd wear on a dungeon dive.

Miles thought he visibly stood out from the business crowd. He was dressed in his tailored off-white robe and brown webbing belt, covered in pouches, with the black pants, white shirt, and warm dark red jerkin underneath.

The blue healer symbol dyed on the chest of his robe probably labeled him as a scavenger to everyone present, even if they didn't recognize that his robe was made of armored fabric.

With the time Miles had taken to reach the platform, he didn't have to wait long for the ship.

It came out of the clouds above him like a sea monster rising from the murky ocean. An enormous, bulbous whale of a vessel half a kilometer long, studded by lights, scabbed with irregularly sized viewports, humming like a live wire as it came down through the mist.

Miles thought that the ship might be an Alfaen design, like the *Starlit Kipper*. It had the same kind of organic curves, evoking an aquatic creature.

It seemed a little extreme to be bringing the entire enormity of the passenger liner into any atmosphere, let alone into a force gradient like the pseudo-gravity around Ialis. Miles thought it would have been infinitely easier to send a shuttle down to make the passenger transfer while keeping the main ship in orbit, but he wasn't the one paying its fuel costs.

The ship came down much lower than Miles was comfortable with. It reached a hundred feet from the platform and kept on coming. It didn't stop at fifty feet, or at twenty feet. Miles had a moment of panic when it looked like the ship was going to crash into the platform, but its speed dropped sharply at the last second, and it came to a stop just ten feet above the heads of the waiting passengers.

A cylindrical cut-out of the ship's belly descended on a telescoping piston, revealing a circular platform that was bounded by railings and packed with disembarking passengers. The disk touched the building's roof, and the sapients leaving the ship flooded out through narrow gates.

When the space was clear, the waiting passengers surged forward onto the platform.

Century Express Passenger Liaison System > Miles Asher
Welcome aboard the Century Express.
As an Independent passenger, you are granted full access to public areas of the ship.
You are granted habitation rights in any of our species-agnostic life support suites on decks D and E.
Nutritional packs, atmospheric top-ups, in-flight entertainment, and souvenirs can be purchased at our commercial facility on Deck E1.
Please consult the attached data pack or any ship data panel for information on our bylaws and conditions of carriage.
Informational briefs will be delivered for each of our destinations for your benefit and enjoyment.
If you have any questions or wish to make a report, this automated system will be happy to help.

Being an Independent ticket holder put Miles on almost the bottom rung of passengers. He was allowed on board the ship, but he had no assigned quarters, no free meals, and no automatic right to access the utilities.

He did have access to a suite he'd have to share with up to twenty other sapients, assuming the suites weren't all full.

He went straight for one of the furthest suites in and was the first passenger to find it. The "suite" didn't look too bad. He was the first one in this compartment, but it looked like it could easily accommodate twenty or more people of Miles's size.

There were sealed-off chambers at one end for waste and washing, with the rest of the space taken up by padded benches.

A soft, padded surface was an almost universal comfort amenity from what Miles had seen. Any species with hard body parts, internal or external, would welcome a place to put themself down that distributed the force over an area rather than a single point. Even Alan, the Welven mage who Miles had met in the Dendril City enclave, had used a cushion while meditating in egg form.

The far wall of the space was completely given over to viewports, though currently they only showed an impenetrable wall of Ialis mist.

Miles picked a bench close to the windows and sat down, moving his shield to stand upright in an out-of-the-way spot in the corner.

Still too unsettled to read, Miles settled down to wait.

The first other passenger to arrive was a Welven traveler, or rather, four Welven individuals of different colors tessellated together to make an even larger flat square.

Miles hadn't knowingly seen any sapient children during his time in the Spiral—neither Ialis or Delatariel Station had seemed like the place for them—but he was certain that the half dozen coaster-sized Welven following the larger square were infants of their species. They wriggled along the floor on their shag-rug undersides, following their larger guardian around the corner and into the room. The tessellated adults picked out a bench for them near the window, and the infants crawled up the sides to sit across the cushion, straining their eyestalks to peer up through the glass.

Miles watched them get situated. Half a minute after he turned his attention to the Welven infants, he started to hear tiny voices coming from the crowd.

"*Fa, what alien is that?*"

"*Fa! I have to freum!*"

"*Fa. I am itchy!*"

"*Fa! Fa! Fa! Fa!*"

The voices were all quiet and high-pitched.

Miles closed his eyes, hoping the translation magic would fade without his attention on them.

Passengers continued to filter in over the next couple of minutes. By the time Miles's comm started beeping with the ship's embarkation message, there were fifteen other sapients in the compartment. Ten of them were the Welven family, plus a rocky coral-like sapient, two Hurc travelers, a Morchis passenger whose hood was so deep their face was lost in shadow, and a Draulean woman.

Miles hadn't seen any other Draulean sapients since Lestiel Dunverde, the first client they'd guided into the dungeon. For some reason, he was surprised to see this one traveling in the public suites. Maybe he thought that because their species was supposedly immortal, they were all rich.

This individual had the same skin effect as Lestiel, alternately ink black and alabaster white depending on whether an area was more in light or shadow, but she had a taller, narrower build, and where Lestiel had a smooth bald head, this person's scalp was textured with raised fractals.

She stood apart from the rest of the passengers, staring out through the viewport.

Miles let *Eyes of the Émigré* fade to bring *Eyes of the Altruist* to the front of his awareness.

A quick check confirmed that she had the same unusual internal structure as Lestiel. No organs at all, except for the large shape in her torso, positioned like a mouth on its side.

A couple of minutes after the last passenger entered, the bulkheads of the ship thrummed like a struck bell and the world outside became tinted with the blue of the ship's shields. There was a minor sense of movement and some swirling in the mist outside.

Soon, the mist was vanishing, giving way to clear skies and an unobstructed view of Ialis's surface. The curve of the planet became clear as the sky turned black, and the ship veered away from the planet to begin its journey.

The rocky cone of a sapient sitting next to Miles struck up a conversation with him once the planet was out of view.

Miles recognized his species as an *Endurer*, which had to be a rare case of a species name being translated semantically rather than phonetically.

They introduced themselves as Stringer, a Euphospher drive technician on their way back from a shipyard contract in Iteration 26,899. It took a few minutes of Stringer describing the world before Miles realized they were actually talking about Torg's homeworld.

The sapient reported an unstable political situation, and a civil war that had left a lot of weave ships damaged. Things were calmer now, and the Spiral had lifted the political embargo, so there was apparently a lot of new work for people in technical fields.

Miles found himself explaining his own job. Stringer was fascinated that Miles was an Ialis scavenger, and even encouraged him to tell some of his dive stories.

Over the course of half an hour, Miles recounted his fight in the cobolt ravine and then his encounter with the Orbellius Ghouls. He kept the Ymn City environ encounter to himself, worried that he'd lose his credibility with the stranger if he started talking about the weirder parts of it. It was probably the kind of account that Fran would call a "ghost story."

After that, they each found they'd reached the limit of small talk and fell into silence. Stringer pulled out a featureless cube which they began manipulating with their tendrils, while Miles grabbed a book from his bag.

There was no day-night cycle on the ship, but after a few hours of quiet reading, Miles began feeling a little stretched.

He wasn't exactly tired. He'd been awake for about eighteen hours and felt like he could go longer, but the stress of packing and travel took its own kind of toll, and his body was worn out, even if his mind wasn't.

When it came to sleep, the passenger suite had the feel of an airport lobby. It wasn't somewhere Miles felt completely comfortable sleeping, exposed and in the company of strangers, but it occupied the weird middle ground where someone could sleep out of necessity without looking out of place.

He found a power port for his levitation unit and set up his sleeping bag on the bench, with his bigger backpack arranged as a pillow and his rain cloak on standby as an additional blanket. He positioned his shield so that it was floating on its side between him and the room, giving him a little cover and the illusion of privacy.

He thought he'd have trouble sleeping, but as he began to drowse, he felt like he was back in the refugee housing of Unsiel Station, where quarters were cramped and everyone was in the same situation together.

Before he had a chance to worry about whether his possessions would be safe, or if he could trust the other passengers, he was already drifting off into troubled sleep.

CHAPTER 26

DAY 1 - IUNIS

Miles stared through the viewport of the liner's community deck. His eyes were gritty from long hours awake, and his skin was dry and itchy from the arid communal-species atmosphere.

He hadn't slept more than three hours since leaving Ialis, and he didn't feel like he could any more if he wanted to.

Miles's Authority in the Harmonizer tradition was still moderate, in his view, but he was already feeling the effects of *Hum of the Enduring*. The magic had promised to reduce the needs of his body, food and sleep, and it was dramatic. He was getting hungry later, and tired more slowly.

If what he'd experienced extrapolated out, then he wouldn't particularly need to eat more than one large meal a day or sleep more than five hours a night.

On an inter-iteration passenger liner, that was a huge convenience.

He could picture a situation in the future where it might stop being convenient, when it started limiting how much he could eat for fun, or got in the way when he was trying to sleep in, but for now, he was happy to live like a snake, gorging himself once a day and subsisting on that for the next few dozen hours.

Miles was passing time in the community deck. The area was busy with seats and tables, interactive games, food vendors, air vendors for passengers who couldn't breathe the communal atmosphere, and information terminals.

Outside the window, Iunis drifted into view. It was a rocky planet, splotched with pink and blue vegetation.

A nearby terminal listed off the world's details.

Stop: Iunis Adjunct (26,200)
Polity: Iunis Corporation
Brief: Iunis is a reserved world in the stellar system of Iteration 26,200.

Precis:
Managed by the Gilthaen-majority Iunis Corporation, Iunis is held apart from the Spiral for the protection of its sapients and its culture. Unsanctioned landings and visitations on the planet are forbidden as Class 3 violations of integrity while the world reconciles with its transposition and its culture evolves to a point where integration can be initiated.

The only Spiral-sanctioned destination within the iteration is Iunis Adjunct, a weave station at the periphery, which stands in for a planetary hub in this region. Iunis Adjunct hosts a full range of amenities, as well as the headquarters of the Iunis Research Directive, an organization investigating the spatial properties of this iteration.

Iunis was a weird case of a world that dropped out of its native universe without anyone already established in the Spiral being able to tell why.
According to the terminal, the inhabitants were land-based quadrupeds, with a pre-industrial technology and a handful of insubstantial magical traditions. There was no grand work that had got them bowered, no huge ritual or technological leap.
The text in the terminal speculated that it'd been the result of either natural cosmic phenomena or the actions of a culture that had stayed behind in their native universe.
Because their technological and magical development weren't at the point where they could communicate with Spiral civilization on their own, the world had been placed under a cultural embargo to protect their evolution.
Sooner or later, the Iunians would discover telescopes or radios and realize there were ships and other worlds up here, but until then all they'd know was that there'd been a cataclysm and the stars had changed.
The policy reminded Miles of the science fiction of old Earth, a kind of enlightened custodianship, but in reality, the Spiral wasn't that enlightened. Only *unauthorized* landings were forbidden. Spiral authorities could and had visited the planet, getting permission from the inhabitants for mineral and land development in the uninhabited parts of their system.
Miles wasn't sure how they'd even done that without giving the game away. The Iunians couldn't have fully understood what they were selling.
It took an hour from first sighting the Iunis system to the Adjunct station coming into view. Miles returned to his passenger lounge.

After the ship docked, half the people in Miles's section left, leaving only Miles, the Draulean passenger, and the Welven family behind. New sapients filtered in a little later, and without much fanfare, the ship was moving again.

Miles began to pay less attention to the other passengers. He was sure that the stops every few hours would soon become routine.

DAY 3 - POLYPOLIS (26,500)

How to Be More Harmonious by Adept Furious was sold as a magical tradition manual, but Miles thought it had more in common with a self-help book. Maybe it really could help its readers to increase their personal Authority, but that wasn't its goal.

To the Purir who developed the Harmonizer tradition, *harmony* was more than just a route to access magic. It was a life philosophy, a religion, a battle strategy, a health plan, and a code of justice. When the Purir went to war, they committed themselves entirely to the attack. They held nothing back, constrained by no rules of morality or concept of mercy, because to pull their punches would be *disharmonious*. When they adopted a defensive position, they literally entombed themselves underground, seeding the stone above them with traps and barriers.

There were no half-measures, no conflicting directives. Purity of intent was their highest virtue, and to lack it was a character fault. It was a demanding philosophy to try and follow.

Although Miles himself didn't ring off-key to the tone of *Strike the Disharmonious*, the book helped him pick out several parts of his life that apparently were sources of disharmony.

He was qualified as a healer, and that was his chosen role on a scavenger team, and yet he carried a weapon. According to the text, that was a source of disharmony. How did the magic know he was selling himself as a healer? Miles wasn't sure. Maybe it was based on his subconscious thoughts. Maybe the magic was an objective force that was watching him from the inside. Even asking the question was something Adept Furious decried as 'mechanistic thinking'.

His problems didn't end there. He was a stranger to the planet Ialis, and yet he maintained friendships there, disharmony again. He wore a robe as a healer, which was apparently good, but he now carried a shield, which was bad. He was a mage but he still used technology freely, also bad.

Miles didn't know how seriously to take the book.

His index offered him access to a core effect called *Stance of Authority*, which would supposedly give him a better instinct for the ebb and flow of Authority. He'd hoped that personal study would have avoided the need to spend the delta on it, but so far the book was asking a lot, and the changes it was suggesting weren't convenient things to experiment with.

It was obvious that none of his supposedly disharmonious qualities were lowering his Authority below the level his index had raised it to, but he felt as far from raising it on his own as ever.

Miles was contemplating messaging Master Curious back on Ialis to ask about the book when Polypolis came into view through the suite's windows.

Polypolis was a world, but not a planet. It was a ring of water in the form of an endless waterfall, tens of thousands of miles in diameter, hundreds of miles thick, constantly spinning and crashing into itself. Something about Iteration 26,500's background fields made a ring the lowest-energy shape for rotating matter to gather in, rather than a sphere.

Enormous waves crested its outer edge, tall enough to sink any naval ship, or even any low-flying spacecraft. There was no atmosphere beyond the water itself, and no solid underlayer.

In any rational universe, the world would have failed. It would have boiled off into space or collapsed into a ball, but in 26,500, the Pulstreen homeworld was normal.

Miles stood at the window of the suite, stunned at the sight and amazed that the life that evolved in such an alien place could even survive elsewhere in the weave.

Of all the worlds he'd seen so far, this was the one he most wanted to visit. He wanted to see those waves from the water's surface.

DAY 5 - DESOLATION III (26,800)

A Draulean's Guide to the Spiral was a bitter, misanthropic take on Spiral culture from an author with a grating superiority complex. It was also clear and concise, and since the author assumed they were writing for ignorant savages, the book explained things that might normally have gone unwritten.

There are only four truly immortal species in the Spiral. Drauleans, of course, stand apart as being untouchable by disease, damage, and even time. The Gilthaens are immortal due to an accident of biology, as every microscopic component of their body contains a copy of their complete biological and mental makeup. The Alfaen are immaterial spirits which dwell only temporarily in physical bodies, their immortality thus an expression of their personal magic, and the Nexilaen are purely informational entities who can exist for as long as their substrate endures. Of the Archaen, I will say nothing, as they are mere pretenders to eternity.

Some of it was uncomfortable reading. The author's value system was pretty different from Earth standard morality. They didn't even ascribe to the "golden rule," which Miles had otherwise found to be a reliable principle in the Spiral.

Miles found that the book had something to say on most of the "century" worlds, including the one that the Century Express was passing now.

Desolation III—a world scorched clean of life by the disaster which brought it here. Many of us believe it was the target of a substrate weapon wielded by one of the powers inhabiting its previous universe, a device either magical or technological that could sever an area and send it crashing down to the bedrock of existence. Perhaps we owe that nameless wielder our thanks, as those worlds which bring resources without yet more clamoring voices to add to our weave are surely the most welcome of arrivals. We may not hope that more such deliveries are forthcoming, but if they were, they would not be unwelcome.

The author wasn't a big fan of the constantly increasing population of the Spiral, and openly admitted that in what amounted to a relatively small, finite universe, the acquisition of new resources was an existential concern.

Miles was just contemplating taking a break from the book when he realized that the Welven adult that was sharing his compartment was approaching him, creeping toward him across the ground, moving like they were shy.

As they got closer, Miles was more sure than ever that the larger body was made up of four adult Welven tessellated together, the pink cilia of their undersides wrapped around each other at the edges like they were holding hands. All four individual squares had their own pair of eye stalks, and all eight eyes watched him as the shape undulated forward

When they reached Miles's feet, the entire square reared up, a little over three feet tall. They touched the tips of their front corners together, and Miles's *Eyes of the Émigré* gave them a voice.

"*Humbly-Pardon. May we ask, are you a healer?*"

The voice Miles heard through *Eyes of the Émigré* was a composite. Four individual voices speaking over each other, the same words at the same times, differing only in pitch and accent.

For a stunned second, Miles tried to work out how they knew what he did for a living, before he realized he had the symbol printed on his chest. *Healer.*

He considered how to respond. He wasn't sure what the other passenger meant by asking.

"I'm a Tier 1 healer," he said, hedging his answer. "I work on a scavenger team."

The other passenger twisted one of their corners to point back over their body, to where the smaller versions sat or scurried over each other on the bench at the far side.

"*Humbly-One of our children is complaining endlessly of itching. Exasperatedly-Would you be willing to check them?*"

Miles folded his arms over his chest, almost unconsciously covering up the symbol there.

Miles hesitated to answer. It wasn't like he had much experience with Welven. He had a magical toolkit that was better suited to obvious injuries.

"Have you tried messaging the passenger liaison system?" he asked. "I bet they have a doctor on board."

The corners of the sapient sagged.

"*No. The price of care on the ship is very inflated. Resignedly-Apologies for troubling you.*"

The sapient began moving away.

"Wait. I can look, at least," Miles said, standing.

He wouldn't have answered anyone asking for a *doctor*—he didn't have that expertise—but he didn't feel that the other passenger had any unrealistic expectations of him.

The sapient paused, then turned back to him. They pressed their front corners together.

"*Thank you. Wearily-The greater part of us were imploring that we at least ask.*"

They turned and led Miles to the bench at the far side of the room. Most of the tiny Welven were quiet. Resting, Miles guessed.

The adult picked one of them up between their front two corners and turned to Miles.

"*This is the itchy one.*"

Miles looked them over. There was nothing visibly different about them. Their topside was white with dark splotches, matching one of the Welven individuals that made up their parent.

Focusing on the infant, Miles let go of his translation magic and fell into *Eyes of the Altruist*.

Just like the Welven pilot on Miles's first ship, the infant had very little internal structure that the magical effect could latch on to. Back when he'd seen his first Welven individual, he hadn't known what that had meant, but he'd studied enough since that he had context for the apparent lack of organs. Almost every function in a Welven body was performed by microscopic structures, and they were all distributed across their entire surface. The organs were individual layers of tissue, sometimes only a few cells thick, performing every function from nutrient extraction to gas transfer and even thought.

One thing about the Welven infant did stand out. The magic was showing a spread of luminous white specks along their upper surface, like they'd been dusted with glowing flour.

The magic had shown him foreign bodies in patients before, like projectile fragments, but here he couldn't tell what these could be.

He let the diagnostic magic fade, switching back to *Eyes of the Émigré*.

The tiny Welven's voice quickly became audible.

"Itchy itchy itchy!"

Miles turned to the parent.

"I can see something on their top surface," Miles said. "I don't know if it's an infection, parasites, an irritant . . ."

I'm not qualified for this.

"Cautiously-Is there anything you could do?"

Miles considered his limited tool set.

Hasten Renewal wasn't something he wanted to experiment with. In his Tier 1 exam, it had outright killed some of the simulated patients. If someone could naturally heal from an ailment, then the spell could help that along dramatically. If they couldn't, then it would accelerate their degeneration.

Temporary Enhancement was safe for him to use, and enhancing the infant's Will would help them endure any symptoms they were suffering, but it wouldn't last more than a few minutes unless he sat next to them, constantly refreshing it. Even that would probably wear him out before they recovered on their own.

Purify seemed like the safest option that might have a chance of helping. The spell promised to "degrade objects and substances inimical to the target's existence." Miles had chosen the spell for its ability to counteract poisoning, but it might work as well on allergens, contaminants, maybe even infections. Could it be that simple?

"I might be able to help. I don't know for sure. I'd need to cast a spell on them," Miles said, speaking to the parent.

The Welven passenger brought a corner to the center of its front edge. "*What spell?*"

"A Harmonizer spell called *Purify*," Miles said.

They lowered their front corners to the ground to support their weight. All of their eyestalks twisted to look at Miles, then the itchy infant.

"*Determined-Please use it on us first, then we will decide.*"

There wouldn't be any adverse effects, but Miles could appreciate the adult wanting to vet the spell for their kids. He was grateful, even. It made him feel a little less out of his depth.

"Okay," he said. "I'll need to touch you."

The Welven adult held out a corner, and Miles took hold of it.

He focused on the litany for the spell. He'd cast it before, but only in practice, never on a dive, never when he needed it to work.

In this being, there is a note of disharmony. The harmonious being purifies themself. **Purity is the natural state.**

Miles's magical core began to spin, expanding, sending energy flooding through his arm. Hot light flickered between his fingers and the warmth passed into the Welven target, where it settled in.

The *Purify* spell wasn't like *Seal Wounds*. It didn't happen all at once. It was closer to *Temporary Enhancement*, embedding a magical structure in the target which did the work over time.

"It's working now. Do you feel anything?" Miles said.

When he'd experimented with the *Purify* spell on himself, he hadn't been able to feel it working any more than he could feel his kidneys working, but he hadn't been suffering from any contaminants at the time.

The Welven adult reached up and touched a corner to its top surface, like a person putting a hand to their head.

"*Respectfully-We feel nothing unusual. Perhaps I feel a little lighter.*"

"Am I cleared to try it on the baby?" Miles asked.

In response, the adult reached down and picked the infant up. It wriggled in their grip as they held it up toward Miles.

"*Aaaahhh.*" The infant thrashed its corners.

Miles reached out and poked it with the tip of a finger. He recited the litany to himself, and felt his core spin up.

The warm light jumped from his finger to the little Welven, and the spell took up residence.

He switched to *Eyes of the Altruist*, watching for any change to the dusting on their surface.

At first, there was no change. He waited in awkward silence for a minute, with the Welven adult occasionally making gestures that didn't translate while Miles was watching through his *Eyes of the Altruist*.

Finally, there was a shift. A patch of the glowing patina vanished suddenly, leaving a gap. A few seconds later, another area of the discoloration disappeared, like something had taken a bite out of it. That continued a few more times, until the effect stalled out and Miles was forced to cast the spell again.

It took four casts of *Purify* in total to completely clear the dusting. By the end of it, Miles was feeling stretched magically, when he'd already been feeling stretched physically. It felt like he was pushing the limits of his Authority.

"Is that any better?" Miles asked, bending down to look at the Welven infant as he switched back to *Eyes of the Émigré*.

The small Welven reached out to him with its front corners.

"*What species are you?*" a tiny voice asked.

Miles glanced at the parent, then back at the child.

"Human."

"*I'm a human!*" the young Welven cried.

The parent flipped the infant over and poked its pink underside with a front corner before putting it back down on the bench behind then

"*Hopefully-They seem to be feeling better,*" the adult said, turning back toward Miles. "*We think that may have helped.*"

"Yeah. There was some kind of contaminant on their top surface."

Maybe the infant had got into somewhere they weren't supposed to be, and been exposed to something, or maybe they had picked something up off the ground.

The adult put their front corners together. *"Thank you for your help. May I have your name?"*

"I'm Miles."

"Thank you, Miles. Do you need payment?"

Miles briefly wondered what he'd charge them, but the thought put a bad taste in his mouth.

"No, of course not," he said quickly.

The Welven turned and picked up the healed infant. *"Your spoken name will be 'Miles'."*

The infant wriggled. *"Miles! I am human!"*

"You are not human."

Were they naming the kid after him? "You don't have to do that," Miles said, feeling panicked.

The adult half turned back to him. Their front edge rose at a couple of points in a movement that was almost a shrug.

"Nonchalantly—*We have more children than we have spoken names. This one will work.*"

The adult put the infant back into a pile with the others, then climbed up onto the bench.

Miles left the Welven family alone, going back to his own seat. A few minutes later, he caught the Draulean passenger watching him, but nobody approached him again.

DAY 7 - INTEGRATION C (27,100)

Integration C was the last stop for the Century Express.

It was the homeworld of the Archaen. Miles got his first look at them as he was disembarking the passenger liner at an open-air upper atmosphere skyport.

Miles's medical reference called the Archaen "technological symbiotic systems." The *Draulean's Guide* said they were "self-engineered immortals, using crude technology to bridge the gaping holes in their biology." To Miles, they activated every negative stereotype of cybernetics that Earth culture had ever produced.

The ones he saw walking around the skyport flight deck were humanoids and quadrupeds, all originally biological, but all now colonized by technological implants in the same way an ocean ship might be colonized by barnacles.

Some had a scattering of devices, skin-deep growths of dull gray or bronze-colored metal, antennas growing from cheeks, noses removed and replaced by membranes kept moist by implants. Others had been modified more extensively. Limbs replaced by segmented black tentacles. Torsos that bulged with metal barrels where organs might once have been. In the most extreme cases, where flesh had been shed completely, the sapients achieved a strange kind of beauty, like living metallic statues.

Under the harsh gaze of *Strike the Disharmonious* most of them clanged and clattered with discord. Miles felt like if he were a real Harmonizer, he would have been disgusted. Which wouldn't have been fair. They were sapients, like everyone else up here, and neither his human prejudices nor his adopted Harmonizer prejudices had any bearing on their reality.

From Miles's left, a hulking humanoid the size of a gorilla stopped and turned a heavily altered face to him. They raised an imploring arm in his direction, and the tech at the end of a wrist stump unfolded into a nightmare of tangled medical instruments.

When they spoke, their voice buzzed like an electrical short buried in a wasp's nest.

"*Will you join us in perfection?*"

Miles watched the twitching surgical limb for a second.

"No, thank you."

The sapient's head lowered. To Miles, they almost looked disappointed. They stomped off without another word.

The skyport reminded Miles of footage he'd seen of aircraft carriers. The flight deck extended hundreds of meters long and about a hundred wide, topped in a high-friction surface that might have been wood, if the wood had been cut from cyberneticized trees. The shape of the structure was aerodynamic, thinner than it was long and squared at the ends. On an aircraft carrier, the flight deck would sit on the top deck of a ship. Here, the skyport extended downward in a massive vertical spire. The descending structure was apparently filled with a lifting gas, taking some weight off the levitation units. The planet below was hidden beneath unbroken cloud cover, giving the impression that they were flying above a white ocean.

Miles slowly scanned the edge of the platform, reading signs that labeled small jetties.

The planet was in Iteration 27,100, just a hundred short of Earth. It had only bowered about fifty years ago, but was already a well-established name in the Spiral.

Earth was in Iteration 27,200. One day it would be a Century Express stopping point as well, but it wouldn't be hooked up until anyone had a reason to go there. Anyone who wasn't human.

From here, Miles would need to travel to the Forward Fleet, and then take a shuttle onward.

Eventually, he spotted the sign for *Fleet Express*.

Grabbing his floating shield cargo, he headed toward it.

DAY 8 - THE FORWARD FLEET (27,201)

This was Miles's last stop. The largest military force in the Spiral.

The Forward Fleet had been Earth's introduction to the weave. Maybe a million ships, from a thousand different iterations, with hundreds of different shapes, aesthetics, philosophies, capabilities, and technological underpinnings, not counting the vessels that were biological individuals of their species, magical vessels, or energy constructs.

It was the Spiral's wall and its hammer, following the cutting tip of the helix as it carved through the void, catching falling worlds in the Spiral's political-economic net.

Struggling worlds would be assisted. Belligerent worlds would be quelled. Isolationist worlds incorporated. And dead worlds colonized.

Earth had been *assisted*. The Fleet's landing shuttles had offered Spiral comm devices and the possibility of evacuation, but they weren't always welcome. For a portion of Earth's surviving population, help from new, strange-looking neighbors was sometimes refused and sometimes forcefully resisted.

The existence of the Spiral created a new, higher tier of political control, which Earth was subordinate to just by existing within its reach. That was never going to be popular among the planet's leaders. Add in the photon burst and cascading disasters, and the new local rulers were left jealously guarding what little they still controlled.

Miles disembarked the Fleet Express onto one of the commercial ships that flew alongside the Forward Fleet like camp followers. This one was a small transport hub, with a few amenities and an onboard hotel. He didn't plan to be there long enough to make use of them.

It was his last stop in the Spiral. From here on, he'd be traveling mostly through Solar space by interplanetary shuttle.

His route would take him through the orbit of Pluto, past the gas giants and asteroid belt, to the rocky interior planets, and then to Earth.

The trip through spacetime would be orders of magnitude faster than anything Earth spacecraft had achieved before the bower break, but it would still be slow compared to the average weave ship. Sub–light speed, and given the cost of accelerating mass in Solar space, not even particularly fast sub–light speed. A journey of thirteen hours or more.

Miles had left Earth on an evacuation ship that wasn't much more than a cargo hauler with sleeping mats. He hoped that the regular shuttle would be a more comfortable ride.

His expectation was fulfilled a few hours later. The information panels lit up with directions to a sixty-seat interplanetary shuttle, the Spiral equivalent of a short-haul plane. He checked his luggage for the shuttle's hold and tried to suppress his concerns as he climbed onboard. Finding his cramped window seat, Miles settled in for the flight.

PART 11

A GREEN PLANET

CHAPTER 27

Through the window of the shuttle, Earth looked just like any other planet. A ball of matter drowned in water and festooned with life. It had one Spiral-acknowledged sapient species: human, C-type biochemistry, humanoid body plan.

It'd been a fourteen-hour journey to reach the world, crawling through viscous spacetime at barely a third the speed of light. Staring down at it, Miles was having to remind himself why he was there at all.

At one point, the night side of the planet would have been rashed with artificial light. Miles had seen photos, pre-bower, taken from the US orbital fleet. Every square inch had been lit up by luminous pinholes, clustering and threading like an incandescent slime mold. Now, every square inch was dark.

The brightest things left down there were man-portable floodlights, and the survivors knew better than to let energy escape into space. Every kilowatt-hour was needed on the ground.

The shuttle window fogged as Miles watched the dirtball grow in the viewport. He could make out a few known locations. Long Island, the Great Lakes, Florida, California. But the places they represented in his mind didn't exist anymore. After the chaos, they'd become new features, with unknown realities.

There were features of the post-bower geography, too. The New York crater, where a stable fusion plant had been abandoned to its ambitions of sunhood. The wildfire scars running the entire Canadian west coast.

Newfoundland was more cove than land, now. It'd been the site of a terrestrial zero-point plant, one of the pins that had burst the bubble.

Miles tried to avoid looking at the place he knew his home settlement was, but his eyes seemed drawn to it.

A hundred miles south of Lake Michigan, where forest met river, a crashing frigate had taken a bite out of the top of the hill.

"Miles Asher, get out here."

The Captain's voice hissed and popped out of the frigate's comm system, burnt wires and demagnetized components reducing the noise to a barely human electronic distortion.

Miles didn't like leaving his room, but the sound wasn't so degraded he could pretend he hadn't heard it.

He unearthed and pulled on plastic boots, straining to pull the material over bare skin, forcing himself to ignore the cold that pressed against his toes. When he was ready, he left the retrofitted storeroom and made his way through the corridors.

The settlement was built into the wreck of a '98er, all rubberized floors and sloping metal walls. The reactor was still hot enough to keep the heat and lights on through the particle winter, for those lucky enough to deserve a place inside. As the son of the Captain, Miles was that lucky.

It didn't matter that Damien Asher had never captained a battleship before the disaster. Only a handful of the residents knew that he'd only been a quartermaster at a Space Force base, and nobody was talking about it.

He had *a* military rank, he had the codes for the wreck, and he had a map of outposts and storage locations. That was enough for people to defer to him. It was even enough for people to defer to *Miles*.

Three teenage men watched Miles from a refuge alcove as he passed. Armed and accustomed to violence, they were the settlement's buzz-cut chosen. All of them were veterans of city raids and population runs, bandits and kidnappers, which made them heroes in the new order.

Assault wasn't a crime for people like them, and their instincts were honed to pick out weakness in a herd. If Miles wasn't untouchable, he would have needed to worry about them. He still kept them in his peripheral vision until they were out of sight.

A hand-painted white line marked the route through the groaning wreck to the entrance, which opened onto a muddy field littered with plastic tents and corrugated plastic lean-tos. Outer members huddled in their shelters, wrapped in silvered plastic blankets against the damp cold.

The frigate that housed the secure part of the settlement had a plastics fabricator that had survived the crash. Scrap plastic was easy to scavenge, and the residents had ended up making a lot of things out of it that they really shouldn't have.

Footprints marked the paths, deep boot impressions that had filled with gray water under the constant rain.

It couldn't be later than three in the afternoon, but the sky was already getting dark. The sun-reflecting particles in the stratosphere were still doing their job months after the world's industries had stopped putting out warming gasses.

The managed climate was another system that only balanced when it had the world's full attention. Another spinning plate sent flying.

Fifty yards away, a man with a short black beard and receding hairline stood on top of a crate addressing his troops. Damien Asher, master of the Frazer settlement.

Damien spotted him and waved him over. Miles started trudging through the mud, trying to stick to the more solid parts of a field that had very little solidity left.

Ratbugs skittered out of his way as he moved through the outer settlement. The giant pillbugs were an invasive species, another gift from the aliens, already everywhere. They bred like flies, could eat anything, including plastic, wood, and gasoline, and they were as happy in the snow as they were hiding under bedding. The more desperate among the settlement's population had been eating them.

Miles reached the group and stopped a little way apart from them.

The assembled troops were men, for the most part. Dark-haired, unshaven, military haircuts and military builds, wearing camo fatigues and modular backpacks.

They could have all been Damien Asher's biological children, by their looks, and it was consistent enough that they had to have been hand-picked for their similarity to him, even if it'd been subconscious on his part. Miles could barely have stood out more in that crowd.

"You're taking Miles with you on this one," Damien said, addressing the group.

"What?" Miles asked flatly.

Damien's patience seemed strained as he spoke to Miles. "We've caught another abduction raid coming down at Eagle Creek. We think they're targeting the Indy holdouts."

Miles's heart sank as he thought of the alien ships. He knew them as lights in the sky and grotesque forms seen from a distance. The raids were getting more frequent. The alien ships touched down at places where survivors congregated, then left with those survivors on board. They'd left whole areas depopulated. There was never any signs of overt violence at the sites afterward, but that just meant they had some way of getting people to come willingly. Miles's father had suggested they were using some kind of mind control.

The Danville refuge had about two thousand survivors. The Captain had been targeting them with his own population raids and proselytizers for a while, but they still had people he wanted, people with skills or expertise, or who he thought would benefit Frazer in other ways.

Miles thought that, for his father, this "intervention" was probably less about protecting fellow humans and more about monopolizing future serfs for his little kingdom, but the problem was that the aliens *were* taking people. Miles couldn't dispute that. He hated that he and his father were aligned on that fear.

"Sir, what's his role going to be?" Seth asked, one of the Captain's favorites.

Damien Asher turned to stare at Miles. "Just let him watch."

Miles was startled by a rattling in the hull. The shuttle's shields had deflected a cloud of space-junk fragments, sending them scattering out of sight to the left.

The view through the window had changed. Now, Miles could see Europe and Africa, as well as their destination.

Iceland had had it comparatively easy in the chaos following the bower break. High food security, energy self-sufficient. The built-in security of being an island had let them dodge problems nearly every other country on Earth had faced. They'd never dabbled in fusion or zero-point energy installations, and the People's Government had been hedging against global instability for the last fifty years. When the Earth had been hit by the equivalent of a massive solar flare from the break boundary, supply lines and modern farming had failed everywhere. Neyjavik had still managed to feed themselves. They'd been the first to welcome Forward Fleet aid ships.

The voice of the ship's comms officer came over the speakers. The translated drawl of a Standard-22 accent explained they were approaching the atmosphere. Next stop, Neyjavik. Local time 11:00 p.m. Prepare for landing.

Miles fastened his seat strap and put his book tablet away.

The shuttle descended quickly, its energy shield parting the atmosphere without heating it. It dropped to a hundred feet over the ocean before skimming forward toward the coastline. The low approach gave Miles a good look at the city.

Neyjavik had been a mid-century attempt at a modern business hub. The original buildings were all 2050s era, four- and five-story blocks of sustainable wood and black solar glass, with their wedge roofs and accents painted in soft primary colors.

It had probably been a prestigious place for companies to have their head offices, once, before the world ended. Now it was the center of a refugee hub.

Beyond the pastel city center, the landscape devolved into an ad-hoc shanty town. Miles recognized the touch of non-human architecture in the mass-produced units organized across the sides of the valley. Boxes that weren't much more than shipping containers were lined and stacked along the grassy slopes in organic rings. He would have bet that inside, they looked a lot like his apartment back on Ialis.

The shuttle passed over the city and turned, aiming for a miniature skyport just outside the city. Lily pads of black metal littered a field at the edge of the city, scattered like they'd just been dropped from the air and left where they landed. It was the same style of skyport as in Dendril City on Ialis. Seeing so much Spiral infrastructure springing up on Earth was jarring.

The shuttle came in for landing with a rattling vibration punctuated by a hissing impact. The vessel's interior lights came up to full, and the doors unlocked almost immediately.

Around the cabin, various sapients equipped themselves with environmental hoods or breathing apparatuses, ready for the unmanaged atmosphere of the planet. A sealed environment could have multiple non-interacting atmospheres at once to cater to multiple biochemistries, but outside, anyone who couldn't live off C-type gasses didn't have that luxury.

Miles queued up to leave the craft. The time it took to shuffle to the door seemed to pass in a blur, but his first step out under the Earth's sky in over a year seemed to trigger an endless, frozen moment.

The air was cold, and the smells of salt, dirt, fish, and the hot electric metal smell of the ship washed over him. He could hear the crashing ocean and the cries of sea birds.

Human skyport techs waited on the ground to service the shuttle, dressed in high-visibility vests with clunky steel toolboxes. There were safety signs labeled with human iconography.

The city was built in a low valley, and even in the dark, Miles could tell that the gentle slopes were drowned in green. Short, hardy grass, tangled shrubs, even a few low, wind-stretched trees.

He only stood in the ship's access port for a second before he was urged out onto the platform by the crowd pressing behind him.

Beyond the black platforms, the skyport was ringed with a tall wire fence, supported by weighted poles and topped with barbed wire. Plumes of black smoke dotted the horizon, blotting out city lights. Miles couldn't tell if they were from campfires or burning buildings.

A squat concrete building stood at one end of the fenced area, showing signs in English, German, Icelandic, and a Spiral language Miles didn't recognize. They all directed new arrivals to report to *Customs and Immigration.*

It'd been a year since Miles had needed to worry about immigration control. Should he have applied for a visa?

He followed the crowd of other passengers around to the rear of the shuttle, where he collected his shield and duffel.

The shield's levitation unit seemed to be working as he pulled it out of the cargo shelf. He piled his bags onto the makeshift levitation sled.

Miles spent the walk over to the office checking his other gear. His index was still working, showing his usual catalog of spells, and he could feel that his magical core was still active.

He could read every language on the customs signs. His *Hum of the Enduring* was still active, a warmth that clouded his core, buffering him against the need to sleep.

He'd cast *Enhance Tool* not long after boarding the inter-iteration ship, enhancing the Durability of his robe. He hoped it would make it better armor. Casting the spell had instantly brought his Authority close to its breaking point, but the effect it had imparted hadn't faded yet. He could still feel it as the distant, muted prickle of external magic.

Miles's comm was still working, the light-speed delay notwithstanding. Trin had kept in touch at first, but having to wait hours for a reply each way had put the scout off from sending casual messages.

The striker he couldn't test. It still reacted to Miles changing the dials, but he wasn't about to fire it in public. It *should* still work. There wasn't anything exotic about a beam of focused light, though his concerns about the weapon started to run in a totally different direction as he approached the administration buildings.

Lists of items forbidden in Neyjavik loomed on every flat surface. Explosives. Intoxicants. Spiral plant and animal products. *Weapons.*

It seemed like the government here was trying to keep a box closed that Miles was pretty sure had cracked when the bower broke. He didn't think it would work. They couldn't control every possible landing site for incoming ships, though from the armed guards, it seemed like they were at least making a sincere attempt at it.

Human security guards patrolled or observed, armed with holstered Spiral-tech pistols. A mixture of black-blister CCTV cameras and Spiral-tech scanner cubes sat at the corners of the building, observing the area, and a drone with a Gilthaen look patrolled the area outside of the fence.

When Miles stepped into the lobby area, he saw Spiral tech screens hanging from the corners, displaying a list of incoming flights. The listed arrivals were both from Spiral space and other parts of Earth.

Miles was surprised at that. He didn't know anyone had gotten local flights running again.

The survivors had to be using military planes, since nothing with civilian electronics would have survived the photon flash that came with the break. Where they were getting the fuel was anyone's guess. There hadn't been a functional oil industry for over a year.

He got into line at the customs desk, standing behind a human in a leather duster with two rolling suitcases. The smell of tanned skin radiated off the coat.

The man had been one of about fifteen other humans on the shuttle with him, interstellar travelers who didn't have the look of the refugee stations about them.

What had they been out there in the Spiral? How were other humans making their way?

There had been a refugee population on Unsiel Station, so Miles hadn't been away from other humans for long enough to miss them, but a month was long enough for him to feel awkward around them in a way he never did around other Spiral sapients.

With other species, the differences in culture, language, philosophy, and biology created a kind of friction in every interaction, and it fostered a lot of patience and leeway.

Interactions with humans, on the other hand, were razor-sharp. Humans were always assessing, always positioning, even in the most relaxed conversations.

He hadn't missed other humans. He missed his roommates. He missed Torg's heat lamp, and finding a comfortable spot in the dumb bed he shared with Trin.

"Reason for visiting?" the human customs official asked the man in front.

The queue had moved. Miles was now in second place.

"Visiting family," the man in the duster said.

He'd barely finished speaking when Miles heard a clanging noise descend around him. It was the ringing of a cracked bell, the dropping of an iron weight, a sound that had more in common with an industrial accident than a musical note.

At first he thought it was coming from a speaker system, until he recognized it. *Ears of the Diplomat*. It was the discordant sound of the truth-telling magic he'd acquired during his last index upgrade.

Whatever reason the man was really here, it wasn't to visit family.

"And your address, while you're staying here?"

The customs official and traveler were both speaking different languages, one probably Icelandic, the other French. Neither were having trouble communicating, suggesting the Spiral's translation tech had made it here.

"The hotel on Astun."

This time, the magic remained silent.

"Are you bringing any alien biological matter or intoxicants into the city?"

"No," the man said.

Ears of the Diplomat clanged again, more strongly. Another lie. Miles wondered if he should keep quiet about it. Accusing the man of lying wouldn't go down well with anyone.

"Are you bringing any weapons or explosives into the city?"

"No."

Ears of the Diplomat rang like falling pots and pans.

Miles examined the man again. Short dark hair, broad build, wearing a tracksuit under his coat. He could have been anyone, doing anything.

Maybe Miles really should say something.

The official finished with his questions and let the man go. Miles stepped up. The clerk began asking the same questions of Miles.

"I think he was lying," Miles said, before the clerk could get started. "He lied about his reason for being here, and about carrying weapons."

The clerk, an older man with wild hair, stared at Miles for a few seconds.

"Why do you think that?" the man asked.

Miles hesitated to explain. No matter how much Spiral tech had made it to this city, "magic" wouldn't be treated as a credible explanation for how he knew something.

"I have a Spiral-tech lie detector," he said instead.

The man seemed surprised. "They didn't tell me I could have a lie detector." He reached under his counter and came up with a handheld walkie-talkie. "Hey, Karen. There's a guy in a leather coat coming through. Give him a scan, will you?"

"Sure thing."

That seemed to be the extent of the action he was willing to take based on Miles's accusation. The man put his radio away and continued with Miles's processing.

Miles hadn't arranged a hotel in advance, but when asked the clerk gave a recommendation for the same hotel the man in the duster had mentioned. When he found out Miles's reason for visiting, redeeming his mineral allotment, he gave directions to the city's Spiral annex as well.

Eventually, the clerk asked Miles the same question about weapons, and he was forced to bring out his striker pistol, as well as the Ymn City metal knife and mace.

The man passed his eyes over the metal weapons, apparently not knowing what to make of them, but seized on the gun.

"I will have to limit this while you're here," he said. He pulled a small device from a cardboard box next to his station. It looked like a translucent plastic postage stamp. "I stick it to the barrel and it drains the energy. It will disable the weapon while it's attached. We'll take it off when you leave."

"Okay?"

Miles surrendered the gun to the process. He wasn't planning on shooting anyone while he was here anyway. When the clerk was finished, Miles packed it away along with the rest of his things and moved on.

He spotted the guy in the duster as he passed into the exit lobby. The traveler was being inspected by a woman using almost the exact same model of scanner as Trin had been using when Miles first met him, a boxy device with a screen covered in scrolling text.

She fiddled with the scanner, an expression of concentration on her face as she tried to interpret a screen of numbers and monochrome graphs. As Miles made his way across the room, she gave the man a pass, letting him go.

Miles watched him step out through the doors.

She obviously hadn't found anything on him.

Had Miles's *Ears of the Diplomat* failed? The wording of the magical effect suggested it could be fooled, but not that it would give him false positives. From Miles's experience, Harmonizer magic was absolute in a way that technology wasn't. On the other hand, he knew for a fact there were devices designed to fool scanners. Brisk had tried to use a signal mask generator to sneak something past the Gilthaen officials on Ialis.

Miles followed the man out.

They were both going to the same location, the same hotel, and after spending longer awake than even his *Hum of the Enduring* could compensate for, Miles found it easier to follow the other man than work out the route on a local map.

He just hoped they hotel had vacancies.

Miles and his unwitting guide moved away from the skyport into the city center. The architecture was very human. Wood, glass, asphalt, and concrete. Straight lines and rectangles, road grids broken up by organic shapes only when the terrain forced the issue, or when the city plan had needed to work around a pre-existing construction.

Outside, at night, the air was bitterly cold. Miles questioned the wisdom of walking to the hotel, but he hadn't seen any other options. There were no cabs, no rideshares. The roads were almost clear, with only occasional passing cars. A few buildings showed signs of life, restaurants and bars with lights or loud music, but there was no foot traffic.

For a while Miles and the man in the coat had an entourage, some of the other passengers from the ship, human and non-human sapients, but the others broke off at various points.

When the cold started to move from uncomfortable to painful, Miles stopped and took his cloak from his bag. That did a lot to keep out the chill, and he resumed the walk.

Miles followed the stranger out of the city center, where the buildings began to shrink to two and three stories, then to single-level warehouses and mass accommodation.

By the time he'd started to catch glimpses of the undeveloped valley through gaps in the buildings, he was starting to realize that something was wrong.

It was late, he was operating on no sleep, still learning the limits of *Hum of the Enduring*, and he'd sleep-walked right out of the city into what classified as its suburbs.

Most of the buildings were now low houses, brick-built, partially submerged in the ground. The refugee settlement that he'd seen surrounding the built-up city center was starting to be visible. There was no hotel this far out.

The man ahead of him cast a glance back from about a hundred yards ahead.

With nobody else on the street, the man spotted Miles easily. He paused, seeming to think for a minute, then turned and started advancing on Miles.

Embarrassed, but not worried about the confrontation, Miles stood where he was and let the man approach.

"Are you following me?" he asked.

"Sorry," Miles said. "I was so sure you were going to the hotel on Astun."

He stared at Miles for a minute. "That's all?"

"Yeah. I heard you say you were staying at the hotel, and I thought I could just follow you there."

It took a few seconds before the man seemed to accept that. If he was concerned before, he seemed amused now.

"You're a fucking idiot, aren't you."

Miles accepted the judgment without comment.

"So, there's nowhere to stay around here?" he asked.

"No. I'm heading to a friend's," the man said. Miles heard the clanging from *Ears of the Diplomat* again. "Hotel's about a half mile back that way. Astun Street."

"Thanks," Miles said flatly.

Forcing his tired brain to process the street names, Miles found his way back to the built-up areas of the city and followed the street signs to Astun.

A row of commercial buildings greeted him. A small mall, what looked like a cinema, and a hotel. It was almost like being back before the break.

The streets here were lit, and even the closed stores were lit. Apparently the city had energy to spare.

Miles stopped at the hotel, stepping through a revolving door into a lobby that was heavy on wood.

The building actually had a night clerk, an alert-looking man in business casual dress sitting behind a curved desk. He was watching something on an LCD screen, and when Miles stepped up to the counter, he realized it was some kind of video streaming service. He was watching a music video.

Miles stared at the screen for a minute, until the man behind the counter decided to take notice.

He turned to Miles with a tight smile.

"How can I help you?"

"Hi. Can I rent a room? I should just need a couple of nights."

After a moment of confusion where the clerk asked for a fee in krona and Miles had to negotiate a custom price in Spiral seln, he was given a room number and a wooden keycard.

The building had a working elevator that he rode up to the third floor.

When Miles finally stepped into the room, he barely stopped to turn the heating all the way up before zombie-walking into the bathroom and taking his first normal shower in a year.

CHAPTER 28

A stratoplane flew into the city the next morning, a jet with wide, flat wings and a pair of piezoelectric fins trailing behind it. It came in low, clearing the ground by a few hundred feet, heading for some local touching-down spot.

It couldn't land at the same skyport that the other spacecraft used. That type of plane couldn't land vertically. When it disappeared out of view beyond the hills to the north, Miles assumed it was being routed to an old-style airstrip.

He wondered where it had come from. The fins were covered in photovoltaics and he remembered that there had been solar planes that could stay in the air indefinitely, sacrificing speed for longevity.

Before the break, they'd been a novelty. Now, they were probably the only type of aircraft that surviving settlements could afford to fuel.

It was already a lot more organization than Miles had expected to see on his return.

His family's settlement had owned an operational light helicopter, but they'd kept it on the ground, fueled and ready for emergencies. If places were able to get tech like the stratoplane working again, it meant Earth was starting to recover.

The world had seemed to grow dramatically when the bower break had hit the edge of Solar space. A wave of light had flooded inward from the shredded boundary, frying GPS satellites and unshielded computers. Container ships had been moored indefinitely. Flight companies hadn't survived, and neither had the planes' electronics.

The other side of the world was no longer a twenty-hour flight away. Anything that wasn't grown, mined, or manufactured locally might as well have not existed.

Some places had been self-sufficient enough to cope, but twenty-four-hour supply chains had broken down across the world. Grocery store shelves had emptied quickly and not refilled. Regional supply centers had been looted, the contents hoarded. The electrical grid went down, and with it water pumping and treatment. If there had been people sitting on grain silos or livestock farms out in the farm belt, they weren't breaking out the horses and wagons to get distribution moving again.

The global banking system crashed, taking all money with it. Police and militaries were no longer being paid, and soon weren't being supplied. There just wasn't enough slack in trade and stockpiles to keep things going. Not enough people to repair damaged systems fast enough. The efficient momentum of the world had hit a stone and broken loose, all that momentum turning to chaos.

The solar plane suggested that was changing. There was no maximum range on those things. They could be coming from Europe, Asia, the US.

Nobody else on the street took any notice of it. It must have been a common enough sight.

The way to the Spiral Administration building wasn't hard to find; it was signposted at every intersection.

The place was an embassy, a chamber of commerce for Spiral economic interests, and, if Miles believed the graffiti scattered around the city, the place from which the "aliens" controlled the local government.

Miles didn't believe the graffiti, if only because the city would be running a lot differently if the Spiral was in control here. He'd be able to access all of its maps and resources through his comm, for one.

The streets weren't crowded as he made his way through the city center. There were people, more humans than he'd seen in one place for months, but it wasn't reaching Chicago at rush-hour levels.

He passed markets selling fish, salvaged and repaired human tech, Earth fruits and vegetables, as well as some of the more basic examples of Spiral tech, including comm units for sale.

Now that it was daylight, Miles could see that the city was backdropped by rolling green hills. It was exactly the shade of green he'd missed. Dark, vibrant, *normal*.

The land here was more than just a comfort to the part of Miles that longed for familiarity, the trees and plants were anchored in his memories. The short, hardy spruces and cottonwoods took his mind back to camping trips along Lake Superior. The rugged grass was the playing fields behind his school. The rowan trees and sassafras were the week he spent in Canada with his family, back when he could still pretend things with them were good. The plants here *were* family, in a way. Everything here had grown from a single ancient ancestor. Nothing was alien. Everything was somehow familiar, even the things he'd never seen before.

When he first caught sight of it through his hotel window, he thought he'd be frozen to the spot forever, just staring at it. He'd found the will to move eventually, but walking through the streets, it kept catching his eye, threatening to captivate him again.

The Spiral administration office was built on top of an older terrestrial building, a chunk of Spiral architecture jammed into the roof of a brick-and-mortar office block. For some reason, Miles had expected the building to have a Gilthaen design, but the angular black plates rising up out of the single-story office were from some other architectural tradition.

Miles stopped across the street to look at the building. It almost looked like a squat weave ship, like a vessel had dropped down from the sky and integrated directly into the pre-existing building.

A pair of motion-sensing doors slid open in front of him when he approached.

Inside, the space had the feel of a militarized DMV. The far wall had a bank of teller stations, part of the original human-built fittings, with armored glass covering most of them. Several angular drones hung in the air around the room, definitely not human-built, and Miles had seen enough Spiral tech to recognize them as armed security. Two of the stations were staffed by Hurc tellers. Both male, one with solid black eyes.

There were a few unattended information stations set against the walls. One was populated with paper-printed pamphlets, the kinds of standard information the refugees on Unsiel station had access to. Another had shelves of basic comm units, similar to the one Miles carried. The comms were apparently free for anyone to just come up and take. Another Spiral initiative to try to integrate as many humans as possible.

Miles had known coming in that anyone wanting to stake a claim would need to have a comm unit, because that was just how the Spiral legal system worked. It looked like they were available here for anyone who wanted one.

One of the tellers was occupied dealing with a human woman in red Spiral-tech armor. It had the same look as the powered armor Miles had fought in the dungeon.

Miles stared at her as he approached the free teller. He'd never seen another human with that level of Spiral tech, himself included. He knew from experience that powered armor like that was *expensive*.

She was arguing with her teller, waving a credit-card-sized comm unit.

"Hey, how can I help you?" the other teller asked as Miles stepped up.

It took Miles a second to realize that beneath his *Eyes of the Émigré*, the clerk was speaking Icelandic.

Weird.

Miles brought up his comm with the message showing from Entrant Allocations.

"I got this message about a mineral rights allocation," he said, laying the comm on the counter so that the teller could read it. "Can I collect that here?"

The teller looked at the message, reading across it.

"Yeah. That's in order, all right," he said. He tapped a device to Miles's comm and the screen changed to show an interface. "Fill this in and we'll get your claim processing."

Miles picked up the device, looking down the fields of what was essentially a piece of paperwork. From the questions, it was obviously trying to match and authenticate him to a known human survivor.

Date of birth, May 11, 2112. City of birth, Fort Wayne. Full name . . .

"Miles Asher," the patrol leader called out, staring out over the crowd.

Seth was one of Damien Asher's favored. He led the raids that another commander might balk at. The hot supply raids, the population runs. His team was just returning from a population run now.

The gas truck was disgorging a crowd of ragged survivors, healthy young men and women, all sleepy-eyed from whatever sedatives the troops had given them at gunpoint to make transporting them easier. Some days it was Xanax, others Ambien. Whatever was available.

The newcomers would rail and fight when they woke up, furious at being kidnapped, furious at being trafficked. They were kept in a different part of the wreck, sequestered behind locked doors. Miles could usually hear them shouting from his room. The fighting never lasted long. The people who'd eventually bring them into the fold had been brought to the settlement the same way. Eventually, they would all accept the settlement as their new home. His father said it was human nature.

It was the main way the settlement grew. There was no automated farming tech left working, and the nascent plots at the boundary needed hands. There were other, unfriendly settlements within thirty miles, and the Frazer settlement needed guards. Most of all, Miles thought, Damien Asher needed his dominion, and having more people under his control fed his ego. Damien was his father, which technically put Miles inside the ruling camp, but within that, he had no control. He could try to run and find himself somewhere as bad or worse, or try to run and be caught, or try to run and die out in the unforgiving new world.

Most of Earth's modern technology had been lost, but there was still plenty of ancient technology within reach. Using violence and survival pressures to control people was a tool the Frazer leadership had found quickly.

Seth spotted Miles standing in the crowd and waved him over.

Miles's feet felt like lead as he approached the truck. Today he was riding along on a defense run, but he wouldn't escape the population raids for long. This was just the start of the process. *Toughening him up.*

The back of the truck smelled of bodies that had gone weeks without washing, of infection, of sewer water. He picked a place on the wooden bench closest to the opening at the back, hoping he'd get more fresh air that way.

A handful of troops joined him over the next ten minutes. Men with dark hair, younger versions of his father, all armed with early twenty-first-century assault rifles, smelling like sweat and oiled metal. They kept themselves apart from him, shooting him glances, but never bringing him into their conversation.

Miles guessed that this outing was also meant to be a kind of initiation for him, but he wasn't yet part of the group. He didn't think he wanted to be.

After the tenth soldier climbed on board, the engine started up, blasting Miles's seat with gasoline fumes. The truck reversed backward, nearly tipping him out when it hit a dip in the mud, then grumbled as the driver pushed it to its maximum speed of about thirty miles per hour. They left through the wire fence enclosure of the outer settlement, then joined a mostly cleared highway going west.

It was maybe three hours to the Eagle Creek settlement.

The location of the raid turned out to be a park on the west edge of the reservoir. The friendly subset of the Indianapolis survivors had set up a settlement in a massive business park on the west edge of the city, close enough to the reservoir to fill up their trucks with good water every week, no pumping infrastructure needed, and defensive enough to keep raids out.

The center of the city had its own survivor population, but they weren't welcoming to visitors, and nobody in the Frazer settlement knew their numbers or dispositions.

Somehow, Seth had known the exact time and place that the alien ship was set to land, and when they got there it was already on the ground.

It wasn't what Miles had imagined. Not because it was alien, but because it looked so normal.

A metal hull, with an aerodynamic shape, wider around the middle than the front, with windows dotted along its length. It wasn't a saucer, or a craft built by unknowable minds according to unknowable principles. It just looked like a slightly weird passenger jet.

The main oddity was that it didn't have wings. Instead, the ship had four round, barrel-shaped devices attached at the corners.

The rear door was down, and a group of aliens were standing behind the craft, doing something to a group of human survivors.

The aliens *almost* looked human. Two arms and two legs each, a head and hands, but they had translucent blue-purple skin, and their tusks gave an animal edge to their features. They didn't look like a species that was hundreds or thousands of years ahead of humans in their technology.

"Go," a shout came from the front of the truck, the order punctuated by the truck's horn. "Light them up."

The fighters around Miles leaped up and hopped out of the back of the truck.

They started shooting even before they were all out of the truck. Miles put his hands over his ears, blocking out the sharp sound of single shots being fired off without any kind of organization behind them.

He had to lean out around the edge of the truck to see what was happening to the aliens.

They didn't seem to mind the hail of gunfire too much.

The purple aliens were still standing around. The humans they'd been dealing with had gone, taking shelter behind the ship and running away in that direction. It looked like a few of the people had gone *inside* the ship, their faces looking out through the windows. Miles tried to imagine what the aliens had promised to get them to come willingly.

The aliens weren't running, or even returning fire. If Miles had to put an emotion to them, they seemed bored.

As he watched, another round of three shots rang out from the soldiers around the truck.

Around the aliens, small plate-sized disks of glowing energy appeared in the air, blocking the shots. They had some kind of forcefield. No wonder they weren't worried.

The aliens didn't even seem to care that they were being shot at. Over the next minute, they spoke among themselves, gesturing in the direction of the settlers who'd run, before unloading some boxes and climbing back into the ship.

The devices positioned at the corners of the ship lit up, lifting it off the ground.

The fighters fired a few rounds at the alien craft as it ascended. The bullets did less to the hull than they'd done to the energy fields.

The ship left at high speed, zapping away faster than a jet and with less ramp-up.

Seth and a couple of the other fighters let out cheers as it receded into the sky.

Miles was left feeling like aliens were departing at their own pace, for their own reasons. The attack hadn't done anything to them at all. It'd scared away the people who were looking to talk, but beyond that, it had been a completely pointless exercise. With the difference in technology, Miles wasn't even sure if rockets or grenades would have gone any good.

While the settlement fighters were celebrating, Miles wandered over to the flattened grass where the ship had been sitting.

It looked like they'd left some trash behind. Along with a few sealed boxes, there were a handful of tablet-sized devices sitting in a small stack on the ground. The screens were active, showing text that Miles couldn't read without picking one up.

"Miles," Seth called from back at the truck. "Come on. We're leaving."

Miles filled out the paperwork, handing them back to the Hurc teller.

"You must have had a lot of off-world humans coming back for this," he said, fishing for how many people were in a similar position to him.

The refugee station had seen a few hundred human residents, and some of them had left for elsewhere in the weave. With the availability of Spiral transport here and in other cities, there must have been travelers who'd departed Earth from other places, too.

With only two terrestrial destinations accessible from the Forward Fleet, at least half of anyone returning would have come through Neyjavik.

"Yeah, a few," the teller said, looking through the form. "Last stats I saw, the scheme had a couple thousand non-residents taking up claims."

That was more returnees than Miles had expected.

He knew he wasn't special for having left Earth and made his way in the Spiral—he'd seen people leave the refugee station for better things before—but the low density of humans in Spiral territory had given him the false impression he was unique out there.

He remembered the woman in armor who'd just left the room. How was she making her living out there?

It was also interesting that these figures were available at all.

"What about total uptake?" Miles asked.

As he understood the scheme, any share which went unclaimed would be redistributed into shares that had been. The lower the overall uptake, the more each individual piece would be worth in the end, after the unclaimed allotments were divided up.

"In this city, about ten thousand. Across the planet, it's coming up to about six million."

That couldn't be right. Miles's message had offered him a certain percentage of the find, and based on that number he'd worked out that the whole had been divided into about eight hundred million parts. That'd been a grim assessment of the state of Earth's surviving population, and Miles thought that was bad enough, but if so few of them were taking what they were owed, then it was a sign that something was seriously wrong.

"Out of how many people who could claim?" he asked.

The Hurc teller checked a comm unit of his own, before saying, "Last scan, it was eight hundred forty million million and change."

"Almost no one is taking it?"

"Fifteen percent of the people in this region are taking it," the teller said. "That's the highest of anywhere, as far as I know." He stared at Miles for a few seconds, then his eyes slid to point in different directions, a Hurc shrug. "I know. I get it. It hurts me to see money being left on the table, too."

That wasn't why Miles had a problem with the figure. This was technically good for him. His claim was going to be worth about two orders of magnitude more than he'd thought coming in. But it was bad news for humanity.

Everyone who claimed their allotment was going to be getting the resources due to more than a hundred other people, if it were properly spread out.

The division had seemed like a brutally democratic distribution in principle. In practice, it was going to create a new class system.

"I don't see why uptake is so low," Miles persisted. "Do people need help getting comms?"

The teller gestured at the stack of comm devices available by the door.

"We give them to whoever will take them. At admin centers, in aid drops. There's special allowances for shared comm units. We even send the same messages out over the local communication channels. Entrant Allocations says ten percent of non-claimants have legit problems getting Spiral tech, forty percent are living in local cultures that prohibit it, and that's not counting the ones who think Spiral sapients are monsters from their mythology."

The teller's description made it sound like the problems Miles had faced at home writ large. People here were so quick to trust their own species over other sapients, even when that trust was clearly being abused.

"It's a trust problem," Miles said.

"It's a trauma problem," the teller said. "Personal trauma. Cultural trauma. Some of the strategists keeping things running up there can't understand it, and they don't account for it. But I get it. A lot of new worlds go through something similar. It's a kind of grieving, pushing anything unusual away."

A few thoughts flitted through Miles's head.

He wanted to ask, "Can I help?" But he knew he couldn't. Miles couldn't fix this global problem any more than he could liberate his home settlement. He was one person, and just getting here had been hard enough.

Both Miles and the clerk were quiet for a minute, both probably weighing the enormity of problems in Earth's near future.

Eventually, the teller spoke.

"You mind having this processed by an automated system, or do you want a sapient to look at it?"

It was the same question Miles had been asked when having his healer accreditation judged.

"Is there any advantage to having it done by a sapient?"

The clerk let out a laugh. "I hear you. I'll send it to the system. It should just take a few minutes."

"That's fine," Miles said. The next shuttle back to the Forward Fleet wasn't until the next day anyway.

Miles thanked the clerk, took the tablet back, and left the office.

The confirmation came in several minutes later.

Entrant Allocations > Miles
This system is pleased to confirm your allotment of a 0.000000119% share of asteroids I9411, I599, and I85591, constituting around 24M tons of recoverable materials. For a breakdown of the mineral content in this allocation, please view the attached file. For information on ventures and corporations who may be interested in purchasing or leasing this claim, message this system with a specific inquiry. Thank you for interfacing with Entrant Allocations.

One ten-millionth of a percent seemed like a small number on paper. Twenty-four million tons of anything, on the other hand, was unimaginably vast.

Twenty-four million tons of mixed metals and rare compounds, most written only in Spiral chemical shorthand.

It was all so much.

On Earth, before the bower break, that amount of any resource would have been worth billions of dollars. Maybe trillions.

In the Spiral, minerals were probably both more common and cheaper to extract, but it still had to be an enormous figure. He was sure he'd find out what kind of value it had as soon as he got back into Spiral space.

The tone of the city seemed to change after Miles had received his confirmation.

Neyjavik stopped being somewhere he needed to be to accomplish something, and became a place he was just passing through on his way out.

He no longer had to mold himself to the city, to figure out its rules and layouts. Now he was just a tourist, and to the extent that he had to interact with it at all, he felt like it was the city's responsibility to conform to him.

As a tourist, Miles passed through the commercial district.

With the pressure off, he felt like he had more time to indulge the offerings. Among the bars and businesses, there were cafes, bakeries, coffee shops. There were none of the chains he'd known growing up around the US, but there was still a lot that *was* familiar.

He stopped outside one restaurant, finding the menu to be pretty fish-heavy, then another, which sold Scandinavian food, none of which sounded appetizing in the translations provided by *Eyes of the Émigré*. He went on down the row, checking menus as he went.

He wasn't particularly hungry. *Hum of the Enduring* had brought his food requirements down to about one good meal a day and he'd bought an in-flight meal on the shuttle from the Forward Fleet, but today and tomorrow would probably be his last chances to sample Solar delicacies for a while.

He finally found a restaurant that had coffee, pizza, and ice cream on the menu.

The board outside the doors listed prices in both Krona and seln, and prices in both were high. A single meal would cost as much as a hotel room for the night, but Miles thought it was probably worth it, given the state of trade and supply routes. The availability of coffee was particularly incomprehensible. In the pre-break regime, coffee production was centralized in a few far-flung countries and shipped all over the world. Post-break, nobody was going to be wasting fuel shipping beans across thousands of miles of ocean.

Miles pushed the door open and stepped inside. A wave of warm air greeted him, along with smells of foods he'd only imagined in the last year. Bread, tomato sauce, bacon. Even the simple smells of vegetable oil and salt were mouthwatering.

The place was popular, and Miles started scanning the room, looking for an empty table.

He froze when he spotted a group of people sitting at one table.

Young men and women, with short hair and athletic builds, all with a similar kind of look.

He recognized one of them specifically. Buzzed black hair, an angular chin. Seth. Damien Asher's lieutenant. He was staring right back at Miles with furious intensity.

Miles's heart stuttered in his chest.

What is he doing here?

Miles backed out of the building, sneakers scraping the sidewalk. He pulled the door closed in front of him.

Turning, he scanned the street, looking for somewhere to run, someone to go stand beside.

Nothing. There was hardly any foot traffic, even during the day. No crowd to lose himself in. There were other restaurants back the way he'd come. He turned back toward them.

Miles had made it fifty feet from the restaurant by the time Seth's group stepped outside. They spotted him straight away and started running down the street after him.

What were they even doing here? Had they come for him? What other reasons could they have? Seth had been shooting at Spiral relief agents a year ago, on behalf of Miles's father. What had changed that he was willing to come to one of the most open ports on the planet now?

Immediately, Miles started sprinting away, heading for the next restaurant along the street.

He felt like he was back in the dungeon, running for his life in the Ymn City environ.

Miles looked inward, casting *Temporary Enhancement*, focusing on his Speed. The litany rolled through him like a personal mantra.

In myself, I am complete . . .

The burst of speed came to him with a feeling like he'd been holding himself back until that moment. His feet rattled against the sidewalk. The gap between him and Seth expanded.

He reached a bend in the road and paused. He stood for a second, breathing hard, and looked back down the street.

He'd already put a lot of distance between himself and the group from the settlement. Miles hadn't measured how fast he could run with his spell-enhanced speed, but from the gap it had to be comparable to a city car.

Seth was still running toward him, his boots hitting the ground with the heavy footfalls of an unaugmented physique.

Miles wasn't weighed down with his shield or bag, and his Authority felt no strain. There was no way they could catch him if he ran. Assuming he still wanted to run.

Miles wasn't the same person who'd escaped the settlement a year before.

He spent long seconds watching Seth approach, deciding what to do.

He could run, but what if he didn't? What could Seth, even with his group backing him up, seriously do to him now?

Weapons were forbidden in the city, so they wouldn't have guns. Knives wouldn't get through Miles's robe. If they tried to hold him, he could break free with enhanced strength. If they tried *anything*, he knew he could get away.

Miles picked a spot on the corner and waited.

When the group realized Miles wasn't running, they slowed down. They arrived flushed and out of breath, fog steaming out of their mouths in the cold air.

"You're Miles Asher?" Seth said. "Miles Asher, the captain's kid? The runaway?"

It hadn't occurred to Miles that Seth might not recognize him. There was an incredulous note in the man's voice, as if he thought finding Miles there was an impossible coincidence.

"Yeah," Miles replied.

"Holy shit. If he could see us now. He'd fucking lose it. You are *the* chip on his shoulder."

Seth shared an amused look with a couple of the group with him.

Miles didn't recognize any of them personally, but they looked like the kinds of guys his father would send out on an errand.

"What are you doing here?" Miles asked.

As an answer, Seth pulled out a palm-sized device from his jeans pocket, waving it in front of Miles. It was one of the comm units that the Spiral administration office was giving away.

The answer was so out of place it took Miles a second to make the connection.

"You're here for the allocation?"

"Yeah. We did all that work kicking the aliens out of our territory, then they go and do *this*. Their payback, I guess. It took us weeks to find somewhere they were still setting down."

"Damien sent you?" Miles asked.

Miles had been completely in the dark until he stumbled across the Spiral comm unit left by a relief ship. At first, he'd thought the messages coming through to it had been propaganda, but there'd been nothing hyperbolic in them. They'd been pragmatic messages offering mundane hope. Food supply drop-offs. Essential equipment. The potential for claiming asylum off-world. Over the following days his world had inverted, and he'd realized that they really were offering help.

Damien Asher had had a comm unit all along. If any of his people were here now, it meant he was the one who'd told them to come here.

Seth lifted a shoulder in a half-shrug.

"Yeah. The faithful. He sent us out to get the payout. He wants everything he can get. Buuut . . . we're not going back." Seth glanced around at the group before turning back to Miles. "You've been living with the aliens, right? What do you think this is going to be worth? Enough to get out of this shit heap?"

A new picture started growing in Miles's mind. An image of his father, not berating Miles to hand over his share of the allocation because he had some special insight or grand plan, not because Miles's allocation was uniquely valuable, but because anyone else he put in a position to claim it had turned around and taken it for themselves.

Suddenly, Damien Asher wasn't a mastermind trying to add one more claim to his pool of hundreds; he was a desperate man trying to add just one more to a meager handful. How many claims did he even have, if even the people he trusted were turning on him? Just his own, Miles's mom's, and his sister's? Or not even that? Miles hadn't had any messages from his mom, even among the deluge from his father.

Miles didn't answer Seth's question. He was done. They weren't a threat to him. They weren't even really interested in him. He turned and started walking away.

"Hey, where are you going, little man? You lived in space while you were gone, right? What's it like up there?" Seth tried to walk alongside Miles, keeping up the questions. "I heard if you can make it to an alien city, everything there is free. Is that how it is?"

Miles didn't answer. He didn't even look at them.

When it was clear to Seth he was just going to be ignored, the group stopped following.

Miles didn't look back to see where they went.

CHAPTER 29

On his last night on Earth, Miles dreamed he was back in the dungeon.
He was back in Ymn City. Blank gray structures loomed around him, vacant streets stretching out for miles.

The distorted giant was there, twitching along the streets, disappearing behind stone buildings before reappearing further ahead than it should have been.

Its eyeless head turned back and forth, looking for him. Slits like vents on its face blasted out a metallic wail, warning him, admonishing him, threatening him.

In the real place, the giant's cry had been meaningless. Here it seemed to be an accusation. There was some terrible crime that Miles was committing, and the giant was both his judge and executioner.

The stone pillar from the environ was there. Miles crouched behind it, silent, breathless.

In the real place, *Eyes of the Émigré* had let him read the inscription, but now it was indecipherable.

The giant flickered out into the street. It turned its head, spotting him. Immediately, it was moving, jerking toward him in an unnatural stop-start sprint, vibrating more than running along the ground.

Miles darted into a building. Inside, there was a stone chest. He pried off the lid. Within the chest were a dozen tiny Welven infants crawling around the hollow space.

He put his hands into the chest, letting them climb up over him. He had to save them from the giant.

At some point, Miles became aware that he was dreaming. He played out the logic of the dream, running from the giant, never fully able to escape, but the fear of the situation was dulled.

Eventually, the dream version of himself pulled out his index and used a new spell to open up a passage in the floor, jumping down into a darkness that became the darkness of closed eyes as he fell.

He started awake.

A noise was ringing out from the corner of the hotel room. A repetitive electronic bleating. It was familiar. At first, he thought it was his alarm, but his comm didn't make that tone. It took him a few seconds to recognize it as the ringtone of the cell phone he'd found on Ialis.

He jumped out of bed. Three steps took him to the pack. He opened the pocket and pulled the phone out.

The last time he'd got a call on the phone, the screen had shown a contact page with a distorted human face. Now, it showed a photo of a dark room. Only a semicircle of light was visible at the bottom of the frame, illuminating a metal floor. In the black background, two points of light were visible in the darkness, like light reflecting on glass beads.

Miles considered rejecting the call. He'd only brought the phone with him because Trin didn't want to have it in the apartment without him, and Miles wasn't totally ready to just junk it.

There wasn't going to be someone on the other end, not really. It was just glitching dungeon tech. The calls had to be random, and any voice he heard must have be coming from some messed-up function internal to the device. It literally *had* to. He was several hours deep into Solar space, so there was no way a synchronous call could come from outside it.

It all added up to Miles simply not having to answer the call. He could live without the temptation to read meaning into it that wasn't there.

He reached for the *end call* button.

A second before he could press it, the call connected on its own.

Miles stood, frozen, looking at the dark scene on the screen. A static hiss came out of the phone's speaker, then a voice.

"Deeper."

It was the same woman's voice as before, with a static sound like it was being played back from a recording.

Miles stared at the device. He pressed the *end call* button. The phone didn't respond.

"Deeper," the phone repeated. *"Deeper. Deeper."*

Every repetition had exactly the same intonation, the same static artifacts, like it was the same clip being played back every few seconds.

Miles dropped the phone on the bed, pulled on his clothes, and left the room.

The coffee shop Miles took refuge in had a radio playing. The presenter was speaking in Icelandic, but *Eyes of the Émigré* let him listen in anyway.

It was a one-person show, the same older woman introducing music, reading poetry, and issuing news broadcasts. The song selection was eclectic, everything from twenty-second-century mainstream titles from just before the bower break to classics from the '30s. If a song had been released on digital media in the last hundred years, it seemed like fair game for the station.

The news was mostly local issues, with some Spiral events thrown in. The story of the day was that the Forward Fleet was massing at the next break point—the location where the next iteration would arrive, when it arrived.

The presenter didn't get deep into the story, but she had enough information that Miles thought that the station must be syndicated to one of those information databases he'd have to pay to access.

The coffee shop's menu finally gave Miles the chance to try all the Earth delicacies he remembered, but hadn't been able to get since the bower break. Coffee, soda, French toast with ice cream and bacon, hash browns, roast pumpkin, and a small bowl of yogurt with red berries.

He found it weirdly easy to just sit and work his way through three plates of it. He hadn't even been hungry, and with *Hum of the Enduring*, this one meal might last him for days.

On the radio, a song ended early, and the presenter's voice resurfaced, speaking quickly.

"More news from events in the Spiral. The Forward Fleet now reports that a new iteration is believed to be imminent. Admiral Nigh Roth says: 'A new world will arrive in our Spiral within the next one hundred hours. There are indications that its arrival will be the result of a magical event. All of our advance forces are positioned to welcome them gently into our association.'"

The presenter was silent for a few seconds before adding, *"If it comes as predicted, Iteration 27,202 will arrive at close to the average time interval for new iterations. It will be one of our neighbors, only two iterations down-spiral of Earth. Our junior in the Spiral by more than a year."*

Miles looked around at the other patrons of the coffee shop, watching how they were reacting to the news.

It seemed to prompt some interested conversation between a pair of local customers, but most of the others paused only briefly to look at the radio before going back to their meals. Miles couldn't tell if they were already jaded to Spiral events, or if the news just seemed too distant or abstract to acknowledge.

Miles was interested, but only in an academic way. He wouldn't be spending enough time in the area for it to make much difference to him. Earth barely felt like his home at all anymore.

Miles went back to his hotel room eventually. The shuttle off-Earth wasn't scheduled to leave until the early evening, but there were only so many places to go in Neyjavik.

He'd returned to find the cell phone as dead as ever, silent, with its screen off. He'd packed it away with reservations, but he'd wait to decide whether or not to dispose of it once he got back to Ialis.

Maybe the Gilthaen officials would have an idea what to do with it.

The new spell in his index was a different problem.

Name: Miles Asher
Traditions: Harmonizer, Sky Quester, Tower Child
Spells (Tower Child)
Boundary Breach (Grasping) *Reconfigure a tower wall to allow passage.*

It was almost easy to miss, sitting innocuously at the bottom of his spell list. *Boundary Breach.*
I did not buy that spell.

It seemed impossible to deny the spell's connection to Ialis. Its similarity to the spell in his dream, its appearance on the morning of the cell phone call, the way the tradition used the word *child*, recalling his first "call" on the cell phone.

Miles teetered on the edge of disbelief. Could it be a coincidence? Could the new spell have been a gift from someone? Or a glitch? Maybe a delayed effect from one of the delta cores he'd absorbed?

His instincts told him the call that morning was somehow responsible, but his instincts would always try to draw connections, even when they were illusory.

Did he dare try to cast it?

Not now, not when he had a flight to catch later.

The only people who might be able to shed light on it were the Morning Star corporation, and they didn't have offices in this star system.

He finished packing the rest of his things—some toiletries, Earth snacks, and spare clothes in human cuts he'd shopped for earlier in the day—and stacked his bags by the hotel room door.

His dungeon-metal shield was a burden. The levitation unit's battery had run down almost to nothing, and there was no universal power connector here in Neyjavik. The wall sockets were all the electric variety.

Running power was a luxury on post-Bower Earth, a benefit of Iceland's geo-thermal and renewables infrastructure, but no configuration of adapters was going to let him recharge Spiral tech batteries from it.

Finally, when the flight was less than an hour away, Miles loaded himself up with his bags, grabbed the handle of his shield, and left the room.

It was probably the last space explicitly designed for humans he'd stay in for a long time.

The man in the leather coat was waiting for the same shuttle out as Miles.

It wasn't a huge coincidence. He recognized half the people in the waiting area from his flight in. A lot of them would be doing the same thing he was, coming back just to redeem their claim, then leaving on the next flight out.

The only difference was that the guy in the leather coat had come with two suitcases, and was leaving with only a weekend bag.

If he could trust his *Ears of the Diplomat*, the man had arrived with items on the customs blacklist, and was leaving without them.

Miles's report to the skyport's security obviously hadn't gone anywhere. The staff seemed like they had too much faith in their Spiral scanners and not enough experience with the countermeasures.

Miles might be the only person on Earth who'd noticed that something potentially illegal was going on, and there was no way the city had a framework for opening an investigation based on a magical intuition.

He picked the seat opposite the man across a walkway, dumping his bags on the chair next to him.

"Have fun staying with your friends?" Miles asked the man.

It felt weird to start a conversation with someone who was much older than him, and who was almost certainly a smuggler, but Miles was still feeling like a tourist, still existing in the liminal psychological space where talking to strangers was a normal thing to do.

The man barely looked up from his comm to see who was speaking.

"Yeah. It was a riot."

"Did you forget your suitcases at their house?" Miles asked.

The man didn't reply.

The doors to the lounge slid open, and the woman Miles had seen arguing with the teller at the Spiral administration building walked in.

She was still wearing her powered armor, metal plates that were dominantly red with white accents, and she now carried a long, single-edged blade at her hip, a circuit pattern etched down its length. Miles had let the customs clerk remove the limiter from his striker, and it looked like the armored woman's weapon had been returned as well.

She looked around for a seat, before walking over and sitting a couple of places from Miles, forming a triangle with him and the man in the coat.

"Hi," Miles said to her once she'd settled.

"Kid from the Spiral building. Hello." She spoke in German, translated through *Eyes of the Émigré* into accented English.

Her eyes fell on the other man. "Nice coat."

The man didn't even look up. "Thanks. It's an Earth original."

Miles found himself looking at the woman while she was looking at the man in the coat. There was more than just the armor and sword to her equipment.

Now that he was closer, he could see the shimmer of augmentation in her eyes. It was some kind of optical enhancement, giving her irises a metallic gleam. When she glanced back in his direction, her pupils flashed with reflected light.

Miles was already doing the most dangerous job in the Spiral he could imagine a human doing. What did she need all that equipment for?

"Is it okay if I ask what you do?" Miles asked her.

She fixed him with a level stare and said, "I kill people for money."

Miles was concerned for a second, before the clanging of cracked bells started ringing around him. *A lie.*

The woman watched his face as his shock turned to unamused disbelief. She laughed.

"I'm a bodyguard," she corrected herself, and this time *Ears of the Diplomat* stayed silent. "Three years ago, I worked for the Gemeinde, the European body, protecting politicians. They took me with them to their bunker when things went bad. Then they kicked us out. All *non-essentials*. That was a hard few months, but it turned out people *up there* also want protection." She lifted her finger to point vaguely upward.

Earth didn't have technology or manufactured goods that were worth anything in the Spiral. It hadn't occurred to Miles that Earth might still have valuable skills to offer.

"I wouldn't have thought being a bodyguard on Earth would qualify someone for that," Miles said.

"Lots to learn," the woman replied. "There are guns that can shoot a thousand miles, and defenses that make those guns irrelevant. So many new threats and countermeasures. A lot of what I know transfers. The philosophy transfers."

Neither the woman nor Miles missed that the man in the coat was paying attention, while still pretending to read his comm.

"And you?" the woman asked Miles. "I've never seen anyone dressed this way."

Miles looked down at himself. He didn't know if she was talking about his robe or the shield.

"I'm a healer working on Ialis," he said.

"Ialis. Is that the maze planet?"

"Kind of?" Miles said. "I've heard it called a dungeon."

The woman waved at her ears. "Translation issue. Yes. The dungeon world."

"Yeah."

The woman stared into space for a second, then shrugged. After a minute of silence, she turned to look at the man in the coat.

Miles thought she was weighing up including him in the conversation, but seemed to decide not to.

"I'm Helene, if you didn't know," she said into the silence.

"I'm Miles."

She reached into a slot in her armor and pulled a credit-card-sized comm unit half the way out. There was a question in her expression.

Miles brought his comm unit from his backpack and they tapped the devices together long enough for each other's contact information to be recorded.

"So, I mostly work out around Iteration 24,000, planet Iun," Helene said, apparently making conversation. "Old world, high civilization, very dense. Twenty-four thousand is a millennium world in four number bases, so it's a popular crossroads for cultures that like round numbers."

"That must take a long time to reach," Miles said. It'd taken a week just to come a thousand iterations from Ialis, and that was on an express ship.

"Yes, four days. Luckily, my client had business at the Fleet."

Four days. He knew that the aggregate physics that worked in the weave didn't have the same speed limit as Earth's spacetime, but Helene's transport must have been traveling an order of magnitude faster than the Century Express.

"I wish you could drop me off at Ialis," Miles said.

He meant the comment idly, but Helene seemed to take the comment seriously.

"Well. Maybe. I can ask. My boss is easy-going."

Miles immediately felt bad. "Oh, no, it's okay. I just meant . . ."

He caught himself and forced himself to stop. His first instinct had been to retract the request, it was too big a favor, but he silenced that voice.

Helene waved him off anyway. "No problem. She's a big spender type. Let me just check." She pulled out her comm, tapping out the start of a message. "You said you're a healer on Ialis?" she asked, not looking up from the device.

"Tier 1," Miles said. He was still only a Tier 1. He was going to need to change that. He was sure he could test into a higher rating with everything he'd learned, and his new spells.

"I can pitch this," she said. She finished the message, then sent it.

She spent the next five minutes typing, reading, and occasionally laughing at replies. Finally, she looked up.

"The boss says you can come with us as far as Ialis. You'll be riding as my understudy."

"That's . . . amazing. Thank you."

"It's okay. I told him you'll work for free."

"That's fine too."

Helene's act of kindness was going to take about a week off Miles's journey. He'd still need to spend a few hours on the shuttle from Earth to the Fleet, but he'd only have about a day of travel once he was back in the weave. He could work for a day.

"And if I'm ever on Ialis, you can put me up."

Miles kept smiling, but had a hard time imagining Helene in the tiny apartment he shared with two other sapients.

"Yeah."

The green-blue circle shrank in the shuttle's viewport. The vessel's chassis rattled around him, despite the energy shields casting blue light over the void. Venus was visible to the right, the only star in that part of the sky.

Beyond the Earth, the night sky Miles had grown up with was absent. No stars and no constellations. It made the Earth, the sun, and the planets look isolated, a white-yellow disk and a handful of white dots floating in an infinite emptiness. The reality was that Earth had never been less alone. When the shuttle turned, he'd see the neighbors. The closest was much less than a light-year away.

Staring down at the retreating planet, Miles wasn't sure what he was supposed to feel.

The space travelers of Earth's history had described awe, a feeling of personal insignificance, and the conviction that Earth was precious.

Miles had to think that being one of twenty-seven thousand worlds re-contextualized the sight a little.

He felt the personal insignificance, but that wasn't anything new. He wasn't one of billions anymore, but tens of *trillions*.

If there was awe, then it was awe at what had been lost. The history of Earth's last hundred years had been a constant rolling disaster, but humans couldn't be blamed for the bower break. It had been arbitrary. A cultural, environmental, technological disaster that had literally come out of nowhere.

Was Earth precious? If another human asked him, he felt like he would have to say that it was, but he wasn't sure if he really felt that way. He wondered if that was unpatriotic, or something to be ashamed of.

As the planet dropped into the distance, becoming a dull star, the warmest feeling Miles could call up was that he didn't hate it.

Elsewhere on the shuttle, Helene was sitting in a window seat, still in her armor. The two of them would ride separately to the Forward Fleet, where the bodyguard would hopefully bring him onboard her employer's ship.

If it all worked out, it meant he'd be back on Ialis in a little over a day. With *Hum of the Enduring*, he wouldn't even need to rely on them offering him somewhere to sleep. He could be on his feet for the next twenty-four hours if he needed to be.

A chirp from Miles's comm drew his attention. He looked down and saw a new message, another one from his father.

It stayed there as an alert, no hint at the content.

He stared at the notification for a minute, then blocked the sender. The new message and entire communication history vanished, deleted or archived, he didn't care.

Eventually, the shuttle turned, and the Spiral came into view.

Looking at it, Miles felt a cauldron of emotions boiling over.

Awe. At the scale of civilization spread out along the coiling chain of worlds, at the fact that it managed to *work* as a unified culture.

Insignificance. There had to be fewer than twenty people out there who even knew his name.

Hope. Because all of those worlds out there had been through a similar catastrophe to Earth, and most of them had recovered.

He felt homesick, as well. Soon he'd be home, in Dendril City, with Trin and Torg, bouncing off the walls of their tiny apartment. And whatever fortune might lie in his future, he still had to work in the present. Soon, he'd be back again, facing down the passageways of the dungeon.

Podium

DISCOVER
STORIES UNBOUND

PodiumAudio.com

Milton Keynes UK
Ingram Content Group UK Ltd.
UKHW011123050624
443649UK00006B/518